PRAISE FOR
BLEEDING HEART SQUARE

"A well-crafted mystery, told with style."   —ANNE PERRY

"A compelling and suspenseful evocation of London in that uneasy period before WWII. In Lydia Langstone, Andrew Taylor has created a protagonist of her time, an intelligent woman coming to terms with her growing sense of self. Intricately plotted and beautifully crafted."

—MARGARET MARON,
author of *Death's Half Acre* and *Hard Row*

"Finely drawn period atmosphere, compellingly complex characters, breath-stopping suspense, then twists that will leave you reeling. Taylor is a riveting storyteller, and *Bleeding Heart Square* may be his best work yet. Absolutely bloody brilliant!!"

—DEBORAH CROMBIE

"It's easy to see why Andrew Taylor's historical mysteries have won so many accolades. The square itself emerges as a major player in this atmospheric, elegantly told mystery, in which you, the reader, are assigned the role of detective."

—RHYS BOWEN,
Agatha, Anthony, and Macavity Award–winning author
of the Molly Murphy and Royal Spyness mystery series

A
STAIN
ON THE
SILENCE

HYPERION
•••••
NEW YORK

A
STAIN
ON THE
SILENCE

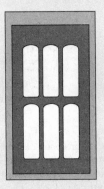

ANDREW
TAYLOR

ISBN: 978-1-4013-0284-9

Hyperion books are available for special promotions and premiums. For details contact the HarperCollins Special Markets Department in the New York office at 212-207-7528, fax 212-207-7222, or email spsales@harpercollins.com.

Book design by Karen Minster

FIRST U.S. EDITION

10 9 8 7 6 5 4 3 2 1

FOR

CHERYL AND SUE,

WITH LOVE

A
STAIN
ON THE
SILENCE

"Are you sure it's here?" the sergeant says.

"Yes." I watch the other man picking his way among the saplings and the stones. "There used to be one further up, but that fell down long before I came here."

The other man drags away a fallen branch and swears as a bramble sucker rakes its thorns across the back of his hand. He works the blade of the spade under a corner of one of the stones, which has been roughly squared. It tapers slightly so perhaps it came from the vault or even from the arch over the entrance. He tries to lever it up but it's too deeply bedded into the tangled roots and impacted rubble. They won't get far with a single spade. They really need a mechanical digger.

The sergeant cocks an eyebrow at me. He's at least ten years younger than I am but, like so many policemen, he believes himself centuries older in the ways of the world.

"Listen, sir," he says. "When it comes down to it, we haven't got a great deal to go on. And it's a hell of a long time ago."

"You've got the fish necklace."

"Which you have to agree is a long way from conclusive. There's no way of telling if it's the same one."

Blood near the gate, I think, and the sound of thunder on a fine day? Doesn't that count for anything?

"We can't even be sure where it was found. Particularly as one witness is no longer with us, and the other was a kid when it turned up. And why here exactly?" he goes on. "It's a big place. Could have been anywhere, surely."

"Because this was special," I say, as I've said many times before to this man and to his colleagues. "This was a secret."

"If we find nothing, it's not going to make things look any better. Have you thought of that? And even if we do find something, it's—"

I sigh. "Nothing's going to make things look better."

"No one likes time-wasters, you know."

"I'm trying to help you. That's why you brought me here. Haven't you got a metal detector in the van? That might save time."

He doesn't like my telling him what to do. "If you're right, there's a hell of a lot of earth and stone on top. Even if there is something worth finding down there, we won't get a peep out of it." He lights a cigarette—a Marlboro Light, as it happens—and turns away to stare down the slope at the stream. He gets out his phone and moves further away from me.

Wood pigeons coo. There are still a few bluebells in the green shade on the opposite bank of the stream. Bluebells mean constancy, Felicity said, everlasting love. And I hear her voice: "The trouble is, I don't know who I'll marry."

A few minutes later, a detective constable appears on the path, carrying the metal detector on her shoulder. I watch the three police officers consult in a huddle among the ruins. The sergeant glances at me. The woman turns on the metal detector. They have the sense to use it near the edge of the stones, where there is almost certainly a thinner layer of debris above the former ground level.

Less than a minute later they have a very sharp signal. The man with the spade comes over. He digs, and the other two try to help by pulling branches and stones out of his way. It's a warm afternoon and it's getting hotter in this little valley, despite the trees and the stream. The air isn't moving.

"I can see something, Sarge," the woman says, crouching. Her fingers scrabble among the stones. "I think it's a wheel of a bike."

A BMX bike. My phone rings. I take it out of my pocket and move away from the sergeant. I know he's watching me. I glance at the caller display and press one of the keys.

"Jamie," the voice says. "Jamie, it's me."

1

*J*AMIE.

That was when it had begun again, nearly three weeks earlier: Rachel told me that someone had phoned the office and asked for me as Jamie. No one had called me that since I was sixteen, with one exception. At the time I was in my early twenties, a student, and very drunk in a pub near King's Cross. I met a man who thought my name ought to be Jamie. He sensed he had riled me, and he kept on using it, Jamie this, Jamie that. I ignored him but he wouldn't stop. He came closer and his voice rose higher and higher. *Jamie, Jamie.* In the end I headbutted him and broke his nose.

I squeezed the phone tightly. After a pause that lasted both a heartbeat and a third of a lifetime, I asked Rachel whether she was sure.

"Yes." Her voice had an edge of curiosity. "I've never heard anyone call you Jamie before so it stuck in my mind. And the second time she said it again. Jamie."

"She phoned twice?"

"Once just after lunch and then about twenty minutes ago to see if you were back."

With my free hand I worried at a spot of dirt on the gear lever. I remembered a lane between a fence and a high hedge, a place where no birds sang in the unbearable silence. I remembered a fish sparkling like a silver stain in the sunshine.

"James? Are you still there?"

"What was her name?"

Rachel breathed heavily and I heard the rustling of paper on her desk. "Lily—Lily Murthington."

"Oh, yes," I said. "I know. And the number?"

I found a pen. Rachel reeled off a telephone number and I scribbled it down on a copy of yesterday's *Independent*. It was a landline number with an outer-London prefix. She was only a few miles away.

"She said it's a switchboard, you have to ask for her." Rachel paused, then added with a little gasp of excitement, "And she said to tell you not to hang about because she might not be staying there much longer. Are you coming back to the office?"

"There's no point now. I'll go straight home."

"Shall I email the agenda for Monday?"

"If you must." My voice sounded quite normal, at least to me. "Any other messages?"

There weren't. I said goodbye and broke the connection. It was Friday afternoon, the end of a long, hard week. I had been working on site in Queen's Park, assessing what needed to be done to convert a redundant chapel into retail premises. If I set off now, I would miss the worst of the traffic crawling out of London on Western Avenue. Instead I stared through the Saab's windscreen at a line of parked cars.

God help me, I had assumed the ghost was dead and buried. Out of sight, out of mind. I said the ghost's name, Lily, trying the unfamiliar shape in my mouth and finding it no longer fitted there. She still called herself Murthington, which suggested that she had not remarried. Who cared? I didn't want her to exist under any name. Had she known where I was all the time? Did she know where I lived as well as where I worked? And, above all, why should she want to break the silence? And why now?

I picked up the phone again. I had no choice. If Lily had found out where I worked, she could also find out where I lived. I couldn't risk her pestering me at the office or—far worse—at home.

The phone rang so long that I almost gave up. At last a woman answered: "St. Margaret's."

"May I speak to Mrs. Lily Murthington?"

"I'm afraid not. The doctor's with her at present."

I hesitated. "When would be a good time for me to call?"

The woman misunderstood me. "You can come any time until about six thirty."

"I meant when should I phone her."

"Whenever you want. She's got a phone in her room but we tend to monitor her incoming calls because she's not always well enough to receive them. Whatever you do, though, I wouldn't leave it too long."

"So she's very ill?"

"Oh, yes. I'm sorry, I assumed you knew."

"Yes, but I wasn't sure how bad it was." I had slipped into the lie without noticing. "She's an old friend, you see, but we've been out of touch for a while. Listen, where are you exactly—can you give me directions?"

The woman gave me an address in Wembley. "You can't miss it—there's a church next door to us. Red brick with a little spire, and a car park beside it. Shall I tell her you're coming?"

"Yes, please do."

"And who shall I say?"

I said, "Tell her it's Jamie."

The first thing I noticed was the sign by the entrance. It wasn't a hospital. It was a hospice, a modern building shoehorned into a small and expensively landscaped garden. Inside there were exposed bricks, gleaming expanses of pale wood, a small exhibition of monochrome photographs, and big windows that filled the place with light. The reception desk stood at one angle of a cloister running round a little courtyard where a fountain played. The staff had been trained to smile.

When I got there it was a little before six o'clock. I asked for Lily Murthington. The receptionist asked me to sit down on one of the leather sofas arranged in a U-shape round a coffee table. She murmured into a phone and a few minutes later a nurse conducted me down a corridor filled with the soft sun of early evening. We passed half a dozen doors, most of them open. I glimpsed old and shrivelled people lying on beds or slumped in chairs. They were dwarfed by the shiny equipment and the brightness of the flowers, and seemingly hypnotized by the chatter of televisions.

The nurse slowed, allowing me to draw level with her. "She tires very quickly. I should think ten or fifteen minutes will be enough." She stopped outside a doorway. "There's a visitor for you, Lily." She smiled at me, as if in encouragement.

I went into the room. A woman was sitting up in the high bed, staring at me. She was very thin and very pale. Her face

and even her arms looked strained and lopsided: it was as
though a giant had gripped her in an enormous hand and
squeezed, and when he let go, she had lacked the elasticity to
return to her former shape. The brown eyes seemed larger
than before because the surrounding face had shrunk. I do not
think I would have recognized her if I had not known whom
to expect.

She raised her right hand a few inches above the blanket.
"Jamie."

"Lily."

The nurse cocked her head. "Anything I can get you? A
cup of tea?"

"No, thank you." Lily smiled up at her. "I'll ring if I need
anything, I promise."

The nurse smiled back and left the room. Lily was good at
making people like her. It had always been one of her talents.
Almost everyone succumbed at some point, even Carlo, I think,
right at the beginning. The only person who never liked her
was Felicity.

I said, "I'm sorry you're not well."

She shook her head and her hair, thinner now but still dark,
trembled round her skull. A layer of gray showed at the roots.
I had never known exactly how old she was and in the past I
hadn't asked, perhaps because I didn't want to know. At least
fifteen years older than me? Twenty? Sometimes it had seemed
more, at others much less.

"I wanted to see you." She frowned. "You don't look as I
thought you would."

"Why do you want to see me?"

"Sit down. It's tiring looking up at you."

I sat in the low chair by the bed, which brought the level of my head below hers. I was suddenly angry. "You wouldn't see me before. God knows, I tried. So why now?"

"There was no point, and it wouldn't have been right. But now there is a point."

To say goodbye? In my mind I stared back at us across a gulf of a quarter of a century. I didn't want to remember. I didn't want to see Lily. I'd said goodbye to her many years ago. All I wanted to do now was to go home and pour myself a large glass of red wine.

"Because you're ill?"

"That's not the reason," she snapped.

I stared at her. "I'm sorry you're like this. Truly. And—and I'm sorry for what happened. But we can't change it, you know, we can't change anything. So there's nothing to talk about. It's all over."

"No, that's just it." She struggled to sit up. "It's not over."

"Of course it is."

She lay back against the pillows. Her eyelids drooped. For a moment I thought she was about to fall asleep. Then she said, "Hugh's dead. Had you heard?"

"No, I hadn't. I'm sorry."

"You've not tried to find out what happened to us?"

"No." I spoke more loudly than I had intended. "Why should I?"

"Hugh was sorry for you," Lily said, after a pause. "Of course, he never knew the truth."

Nor had Lily, come to that, not the whole truth. Anyway, I didn't want Hugh Murthington's pity. I had liked him, and I felt guilty for what I had done to him. "Is there anything I can do for you?" I asked.

"Not for me." She grinned unexpectedly, another twist in the twisted mouth. "I didn't want you to come here for me. I wanted you to come for your daughter."

I stared at her. At first I thought I must have misheard. She shook her head slowly, as if to reject that possibility. I held my tongue. I have learned over the years that it is always better to say less rather than more and when in doubt to say nothing, if nothing will do.

My daughter, a voice said in my head. *My daughter.*

"You didn't know," she went on slowly, speaking as if each word cost her an effort. "I realize that. You couldn't have. I didn't know either, not when I last saw you. And afterwards it was too late."

At last I found my voice. "What about Hugh? Why can't it have been his?"

"It?"

"I'm sorry. She."

The broad mouth twisted again, but this time there was no trace of humor in it. "Her name's Kate."

I wasn't surprised. The only surprise was that I remembered her saying, all those years ago, that she liked the name Kate.

"I was quite sure she wasn't Hugh's for the most obvious reason in the world," she was saying. "I had to pretend that she was premature, which involved a lot of juggling with the dates."

"I'm not sure you should tell me this, for her sake or mine. We should forget it."

Lily shook her head. "She needs a father."

"She's got one. Hugh's her father. I'm sure he made a very good job of it, and it's better to leave it at that. I don't think there's any need to drag me into her life at this stage. Or at any stage."

"You've changed."

I looked out of the window. I saw a square of grass and a bird table, beyond which was a leylandii hedge. I wished I hadn't come.

"She needs you," Lily said.

I didn't turn round. "Nonsense."

"I'm no good to her. She's got no one else."

"I can't believe that. She must be—what? Twenty-three, twenty-four? She's not a child. I'm sure she's got scores of friends and relations." I hesitated. "She's got Carlo."

"Carlo's part of the problem."

"You haven't told me what the problem is."

There was silence in the overheated room. A couple of nurses passed across the open doorway. They were laughing at something but one glanced in and smiled at us.

"She's in trouble," Lily said. "That's why she needs your help."

"I'm sorry but it's nothing to do with me."

"She's got no one else. And, Jamie—"

"What?"

"You owe me something. You owe us all something. Don't you think so?"

I looked at her. Perhaps my face showed the hatred I felt.

"You owe me," she repeated. "Don't you?"

"We both made mistakes," I said. "I don't owe you anything."

Lily lifted the glass beside her. Her hand was trembling so much that she spilled a few drops of water.

"Let me." I stood up and took the glass from her. Feeling as awkward as a teenager, I held it to her lips. She put her finger to the base of the glass to steady it as she sipped. Her skin brushed mine. I glanced at her face, and found her looking at me.

"Not quite the same, is it?" She pushed aside the glass. "Touching me, I mean. Nothing's the same. I'm scared to look in the mirror."

"What's she supposed to have done?"

"The police believe she killed someone."

"I don't think I heard you properly."

"I haven't much energy so don't waste time. They believe Kate killed someone. Or if they don't now they soon will."

"Who?"

"His name's Sean. They used to live together. She was going to marry him but then she changed her mind."

I said, in a tight little voice, "If there's been some sort of accident, the best thing for her to do is to find a solicitor and then go to the police."

"You don't understand." Lily sounded weaker now.

"I'm sorry, but I understand more than enough. Tell her to find a solicitor and go to the police."

"It's more complicated than that." Her head swayed on her narrow neck. "She needs time to decide what to do, and somewhere to catch her breath. And then there's the problem of Carlo."

I shook my head and stood up.

"Jamie," Lily said. "Please, Jamie."

I stared down at her.

"You owe me something," she said. "Remember?"

She stretched her hand to a book, a biography of a dead actress, which was on the table by the bed. She pulled out a white envelope that had been marking her place. Its flap was unsealed. She fumbled inside and took out a tarnished fragment of very fine chain with a scrap of metal hanging from it. I glanced at it and looked away. Lily let her hand drop to the white sheet, and curled her fingers round the chain.

It can't be, I thought. *It can't be.*

"Do you recognize this?" Lily asked.

"No," I said, and looked away.

"It was Kate who found it. Isn't that strange? It was when she was a little girl. We went for a picnic by the stream. You remember? There were some ruins, and that's where it was, among the stones. No point in saying anything, I thought, not then. Far too late. Better to let sleeping dogs lie. Kindest thing for everyone."

"I have to go now," I said. "Goodbye."

"But now it's different," I heard Lily saying as I left the room. "You said it was a fox, didn't you, Jamie? But it wasn't."

2

LILY HAD BEEN RIGHT: IT WAS DIFFERENT NOW, AND IT WAS also true that I owed her something, and that it was the sort of debt you can never finish paying. But she didn't know that she had destroyed the last shred of hope, that now I could no longer pretend there might be another explanation.

When I was younger I wanted so badly to find a scapegoat for what had happened. Anyone but me. Carlo was the obvious candidate. In the darkest time, blaming him became a sort of lifeline, and it was good to have one to hold on to even though the other end wasn't attached to anything. Of course, it wasn't really Carlo's fault, though it's true that he introduced me to Lily.

I first saw him in September 1976. I was nearly thirteen, and he was five months older. He had already been at the school for a year, but this was my first term. I am not sure when or how we became friendly. Friendships often grow imperceptibly. You realize that they have begun only in retrospect.

Carlo and I played on the same teams, we slept in the same dormitory, we liked the same TV programs and bands. He lived in Chipping Weston with his father and his younger sister. One of the things that brought us together was that he had no mother. Both she and the child she was carrying died in childbirth, though I didn't know about the baby until much later. But it gave Carlo and me something in common: my father was dead, the victim of a car crash in Birmingham on the last Friday before Christmas in 1970.

I liked it when Carlo talked about his home, his father and sister. Not that he did so very often—a boarding school is a self-contained place, especially for boys of our age, and we were bound up in its events and rituals. But when people talked about their home lives, it was as though they were travellers who had returned from exploring an exotic foreign country: their stories were touched with the glamour of the unknown. My own home and family existed in theory rather than practice. I was hungry for the reality of other people's.

I remember a Saturday afternoon near the end of my first summer term. Carlo and I were sitting on the boundary that ran round the perimeter of the cricket field, watching the school's first eleven being beaten by the visitors. Those of us who weren't playing in one or other of the school teams were obliged to watch and clap at appropriate moments. We lay on the grass in the shade while white-clad figures moved like sunlit ghosts. It was a tedious way to spend an afternoon but oddly restful too. Carlo and I lay side by side and lobbed sentences between us.

"I'm getting an electric guitar at the end of term," he announced.

"Jammy bastard," I said. "What sort?"

"A Fender Strat." He plucked a piece of grass and pretended he was smoking it like a cigarette. "Brand new. With a practice amp."

"It's not your birthday. What's your dad up to? I thought he didn't like any sort of music since Beethoven."

"It's not from him," Carlo said. "It's from Lily."

"Who's she?"

He turned his face away. The tips of his ears reddened. "A friend of my dad's."

"Are they—you know?"

"I don't know. Probably. She was around quite a lot in the Easter holidays, and I met her again at half-term."

"Ooh-er," I said, trying to sound lascivious. Then: "What's she like?"

"OK. Quite nice, really. She's a nurse. She's giving my sister this amazing doll's house. It's because they're getting married, her and my dad."

I wondered how long he'd known this. "You going to be a bridesmaid, then?" I asked. "Are you going to hold her flowers?"

He kicked me in the shin and we scuffled discreetly for a moment where we lay on the grass.

Afterwards he said, "Lily." He let the word linger. "She says I have to call her that. Lily, like my dad does."

"Lily," I repeated, in the soppiest voice I could manage, rolling my eyes and placing my hand upon my heart. "Lily, darling!"

The footsteps behind me were a woman's, light and fast. I pressed the remote control as I crossed the car park and the Saab's lights flashed in welcome. I stopped. The footsteps behind me stopped too.

A woman said in a low, husky voice: "Hey. You're Jamie, right?"

I turned and stared at her. She hadn't been in the hospice's reception so she must have been waiting outside. It had been raining during the afternoon and her blue waxed jacket was still damp round the shoulders. She looked younger than I'd expected—if I hadn't known better I would have said that she was still in her teens. She was small and slight, brown-eyed and dark-haired like her mother, with a generous mouth and high cheekbones. She was attractive. I liked that, which I suppose was a form of vanity. If I was going to have a daughter wished on me, I preferred her not to be ugly.

"Kate," I said.

"You've seen my mother?"

"Yes."

"Then you know—"

"I don't want to know anything," I interrupted.

"It's too late. You already do."

"That doesn't matter."

Kate came closer to me and said, more quietly, as though afraid her mother might hear: "She's dying."

"I'm sorry." I wasn't sorry at all, not really. I just felt uncomfortable.

"Did she tell you about Sean?"

I edged towards the car. "Yes."

"Did you believe her?"

"I wondered if she knew what she was saying."

"Because of the drugs?" Kate glanced over her shoulder, a fugitive's reflex. "I wish to God she'd made the whole thing up."

"If you're in trouble, the best thing for you to do is to see a solicitor. That's what I told her."

She looked up at me. "All I need is time. A little breathing space."

"She said the police think you killed someone."

She flinched. "But I didn't."

I said nothing. Silence is safer.

"I'm not asking for—"

"I can't help you."

"But you're my *father*."

"No," I said. "I'm not getting involved."

"Why? Have you got children of your own?"

"No."

She stared at my hands, at the ring on my finger. "But you're married, right? Are you afraid your wife might—"

"I just don't want anything to do with this, or with you. Is that clear enough? Find a solicitor."

I climbed into the car and locked the doors from the inside. I started the engine. Even if Lily had realized the significance of what was in the envelope, she couldn't have told Kate because Kate would have used the knowledge just now. And Kate wouldn't know what it meant unless someone told her. No one else could even begin to understand its meaning—not now. Except, of course, Carlo.

Kate could have stood in front of the parking space and blocked me. But she moved to one side, waited and watched. I drove slowly out of the car park. As I turned into the road, I glanced into the rearview mirror. She was still waiting, still watching.

I thought I was handling everything perfectly well. I thought I was still in control. But I don't remember driving home to Greyfont, the route I took or even what I thought about. There's a gap in my memory. There must have been a lot of traffic on the A40 and the M40, with everyone rushing out of

London for the weekend. I must have thought about what had happened, about Lily and Kate. I must have thought about Nicky.

But I do remember turning into the driveway, the sound of the tyres leaving Tarmac for gravel. I switched off the engine. Nicky's Mini Cooper was parked exactly parallel to the boundary fence. The kidney-shaped patch of grass needed cutting.

My home looked like somebody else's. We had lived there for less than three months and I still found it hard to think of it as mine. It was about eighty years old, a solid, detached house built of red brick, which had expanded during the intervening decades to the side and back. There was nothing about it to like and nothing to hate. It looked as if it had what it deserved, as if it belonged to careful, comfortable people living respectable suburban lives. It was a sensible house, a good place to bring up a family if you happened to have one.

There was a raku bowl on the sitting-room windowsill. It was one of Nicky's favorite possessions. I looked at it now, and its curves reminded me of the first time I had seen Lily naked, the neat little waist and the swell of the hips, the most alluring shape in the world.

I forced myself to leave the sanctuary of the Saab. The hall smelt like a stranger's. I noticed the clean paintwork and the lack of clutter, the way the colors in the picture on the wall harmonized with the flowers on the table below it. Perhaps we'd tried too hard to make it attractive, homely. All we had achieved was something tastefully sterile, like an operating theater in a private hospital.

Nicky was in the kitchen at the back of the house, sliding a dish into the oven. Her bag was on the table, her coat draped over the back of a chair. She was wearing navy jeans and a pale blue polo-necked ribbed jersey that emphasized her waist. She looked five or ten years younger than she was.

She closed the oven door and straightened up. "Your supper's in there. It's an aubergine and mushroom bake. It should take about half an hour."

"You're going out?"

"My book group." She smiled. "Don't you remember?"

"I thought that was next week."

"It was, but we had to change it. It's all been a bit of a rush because I was late back from work." She glanced at her face in the mirror on the dresser, and pushed back a stray hair. "There's salad in the fridge."

"Thanks. What is it?"

"What's what?"

"The book."

"Henry James. *The Turn of the Screw*." She pulled a face as she picked up her coat. "Horribly spooky. You're later than I expected."

"Something came up. I was going to come straight back from Queen's Park but I made the mistake of phoning the office first."

She pecked my cheek. I smelt her familiar smell and felt the touch of living, healthy skin.

"You're tired," she said.

"A long day. You know."

"Are you feeling OK? You look cold."

"I'm fine. But it's getting quite chilly out there. Not like May at all."

"Have a bath—that'll warm you up. I'll be back about ten."

Like a doting husband, I walked Nicky to the front door, kissed her, and waved as she drove away. I went upstairs and changed into jeans. The suit Nicky sometimes wore to work was hanging on the back of the bedroom door. Her colleagues usually wore jeans but Nicky thought appearances mattered.

Afterwards, I fetched a bottle of Burgundy from the rack in the garage. I uncorked it and carried the bottle and glass into the sitting room. I wanted to drink too much tonight, partly because of Lily and partly because of the tarnished scrap of metal in the white envelope.

It was almost time for the Channel 4 news. I wanted to know if there was a report of a man named Sean being murdered. Whatever happened, I knew that later this evening I'd be trying to track down more details on the Internet. I didn't feel guilty about refusing to help Kate—it was what anyone would do, anyone with an atom of sense—but I admit I was curious. Part of me hoped that the whole thing was a pack of lies, that Lily and Kate had been playing an elaborate joke or fabricating the story to manipulate me for reasons unknown.

As I picked up the remote control, there was a tapping on the window. I looked towards the source of the sound. Kate was standing outside, her face pressed against the glass.

My first reaction was anger mixed with relief. At least Nicky had gone out. I put down the remote control. Kate was still staring at me. She looked like a refugee or a beggar or a prospective burglar. Her face was expressionless. She might have been examining an empty room. I felt another spurt of anger. This was no better than emotional blackmail.

But I couldn't leave her there. She was at the front of the house, overlooked by two of our neighbors and easily visible to anyone passing along the road. Someone would notice, someone would wonder—someone might mention the strange woman to Nicky. People who lived in Greyfont prided themselves on their community spirit.

When I opened the front door, cold air eddied into the hall. Kate was waiting for me on the step. It had started to rain again and the collar of the blue jacket was turned up. There was a long rip in the left sleeve and a smudge of white paint on the shoulder. She looked unkempt—not at all the sort of person who lived in Greyfont, or not in our road.

"Go away," I said. "I don't want to see you."

"I just need a little help."

"It's not possible. Please go."

"It's not much to ask. In the circumstances."

I said nothing.

"Is your wife out?"

I nodded. I wondered what would have happened if she had called while Nicky was here. I would have liked to find out how Kate had discovered where I lived, where I worked, but I knew it was better not to start a conversation. In the long run it would be better for everyone if I kept her at arm's length. I began to close the door.

"All I want is somewhere to stay for the night," she said, in a gabble. Her forehead was shiny with perspiration. "Time to work out what's best. It's not much to ask."

"Please go, or I'll have to phone the police."

"You really want to phone the police?"

I said nothing. I thought about Lily and the little tarnished chain and wondered what the police would make of it all.

Kate put her foot on the threshold. "I don't think so. And if you shut that door on me, I'll just wait here till your wife gets home."

"I wouldn't be so sure of that."

"Sure of what?"

"That I won't phone the police."

"I didn't kill Sean," she said. "And there's one more thing you should know."

I hesitated a moment too long. Kate undid the jacket and opened it. Underneath she was wearing jeans and a loose white T-shirt, which she smoothed over her belly and hips. The soft material flowed over and round the gentle hump below her breasts. "I'm pregnant," she said.

3

YOU COULD SAY THAT THIS IS A STORY ABOUT LOST CHILdren. The world is crowded with their absences. Sometimes we lose children because we love them too little, sometimes because we love them too much. We lose them to drugs, or to faceless men with obscene desires, or to those arbitrary catastrophes that punctuate the most orderly lives. Sometimes we're too careless, sometimes too watchful, too rich or too poor. Most often, though, we lose them to their own mysterious futures, which have no room for us.

Lily was almost certainly pregnant when I first met her. That was in May 1978, when Carlo took me to Chipping Weston for the first time. She had been married to Hugh Murthington for nearly a year.

We'd had a half-term holiday when the boarders were allowed to go home for a long weekend. They were occasions I dreaded, whether I went to my grandmother's or stayed at school. My grandmother lived not far from Hastings in a bungalow among an army of similar bungalows about two miles from the sea. She saw few people and most of them were over seventy. When I was there I felt I was living at the edge of the world among a race of zombies, about as far from the beating heart of humanity as it was possible to be.

To go to my grandmother's at half-term was bad but to remain at school was worse. There were usually others in the same forlorn position, though rarely more than half a dozen. One of the married teachers would take responsibility for us. There would be outings, perhaps picnics, visits to the cinema. We watched a lot of television and were jollied into playing games, like rounders and Monopoly, that most of us believed we had outgrown.

You would have thought that our abandoned condition would bring us together, comrades in adversity, but it rarely worked that way. Even to each other we were pariahs. The boys who were left behind were always the ones I didn't like or who were the wrong age, had the wrong interests or didn't like me. We knew ourselves for what we truly were—lost boys: the ones who weren't wanted, the ones who had been mislaid. Afterwards, we suffered the exquisite torture of hearing what the fortunate majority had done when they returned home to their families at half-term.

So when Carlo asked me to stay for half-term I was glad to accept, though I tried to conceal this from him. The weekend had an air of celebration about it, too, because the Sunday would be Carlo's fifteenth birthday.

We left school after breakfast on Friday morning and took the train to London. This was the familiar part of the journey for me: I took it when I went to my grandmother's or, less frequently, when I went to the airport on my way to my mother and stepfather. In London, however, we caught the Underground to Paddington, then boarded a train going to towns I had never been to before.

Chipping Weston, nearly two hours from London, was folded among hills. The train approached through a winding valley, threading its way through a disorderly maze of contours and following the course of a weed-choked canal. The slate roofs and stone buildings slipped in and out of view as though the town were trying to hide and making rather a bad job of it.

Carlo was smoking a cigarette as quickly as possible, hoping to finish it before the train drew into the station. He looked up as it crawled along the edge of the platform. "God, what a boring place this is," he said. "Almost as bad as school."

There was no one to meet us. We picked up our bags and walked through sun-baked streets that climbed up and down the hills. The warmth and exercise made me sweat, and I wondered whether Carlo's family would be repelled by my smell. If they weren't, I thought, they would probably find the two spots on my forehead offensive instead. I was fourteen, and ready to be unwanted.

The Murthingtons lived in a Victorian suburb to the west of the town. Their house was in a broad, curving road lined with London planes. The houses were set back from the road behind iron railings and dusty shrubberies. Each had a short driveway with enough space to take a couple of cars. Most were shabby but there was something solid, spacious and settled about the neighborhood. My grandmother's bungalow belonged in a different world.

The Murthingtons' house was built of dirty yellow brick beneath a slate roof, the openings for windows and doors framed by improbably Gothic arches. It looked oddly incomplete, as though it formed only a single wing of what had been designed as a much larger building: municipal offices, perhaps, or a modest lunatic asylum. It stood at a right angle to the road, with the front door facing the garden at the side.

After the sunshine, the hall was cool and dark. A pitch pine staircase stretched into the gloom above our heads. We dumped our bags at the foot. Carlo poked his head into one room, then led me down a long hallway into a big kitchen at the back of the house.

"I suppose we'd better go and say hello." He opened a tin on the table, took out a couple of biscuits and tossed one to me. "They're probably down the garden."

We found them sitting in deck-chairs outside a little summerhouse tucked into the angle where two walls met. The branches of an ash tree formed a green canopy overhead and the lawn was dappled with shadows. Carlo's stepmother, Lily, was playing cards at a wicker table with his little sister. Felicity was still wearing the white blouse and navy-blue skirt of her school uniform. She looked at us, smiled shyly, blushed and stared down at her cards.

Lily stood up, kissed Carlo and shook hands with me. "Lovely to see you both. Did you have a good journey?"

Carlo grunted ungraciously.

Her perfume seemed very strong—an uninvited intimacy like someone flaunting themselves in their underclothes. I noticed Felicity was staring at me.

"Charles dear," Lily went on, "your father hoped to leave work early but he must have been held up."

So that was the first time I saw her. Later I used to wish that the meeting had had more of an air of importance. In view of what happened afterwards, I came to feel, it would have been more appropriate if her beauty had immediately dazzled me, or if Fate had underlined the significance of the occasion with a clap of thunder or a small earthquake. Later still, I wished I had never met her at all.

"So, what are you boys going to do now?" Lily asked. "Would you like some tea?"

"Is there any Coke?" Carlo said.

"In the fridge. Is that what you'd like too, James? There's squash or milk, or—"

"James'll have Coke," Carlo informed her.

I nodded.

"Can I have one, too?" Felicity asked.

Lily laughed and said Felicity had a perfect sense of timing. The girl glanced at her stepmother and for an instant I glimpsed something in her expression that was at odds with this snapshot of happy family life. In May 1978, Felicity was ten years old, almost eleven, but sometimes she looked older and sadder than she had any right to look.

"Why don't you two go and get the Coke and bring me some orange juice at the same time?" Lily said to Carlo. "I want a word with Jamie about something."

"It's James," Carlo said.

I stared at the ground. Carlo and his sister went back to the house.

Lily patted the chair beside her. "Come and sit here. I'll try to remember to call you James, but you look much more like a Jamie to me. Now"—she leaned towards me, drawing me into her confidence—"I want to ask your advice. It's Charles's birthday on Sunday. His father and I were thinking of having a family outing. Do you think he'd rather go to the cinema or to a bowling alley?"

I muttered that I wasn't sure. She refused to let me get away with that, however, and maneuvered me into saying that I thought Carlo would prefer to go bowling.

"And what about afterwards?" she continued. "We thought we'd go out for a meal. Is steak and chips still his favorite?"

I was more relaxed now. "Carlo was saying on the train that he could spend the rest of his life eating pizza."

"Pizza? Great—that's settled. Luckily Felicity likes it too, and she hates steak." She smiled at me. "Carlo? Is that your name for him?"

I nodded, suddenly awkward again. "Everyone calls him that."

"It's rather nice. Charles sounds a bit formal." She put her head on one side and grinned. "A bit snooty."

Carlo and Felicity were returning with the drinks. He was walking ahead very rapidly, and in silence, with Felicity almost running after him, chattering.

"Well done, Carlo," Lily said. "You remembered the ice."

He put down the tray without saying anything, glanced at me and then away. She never called him Charles again, not in my hearing. The name stuck to him. Soon Felicity was calling him Carlo too, and her friend Millie, and at last even his father.

I think now that Lily liked to give people names. It was a way of drawing them into her circle. It gave her a special relationship with them, perhaps even a form of power over them. That's why she called me Jamie, and it didn't matter to her that nobody else did. She appropriated Carlo. She turned Carlo's father, Hugh, into Hughie. Outwardly, at least, he was a stern, formal man and the pet name sat awkwardly on him, like a party hat on an undertaker. Carlo told me later that, in the early days, Lily had tried to call his sister "Fee," but Felicity became so angry about this that she had been forced to stop. Felicity was always Lily's failure.

I don't remember a great deal more about the first weekend I spent with the Murthingtons. Everything was overshadowed at the time and in memory by what happened on Sunday evening. But memory is selective and perhaps as liable to change as everything else.

Sunday was Carlo's birthday. In the morning it was raining, which everyone said was unfair after all the fine weather we'd been having. I gave Carlo a tape of Elvis Costello's *My Aim Is True*. I knew he liked it because he rubbed it with his fingers over and over again, almost stroked it, which was what he often did with something he liked. Lily gave him clothes, and Mr. Murthington a music center with a turntable, a cassette player, a radio and a couple of free-standing loudspeakers. I was envious but pretended not to be.

Felicity presented him with a book, a biography of Eric Clapton, and Carlo said how wonderful it was, just what he wanted, although I knew he wasn't interested in dinosaurs like Clapton anymore or in the music they played. She had also made him a card, and she stood watching him as he opened it, her eyes huge and blue in her pinched white face. On the front was an ink and crayon drawing of a long-haired man in dark glasses playing a red Fender Stratocaster.

After lunch we piled into Mr. Murthington's Rover SD1 Vitesse. The car impressed me, as Carlo intended it should. He murmured that it had cost over fifteen thousand pounds. "It's the manual model," he said, with an almost equally impressive assumption of expertise. "Much sharper acceleration than the automatic, of course. It's even got central-locking."

We drove down to Swindon, where the ten-pin bowling center was. Carlo and I had been bowling before and were at least half familiar with the sport. Felicity was eager to learn, if only to emulate Carlo.

But she found the bowls much heavier than she had expected. Her first throw ended up halfway down the alley, stranded in the gully along the side. I thought she was going to burst into tears but she didn't. She chewed her lip and hugged herself instead. Carlo said that, as it was his birthday, he made the rules and she could have her go again.

Mr. Murthington and Lily hadn't played before either, and they didn't really want to play now. They tried to conceal this from everyone, even each other. Mr. Murthington retreated into himself and became even quieter, calmer and more abstracted than usual. Lily manufactured an ersatz excitement and pretended to be overjoyed when at last she knocked down a single pin. Carlo tried to jolly things along, for Felicity's sake as much as for his own, but he couldn't keep it up forever.

I don't know what pushed him over the edge. It might have been the sight of his father looking surreptitiously at his watch. It might have been Lily clapping vigorously and crying, "Hooray, darling!" when Felicity knocked down two pins, thereby attracting glances from the people using the alleys on either side. Or it might have been the heat—it was very warm in there—or the monotonous muted thuds and rumbles of the bowls or the rubbish they were playing on the jukebox. Anyway, quite deliberately, he let the bowl he was carrying slide through his fingers. He jumped aside before it hit the ground. He had been standing next to Lily. The bowl missed her foot but for an instant her face went perfectly blank and her mouth hung open. As it hit the floor, she sprang to one side like a startled deer and stumbled on an empty Coke can. She fell awkwardly, and the air rushed out of her lungs with a great gasp of surprise.

"Sorry," Carlo said. "It slipped."

Mr. Murthington helped Lily to her feet. Everyone was very nice to each other. We carried on for a little longer, but Lily said she was tired and went to sit down. She fussed over her tights, which had laddered. Mr. Murthington joined her and they talked, his head close to hers. All the enjoyment had gone out of the afternoon, not that there had been much to begin with. Nobody disagreed when Mr. Murthington suggested it might be time to go and find some pizza.

We trailed back to the Rover, but we didn't find any pizza. Lily murmured something to Mr. Murthington. He turned to the three of us on the backseat and said Lily wasn't feeling well, perhaps we would go back to Chipping Weston after all.

No one spoke on the drive back. Lily gave a little cry. Mr. Murthington glanced at her. She leaned towards him and said something I couldn't hear above the noise of the engine. We drove on. Lily moved continuously in her seat as if she couldn't get comfortable. At one point I thought I heard her moaning but I wasn't sure.

I felt uncomfortable—not because of what Carlo and Lily might be feeling but because I was witnessing it. It was a private matter, not for strangers, and with the effortless egocentricity of the adolescent, I imagined they were blaming me for the afternoon's problems. I stared out of the window at the outskirts of Chipping Weston and wondered whether they were all wishing I were somewhere else.

But we didn't drive back to the house. A few minutes later we reached the broad main street of the town. Mr. Murthington pulled over to the curb and braked. With the engine still running, he turned to the three of us on the backseat, Felicity in the middle, Carlo and me on either side. "Lily's a bit under the weather," he said, in a heartier voice than I'd ever heard him use before. "Um—I might take her down to the hospital and have her checked over. Nothing to worry about, but it's always wise to make sure, eh?" He took out his wallet and removed a couple of notes, which he handed to Carlo. "Why don't you get yourselves some fish and chips or something? Go and have a—a feast at home. I'm not expecting any change."

"There's ice cream in the freezer," Lily said faintly. "And a chocolate cake in the larder."

The three of us scrambled out of the car. We bought food and took it home. The evening that followed had a dream-like quality. In the absence of Lily and Mr. Murthington, the house became unfamiliar, even threatening. Felicity stayed up much later than she normally did. Mr. Murthington phoned from the hospital to say that everything was fine but they were keeping Lily in for a night just to make sure. He would be back in an hour or two.

Carlo told Felicity to go to bed—and to make sure she had a bath and did her teeth.

"Yes, Carlo," she said, with a meekness she never showed to Lily.

When she was upstairs, Carlo raided the sideboard in the dining room and poured us both large vodkas, which we topped up with Coke.

"Vodka's better than Scotch," he said, with a worldly air I envied. "They can't smell it on your breath."

We clinked glasses solemnly and I wished him a happy birthday. "Is she going to be OK?" I asked. "Lily, I mean."

Carlo swallowed a third of his drink. "I couldn't give a fuck."

Glasses in hand, we strolled round the garden, still full of the long twilight of early summer, and smoked cigarettes. Afterwards we gave ourselves more vodka and put Elvis Costello on the music center. Soon I had drunk enough to feel unsteady. Carlo suggested a nightcap and I became even unsteadier. When at last we went to bed, Mr. Murthington had still not returned.

At breakfast, Mr. Murthington said Lily was fine but she needed a rest in hospital. "Um—women's trouble," he murmured, staring at his cornflakes. "It may be better if you boys go back to school on the earlier train—there's one at ten thirty-five." He smiled at Felicity. "And you're spending the day at Millie's, aren't you? I don't have to worry about you."

Lily sent her love, he went on, as an afterthought. Carlo winked at me and sent his back. I muttered something about thanking her for her hospitality.

Mr. Murthington took us to the station but didn't wait for the train to come.

"Trust that woman to ruin my birthday," Carlo said, as his father drove away.

"What's wrong with her?"

"She's a bitch."

"No—I mean why's she in hospital? The bowl didn't hit her."

He shrugged and stared down the line. The train was a small black dot, growing slowly louder and noisier. Neither of us spoke.

Once we were on our way, Carlo took the Clapton biography out of his bag and opened it. I picked up a *Daily Mail* that somebody had left on a seat across the aisle. I read about terrible things happening in other parts of the world. We travelled most of the way to London in silence. It was only when we were on the Underground that the shadows of Chipping Weston dropped away and everything was normal again. We talked about music and football and how, when we were rich, we were going to build the perfect stereo system together.

I never found out for sure what happened to Lily in the bowling alley but I can guess. From something she let slip later, I know she had had a miscarriage in the first year of her marriage. It seems more than likely that when Carlo dropped the bowl it triggered a sequence of events that led to her losing the baby.

A commonplace family tragedy—up to fifty percent of all pregnancies end in loss, most of them during the early stages and often before the mothers even know they are pregnant. Miscarriages happen all the time.

Millions upon millions of lost children. And one was Lily's.

4

I HAD TO BRING KATE INTO THE HOUSE. IF I LEFT HER ON THE doorstep, it would increase the chance of someone noticing her. There was, of course, the possibility that someone had already seen her, or that they would see her when she got into the car with me, but there wasn't much I could do about that. So she sat on the chair in the hall while I wrote a note to Nicky and found the car keys. She folded her arms across her chest, and looked around her. "It's a nice house, Jamie. You and your wife must be very happy."

"How did you find me?" I said.

"Carlo told me your name the other night. I found you on the Web."

Her answer just gave me more questions to ask. I remembered the aubergine and mushroom bake. I turned off the oven and left my supper to cool, uneaten. The smell made my mouth water. I scooped up my jacket and took her out to the car. Once inside the Saab, we would be screened by the tinted glass of the windows.

"Where are we going?" Kate asked, as I started the engine.

"Somewhere you'll be safe for the time being. That's what you want, isn't it?"

She put her right hand on the steering wheel, forcing me to look at her. "If you take me to the police, I'll make sure it all comes out. Everything."

Everything? But what did she mean by everything? No one knew everything, not even Lily, not even Felicity. Not even me.

"I mean it," she said.

"It's all right." I pretended to alter the heating controls so she couldn't see my face. "I'm not taking you to the police."

"And it mustn't be a hotel or anything like that." For the first time her voice had an edge of panic. "There mustn't be people."

"OK," I said gently, as though she were a fractious child. "As a matter of interest, though, why not? There's a hundred places in London where they never really look at you, as long as you pay your bills. And if you pay cash—"

"No." Her fingers tightened round the steering wheel. "I don't want to be with anyone. I want to be alone."

"Why?"

"Because—because someone might see me. I can't take the risk, not yet. I need to change how I look. I need to know what's happening. And I need time to *think*."

"In that case, I've got an idea where you can go, but I'm afraid it won't be very comfortable."

"That doesn't matter."

"We'll have to stop on the way and buy a few things. You'll need some food and a toothbrush, that sort of thing."

I expected Kate to ask where I was taking her, but she didn't. I drove first to a big branch of Tesco. I made her stay in the car. She noticed me taking the keys from the ignition. As I was walking away, she opened the car door. "Jamie?"

I stopped.

"Would you get me a packet of cigarettes and a lighter?"

"What sort?"

"Marlboro Light. Thank you."

It was the first time I had seen her smile. I went inside and bought the lighter and the cigarettes. She had made no other requests so I used my imagination. I bought water, fruit, milk, cereal, cheese, ham and a torch. I remembered toothpaste, a toothbrush, soap and toilet paper. I joined a queue at a checkout but had to go back for picnic plates and plastic cutlery.

As I waited to pay, I found myself glancing round for the cameras. I read somewhere that ten percent of the world's CCTV cameras are in Britain: the average person is photographed three hundred times a day. These are not reassuring statistics if you are aiding and abetting someone suspected of murder. I paid cash and felt like a criminal on the run.

Kate was sitting in the car just as I'd left her. I put the shopping into the boot beside a down sleeping-bag I had last used in Ireland the previous summer. She said nothing when I slid into the driver's seat.

"Are you OK?" I asked.

"I feel—" She broke off and looked directly at me. "If you really want to know, I feel naked." Suddenly she smiled again. "It has its good side. It's like being a child again, I suppose. A baby. I don't own anything. I don't have many choices to make." Her voice wobbled. "If you wanted the short answer, though, I'd have to say I feel like shit."

I gave her the cigarettes and lighter, which earned me another smile. "Smoke if you want."

I started the engine and drove out of the car park. Kate ripped the cellophane from the packet but she didn't light a cigarette. For a few miles neither of us spoke. I glanced surreptitiously at her more than once, and I caught her doing the same to me. *I may have a daughter. She may be in the car beside me.* For the first time the full realization hit me, so hard that I couldn't find any other words to say, even to myself.

Kate was the first to break the silence. "So, where are we going?"

"London—to an empty building in Queen's Park. Rather primitive, I'm afraid, but it's vandal-proof. You shouldn't be disturbed, at least not by humans."

"Then by what?"

I shrugged. "I don't know. It's been empty for a while. There may be rats or cats."

"I see."

I glanced at her. "Unless you'd rather go to a hotel or a bed-and-breakfast. It's not too late to change your mind."

"No. What do you do, anyway?"

"I'm an architectural engineer. The company I work for maintains the infrastructure of buildings."

"Like the drains and stuff?"

"And the electricity and the water supply. And the insulation, the ventilation and the heating system. We don't actually design the buildings, but we design and take care of all the things that make a building work."

We drove another mile in silence, crawling along Western Avenue towards the great gray heart of London. The evening was overcast. The rain had stopped, apart from the occasional flurry of drops against the windscreen. I expected her to ask more about where we were going, but she didn't. In the end, I said, "I'm taking you to an old chapel. I went round it today so I've got the keys. There's a room at the back with a sink and a lavatory. The odds are that no one will go there for weeks."

"A chapel," Kate said. "Is it old?"

I thought she probably meant, "Is it spooky?"

"Not as chapels go. It looks like a glorified Scout hut. Even in its prime, it can't have held more than a hundred and fifty people. And I doubt there's been a service in it for forty years."

"What are you doing there?"

"It's a change-of-use job. The architects have been in, and we've been in, and now we have to sort out the planning permission before it goes to tender."

The chapel was in a side road between Kensal Vale and Kilburn. The area was largely commercial now, and there weren't many people about at this time. I parked the car fifty yards up the street. We walked quickly to the chapel, carrying the sleeping bag and the shopping. I ignored the main doors and made for the tall gate at the side, which was faced with corrugated iron and topped with loops of rusting barbed wire. It took me a moment to find the right key from the bunch the agents had given me. Kate was nervous, looking up and down the road, her breathing fast and jagged.

I found the key, and the gate swung back with a creak, opening into a damp alleyway running between the wall of the chapel on the right and a tall chain-mesh fence topped with more barbed wire on the left. Beyond the fence was the gated car park of a small office block, closed for the weekend.

We slipped into the alley. I shut the gate behind us and locked it, then led the way down the path, Kate's footsteps keeping pace behind me. I could do anything to her, I thought. Here she was, a small, attractive young woman, trusting herself to a middle-aged man she had met only a few hours ago, alone with him in a place without witnesses where no one would come for weeks.

At the far end of the alley was a doorway with a boarded-up window. The door was secured with a five-lever lock and a Yale. More minutes crawled by as I fumbled for the keys. Kate breathed noisily behind me. I tried to work as quietly as possible. Even here people might be listening. I knew from long and often bitter experience that empty buildings were not always as empty as they seemed.

The second lock yielded. I pushed open the door and stooped to pick up the carrier-bags. The room was small and narrow. It smelt of damp and rot and the charred ghosts of old fires.

"Shut the door," I murmured. Kate obeyed and the room became entirely dark. I switched on the torch and its wavering beam found her white face. "At least you can have a light," I said, feeling like an inadequate host trying to emphasize the virtues of the accommodation on offer. I put down the carrier-bags and blundered along the room to a door at the end. "The sink and the lavatory are in here. Not very clean, I'm afraid, but the water's still on. Try not to use it unnecessarily. I'm not sure who's in earshot."

Kate said nothing. I turned and let the beam of the torch play up and down the room. In its spotlight we saw empty cans, a pile of old newspapers, and the blackened remains of a wooden kitchen chair. In the wall on the right was a third doorway, also smoke-blackened. It was padlocked shut.

"Someone squatted here for a while," I said. "There was a fire. That was when they boarded up the window, and put on the extra locks." I found the key for the padlock and opened the door. "That's the chapel itself. Be careful about light. Don't use the torch in there. There isn't a blackout."

"I don't want to see it," Kate said. "I can feel it."

It was not a rational thing to say but I understood what she meant. You could sense the cold, musty silence in the chapel, the empty space, the smell of decay, the smell of a place un-loved and abandoned. I shut the door and re-fastened the padlock.

"We'd better make you comfortable." I sounded falsely jolly. "I'll put the sleeping bag here, shall I? Food and drink in that bag, loo rolls and so on in the other. I'll leave you the torch, of course."

"When will you come back?"

I thought quickly. Nicky and I had planned to go to the garden center in the morning. I'd have to find a way of post-poning it. "In the morning. I'll try to get here between ten and eleven." I hesitated. "We'll have to have a proper talk then. You'll have decided what you want to do, I expect."

Kate laughed, almost a giggle, a sound that teetered to-wards hysteria.

"Well, then." I handed her the torch. I felt the warmth of her hand as her skin brushed mine and for an instant I felt a twinge of desire, as unexpected as it was unwanted, because she was so completely at my mercy in this place. Power is an aphrodisiac. Nobody knew she was here. I could do any-thing to her.

"Jamie?"

I sucked in my breath. It was as though her mother had spoken. Not just that she'd called me Jamie but the way she'd said my name. Something in my body responded faintly to the timbre of her voice. The ghosts of old emotions touched

me. I felt edgy, desperate and unsatisfied—*sixteen again.*
"What is it?"

"Can I ask you a favor? Another." Kate was calmer now,
and she moved away from me. "Can you buy me a phone on
the way here tomorrow? I'll pay you back, I promise."

I wondered how she would manage that. I said, "OK."

It was easier to say yes than no. Time was moving on.
Nicky would be back before me, which had a number of
unwelcome implications.

I jingled the keys. "I'm going to have to lock the gate at
the end of the alley. I suppose at a pinch you could always
climb over. I won't lock this door, though." I ran the torch
beam over it. "You can put the Yale down when I've gone,
and there's a bolt." I worked it to and fro to make sure it was
still usable. "It's not too late to change your mind. You don't
have to stay here."

"I'll be all right."

I shrugged, then realized she probably hadn't seen the
movement.

"Jamie—do you mind if I call you that, by the way?"

"Of course not."

"Thanks for everything. Anyway, you need to go home.
I'll be fine—see you in the morning."

I gave her the torch and she shone the beam on my face. It
was deliberate. As I walked down the alley, it occurred to me
that perhaps she'd been searching for a resemblance between
my face and hers. If I'd found my father after twenty-five
years, that's what I should have wanted to do—to gaze into
his face for as long as I could in the hope of finding a reflection of myself. Whether I would have done it is another matter. But a lost child is always on the lookout for a parent.

. . .

My father had left little of himself behind, besides his genes, a handful of unreliable memories and a creased photograph. All the rest is silence.

I was seven when he died. The photograph shows a slim, dark man with a slim, dark moustache and what seems like very long hair. It had been taken on his wedding day, and he is wearing a suit with wide lapels and an even wider tie. My mother is in a very short dress and a hat with an enormous brim. In the photograph she is gripping his arm with both hands as though she is afraid he might blow away if she doesn't hold on tight.

I don't have a direct memory of my father's clothes, face or hair. But I remember the feel of the moustache, the way it tickled my skin when he kissed me goodnight, and how he often smelt of sour masculine things, like alcohol and sweat, cigarettes and aftershave.

He worked for a wholesaler's firm specializing in office products, especially stationery. It was based in Bristol, where we lived, and his territory covered much of the West Midlands. That was why he was in Birmingham on the last Friday evening before Christmas in 1970. It was about half past six in the evening, and he was hurrying home. A white Transit van ploughed into the side of his red Capri as he was driving down the Bristol road. The driver, who had been celebrating his last day at work since half past eleven in the morning, wasn't wearing a seat belt. He was killed too.

The most important thing I remember about my father, with blinding clarity, is that I loved him. Love seems a pallid, inadequate word for what I felt. It was a form of adoration.

I can't remember his face but I can remember waiting at the gate for him to come home. If it was raining, I watched from the front window. I carried his empty briefcase about the house and pretended I was him. When, suddenly, he was no longer there, I persuaded myself that he was away on a longer trip than usual. Although I was told many times that he was dead, I clung to this belief as the weeks became months. Day after day, I waited at the gate or watched from the front window.

Before we married Nicky once said to me, when she was asking about my childhood, that the further back you go, the more fictional memory becomes. We create myths and legends from the debris of our past. She said we make patterns to keep the chaos from overwhelming us.

So I don't know for certain that my parents' marriage was unhappy. I think I remember feeling uncomfortable if I was in a room with the two of them, and raised voices as I lay in bed at night. But I may have invented all that. It may have been a hypothesis that I constructed to explain what happened afterwards, a hypothesis that subsequently solidified and became indistinguishable from fact.

When she met my father, my mother had been a secretary working for the sales director of the company that employed him. After he died, she brushed up her typing and shorthand speeds and went back to work. Gran came to live with us, to look after the house and me. My mother found employment with a local construction company, which did a lot of contract work in Saudi Arabia. That was how she met the man who became my stepfather.

Ed was an American engineer spending several months in England because his company and my mother's were working on the same project in Jeddah. He and my mother became friendly but she rarely asked him back to the house. On the few occasions when I met him, it was on neutral territory, like a restaurant. He seemed infinitely tall and remote. His American accent made him unreal and mildly glamorous. He was also very generous. I had no objection whatsoever when my mother said she and Ed were going to get married. It seemed rather a good idea.

It proved a good idea for my mother but less so for me. Ed's job took him all over the world. While he worked on the project of the moment—a dam, a hospital, an office block, a freeway—she lived in a compound with all the other American employees. Surrounded by barbed wire, and with the perimeters patrolled by armed guards, these were green enclaves, studded with single-story houses arranged with military neatness along miniature suburban roads. The inhabitants drove everywhere, even if it was only a hundred yards—to the PX store, the bridge party, or the little open-air cinema.

I hated it. And I also hated my stepbrother from Ed's previous marriage: Danny, three years older than me. He once stole my clothes when we went swimming in a neighbor's pool and made me run home in my swimming trunks. He laughed at my accent and my ignorance. He put salt on my cereal and stole my pocket money to buy cigarettes. At night he gave me Chinese burns in the bedroom he was forced to share with me.

Ed ignored me wherever possible. As far as he was concerned, I wasn't really there. Eventually he and my mother decided there wasn't much room for me in their busy and otherwise satisfactory lives. This was especially obvious when my mother became pregnant with the first of the three

children that she and Ed were to have together. I was an unwanted reminder of another relationship.

It seemed like an eternity but it was less than a year after
my mother's remarriage that she and Ed made up their minds
to send me to school in England. They persuaded themselves
that this was the best thing they could do for me. The sad
thing is that they might well have been right. Money was not
a problem. Ed's employers paid for most of my upbringing—
for my education and the return flights once a year between
the UK and wherever my mother and Ed were living.

I remember my first day at boarding-school, when I wept
among the lank, dusty bushes at the bottom of the housemaster's garden. I decided then that the best way to survive
was to cut myself off. My father was dead, and so, for most of
the time, to all intents and purposes, was my mother. I told
myself I no longer loved her and after a while I believed it. It
was better that way. If someone is effectively dead, they cannot hurt you.

All this helps to explain why Carlo Murthington was so
important. It wasn't only him I liked: it was his family as well.
They weren't perfect but for most of the time they seemed to
live together in reasonable harmony, which was more than
my own did. Lily was stepmother to Carlo and Felicity, as
Ed was my stepfather, but she never stopped encouraging
them to like her. They talked to each other.

The second time I went to stay in Chipping Weston was at
the end of the summer holidays in 1978, after I had returned
from visiting my mother and stepfather and their other children in Turkey. For me, the highlight of the visit was when
Mr. Murthington took Carlo and me to Rackford.

Hugh Murthington was a tall, thin man who, as a boy, must have been very fair. Now his complexion had weathered to a mottled red and the bright hair had turned wiry and gray. He seemed very old to me—at the time he was probably in his fifties. He had a small moustache that gave him a military air at odds with his hesitant speech. Not that he said much. Carlo made a joke of this and if he wrote to me during the holidays would sometimes refer to his father under the codename CTCL, which stood for the wartime slogan "Careless Talk Costs Lives." Carlo's grandfather had been a partner in the town's auctioneers, and he had left his son comfortably off. Hugh Murthington still worked in a vague and not very arduous capacity for his father's firm, but he also pursued business interests of his own.

He had bought the decommissioned RAF airfield at Rackford as a long-term investment. The first time we went there was on a Sunday afternoon. The Rover Vitesse had just been cleaned, and its metallic blue paintwork gleamed in the sun. Mr. Murthington drove on to the larger of the remaining runways. He stopped and switched off the engine. He turned round to Carlo and me, sitting on the backseat. Carlo was pretending to be blasé about the outing—he was reading a magazine, whistling under his breath and rolling his eyes at the same time. He had been there before, of course, and treated the occasion with the disdain he felt it deserved.

"All right, boys," Mr. Murthington said. "Um—your turn now."

Carlo went first. He chugged along the runway in second gear and only stalled twice, once when he mistook the brake for the clutch, and once when he accelerated, changed up to third gear and tried to break the land-speed record, where-upon Mr. Murthington hauled on the handbrake.

Then it was my turn. While Carlo laughed unkindly in the backseat, Hugh Murthington taught me how to find first gear, second gear and reverse. He showed me how to balance the clutch against the accelerator. He allowed me to drive fifty yards, very slowly and mainly in first gear, charting a waver-ing course like a nervous kangaroo. I was terrified and exhila-rated, and by the time I'd finished, my shirt was soaked with sweat. I was also amazed that he trusted me enough to let me drive his car.

"Well done," Carlo's father said afterwards. "Your first try? Um, not at all bad."

He was a kind man, Hugh Murthington, and in some ways I wish he had been my own father.

5

NICKY WAS ALREADY HOME WHEN I GOT BACK FROM Queen's Park. She was in the sitting-room, watching the news with a glass of wine. I could tell she was in a good mood.

"How was Henry James?" I asked.

"Scary. What happened to you?"

I had been deliberately vague in my note to her, saying simply that I had had to go out. "You remember that place I went today? The old chapel they want to turn into a carpet warehouse? Someone thought some kids were trying to break in. The police had our office number—Rachel was working late and phoned me. I've still got the keys so it was easy enough to pop over. But the traffic was heavier than I thought it'd be."

"And had they?"

"Had they what?"

Nicky looked puzzled. "Had they broken in, the kids?"

"No, luckily not. False alarm. There's an alley at the side, and they'd climbed over the gate but they hadn't got any further. Still, we may have to review the security."

I went into the kitchen to fetch myself a glass of wine and retrieve my supper from the oven. Nicky and I watched the rest of the news. There was nothing about a dead man called Sean. Afterwards we watched something else, but I cannot for the life of me remember what it was. All I could think of was Kate and the unanswered questions she had brought with her.

Nicky went to bed before I did. I went into the little room I used as a study and switched on the laptop. I searched for the name "Sean," looking for an entry that included at least one of the words "died," "murder," "death," "murdered." I asked the search engine to return pages written in English and in any format. I wanted pages that had been updated in the last three months. This brought up nearly two million hits, many of them emanating, as I should have predicted, from Ireland. I ploughed through the first couple of hundred and found no Seans whose death appeared to have a plausible connection with Kate. I had not realized that the Worldwide Web contained so many dead Seans.

My next problem was how I was going to explain my absence tomorrow to Nicky. In the event, I was lucky—or so I thought at the time. When I got upstairs, she wasn't asleep but reading in bed. "What's this?" I said. "The next one for the book group?"

She looked at me over her glasses—she had recently taken to wearing them for reading, and I thought they made her look voluptuously prim. She held up the paperback so I could see the jacket. It had a photograph of a little girl, monochrome and forlorn. "That reminds me," she said. "I know we were planning to go to the garden center tomorrow but would you mind if I gave it a miss? Miranda asked if I'd go up to London with her. She wants me to help her choose a dress for a wedding."

"Of course not. When will you be back?"

"I'm not sure. She's picking me up at about ten. We should be back by early evening. We'll have to be—I think they're going out. Anyway, I'll phone."

So the deceit was easy. In the morning it was sunny, and Nicky and I had a leisurely breakfast in the conservatory. After she had left, I went into my study and phoned the hospice. I asked to speak to Lily Murthington. The nurse said she had had a bad night and was sleeping now. She didn't want to disturb her.

I had told Nicky I might go for a walk so she wouldn't be surprised if she phoned the house and found I wasn't there. I drove to a supermarket, not the one we'd visited yesterday evening, and withdrew some cash from an ATM. I felt both ridiculous and paranoid as I took these precautions. Either they were unnecessary or they were inadequate, but they were like touching wood or crossing my fingers: a way of tipping my hat respectfully to the supreme power of Fate.

I bought another packet of Marlboro Light, a phone and an in-car charger. On the way to Queen's Park, I listened to the news on both national and local radio stations. There was no mention of a young man called Sean, living or dead. I didn't want to ask Kate for information because the more she told me the more I should be involved with her. But I had to know what was going on—for my own protection, and for Nicky's. At the back of my mind was the tarnished chain that Lily had shown me.

I parked several streets away from the chapel. It was a Saturday morning, and there were plenty of people about. I tried not to glance over my shoulder as I unlocked the gate to the alleyway beside the chapel. After all, I had a perfect right to be there—I was a keyholder, with a legitimate purpose for visiting the place. It wasn't enough to reassure me.

The alley was damp and airless. The noise and smells of the street dropped away. I walked to the end and tapped on the door of the little room at the back. I heard nothing. I tapped again and said, as loudly as I dared, "It's me, Jamie."

The name "Jamie" slipped out by accident. It seemed to belong to someone else, not to a respectable architectural engineer but to a wild boy who had taken risks and paid the price, and was now taking even more risks.

A bolt scraped on the other side of the door.

"Kate, it's me," I whispered.

The door swung backwards and I stepped quickly into the room. She closed it gently and for a moment we were alone in the darkness. I heard her breathing. The atmosphere was thick with stale cigarette smoke. Mixed with it was the faintest hint of perfume, perhaps soap.

Kate switched on the torch. In the artificial light, she looked pale and unhealthy. My eyes struggled to adjust. The smoke was making them smart. She was still wearing the blue waxed jacket. I wondered whether she had taken it off. "How did you sleep?" I asked.

"I didn't—not much."

"I rang the hospice this morning. Your mother had a bad night, too."

Kate took a step towards me. "You talked to her?"

"They wouldn't let me. She was asleep and they didn't want to disturb her. I left my number with them."

"Have you got a phone?"

"For you? Yes, but it's in the car. It needs charging."

The torch in her hand dipped and my shadow swooped along the wall. I wanted to see her properly, and also to breathe fresher air. I said, "Let's go next door. There's natural light and a few chairs."

"If you want."

I unlocked the connecting door. Most of the windows in the chapel had been boarded up but there were two fixed lights in the roof and another over the main door to the road.

"Avoid the wall on the left," I said. "It's not safe underfoot." The chapel had a sprung floor and on that side the ends of the joists were rotten. "We shouldn't be overheard if we talk quietly."

I led the way down the chapel to a pile of wooden chairs with elm seats and racks for hymnals. I found two that were usable. Kate and I sat facing each other and a couple of meters apart. It was a formal arrangement, as though we had business to transact. It was much colder in the chapel than it was outside and the high space was filled with pale, grubby light. Kate wrapped the jacket around the bulge of the growing baby, fumbled in her pocket and brought out the packet of cigarettes. She stared at me. Then she sighed, shook out a cigarette and lit it.

"I need to know more," I said. "What happened to Sean? There was nothing on the news."

"There wouldn't be, not necessarily—not if they haven't found the body yet."

"What's his surname?"

She seemed not to have heard me. She bit her lower lip and blurted out a question of her own: "You know Chipping Weston?"

"I used to. I haven't been there for years, since I—I knew your mother."

There was silence, short but uncomfortable, while we both thought about that.

"I grew up there," Kate said. "My mother still lives in the same house. I mean, she did, until she and Dad got too ill. They leased a flat in Ealing to be nearer hospitals. That's why she's in St. Margaret's. She's given up the lease on the flat now but she's still got the house, and I've been living there off and on over the last few months. Are you sure you want to hear all this?"

"I don't think I've got much choice."

"Wouldn't it be safer for you not to know?"

I wondered whether she was right. I said, "But I want to know. And if I'm going to help you, I need to."

She inhaled. "Carlo did it," she said, in a flat, dull voice, and the smoke drifted out of her mouth and nostrils.

"Carlo did what?"

"Carlo killed him, of course. Killed Sean. Bloody Carlo, the prodigal son. My brother—except he's not my brother, of course. That's the whole point. That's—that's *important*."

"You're not making much sense."

She smiled and, to my surprise, I smiled back at her. "I'm sorry. I keep forgetting there's so much you don't know. I'm not thinking straight. Until my father died, I hardly knew Carlo."

"Your father."

She blushed. "I can't stop calling him that. He thought he was my father, and I thought he was too. I still do."

For a moment, neither of us moved or spoke. I listened to the rumble of traffic outside. Someone sounded a two-tone

horn. Music rose and fell as a car went by with its windows
open.

"When did he die?" I asked. "Hugh, that is."

"In October last year. He had a stroke in the summer, and
he never really got over that. My mother had been diagnosed
with breast cancer by then. She had a lumpectomy, then ra-
diotherapy and chemotherapy." She wrinkled her face. "But
there were secondaries, first lung and then bone."

"Who's the father of your baby?"

She blinked. "Sean."

"Your mother said you were going to marry him."

"That was earlier. I met him in London. I was temping, and
I met him through work." She glanced at me, then away.
"And things sort of went on from there. We lived together for
a while. But after my father died, we quarrelled." She laughed
without humor. "Sean always wanted his own way. It's one of
the things I used to like about him, actually. He seemed so
certain about everything."

I looked at her belly. The pregnancy wasn't showing
much. "When did you break up with him?"

"October. But it was the other way round—he broke up
with me." Kate's eyes widened. "Oh, I see what you mean. He
came down to Chipping Weston after Christmas. That's when
I got pregnant. We had a sort of reconciliation." She patted
her stomach. "But it didn't last."

She stubbed out her cigarette. I waited.

"He didn't want *me*, anyway," she said. "He was out for
what he could get."

"He needed money?"

"He did by then. He used to have it coming out of his
ears—he earned at least ten times what I did. He had this

amazing flat near Covent Garden. The trouble was he spent it all, and the flat was only rented. So when they fired him, he didn't have anything to fall back on." Kate rubbed her forearm as though feeling for old bruises. "Results were down, and he had a row with his boss. He actually hit him. And the sort of job Sean was doing, it's a very small world. Word got out. He knew it wouldn't be easy to find another job, even if business got better. So that suddenly made me attractive again. In financial terms, that is—until he found out the truth."

I remembered the house, the partnership in the auctioneers' firm, the investments. "He thought your father had left you something?"

Kate shook her head. "He knew my father had been fairly well off. But things hadn't been going so well the last few years. Anyway, there was nothing for Sean. What's left of Dad's estate will come to me and Carlo in the end, but Mum has a life interest."

When you're young, I thought, everything seems permanent, from your own youth to other people's money. "Who's the executor?" I asked.

"Carlo. Anyway, Sean went off, and I didn't see him again until earlier this week when he came back to Chipping Weston." She traced the outline of the packet of cigarettes in her pocket. "And Carlo was there. You don't know about Carlo yet, do you?"

"How can I?"

She shivered. "I didn't see much of him when I was growing up. He was married for a while and they used to live quite near us. But after the divorce he moved away. He lived all over the place—Canada, Africa, the States."

She paused, as though she was expecting me to say something. I stared at the floor.

"Things changed after Dad's first stroke," she went on. "Carlo came back. First it was just a visit, and then, after the funeral, he decided to stay. He's living in London now." She hesitated, and I had the sense that she was on the brink of telling me more. But she shook her head violently as though shaking away unpleasant memories. "He never liked my mother, you see—that was why he stayed away. He never liked me, either."

"Did he know?"

"About you and my mother?"

I nodded. Even now I found it hard to put it into words.

"He does now. I don't think he did before. But maybe he suspected." Kate ran her tongue along her lips, as if her mouth was dry. "Have you heard of Rackford?"

"The airfield?"

She nodded, licking her lips again and feeling for another cigarette.

"What's Rackford got to do with this?" I said loudly, far too loudly.

Surprised, she stared at me. "Because that's what they both want, Sean and Carlo. They want the old airfield."

"Why?"

Kate wasn't listening. "Except Sean doesn't want anything now." She gave a high, nervous laugh. "But in a way he's got it because that's where his body is. He's at Rackford, Jamie, and he's waiting for the police to find him."

· · ·

Every time I stayed with Carlo at Chipping Weston, apart from that very first time, we went to Rackford. Mr. Murthington would take us, or sometimes Lily. In those days most of the land was let to a farmer in the village. He had ploughed some of the ground. Whenever I see a field of oilseed rape glowing improbably yellow in the early summer, I think of Rackford.

Rape was still a novelty in England during the 1970s. Mr. Murthington explained that the farmer was methodically breaking up the ground to grow wheat. Year after year, as more and more of the former airfield came under cultivation, the patches of rape moved from one area to another. Its vivid color was exotic and its smell—a combination of oil and fresh urine—faintly disturbing. Even now, the strange, ambiguous scent takes me back to Hugh Murthington's Rover Vitesse.

The farmer used some of the less fertile ground for grazing. Along the western boundary of the airfield, where the land began to rise, there was an irregular strip of ground so broken up that it was little good to anyone. It was enclosed by the airfield's perimeter fence only because it bordered the lane, and it would have been more trouble than it was worth to leave it out. There was a side entrance to the airfield here—if you walked briskly, you could reach the village in ten minutes, or even less if you cut through the fields behind the church.

Most of this wasteground was filled with a patch of woodland lining the sides of a steep little valley. A stream ran—or, rather, strolled—along the bottom, and near the banks in the spring were cuckoo pints, wild garlic and wood anemones. Here, too, were places where ferns grew, natural bedding, their leaves curling like green intimacies in the spring, then growing broad and dusty in the summer. On the far bank, the land rose sharply towards the fence and the lane beyond.

Before the Second World War, the land at Rackford had been the property of a local farmer, who had made a tidy profit when he sold it to the Ministry of Defence in 1940, and whose son subsequently paid Hugh Murthington a token rent to use it for agriculture once again. When I knew the airfield, in the late 1970s, the longest runway had been broken up and sold for hardcore. But the smaller runways and the perimeter road were still there.

Many of the buildings survived—the control tower, the two hangars and an untidy cluster of Nissen huts and single-story brick buildings. The farmer used the larger hangar for storing winter fodder, rusting farm machinery, tractor tires worn smooth and all the rubbish a working farm accumulates. The other buildings were sliding towards ruin.

Hugh Murthington had bought the airfield in the early 1970s, when a property developer had lurched into bankruptcy. From his point of view, the most important thing about it was the road access. Sooner or later, he explained to Carlo and me, this would make the land soar in value. The main road ran east–west a few miles south of Rackford. A broad minor road led north towards the village, passing what had once been the main entrance of the airfield, still with its guardpost and padlocked gates. In the long run, he was right about the significance of the road access but, of course, by that time it was far too late for him to profit by it.

The second time I went to Rackford, it was winter, January 1979, in the last week of the Christmas holidays. There had been a hard frost overnight and it was a cold, brilliant day. The sun made the hard edges of the buildings gleam and there were puddles of black ice in the potholes of the runway.

The plan had been that Hugh Murthington would take us, but at breakfast that morning he had had a phone call: a pipe had burst at his office, and he had to deal with it. So Lily said that she would drive us instead. I sat in the front of the Rover with her. Carlo was in the back behind me, and Felicity bounced up and down beside him. As we turned into the airfield, we saw a fox trotting with fluid elegance not far ahead of us. It was at least a yard long, its coat rich and glossy. Ears cocked, it glanced back. The white tip of its tail twitched and then the fox slipped without haste into a dense patch of brambles.

Lily allowed all of us to drive that day, even Felicity. It was her first lesson. We pushed the driver's seat as far forward as it would go. Even so, she had to perch on the edge to reach the pedals, with Carlo's coat wedged between her little body and the seatback, and my coat underneath her so she could see through the windscreen. The Rover jerked and stalled repeatedly. In the end Felicity hammered the steering-wheel in her frustration.

"Don't worry, darling," Lily said. "That's how everyone starts."

"But I'm not everyone," Felicity shouted. "I'm me."

Lily laughed, which made matters worse. It was not only that she laughed but how. When I came to know Lily better, to study her, I discovered that she had a small repertoire of laughs. This one had ended in a discreet gurgle and was accompanied by the arching of the eyebrows. She used it especially with those she felt she could safely patronize.

Felicity blushed, and her pale complexion cruelly betrayed the rush of blood. Carlo muttered something under his breath. He leaned forward and put his hand on his sister's shoulder.

"Handbrake on," he said, in a low, monotonous voice. "Good. Press down the clutch. Put the gear in neutral. No, find where you can wiggle it from side to side—yes, that's it. Now start the engine again. Good."

The touch of his hand and the calm instructions quietened her. She obeyed. Carlo taught her how to lift her foot slowly off the clutch until she felt the biting point. He was good with mechanical things, and with Felicity too. All the impatience and surliness he showed towards Lily and his father dropped away. Felicity would have done anything he asked of her.

Lily watched with a smile fixed on her face. Soon Felicity, under Carlo's instructions, was edging along the runway in first gear. A few minutes later, he talked her into changing up to second. In another five seconds, she stalled, but by then it no longer mattered. "Good girl," Carlo said. "You're a quick learner."

When it was my turn, Lily made a determined effort to redeem herself as a driving instructor. She rested her arm on the back of my seat and told me what all the controls did, what all the dials were for. I had never been so close to her. I saw a tiny mole on the side of her neck and noticed how her lashes curled, which I now realize may have had something to do with art rather than nature. Her perfume—I learned later that she always wore Chanel No. 5—seeped into me: it was a smell that, like the oilseed rape, both repelled and attracted. When at last I started the engine, I forgot the car was in gear—it bucked as the engine stalled.

Lily touched my shoulder. "Silly boy. Come on. Try again." Felicity giggled.

Lily rounded on her. "Do be quiet, dear. You'll distract Jamie. After all, you know how difficult it can be."

Despite my own experience, I had assumed that adults had a duty to love and protect the children in their care. In those days it never occurred to me that liking or disliking could come into it. I realize now that Lily must have disliked her stepdaughter, that perhaps she repaid hatred with hatred.

I was a slow learner. Unlike Felicity. And most unlike Carlo.

Carlo terrified Kate. She made that very clear.

"He killed Sean at Rackford." She turned her head to look at me. We were sitting side by side in the decaying chapel, and I was growing colder by the minute. "It was only yesterday but it seems like weeks ago."

"How did he do it?" I said. *Why did it have to be Rackford?*

Kate stroked her belly with both hands, an unconscious movement, as though she wanted to reassure the person who was growing inside. "Just lost it and went for him. I saw him do it."

"I don't understand. Why?"

"Carlo started hitting me and Sean tried to stop him. So Carlo knocked him down. Then he kept hitting him and kicking him, and there was all the blood." As the hands stroked the belly, Kate's voice wavered in volume and quality like a poorly tuned radio program. "I told you—he just lost it. He's always scared me. Carlo, I mean. Even before Daddy died." She looked quickly at me out of the corner of her eyes, something her mother used to do, and her shoulders lifted and fell with the smallest of shrugs, simply to show that she knew I had heard it too: *Daddy.* "There was blood all over the place," she went on. "And Carlo said, 'And now I'm coming for you. If the police don't get you first.' "

"What did he mean by that?"

"That he was going to make it look like I killed Sean."

"Are you sure Sean was dead?"

Kate screwed up her face and rocked to and fro, her whole body nodding. The chair was digging into my back. I stood up and stretched. Her eyes followed my movements. I felt very tired. I like problems to have boundaries or at least a framework for describing them. But Kate's were messy and shapeless. There was no telling where they began or where and how they would end.

"You don't know what Carlo's done," she said, in time with her nodding body. "You just don't know what he's capable of. I do."

"There's something else? Something you're not telling me?"

She did not reply. She rocked to and fro like a child in a swing.

"You have to do something," I said. "You can't stay here."

She lowered her head to stare down at her hands and her belly. I prowled up and down the chapel, avoiding the holes in the floor and the piles of rubbish. According to Kate, she had seen Carlo kill Sean yesterday. So how had she got up to London? At some point she must have phoned her mother, who had then phoned me. If Kate didn't have a mobile, where and how had she contacted Lily?

Kate still had a jacket but surely she must have had some sort of handbag as well. Where was it? What else was she leaving out? It struck me then, with full force, how vulnerable I had made myself. Did Kate want more than help? Did she want a scapegoat as well? We're used to trusting people.

In most relationships, we make assumptions about the nature of those we meet, and generally the assumptions are more or less correct. But take away those assumptions, take away trust, and all that's left is chaos.

She shook yet another cigarette from the packet and lit it.

"Surely you shouldn't be smoking," I said, before I could stop myself. "Not if you're pregnant."

"At present it doesn't seem very important. All right?" She blew a smoke ring, angling it so it wobbled across the air towards me. The hand holding the cigarette was trembling. "I—I need to know if they've found Sean yet."

"Who? The police?"

She nodded. "If they haven't, everything's easier, and it's only Carlo I have to worry about." She wrinkled her nose. "Only Carlo," she repeated. "Christ."

I watched the coils of cigarette smoke writhing like blue snakes above her head. "There was nothing on the national news this morning," I said. "And I couldn't find anything on the Web last night."

"That's something."

"But I didn't know Sean was at Rackford then. And you still haven't told me his surname."

"It's Fielding." Her eyes narrowed. "Would you go there for me?"

"What?"

"Would you go to Rackford?"

I stared at her. She seemed perfectly composed now. I was the one in danger of losing control.

"Not to the airfield," she went on. "There's no need for that. You could just drive through the village, maybe have a drink at the pub. Did you ever go there?"

"Yes," I said. I remembered the Eagle. I remembered Carlo with the baby punk in the yard. I'd wanted to be sick but there hadn't been time. "And I don't particularly want to go back."

"But no one would have any idea who you are. You'd soon know if the police were around. You'd hear if they've found a body."

Which body? "And if they have?" I said.

"I'd have to think again. But if they aren't there, maybe you could fetch a few things for me from home—from Chipping Weston, I mean. It shouldn't be a problem, if you're careful."

"Then what?"

"Then I'd leave." Kate flicked ash on the floor. "I'd be out of your life forever. You'd never see me again." She smiled at me. "How's that for an inducement?"

"It certainly has its attractions."

Neither of us spoke. We avoided each other's eyes. She had found a father to replace the one she had lost, only to learn that he didn't want her. I wondered whether that mattered to her. It would have mattered to me.

At last she dropped the cigarette and ground it out under her heel. "But you'd have to be careful if you go," she said. "Do you think you'd recognize him now? When did you last see him?"

"Carlo?" I knew the time, the date and the place of our last meeting. I remembered what he had said, too: *Christ, what a mess. It's a fucking nightmare.*

"It was years ago," I said. "He was seventeen. What does he look like now?"

It was a capitulation, and Kate knew it.

"He's taller than you, and heavier. He's got a beard. Close-cropped. So's his hair, and they're both going gray, although the beard's less gray than the hair." She closed her eyes as though visualizing him. "But he's in good shape for his age. Looks as if he works out."

I tried to mesh her description with my memory of the Carlo I had known: a tall, slim boy with wide shoulders, floppy hair and a sharp nose. I remembered his hands, which were large, with powerful, agile fingers: a guitarist's hands, he used to say. He had been very good at Chinese arm wrestling.

"The other question is," Kate went on, "would he recognize you?"

"That's assuming I go, of course." It occurred to me that Kate might be off her head, and that perhaps the story was a fabrication from start to finish. After all, Lily was hardly a trustworthy witness now—if, indeed, she ever had been. I smiled and pretended a confidence I didn't feel. "Anyway, would it really matter if Carlo saw me? Even if he recognized me, what's he going to do about it?"

Kate took a deep breath and let it out slowly. "You really don't understand, do you, Jamie? Even now. Carlo's not like me and you. He'll do whatever he wants. And what he wants to do right now is kill me."

6

I SUPPOSE I WAS ALWAYS A LITTLE SCARED OF CARLO. IT WAS one of the things that made our friendship interesting. With most people you know how far they will go when you push them. But with Carlo it was hard to be sure. His boundaries were more elastic.

At school this gave him a dark glamour, which made his liking for me all the more flattering. Once I was fighting with another boy in the changing-room. It wasn't serious—just a squabble over a disputed towel, an excuse for a mock duel. But Carlo came out of the showers and misinterpreted what was happening. Naked and dripping, he grabbed the boy by his collar and his waistband and rammed his head against the wall. The boy was concussed and needed three stitches. Carlo was punished, of course, but the incident increased his prestige.

Sometimes he worried me. After Felicity's first driving lesson, for example, he was like a baited trap waiting for a mouse. The hatred he felt for Lily would have to find an outlet, but I didn't know how or where. All I knew was that I had a dull ache in my stomach and would have preferred to be somewhere else, even in my grandmother's bungalow.

In the afternoon, Carlo and I went to the high street and prowled through shop after shop. We were adrift in the limitless boredom of the adolescent. At length we wandered into a café near Woolworth's where we drank Coke, ate greasy chips and fed the jukebox. The place was full of local teenagers who glanced at us with wary eyes and talked with lowered voices. Carlo said little, but I knew he was tense, waiting for whatever needed to happen.

Our table was beside a window that had steamed up. In an attempt to divert Carlo's attention, I rubbed a peephole in the mist and began to make scurrilous remarks about the passers-by. Eventually he rubbed another and joined in. It was growing darker outside, and even colder.

I was the first to see Felicity. She was standing on the opposite pavement, her back to the window of a shop selling washing machines. She was clutching a parcel and chatting with a couple of boys. She had the parcel in the crook of one arm, and a little white handbag looped over the other.

"Look," I said. "Your sister's over there."

Carlo enlarged his peephole. As soon as I spoke, I realized I had misread the situation: Felicity wasn't chatting—she was being interrogated.

"What's she carrying?" I asked.

"It's a present. She's going to Millie's birthday party this afternoon."

Even as Carlo was speaking, the taller of the boys lunged at the parcel. Felicity pulled away, turning to evade him, which brought her face to face with the other boy, who stood over her with his hands on his hips.

Carlo swore. He stood up and ran from the café. I scooped up our coats and followed. By the time I reached the doorway, Carlo was almost across the road. A cyclist rang her bell and screamed at him.

The taller boy pulled Felicity's parcel, and his friend tugged the handbag. Carlo cannoned into the smaller one and knocked him into the shop doorway. The other boy's reactions were too slow. Carlo caught him by the throat with his left hand and punched his victim's ear with the right.

I ran across the road.

"Get the fucker," Carlo said, as he hit the taller boy full in the face.

I dropped the coats, shoved the younger boy against the side of a phone box and punched his nose. His friend shouted something and broke away from Carlo. The two sprinted down the road. Carlo snarled and gave chase.

"Help him!" Felicity shouted in my ear. "Go on."

I ran after them. We stampeded along the pavement, scattering shoppers. Our quarry turned into a small park. Carlo swung through the gates in their wake. I hesitated and glanced back. Felicity had picked up the coats. She waved me on.

I had never before been inside that park. It was dusk already, and the streetlights cast a dull yellow glow over the grass and the leafless trees. I heard shouting at the far end away from the lights and road. I ran towards the noise.

I found Carlo in the children's playground. He was underneath the infants' swings with the smaller of Felicity's attackers. There was no sign of the other. The boy was lying on his side on the Tarmac underneath the iron frame and curled into a fetal huddle. Carlo crouched over his body, hammering it with his fists. Neither said a word. Carlo grunted. The boy cried, gasped and wept. I took Carlo's arm and tried to drag him off. He pushed me away.

"Hey—that's enough," I said. "You don't want to kill the little bugger, do you?"

"Why the fuck not?"

The blows continued. The boy on the ground was screaming, calling for his mother. I glanced round, afraid we were attracting attention, afraid of the police, afraid most of all that Carlo might really kill the boy.

"Come on," I whispered. "Felicity's over there."

For a second or two, Carlo's fist stayed in mid-air, poised above the squirming, moaning body. The boy must have been a couple of years younger than us. I caught sight of his face, which gleamed with dark moisture—blood, I suppose, mucus and tears.

Carlo sighed. He stood up. He looked towards the gates, where Felicity was waiting. He turned back to the boy and gave him a kick in the ribs. Then he bent down and spat in his face. The boy muttered something moist and gurgling. Carlo kicked him in the head and the boy howled like a dog.

I touched Carlo's arm. "Felicity's waiting."

The Eagle was in Lower Rackford. I drove into the car park at the side. The last time I'd been here was the night the fox was killed, the night Felicity cried. I couldn't help looking towards the corner at the back, beyond the toilet block. There was a line of wheelie-bins there now. That was where Carlo had taken the baby punk, another thing that had happened that evening.

The pub's main block was two stories high and separated from the road by a strip of garden. Smaller, single-storied extensions projected from the ends. At the back, at right angles to the road, were two roughly parallel rows of outbuildings. Over time the stone tiles had settled on the timbers beneath and the cluster of roofs had acquired shapes and curves that seemed organic, almost animate.

I got out of the Saab. The car park contained a sleek herd of Jaguars, BMWs, Mercedes and sparkling SUVs. The shape of the place was the same but much else had altered. While time had been moving forward elsewhere, at the Eagle it had apparently been moving backwards. I remembered metal windows and pebbledash rendering. Now there were wooden sashes and casements. The door to the bars was flanked with a couple of brass coach lamps.

Inside, framed on the wall, was an eighteenth-century bill of fare. On the floor were flagstones where I remembered a purple carpet with ranks of orange flowers. What had once been the public bar was now a restaurant. Every table was full. In the lounge bar, the jukebox and the fruit machine had been swept away in favor of oak settles and Windsor chairs. Wooden casks squatted behind the bar and blackboard menus hung on unplastered stone walls. Despite the warmth outside, a log fire burned in a grate that had not existed at my last visit a quarter of a century ago.

The people in the bar went with the cars outside. No one took any notice of me, which was another thing that had changed. When Carlo and I had come here, pretending to be eighteen, conversations had faltered and people glanced at us, then away. In those days we drank vodka if we could afford it and cider if we couldn't.

I asked for mineral water and wedged myself into a corner at the end of the bar. I sipped my drink and let the conversations around me ebb and flow. I dipped into a discussion about Henrietta's new pony, another about a planning dispute over an extension, and a third about what Ursula had said of Giles's asparagus last night, and how terrible it was.

But there was nothing about a body at Rackford airfield.

I stared out of the window at the children making life hell for the parents in the beer garden at the front of the pub. The airfield was a little over a mile away from the village. If a body had been found, if the police had been there, everyone would have been talking about it. Yes, on the whole, no news was good news. It meant that by the end of today I should have Kate off my hands and, with luck, that I should never again have anything to do with the Murthingtons. It was less than twenty-four hours since Lily had come back into my life, yet I could hardly remember a time when I had been free of her.

Had I ever been truly free of her? Lily's death wouldn't mean the end of it either, not necessarily—because now there was another reason to be afraid: she might have told Kate at least some of the truth.

I needed a distraction. Through the window I noticed a little post office and general store across the road. After I had finished my drink I went over there to buy an Ordnance Survey map. I sat in the car and unfolded it.

RAF Rackford had had a typical wartime layout: three intercepting runways, forming a pattern like a folding camp-stool in profile. Across the top had run the broad main run-way, intersected near the ends by the tops of the cross made by the two lesser runways below. All three were linked by the wavering line of the perimeter road, from which pro-truded the frying-pan shapes of the aircraft dispersal areas scattered around the edge.

I found the patch of woodland on the west of the site with the thin blue thread of a stream running through it. According to Kate, Sean was somewhere down there. Well, there was a coincidence. Beyond the woodland one of the lanes from Rackford zigzagged along the western boundary of the airfield and eventually joined the main road to Chipping Weston. I laid the palm of my hand on the map, obliterating both woodland and lane. "You don't exist," I said aloud. "Not now."

I folded the map and started the engine. Fortunately there was more than one way to get to Chipping Weston from Rackford. I took the shorter route, a B road that skirted the eastern boundary of the airfield and passed the main entrance.

The road was wider than I remembered. There were roundabouts where before there had been only crossroads. Hedgerows had vanished. The fields on either side had become larger. I felt oddly aggrieved: it was as though someone had been making unlicensed alterations to my own past. I drove fast, keeping my eyes on the Tarmac and white lines in front of me. The airfield's boundary flickered along the edge of my vision like a soundless and almost monochromatic cine film, a home movie from somebody else's childhood.

After a few miles I joined the main road from Oxford and, after another mile, turned left towards Chipping Weston. I drove down the old London road—the town was now by-passed by the trunk road to the north. Familiar buildings appeared like ghosts. Among them was the Newnham House Hotel, sprawling among a rash of new houses on the left-hand side. It was a large, red-brick Victorian place, which had sprouted modern wings since I had last seen it. Once it had seemed the height of sophistication. Now it was just another chain hotel with a gym, a swimming pool and a very big car park.

The nearer I came to the Murthingtons' house, the worse it was. There was a chance that someone might notice me or the car. Perhaps I shouldn't have gone to the Eagle or called at the village shop. Once you start worrying about the possibility of unpleasant consequences, it's not easy to stop.

I turned into a side road and found myself driving along the boundary of a cemetery. I had never been there before. There was parking on the road so I pulled over and switched off the engine. It was as safe there as anywhere.

I left the shelter of the Saab and walked in a broad arc round the southern part of the old center of the town. I found a callbox and phoned the Murthingtons' number—it was the same number, though prefixed with a sixth digit. The phone rang on and on. The ringing stopped and the voice mail's standard recorded message began to play. I put down the receiver. I had lost my chance of a last-minute reprieve.

In the Murthingtons' road, some of the old houses had gone, replaced by newer, smaller ones. Gardens had been subdivided. Although more and more families had been crammed into the space, the road had acquired an air of glossy affluence. Wherever they looked, I guessed, the owners of these houses saw double: two kids, two cars, two homes, two foreign holidays a year.

The only house that was out of place was the Murthingtons'. Since I had last seen it, it had become shabbier, more ramshackle: slates were slipping over the bay window and one of the bedroom windows at the side of the house was broken. In the garden, the shrubs had grown enormous and the lawn had run to seed. The house wasn't quite an eyesore but it was getting there. If houses were fairy tales, then this one was *The Sleeping Beauty*, its heroine grown older and no longer beautiful.

I walked rapidly down the opposite pavement. Children were playing in back gardens and someone was having a barbecue, a late lunch or an early supper. A man was mowing his lawn two doors up. He paused and waved to me. I waved back and hoped he would not remember my face. As I passed the Murthingtons', I glanced over the road at the house and garden. There were no cars in the driveway, and the curtains were drawn across the downstairs windows at the front. It looked empty, just as Kate had said it would be.

At the end of the road I turned left. Sixty yards further down, on the left, was a path surfaced with Tarmac between tall creosoted fences. When I had known it as a teenager, it had been a narrow, muddy track bounded by hedgerows running between the backs of the gardens of the Murthingtons' road on the left and open fields on the right. The fields and the hedges had gone but the path was still there.

"Some of the people in our road put gates in," Kate had told me. "Ours is the fifth on the left."

I met no one. At the fifth gate, I stood on tiptoe and glimpsed the thick, fresh greenery of trees in early summer.

"Put your hand over the top of the gate," Kate had said, "and feel to the right, round the post. There's a key hanging on a nail."

It was a Yale, the metal warm from the sun. I opened the gate and slipped inside. I left the key where I had found it and advanced slowly up the garden, like a soldier moving through potentially hostile jungle. The path was still there— cracked stone slabs running through a forest of weeds where once there had been a vegetable garden. There was a little potting shed with a greenhouse leaning against its side. Two of its glass panes were broken, and nothing green grew inside except weeds. I remembered this place too well and I was a little afraid of it. It contained a ghost who hated me.

People still came this way—the path was clear and, where it passed under an iron-framed archway, the box hedge had been cut back. The cuttings were lying in the lee of the greenhouse, brown and brittle.

On the other side of the archway was the ash tree. This was where I had first seen Lily. One of the branches had fallen off—years ago, by the look of it—and landed squarely on the roof of the wooden summerhouse.

The shrubs and trees were so high that this part of the garden had become a green tunnel. I glimpsed the chimneys and slates of neighboring houses, but no windows. The remains of the lawn rose to my knees. The tips of the grasses had tiny purple fronds, and among them were wild flowers—clover, vetch, cow-parsley and the drying stalks of cowslips.

"You'll find a spare key to the front door underneath the bowl of the little birdbath near the shed," Kate had said. "The shed by the scullery. You just lift up the bowl of the birdbath and the key's on the—"

"I know," I had said. "There's a hollow in the base. That's where they always kept it."

The key turned easily. Someone had recently oiled the lock. I remembered Carlo oiling locks, both there and at school. He always planned ahead if he could, and oiled locks made it easier to slip in and out late at night without anyone knowing.

I turned the handle, pushed open the door and stepped from the overgrown, sunlit garden into the stillness of the house. Once inside I closed the door and waited while my eyes adjusted. I listened to the silence of the house and felt the thudding of my heart.

Slowly the details emerged. The hall was smaller than I remembered but I had expected that. A faded runner stretched across black-and-white tiles to the foot of the stairs. There were splashes of color on the tiles, where the sun filtered through the stained glass in the fanlight of the front door. I heard, very faintly, noises from the outside world—a child wailing, a car on the road. Inside the house, everything was quiet—more than quiet: the silence had a thick, smothering quality, gray and feathery like dust.

As the seconds slipped by, my pulse slowed. There was an odd smell in the house, dry and papery, with an unpleasant underlayer of sweetness, and beneath that something worse. Stacked along the right-hand wall was an irregular inner barrier made up of newspapers, piled into stacks, each leaning against the wall and its neighbors. There must have been years of news in those crumbling pages. Two or three of the piles had bellied out under their own weight and collapsed across the strip of carpet.

I don't know how long I waited. The silence of the house settled around me like a blanket, the sort that stifles rather than comforts. In the end panic pushed me forward, the sense that if I didn't move now I would lose what little courage remained.

I edged past the wall of newspapers. Some time after my last visit to the house, the dark-stained stairs had been painted white, although the paint had mutated now to a blotchy yellow. An island composed of black plastic sacks rose like shiny volcanic rock in the middle of the floor. Old clothes dribbled from their open mouths.

The drawing room door was ajar. I edged inside. It was here that I truly appreciated the scale and the nature of the changes. The Murthingtons' house had always been untidy—as a teenager, I had thought its casual clutter much more distinguished and homely than the spotless order of my grand-mother's bungalow—but it looked as if in recent years the Murthingtons had simply stopped caring. The drawing room was now like an overcrowded second-hand furniture shop. Smaller objects were heaped on every horizontal surface in-cluding the floor. A chesterfield with a broken back supported an old-fashioned tin bath containing a pile of sheet music. The shelf above the fireplace housed a collection of clocks and china ornaments, as well as a cut-glass vase crammed with brown stalks. A pile of overcoats had been dumped over the wing-backed armchair where Hugh Murthington used to sit.

The same story, with minor variations, was repeated throughout the house. Carlo's father had been a man who col-lected things, and there's a fine line between collecting and hoarding. It was clear that in his later years he had found it hard to stop acquiring and even harder to throw anything away. Lily's casual approach to housekeeping, which had seemed endearingly carefree, had turned into something darker: a surrender to chaos. I wondered how long the two of them had been living there alone.

In some rooms, however, there were pockets of order, as if Kate or Carlo had tried to introduce limited areas of tidiness. The desk in Hugh's study, for example, was clear of every-thing, including dust, apart from a photograph in a silver

frame, in the corner of which was a small card. I went closer.
The photograph was a head-and-shoulders shot of Felicity
grinning up at the camera. The card gave the address of St.
Margaret's Hospice.

Someone had also made an effort in the kitchen. The big
Belfast sink, though stained by decades of use, was clean and
smelt of bleach. The draining-board was empty apart from
a mug and a plate. Yesterday's paper—the *Guardian*—lay
folded open on the table.

Slowly I mounted the stairs. The runner was beige in color
and years of use had worn a dark track through the center
of it. My limbs seemed heavier than usual, my movements
slower. The stairs creaked. If someone was in the house, they
would have heard me by now. The air smelt unclean. The
higher I went, the warmer the temperature and the worse
the smell.

On the landing, I paused. A passage led to the back of
the house. Another flight of stairs climbed into a deeper
darkness. The paneled doors were all closed. I pushed open
the one on my right.

The room had belonged to Lily and Hugh. It was large
and high-ceilinged with two big windows, both with pointed
heads, looking through overgrown trees towards the road.
But the furniture made it cramped. There were three tall
wardrobes, all with clothes hanging from their doors and
sides. One of the two dressing tables still held a man's
brushes and a strop for a cutthroat razor. Shoes, mostly in
boxes, filled the gap between the end of the bed and the window, and these at least were tidy, the corners squared off,
drawn up in ranks like soldiers on parade. A pile of hatboxes
towered between two of the wardrobes. A zimmer frame and

a commode stood beside the high double bed with its dark wooden headboard.

Two other bedrooms opened off the main landing. They had both silted up with clothes, magazines, suitcases and cardboard boxes. But the smallest bedroom was different. It was set apart from the others at the end of the passage, next to the bathroom. According to Kate, this was where Carlo slept when he stayed there. The room had once belonged to Felicity but there was no trace of her now.

Here, as nowhere else in the house, I felt I was truly a trespasser. I was also aware of panic nibbling at the edges of my mind. This was so clearly a room whose owner intended to return. Everything was very clean—scoured, scraped and polished until not a speck of dust or dirt remained. The single bed was made up. A radio stood on the bedside table. A big backpack was leaning against the wall behind the door. Carlo had not been particularly tidy as a boy but now he appeared to live in surroundings that were almost monastic in their organized simplicity.

I glanced into the bathroom, which was empty, and again surprisingly clean. The bath was still the Victorian one with the high sides of scarred enamel and iron legs with claw feet. I walked back quickly to the main landing and up the attic stairs.

This had been Carlo's domain—a bedroom with a sloping ceiling and two dormer windows, with a tiny boxroom lit only by a skylight next door. On Christmas holidays we piled the contents of the boxroom against one wall, thereby clearing just enough floor space for ourselves and our guitars. We referred to this as the studio and played music under its sloping ceiling with religious solemnity. Music was our secret cult and in this airless little room we worshipped the gods of punk with the fervor of the newly converted.

But there was no trace of this now, and had not been for years. It was obvious that Kate had spent her childhood and her teenage years in the attic. An archaeologist of the individual would have been able to find layers relating to every stage of her life, from infant to student. Overlaid upon this older and longer period of occupation were glimpses of the adult. The bed was unmade—the duvet thrown on the floor, the sheet twisted and crumpled, the pillow still dented by the head that had rested on it. On the dressing table stood a mug half full of what looked like herbal tea and an ashtray containing a solitary butt. The room was untidy but in a different way from the rest of the house, suggesting the mess had been made recently and in haste. I wondered who had been responsible for that.

I was in sight of the end at last, which made me hurry. Originally Kate had asked me to pack all of her clothes but I had persuaded her against this. It would make me far too conspicuous, whether I brought the car to the house or simply walked off towing suitcases. Besides, I had added, I would pay for her to buy new clothes, then no one could circulate an accurate description of what she was likely to be wearing.

Her passport and other papers, she had told me, were zipped into the inner pocket of the smaller of two suitcases. The suitcase was there but its inner pocket was empty.

While I considered what to do, I dropped a couple of T-shirts and a change of underclothes into a nylon overnight bag with a shoulder strap. I had arranged with Kate that I would phone her only in an emergency because the call would leave a record. But now I had no option. She answered on the first ring.

"It's me," I said. "Look—"

"Have they found him?"

It took me a moment to realize whom she meant. "No, I don't think so. Not yet."

"Thank God." She drew a long, shuddering breath.

"I'm at the house now. The trouble is, some of your things are gone. The important stuff."

"Any sign of him? The—the other one."

"No. But his things are in his room."

"Shit."

There was a silence.

"I'm leaving," I said. "He could be back at any moment."

"No—wait. You could have a look for them. He might have—"

"There's no point. You know what this place is like. It could take years to search." The revulsion in my voice took me unawares. Suddenly angry, I went on: "I'm leaving. That's that."

"If they're still there, they'll be in his room."

"I'm going."

"Please, Jamie."

I hesitated.

"Is his backpack there? He always brings it when he comes. That's where it'll probably be. It's all I need—the building-society stuff and the passport."

It occurred to me that perhaps the risk was worth running for my sake as well as hers. Sean hadn't been found yet. Nothing incriminated her so she was free to go abroad, to go anywhere as long as it was away from me. But once Sean was found, it would be too late.

"I won't spend long," I said. "Just a couple of minutes. If that."

"Thank you."

I rang off and went down the attic stairs. It seemed incomprehensible that I'd ever liked this ugly, overcrowded house, as incomprehensible as my obsession with Lily. I walked down the passage into the bedroom that had been Felicity's and now was Carlo's.

The backpack was enormous. It had a wealth of outside pockets and I decided to start with those. There was one held with Velcro at the top of the main flap. I pulled it open. It contained a map—the same edition of the Ordnance Survey map I had bought in Rackford earlier that day—and also a manilla envelope, foolscap size, folded in two, the flap unsealed.

I pulled out the contents and wished I hadn't. I found myself looking at another photograph of Felicity, this time when she was older, self-conscious and wearing a dress that was probably new and the reason for the photograph. Her long hair hung beside her pale face. Adult features were just beginning to emerge from the gentle, rounded contours of puppy fat. She was almost beautiful, not a word I'd associated with her before. I didn't want to look at her.

Beneath the photograph was a homemade card. I was standing near the window and I angled it towards the late-afternoon sunlight. "For Daddy—happy birthday, with lots of love and hugs from Felicity."

I turned the card over. Felicity had done a picture for her father, just as she had for Carlo on his birthday on my first visit to Chipping Weston. Technically, it was surprisingly good in many ways. It showed a group of flowers carefully drawn in ink, with delicate dabs of watercolor that even now made them glow. Yet the composition was oddly stiff. She had lined up the flowers in a row with no apparent thought to the effect they made together. They didn't belong with each other.

I was about to slide the card and the photograph back into the envelope when I heard a sound from outside. I glanced out of the window. I was in time to catch only a flash of movement at the edge of my vision. Someone had just turned into the little porch.

Carlo, I thought. At last.

I stuffed the envelope into the bag and slipped out of the room. I heard the sound of the key turning in the distant lock. If Carlo came straight upstairs, he would meet me on the landing. If he went somewhere downstairs first, he would hear me moving about or on the stairs.

I backed into the bathroom, because that put more space between us. I bolted the door and glanced at the window over the basin. It was the original Victorian sash with stained glass in the lower half. A memory came back to me—Carlo and I together in the bathroom: we were teasing Felicity. We'd locked the door and she was on the other side, banging on the panels, almost weeping in her anxiety to join us. Carlo had winked at me. "Hang on a moment," he called out to her. "I'm going to make James vanish. I'm going to flush him down the bog. Then you can come in."

He pulled up the lower sash. "There's a way down over the shed roof," he whispered. "She doesn't know."

I had climbed onto the sloping slate roof of the scullery. I heard Carlo flushing the lavatory and gently closing the window. Then he let Felicity into the bathroom—and into the secret, too. He would never tease her for long.

I was too desperate for caution. The window went up with a screech. I glanced down, wondering where to put my feet. And that was when I saw the blood.

The shock made me catch my breath. For an instant I forgot the desperate need to hurry. A white plastic bucket was standing on the floor, tucked between the basin and the bath, full almost to the brim with blood. Something pale and slimy floated just below the surface.

For Christ's sake. Brains? Intestines? What the hell is Carlo—

I snatched a toothbrush from the jar on the side of the basin and poked its handle into the bloody mess. I fished up the cuff of a pale blue shirt, dripping with watery blood.

Relief hit me like a blast of warm air. Then I heard rapid footsteps somewhere in the house—on the stairs? the landing?—and another form of panic set in. I clambered on to the side of the bath and poked a leg through the gap. I pushed my head and shoulders through, then the other leg. I let go of Kate's overnight bag and it slid down the slates, snagged for a moment on the guttering, and vanished. I slithered down the roof.

When I had done this before I had been fifteen, lighter, smaller and much more supple. My adult body was cumbersome and fragile. A slate gave way beneath me. My foot jarred against the guttering and for a moment I thought that that, too, would give way. But it held. I dropped down four feet to the flat roof of the shed below. I grabbed the bag. The roof cracked and sagged beneath my weight.

On the far side of the shed, in the corner where its back wall met the boundary fence of the garden, there had been a compost heap. It was still there but now it was covered with a dense forest of nettles. I sucked in a breath of air and launched myself into the green leaves. I landed awkwardly. My ankle twisted. My leg gave way. I fell head first to the path below. Grunting with pain, I staggered down the long, overgrown garden.

A terrified gray squirrel scrambled up the trunk of the ash tree and vanished among the leaves. As I reached the gate I heard the bathroom window close and, somewhere in the distance, the seesaw wail of a police siren.

7

DURING THE DRIVE BACK TO LONDON I CHECKED THE rearview mirror repeatedly. On the eastern side of the Oxford ring road, a few miles before the motorway began, I stopped at a pub where I ordered a cup of coffee and phoned Nicky. When her voice mail cut in, I said I hoped she was having fun, and I'd see her soon. It didn't occur to me to worry about her. My mind was on other things.

I didn't want to talk to Kate. But before I left the pub I texted her: "No luck. C came back."

The motorway unrolled before me, a gray carpet stretching all the way to London. Most of the traffic was coming the other way. Thoughts scurried around my mind like a pack of monkeys. For a moment those monkeys were more real to me than my hands on the steering wheel and the vehicles in the other lanes: I saw their little black hands gripping the bars, rattling them, trying to get out. Then I stopped being metaphorical and thought instead about Felicity's photograph and the bloody shirt soaking in the white bucket. I thought about Lily lying in her room and holding the tarnished chain with the twisted shred of metal attached to it.

All the while, I watched the cars behind me, fixing on first one, then another. I slowed, I speeded, I changed lanes. I passed the Greyfont turn-off and drove on to London. When the motorway petered out, I pulled over and phoned the hospice. A pleasant, concerned voice told me that Lily Murthington had woken up in the afternoon and had some food. She seemed happier in herself, the voice said, and in less pain, but now she was sleeping again. No, if I wanted to pay her a visit it would probably be better to do so in the morning.

I drove to Queen's Park and left the car in a side road. At a general shop I bought two egg-mayonnaise sandwiches and, as an afterthought, a packet of Marlboro Light. I took my time walking to the chapel, following a roundabout route and using shop windows as mirrors. I entered a pub by one door, walked rapidly through the bars, glancing about me as though looking for a friend, and left by another.

Paranoid logic is irrefutable. If I could not see a pursuer, it did not mean that one was not there; if anything, it confirmed his or her fiendish cunning. I walked past the chapel once, then again. Only on the third time did I decide it was safe to go in. I unlocked the gate, went rapidly up the path, and tapped on the door of the little room behind the chapel. There was no answer. I pushed the key into the lock. To my surprise, the door opened.

The room was empty. The inner door on the right was ajar. Panic spurted through me. I kicked the door fully open. The main body of the chapel was as bright as I had ever seen it. Sunshine streamed through the grimy window above the doors to the road. The skylights glowed golden. There was more than enough light to see the stained floorboards, the crumbling plaster, the dust that swirled lazily in the air and the huddle of chairs at the end. There was more than enough light to see that I was alone.

I walked slowly towards the chairs. Beside the one where Kate had sat there was a heap of squashed cigarette butts and some ash, which formed a gray smear the size of a dinner plate. In places I could see the swirls and curves that Kate's fingers had made. She hadn't had a pen or anything to write on so she'd used the ash as her paper and a fingertip as her pen. Only two words were written there.

Sorry. Goodbye.

I ground the ash under my heel until the message was gone, until all that remained of Kate was a little pile of cigarette ends. It was better that way.

By the time I reached Greyfont it was after half past six. I drove slowly along our road and turned into the drive. Nicky's Mini wasn't in front of the garage. She must have come back and gone out again. In a way I was glad—I wasn't looking forward to explaining how I'd spent my day. I didn't like having to lie to her, even by implication.

Inside the house the air was cool and musty. I switched off the burglar alarm and went into the kitchen. There was no sign of an evening meal.

To my surprise I found the trousers Nicky had been wearing folded neatly over the back of a chair in our bedroom. So she'd come back and gone out again. I picked up the phone by the bed, intending to ring her. When I put the receiver to my ear I heard the broken tone indicating a new message on the voice mail. I punched in the access number. Then Nicky's voice, thin and remote, was speaking rapidly, saying words that at first I didn't understand: "James, it's me. I can't believe what you've done. I need time to think about it, about what I'm going to do. I'll be away for a night or two."

The message ended abruptly, as if she had slammed down the phone. I played it again, then again. I phoned her mobile. It was switched off and I went straight through to voice mail: "Nicky, it's me. Can you call me? Where are you?"

Nicky had come home to change. It occurred to me that if I worked out which clothes she had taken, I might get an idea of where she had gone. I opened the wardrobe and pulled out drawers.

It didn't take me long to realize that I had the wrong sort of mind for this. I vaguely recognized some of the clothes and shoes I saw but it did not follow that I was aware of the ones that weren't there. I glanced round the room. I noticed one absence—her novel was gone from the bedside table.

My head buzzing, I went back downstairs. It occurred to me that my message must have sounded curt to her, as curt as hers to me. I picked up my mobile from the table, leaned against the wall and began to text her. "Please call." I'd already said that on the phone so I deleted it. "I can explain." That sounded unduly defensive. I knew I had a good deal to defend but there was no point in making a tactical error at the outset. In the end I wrote, "I love you," and pressed the send key before I had time to change my mind. I couldn't think of anything else to say to her.

An idea slipped into my mind. Nicky had taken her novel with her, the current book-group selection. She had gone up to London today with Miranda, another member of the book group. So Miranda might know something.

I found their number on the pad in the kitchen and phoned them. Their baby-sitter answered—Miranda and Dave had gone out to the Furstons' round the corner. I grabbed my jacket and left the house. Nicky and I knew the Furstons, though not as well as Miranda and Dave did because we didn't have children. In this neighbourhood, children act as the principal form of social glue, binding together the most ill-assorted couples in an unending round of competitive hospitality.

The Furstons were having a party. As soon as I turned into their road, I smelt the barbecue and heard the sound of raised voices and laughter. I rang the front-door bell and one of their children answered the door. This one was a girl, and she scowled at me from beneath a long, straight fringe. "Is your mum in?" I asked unnecessarily, as I could hear the shriek of her laughter from where I was standing.

The child, who couldn't have been more than ten, clung to the edge of the door and said nothing.

"I'm James," I reminded her. "I live round the corner. I'm looking for Miranda Hammett."

"Round the back," the child said, and shut the door in my face.

I took this as an invitation and went through the gate beside the double garage. Guy Furston was the director of marketing for an IT company. The children went to the prep school in the next village, and his wife described herself as a homemaker. They ran three cars, and in the two years since they'd lived there they'd converted the loft, built an enormous conservatory on to the sitting room at the back and added a swimming pool.

This was where the barbecue was—on the patio area that spread from the hardwood doors of the conservatory to the sparkling blue waters of the pool. Elton John throbbed and warbled in the conservatory, mingling with what sounded like an episode of *The Simpsons* from one of the upstairs windows. A dozen people were talking and drinking. Guy was arranging steaks, burgers and sausages on the barbecue. He saw me coming and waved an uncooked sausage in my direction.

"James! Come and join us—beer? Glass of wine?" He was a big, efficiently sociable man with a smile that split his fat red face in two. "Nicky with you?"

"Actually, I wanted a word with Miranda. She and Nicky went to London today."

"I know. Dave said he didn't realize you could cram that number of carrier-bags into an M-class Merc. Probably a world record. After all, the poor girls only had two thousand liters of luggage space to play with." He laughed, spreading his arms in uncomplicated enjoyment of his joke. Then he bellowed across the pool to Miranda, who was standing in the evening sunshine with a glass in one hand and a bottle in the other. "James wants a word with you. Why don't you get him a drink while you're at it?"

Miranda broke off her conversation and gave me a little wave. I watched her walking along the edge of the pool. Her long, flowery dress billowed like a tent on the move. She was a heavy woman, and growing heavier. Her pretty features were framed by artfully cut hair lifted by blonde highlights, and they were sinking slowly into thickening jowls. There was no surprise in her expression. I guessed she had been expecting me.

She pecked my cheek with soft, heavy lips, and her hair swung forward, revealing glimpses of gray and ginger at the roots. She nodded at the table where the drinks were. "What would you like?"

"Nothing, thanks. I was wondering if you'd seen Nicky."

"Not since we got back from London. Is she coming here? She didn't say."

"I thought you might know where she was—she's not at home."

She brayed with laughter. "You mean she's vanished?"

"No, of course not."

Miranda smiled. "But you don't know where she is?"

"She came home, got changed and went out in the car. She must have forgotten to leave a note. I wasn't there, you see—I've been out all day."

"Have you tried phoning?"

"Of course. Her battery must be flat or something."

Miranda shrugged, which sent a ripple through the floral tent. "All I know is I dropped her off at yours at about half past five. She didn't say if she was going out or not."

"Was she OK?"

Her smile slipped. "She was fine. All things considered."

"How do you mean?"

"Well, the thing is, James, she's a bit upset. Naturally." There was no mistaking the malice now. "As you would be, wouldn't you?"

"I don't understand."

"If it was Dave, I'd go after him with the frying pan. But Nicky's different." Miranda sipped her wine. "We're good friends, you know, me and Nicky—she tells me quite a lot."

"I'm sure she does. So what was the problem today?"

"You were, of course."

"I really don't understand what you're getting at."

Miranda gave another metallic laugh. "Come on, James, there's no point in pretending. If you don't want people to notice when you play away from home, you'll have to do it a bit more subtly than that."

I stared at her. Late one evening, at a party just after our move to Greyfont, Miranda had made a pass at me. I'd backed away as if she'd stung me and muttered something about needing to ask Nicky something. I wondered whether she disliked me because of that.

Suddenly she stretched out the hand holding the glass and touched my arm. A few drops of wine slopped onto my sleeve. "You OK?"

"Yes. I think there's been a mistake."

"Well, that's something for you to sort out with her, isn't it? But it's only fair to say you're going to have an uphill job."

"What did she say? Tell me exactly what she said."

Miranda waved a finger in front of my face. "It's been going on for a while, hasn't it? And then, of course, Dave saw you with that girl yesterday evening. I mean, that's what really did it—letting her come to the house. All very surreptitious, I gather." She glanced slyly at me with little eyes wedged in folds of fat. "I had to tell Nicky, you do see that? I mean, us girls have to stick together." She took another sip of wine, examining me over the rim of the glass. "Dave said she was a pretty little thing, your young lady. Ravishing—that was his word. Mind you keep her away from him. I don't want him straying."

I nodded, I didn't trust myself to speak, and turned to go. Guy shouted something about sausages. Dave barged into me and laughed as if I'd made a joke. But Miranda hadn't finished: her voice pursued me as I escaped from the patio.

"You know what they say, James? Sauce for the goose is sauce for the gander. It works both ways, doesn't it?"

It was a long evening. I went home and poured myself a glass of the Burgundy I had opened the previous evening. I took the glass and the bottle into the garden. I didn't want to stay in the house. It was heavy with silence, pregnant with Nicky's absence.

Time stretched. I sat on a wooden bench in the last of the evening sun beside a little herb garden that Nicky was making. Felicity had liked flowers, gardens and plants, and so did Nicky. I looked at lovage and parsley, chives and rosemary, garlic and thyme. I didn't think much about Carlo, Kate or Lily. I didn't wonder about what had happened at Rackford or whose blood was in the bucket. Instead I thought about Nicky. I listened for the phone, which didn't ring, and tried not to glance at my watch too often. I was a failure as a husband in more ways than one, but at least I had been faithful. With Nicky that had come easily.

I tried to phone her. Once again I went straight through to voice mail. So I wrote her another text: "It's not what you think, I promise. We need to talk." But I deleted it without sending. There was no way round the fact that I had lied to her about Kate. Nicky was right to be angry. She was only wrong about the reason. Much as I loved her, though, I couldn't tell her the truth. Because if I did, one thing would have to lead to another. I would need to explain about the Murthingtons and Chipping Weston, and then she would have a far more powerful reason to leave me. It was better left alone, dead and buried.

And there was another reason for silence: I had no right to involve Nicky in Kate's problems.

I drank another glass, then a third. In the end the cold drove me back inside the house. I forced myself to eat a slice of toast and a slab of cheese. While I ate, I watched the news in case there was mention of a body near Lower Rackford. Sean still hadn't been found. I almost wished he had been. At least the waiting would be over.

Miranda's parting words turned and twisted in my mind. Were they a broad hint that Nicky had found consolation with someone else? Or had they been merely an instinctive attempt to correct an imbalance of injury?

The wine bottle was empty. I considered opening another but a shred of sanity held me back. Nicky might ring. I needed to have at least some of my wits about me. I staggered upstairs and stood in the shower. I held my face up to the showerhead so the water washed down my cheeks. The tiled enclosure was slippery and seemed to sway as if it were floating on a choppy sea.

I would have liked to cry. I could not remember crying since that first day at boarding-school when I had wept in the housemaster's garden and told myself that I would no longer love my mother. I knew what would happen if I didn't find a way to deal with Nicky's absence: it would turn into something sad, sour and hard, just as it had when my mother and stepfather packed me off to school in another country.

But perhaps, in the long run, that would be better than the alternative. If I cut myself adrift from Nicky, if I stopped loving her as I had my mother, then at least one of my problems would be solved. It wouldn't matter if she thought I was having an affair. It wouldn't matter if I was or, indeed, if she was. The trouble was, I did love her. And I didn't want to stop.

It was still early—not much more than ten o'clock—when I left the shower. I went to bed because I couldn't think of anything else to do. I lay with my head on a pillow that smelt faintly of her perfume and thought about how we had met, when I had been working in London and she was still living in Winchester. The first time I saw her was at the house of a client, a man with more money than sense who had bought a half-ruined Jacobean mansion on a whim and was trying to find out whether it could be made habitable again. There were dead sheep among the brambles in the garden and no mains services. Most of the land had gone and an industrial estate had grown up on the other side of the garden wall.

The client had wanted everything done in a hurry. Nicky, who worked for a firm of interior decorators, had been summoned about three years prematurely to advise on color schemes. After the client had driven away to his next appointment, she and I had had lunch in the local pub. Then we picked our way through the ruined garden, trying to imagine what it had once looked like. We compared notes on the sanity of our client and discovered that we were both intending to see the same exhibition that weekend. The following Saturday afternoon, I contrived to bump into her at the Barbican.

I knew from the first weekend that Nicky was different. I wanted to be with her when she woke up in the morning with her eyes gummy from sleep. I wanted to share the Sunday newspapers with her. If I had to trail round a supermarket, I would rather do it with her than with anyone else. I wanted to buy a house with her and make it into a shared home, something I had never had since my father died, a home I shared on equal terms with other people. At the end of all my long days, I wanted to drive into the sunset with her. It was that complicated and that simple.

We got to know each other slowly. We spent a lot of time walking, looking at buildings and gardens, sitting in parks and restaurants. And all the time, in those early months, we were talking. I had never talked so much about myself. I unlocked doors in my mind that had been shut since childhood. I was amazed at Nicky's power to liberate me and amazed at my own willingness to let her.

But there had to be a limit. Some doors remained closed, as much for her sake as mine. It wouldn't have been fair to ask her to share the burden of what had happened all those years ago. Besides, I thought that if she knew, she would no longer want to be with me. So I told her about school, my parents and my stepfather, but I said little about the Murthingtons. I mentioned Carlo's name once or twice—it would have been hard not to—but only in passing.

"How could your mother bear to send you away?" Nicky said. "It's weird. Have you ever asked her why she did it?"

I shook my head. "I haven't talked to her for years."

"Don't you want to?"

"I don't even know whether she's alive."

Nicky laid a hand on mine. We were sitting on a bench near the summit of Primrose Hill and London rolled away from us, wave after wave of brick and concrete, Tarmac and glass, surging towards the distant shore of the horizon.

"I'd never send a child to boarding school. What's the point in having them if you send them away?" Nicky's eyes were large and serious. "What do you think?"

"I agree."

She worked a finger into the gap between two of mine. Our hands curled together on the warm bench. "Do you think we should have children? You and I?"

"Oh, yes," I said. "We must have children."

I dropped a kiss onto her warm hair. It seemed to me that she had given me a chance I had never had before. I couldn't mend what was broken. But at least, with Nicky's help, I might make something that was whole.

Despite the wine, I couldn't sleep. The hours crept by. I lay on the double bed with the curtains drawn. I shuttled to and fro between two sets of terrors. When I wasn't thinking about what had happened at Rackford, I was creating scenario after scenario that showed in graphic detail what Nicky was doing now.

She was sitting up in bed in a big, anonymous hotel reading her novel for the book group, the one with the little lost girl on the cover. She was lolling on a faceless friend's sofa, eating chocolate and watching a DVD. She was in an airport departure lounge, waiting for her flight to be announced. Worst of all, she was writhing under another body in the oldest dance of all.

Slowly I slid into the trance-like state between sleeping and waking, where thoughts merge imperceptibly with dreams. But I didn't dream of Nicky. Instead the logic of the sleeping mind led me back to Lily—not as she was now but as she had been then.

It was half memory, half dream, the summer of 1979, when I had spent the last ten days of the holiday at Chipping Weston. Carlo was already sixteen, and my own sixteenth birthday was only a couple of months away. Lily took the three of us—Felicity, Carlo and me—to a falconry center near the Malverns, where the green hills shaded into the blue horizons of Wales.

Felicity enjoyed watching the peregrines and goshawks swooping at the lures, and examining the birds on their perches, and so did Lily. Carlo and I, however, were at an awkward age: too old to take a child's pleasure and too young to take an adult's. We trailed behind the others in sulky silence. When the tour of the center had finished, we had a late lunch in the picnic area beside the car park. Carlo and I spread a rug in the shade of an oak tree. Lily and Felicity unpacked the contents of the icebox and the picnic basket.

Looking back, I realize that Lily had gone to some trouble, although at the time none of us was very grateful when she produced sausage rolls and pâté, ham and chicken, several sorts of salad, bread, crisps, cheese and fruit. We ate quickly and in silence, washing the food down with fruit juice and Coke. Lily had also brought the remains of a bottle of Frascati that she and Hugh had shared the previous evening. She ate little but drank quickly—first one glass, then another, then the half-inch at the bottom of the bottle.

After lunch, she shook the crumbs from the rug and lay down on it. She said she was going to enjoy the sunshine for a few minutes. Felicity tugged at Carlo's hand, pulling him to his feet. She wanted to go back to the shop attached to the center to buy souvenirs. He pretended to be angry and chased her, shrieking with laughter, across the picnic area in the direction of the shop.

I lay on my side in the grass. My head rested in my right hand and with my left I plucked idly at blades of grass.

I glanced at Lily on the rug. She was lying on her back, her eyes closed. Her cheeks were pinker than usual. The picnic rug had a pattern of red-and-white checks, and her cheeks were almost the same color as the red checks.

I stared at her. She was wearing a pale green cotton dress. It was sleeveless and came above the knee. Her legs were bare and there were sandals on her feet. For the first time, it seemed to me, I was seeing her properly—as herself, rather than as a figure in Carlo's background defined only by his relationship to her.

There was no reason for this—or, rather, nothing for which she could be held responsible. After all, I had seen her before in poses that were far more obviously alluring—in a bikini, for example, or in a nightdress. It wasn't her doing. It was mine. None of this would have happened if it hadn't been for me. It was my fault.

I looked at the faint sheen of sweat on Lily's forehead. I noticed the soft dark hair on her neck just behind the ear. It was as fine as a baby's. I watched her breasts rise and fall as she breathed. There was a slight breeze, enough to send the occasional ripple through the hem of her skirt. I stared at the place where the dress ended and the legs began, almost willing the breeze to grow stronger, to push the light cotton higher up the leg.

Something changed.

At first, I didn't know what was happening to me. I had heard people at school talk about this, usually with a knowing laugh. I had read about it in books and seen it on the screen. But it had never happened to me. I was simply not prepared for it. For several minutes I didn't recognize it for what it was.

Though I had recently eaten I had a sensation curiously close to hunger. I felt something in the back of my throat, too, an anticipation, an excitement, as if a momentous event was just round the corner. I couldn't tear my eyes away from Lily. She drew me towards her, like a falling body to the earth, and I could no more resist the force of her gravity than I could live backwards in time.

Running footsteps pounded across the grass. Felicity shrieked with laughter.

I was acquiring an erection, which was increasingly obvious as it pressed with painful urgency against the crotch of my jeans. Lily opened her eyes and stared at me.

8

SUNDAY MORNING. IT WAS DAWN AND I HAD A HEADACHE from the wine. I had slept for an hour or two. My body felt brittle. A well-placed blow could have shattered it into a million pieces. I lingered in bed because it was easier than getting up.

The red digits on the LCD display changed from 05:59 to 06:00. I panicked—I hadn't checked my phone: Nicky might have texted me in the night or, if she hadn't, she might have emailed. I rolled out of bed, tripped on the rug and stubbed my toe.

But there were no messages on the phone. I went downstairs to my study and switched on the laptop. Emails were waiting, but not from Nicky. Afterwards I checked the news. Still nothing about a body at Rackford.

I closed the laptop. Beside it on the desk was the brown envelope I had stolen from Carlo's backpack during the abortive trip to Chipping Weston. I slid out the photograph and the card. There was Felicity, eternally poised between child and woman, doomed always to be neither one nor the other. I glanced at the card, with its row of brightly colored flowers strung across the front like a line of washing. "For Daddy— happy birthday, with lots of love and hugs from Felicity."

It made me feel worse than ever. I had another shower because I felt unclean. The morning crawled slowly by. At eight o'clock I tried to phone Nicky. At eight thirty I tried again, and at nine o'clock too. I called Kate's number. She wasn't answering her phone either.

I needed to do something. I wrote a message for Nicky and left it on the kitchen table. I drove to Wembley. The hospice car park was full. The reception area was thronged with Sunday visitors.

"Yes, go on in," the nurse said. "Lily's had quite a good night but she's finding it hard to concentrate."

"Is she worse?"

"It's not so much that—it's the medication."

"Has her daughter managed to visit?"

"Not that I know of. But her son came yesterday afternoon."

"Her son?"

She looked sharply at me.

I said quickly, "Oh, of course—her stepson, you mean. Carlo."

"Try not to excite her," the nurse went on, as we walked along the corridor. "I think he did. I'm sure he didn't mean to. But Lily was quite agitated after he left."

Lily was sitting up in bed with her arm attached to a syringe driver. The biography was no longer on the bedside table. When she saw me, her face brightened. "Jamie." She held up her cheek for me to kiss. With the nurse looking on, I lowered my head and brushed the dry, wrinkled skin with my lips.

"Come and sit here." Lily touched the arm of the chair beside the bed. "I want to see you."

The nurse left us. Lily smiled at me, and the ghost of her old charm reached out and touched me. "I'm so glad you're here," she whispered. "You're the only one I can trust."

This was a technique she had always used. She made you feel special. She made you feel that there was no one in the world who could do whatever it was as well as you could. She made you feel unique and wonderful.

"How are you feeling?"

She waved the question aside with a hand that was all skin, bone and tendon. "Carlo came, I think," she said, in the same hissing voice. "He scares me."

"Did he try to hurt you?"

"No, not that. He doesn't want to hurt *me*." She frowned, groping in the cloud-filled recesses of her memory. "She phoned, Kate did. She said you were helping. I knew you would, Jamie, I knew I could trust you. Only you."

Carlo must have come in the early afternoon, I thought, before driving down to Chipping Weston where he had flushed me out of the house. I glanced about the room, hoping to see the book with the white envelope in it. *Surely she hadn't shown it to Carlo?* "What did he want?" I said.

"Kate, of course." She stared at me, and the brown irises of her eyes were enormous, the pupils reduced to minute dots. "He's going to kill her, you see."

"I'm sure that's not true," I said gently.

She shook her head. "He wants me to stay alive until she's dead because then he'll get it all. Everything from Hugh, I mean."

"Did she say where she is?"

Lily looked blankly at me. "She's with you."

"Not anymore. I found her a place to stay but she left yesterday afternoon. No warning. I went there and found she'd gone."

"Why?"

"I don't know." In fact I thought that Kate might have calculated that if the body hadn't been found, no one would be looking for her. Yet. So in the meantime it was safe for her to leave.

Lily yawned. She poked a fingertip into a nostril, then took it out and stroked her cheek with it. She yawned again. Her eyelids were closing. I moved a little closer, hoping to catch sight of the envelope. I cleared my throat. "Maybe Kate told you where she was when she phoned?"

Lily blinked.

"Try to think. Lily, you must think."

She rubbed her claw-like hands together. "I—I'm not sure."

The harder I pressed, the vaguer her replies. Her memory had become treacherous: it allowed her to lurch from time to time, from place to place. In the end she gave up all pretense of listening to me. She rested her head on the pillows and closed her eyes. I sat back in the chair and watched her sleeping. Except she wasn't quite asleep. Slices of brown iris showed between the lids.

"Hugh," Lily said, opening her eyes wide. She smiled. Then her face crumpled and she frowned.

"Not Hugh," I said. "I'm Jamie."

Her head nodded, a heavy, dying flower on a brittle stalk. "Look after Kate. Promise me."

"I'll—I'll try." As I spoke I thought of Nicky, and my need for her was so extraordinarily painful I almost cried out. "But I don't know where she is."

"At Sean's?"

I frowned and whispered: "But Sean's dead."

"His house. She lived there for a bit."

"Where is it?"

Lily thought—for so long that I wondered whether she'd forgotten the question. "I don't know." She gave another wave of the fleshless hand. "I used to know. I've forgotten."

"I expect you wrote it down somewhere," I suggested, without much hope.

But she nodded. "Of course I did. It's at the back of my diary."

"And where's your diary?"

She wasn't listening. "I'm tired, Hughie, so tired."

"I know. The diary—where is it?"

Lily blinked. "It's bedtime, Hughie."

The lids slipped over the eyes. She turned her face away from me on the pillow. Her breathing became heavy. She began to snore.

The door was wide open and every few seconds someone would pass along the corridor. I stood up, slowly and quietly. The snoring continued, growing louder. With my eyes swinging between Lily and the corridor, I sidled round the bed. I stooped over the locker beside it. The door creaked when I opened it. The snoring stopped. I straightened up and pretended to stare out of the window. The snoring did not start again but in a moment the breathing resumed its regular rhythm.

I turned back to the locker. There was no sign of the biography, but a blue suede handbag was on the bottom shelf. I eased open the catch and rummaged quickly through the contents. A black appointments diary was in a side pocket.

I flicked through its pages, which were mainly blank. At the back was a section of addresses and phone numbers. Carlo's wasn't among them, but the name Sean Fielding was halfway down the second page. He lived in St Albans: 9 Laburnum Lane. As I was trying to memorize the phone number, Lily stirred. She opened her eyes.

I smiled at her. "Had a nice rest?"

"Did I drop off?"

I put the diary into the open mouth of the handbag and closed the locker door with my knee. "You nodded off for a couple of minutes."

"I do that all the time now. It's so silly. Sometimes I don't know if I'm waking or sleeping."

"I'd better go. I don't want to tire you." I lifted up the glass, which was on top of the cupboard. "Would you like some water?"

"Thank you."

She leaned against me. I slid my right arm round her and supported her. She took several sips. Water dribbled down her chin. I dabbed it dry with a tissue.

"Thank you," she said, and sank back against the pillows.

At that moment I saw the book. It had slipped between her arm and her body, and most of it was concealed by the folds of her nightdress. "Shall I move your book? It can't be very comfortable there."

"No," she said. "It's all right where it is."

Her eyelids closed and her breathing slowed again. I looked down at her. For a moment I forgot about Nicky and Kate. I forgot about the tarnished chain in the white envelope and the address in my memory. For a moment there was only Lily. Lust had evaporated and love had run dry. But something remained—a connection, perhaps, or a responsibility; a sadness for what had been and what might have been.

I bent down and kissed her cheek. I wished her a gentle death.

In December 1979 I went to stay with the Murthingtons at the beginning of the holidays. Since the previous summer I had spent a surprising amount of time thinking about Lily and constructing dramatic situations designed to make her realize how wonderful I was. I didn't want to think about her while I was at school but I found I had no choice in the matter. I even encouraged Carlo to talk about his family in the hope of eliciting scraps of information about her, however small and inconsequential. I needed something to feed on.

But it didn't mean anything. I told myself that over and over again. I couldn't fancy Lily, not really. It would be too sick and weird for words. After all, she could have been my mother. She was *old*.

Life, I already knew, was full of private embarrassments and secret fears. You just had to keep quiet about them and pretend that they didn't exist, and hope that sooner or later they wouldn't matter. My mother didn't want me. My penis was smaller than anyone else's in the history of the world. I would never pass my A levels. I was terrified that my grandmother would die, and sometimes I had nightmares about finding her dead body in the bungalow. So Lily was just another item for the list. Something to grow out of as quickly as possible.

During that visit to Chipping Weston, Christmas spread like an infection throughout the house. The freezer filled up with mince pies. Cards dangled on ribbons attached to the picture rails. Wrapping paper, Sellotape and scissors appeared and disappeared all over the house. The sitting room, the hall and the stairs were laden with golden and silver streamers. The landing windowsill became the setting for Felicity's nativity crib with scenery and figures she had painted.

Lily seemed hardly to notice me, except as another pair of hands to help with the preparations. There was something ruthless and single-minded about her desire to ensure that Christmas conformed to the rigorous expectations she had of it. She sent Carlo and me to dig up the tree from a damp, sunless corner of the garden beyond the summerhouse. We lugged it into the house, scattering a trail of earth down the hall and into the sitting room. Felicity took control of decorating it, spurning any advice from Lily but graciously accepting Carlo's assistance and even mine. Carlo was cooperative but less than enthusiastic.

"I mean, for God's sake," he said to me afterwards, "all that bloody holly. And the mess the tree makes, you wouldn't believe it. I hate Christmas. Everyone buys everyone else presents they don't really want, and they spend about four weeks wrapping them up. Why don't we just give each other money? And, Jesus, you should be here for Christmas Day. They couldn't make more fuss about lunch if it was a blood sacrifice with a couple of underage virgins. And on Christmas Eve we all have to go to the midnight service at church. It's full of people like us who never go for the rest of the year. It's pathetic. Bloody hypocrites. Why do they have to pretend it's so wonderful when it's not?"

But it sounded wonderful to me—what Christmas ought to be. When I spent Christmas with my mother, my stepfather and their family, I was a stranger, the boy perpetually on the wrong side of the window with his face pressed up against the glass. It was slightly better at my grandmother's, where I was going this year, because my expectations were so low as to be almost invisible. We would pull a solitary cracker and chew our way through a roasted turkey roll. Afterwards my grandmother would go to sleep in front of the television while I slipped into my room or outside for a quick cigarette in the garden.

In the meantime, being in the same house as Lily wasn't easy. There were two main problems. First, I discovered that she still had a profoundly unsettling effect on me. I tried not to look at her too often, which was hard. Second, it was painful to discover that the real Lily was so far removed from the obliging woman in my carefully nurtured fantasies.

On my last evening at the Murthingtons', I met her coming out of the sitting room. She stopped, and I stopped too. "That's for you." She held out a small parcel. "For Christmas."

I looked from the present to her unsmiling face and back again. I felt my skin growing warm. Her cheeks were flushed too, perhaps from the wine she had drunk at supper. "Thank you," I said, and my voice emerged as a strangled whisper.

"Jamie."

"What?"

"Mind you don't open it until the day itself." She rested her fingers lightly on my arm and the hairs rose on my skin. "Promise."

"I—I promise."

"Good boy."

She raised herself on tiptoe. Still holding my arm, she brought her face up to mine and kissed my lips. I was too surprised to kiss her back. She released my arm and walked away. I heard her saying something to Hugh in the kitchen.

That was the first time Lily kissed me. They say you always remember the first time. In every kiss is the ghost of that first one—the first, I mean, that expressed something other than duty or affection. The first that tasted of desire.

I reached St. Albans at lunchtime. Laburnum Lane was part of a former council estate. As it was Sunday there were plenty of people about but none paid me much attention. Most of the semi-detached houses were now privately owned. Owners had expressed their individuality with doors and windows, coats of paint and extensions. The gardens offered a guide to the rich variety of human life.

Some houses, however, were still trapped in an unwholesome past. If Sean's, number nine, had had any money invested in its exterior over the last ten or fifteen years, it kept its secret well. I drove past it, parked round the corner and walked back.

The garden contained weeds, discarded food wrappers, a dustbin without a lid and two bicycles, neither of which had any wheels. I pushed open the gate and walked up the cracked concrete path to the front door. I tried the bell but nothing happened. I thought I heard a child crying inside but the sound might have come from a neighbor's. I rapped on the door with my knuckles.

Nobody came to ask what I wanted so I followed the ribbon of concrete round the side of the house. The back door was open, and just inside it a small child, naked except for a pair of shorts, was sitting on the floor with his legs spread out before him. A litter of discarded objects surrounded him—a plastic bath book, a wooden spoon, a handful of large, brightly colored plastic bricks and a soft purple object, which bore a faint resemblance to a monkey. The child was crying in a half-hearted way—not from pain or sorrow, I guessed, but because he could think of nothing better to do.

When he saw me looming over him outside the door, the crying stopped. He looked up at me with round blue eyes and his mouth opened in astonishment. Behind him was a grubby kitchen in need of a complete refit. I tried the effect of a smile. The child stared blankly at me and his mouth opened wider. I nudged the door further open with my foot.

"Hey!"

I turned in the direction of the sound. A sturdy woman was walking quickly toward me. She had short dark hair and wore a paint-stained T-shirt and jeans. She looked in her late twenties or early thirties. "What do you think you're doing?"

I smiled at her. "Sorry—I hope I didn't surprise you. I tried knocking and ringing the bell but there was no answer. Maybe I've got the wrong house."

"More than likely."

Some of the hostility had gone. I don't sound or look like a debt collector or a burglar, which probably counted in my favor. Another child appeared behind the woman—this one was definitely a girl of four or five. She clung to her mother's T-shirt and stared at me. There was a ring of chocolate round her mouth.

"So who do you want?" the woman said.

"I'm looking for Sean Fielding."

"He's not here."

"So he does live here?"

She nodded. "But if you've come about the car, I might as well tell you you're wasting your time."

"The car?"

"The one in the paper this week."

The girl yanked her mother's T-shirt. "It's not Daddy's car, it's yours."

"In theory," the woman said. "It's Daddy's, really. Anyway, I don't think anyone will want to buy it now."

"What's happened to it?" I asked.

She glanced at me. "Someone took the wheels off and set it on fire. So now it's not a car. It's a piece of scrap metal somewhere in Peckham." She detached the child's hand from her T-shirt. "Don't do that, Maisie."

"I'm sorry," I said. "I've come at a bad time."

The woman's mouth was a thin straight line. "Where Sean's concerned, it's always a bad time." She ruffled the little girl's hair. "Still, we'll manage."

"I haven't come about the car, actually."

She bent and gave the child a gentle push towards the doorway. "Go and look after Albert, darling. He wants to play with you."

The girl went into the house, squeezing herself against the wall, as far away from me as possible. She tried to pick up her brother, who shouted until she stopped.

"Why do you want him?" the woman said quietly. "Does he owe you money?"

"No. It's not him I'm looking for, really—it's a friend of his. Her mother's ill."

Albert howled with rage. Maisie had taken the monkey.

"Play nicely, darling," the woman said, without much conviction. Her voice hardened. "Her? Is it Kate?"

I nodded.

"It's my monkey," Maisie said. "Albert stole it. He's a thief."

"Are you a friend of hers?"

I said carefully, "I hardly know her, but I used to know her mother quite well. That's all."

Albert lost interest in the monkey. He fell silent and chewed a plastic car.

"I don't know where the cow is, and I don't care."

"What about Sean?"

"Your guess is as good as mine. I thought he was here. The first I knew was when I had a call from the police about the car—it's still registered at my address and in my name. I tried to ring him but I couldn't get an answer so I thought we'd better come over." She wrinkled up her face. "He was going to sell the car and split the proceeds with us. Some hope. With Sean, it always goes wrong."

"Any idea where he might be?"

"Somewhere with Kate? Maybe she's living in Peckham, these days. Bit of a comedown." Her voice was jerky now, the words coming in spurts as though pumped out under pressure. "I thought she was ancient history as far as Sean's concerned. She wasn't going to hang around after he got fired. Not her style at all."

I glanced into the kitchen. The children were playing in a more or less cooperative manner with the purple monkey, the plastic car and an empty cereal packet. "I didn't realize that Sean—"

"Was married with two kids? Nor does he, half the time. That's the problem. And Kate never gave a toss anyway. If it wasn't for her, we'd still be together."

"What happened?"

For a moment I thought she would tell me to mind my own business. Then she shrugged and said, "You really want to know?"

I nodded.

"You won't get the truth from Kate so you might as well have it from me. The first thing you need to know about her is that you can't believe a word she says. Come and sit down—if you can find a chair you can trust in this tip."

For an instant I was surprised she had invited me into the house. Then I grasped that she didn't really care anymore and she was desperate for someone to talk to. We went into the kitchen and squatted on stools at the table. Maisie and Albert scrapped and scuffled like a pair of puppies around our feet.

Her name was Emily, she said, and she had met Sean Fielding at university when she was in her first year and he was in his third. Two years later, she had married him. It had seemed like a good idea at the time because she had been pregnant with Maisie.

Sean was working for a firm in the City. They invested other people's money. His face fitted; the timing was right. His employers showered him with promotions and bonuses. Soon the Fieldings could afford to buy an early-Victorian farmhouse with five acres in south Cambridgeshire. Sean leased a flat in Long Acre with a garage in the basement for the Lotus. It was more convenient if he had an early start at the office, which he increasingly did. Emily spent most of her time with Maisie in Cambridgeshire. A woman came in five days a week to help with the cleaning and the more mundane side of the housekeeping, and a firm of contract gardeners kept the garden in trim.

"I suppose I thought it would always be like that," Emily said. "I'd never known any different, not since I left university. I used to worry about whether my soufflé would rise when we had people round for dinner. Or whether we'd get Maisie into the right pre-prep school."

I didn't have to prompt her much. Bitterness fueled her, and perhaps loneliness too. She wasn't really interested in why I was there, except in so far as it might affect herself and Sean. She had enough problems of her own without worrying about other people's.

"But it started to fall apart after Albert was born. I sort of lost interest in Sean. I took him for granted, I suppose. What I didn't know was that he was having a hard time at work. The market had changed. Suddenly he wasn't the favorite face in the office anymore."

Beneath us, the children wriggled through the forest of legs—the chairs', the table's, Emily's and mine. Albert tripped over my foot, fell on his face and started to wail. Emily bent down and scooped him up. Still talking, she held him against her and patted his back until he quietened.

"Sean wasn't very good at handling that. He needs to feel loved—don't we all? Spoiled rotten by his bloody mother, that's his problem. If he doesn't feel loved, he does stupid stuff. He was making mistakes, and that made everything worse. Then he started losing his temper. It was just before that he'd started seeing Kate."

"How did they meet?"

"She worked for one of his colleagues. Must have thought she had a meal ticket for life. Well, she had a nasty shock in September. Sean got the sack. They told him to clear his desk by the end of the afternoon, and don't bother coming back.

He phoned me with the news but I was out, so he left a message. I tried to call him back but he wasn't answering so I picked up the kids and went up to town. I turned up at the flat and there was Kate." Emily shrugged. "The bastard didn't know what had hit him."

The Fieldings' lives had disintegrated in a matter of weeks. Sean had lost his job. He had lost his wife and children because of the girlfriend, and he lost the girlfriend because he'd lost his job. He lost the flat because he couldn't afford the lease. Neither he nor Emily had had much in the way of savings because they had always lived up to their income.

"And Kate was always going on at him too. He didn't know what he'd let himself in for." Emily glanced across the table. "Tell you one thing, I feel sorry for Kate's mother. That girl's weird. Seriously weird."

Sean had sold the Lotus. He and Emily put their home on the market. Once the mortgage was paid off there was just enough money for Sean to put down a deposit on this house and for Emily to put down a deposit on an even smaller one in Bedford.

"We keep in touch, of course," Emily said. "For the sake of the kids. Give him his due, he's quite fond of them as long as he doesn't have to spend much time with them. Anyway, the divorce hasn't come through. Both the cars are in my name—it's cheaper to insure them that way." She picked at a congealed smear of tomato sauce on the chipped Formica top of the table. "Are you sure he's seeing Kate again?"

"I think so."

But if Kate was right, Sean wasn't seeing anyone or anything. He would never see his children again, and they would never see him. Emily lifted Albert from her lap and lowered him gently to the floor. Maisie hugged him fiercely and hit him with the purple monkey, which made him giggle.

"What do you think?" I asked.

Emily rested her elbows on the table. "I can't help wondering if he's gone off for good. With her, I mean."

"Why?"

"If she whistled, he'd go to her—no question. When I saw them together he was always watching her. Like a dog, you know. A dog that's worried it's going to be left behind. And there's nothing to keep him here, is there?" She hesitated. "I had a look round. I can't find things like his passport. Or his bank stuff. I phoned his mum but she hasn't heard from him and that's odd. They're really close—he told her he'd been sacked before he told me." Her face quivered. "I—I just hope he's OK. He's such a bloody fool. He needs someone to look after him. He's like a kid in some ways. Maisie's got more sense than him."

She gave me her telephone number in case I heard any news of him, and I gave her my mobile number in return.

"And another thing," she said, as I was leaving. "He's not answering his mobile. That's not like him."

When I left the house, she was still sitting in the kitchen. The children were getting fractious but I think she was waiting for Sean.

I drove home to Greyfont. Emily's Sean seemed to bear little relation to Kate's. They might almost have been different people. And I was no nearer to finding Kate, let alone Sean. I was just more confused. If there was more than one version of Sean, perhaps there was more than one version of Carlo.

Before I reached the motorway, I pulled over and phoned first Nicky, then Kate. Neither answered. I phoned the hospice.

The woman on the switchboard told me that Lily was asleep. I asked her to say that Jamie sent his love and that I would be in touch.

It was mid-afternoon before I turned onto the patch of gravel outside our house. Nicky's Mini Cooper was parked outside the garage.

9

NICKY SAID, "THERE'S SOMEONE ELSE, ISN'T THERE?"

"No. No, there isn't."

We were upstairs in the bedroom. She had two suitcases open on the bed, the big blue one we took on holiday and the smaller one we used for weekends. She was carefully folding shirts, skirts and trousers and putting shoes in bags.

"You haven't been talking to me for weeks. For months, even. Not properly—not since we moved here. I thought you might be seeing someone else but I wasn't sure, not till this weekend." She slipped a new toothbrush into the smaller suitcase. "Now it all makes sense."

"It makes nonsense. Where do you think you're going?"

"It's not nonsense. And where I'm going is no concern of yours."

I glared at her and she glared at me.

I tried to throttle back my anger. "I'm sorry if—"

"I don't care if you're sorry or not. You lied to me. It's the one thing I thought you'd never do. I can put up with your moods and your silences but not lying. I thought you understood that."

"There's been a mistake."

"You mean you've made a mistake."

"No. I mean you're jumping to the wrong conclusion."

"I don't think so. Where were you on Friday?"

"I told you, I was working."

"Not according to Rachel."

"You asked *Rachel*?"

Nicky put a towel in the big suitcase and concentrated on smoothing away the wrinkles. "Of course I did. I often talk to her. You probably haven't noticed but we're quite good friends."

"That's spying."

"Don't be stupid. I haven't tried to conceal it. Anyway, I like her, and she's your assistant. She sees more of you than I do, so it makes a lot of sense."

"But why didn't you mention it?" I asked.

"You never asked. You never *noticed*. Which did not surprise me. You spend most of your life hermetically sealed in a bubble. She tells me a damn sight more about what's going on at the office than you do." She picked up two pairs of shoes and considered them. Then she held first one pair, then the other against a dress that was already in the suitcase. "And you weren't working. That's a direct lie. Rachel said you phoned in and—"

"I was working before that."

"Before what? Before you went off to your lover? Is that what you call her? Or is she your bit on the side? Your young woman? Did you know Dave Hammett saw you on Friday night with your—your young woman? Is that why you like her, by the way? Because she's young? Younger than me? Because she can have—"

"She's not my young woman," I interrupted. "And I don't—"

"Then who is she?"

"She's—she's just someone I'm helping. I will explain, I promise, but not now. I can't."

"Is she called Lily? Rachel said she kept ringing the office on Friday, that she sounded quite upset."

"That's someone else. An old friend who's very ill. In fact, she's dying."

"So that's another person I haven't heard of. What else haven't you told me?"

Nicky continued packing, her movements deft and methodical. My head hurt. I dropped my jacket onto the bed and went into the bathroom. I opened the cabinet and took out the paracetamol.

"Miranda says she's very attractive, according to Dave. Very sexy." Nicky had pursued me and was standing in the doorway. "Whatever her name is. She said Dave was quite smitten."

Nicky's face was still beautiful, but bleak. I told myself that jealousy corroded not only other emotions but also how the sufferer thinks. Nicky feared this: therefore it existed. My apparent affair with Kate had taken on independent life.

"This has been coming for a long time, hasn't it?" she went on. "You know what really hurt? That you let her come here, to our home. This house was meant to be special, remember?"

I poured myself a glass of water and popped one of the capsules out of the foil. "Look, this business is something out of the past, long before I met you."

"Does that make it any better—assuming what you say is true? The point is, it's not in the past, it's now, and it's affecting you and me."

I swallowed the second capsule. "It's over."

"Is it? Not for me."

"I'm not having an affair. I never have and never will." I followed her back into the bedroom. "This was about something else."

She closed the lid of the smaller suitcase, snapped the locks and straightened up. She stared at me like an accuser, like a judge. "We started to go wrong a long time ago, didn't we? You know why."

I looked away.

"I need time to think," she said. "I'm going away for a few days to work out what to do. But I tell you one thing, James. I've had enough. I can't go on like this."

At that moment my mobile gave two sharp bleeps. Someone had sent me a message. Nicky swung round as though the sound had stung her like a wasp. She picked up my jacket and patted the pockets until she found the phone. She stabbed at the keys and stared down at the tiny screen. Her face changed. Still bleak, still cold and now, I thought, suddenly much older.

"You see?" She tossed the phone down on the bed. "You bastard. It's not over."

When Nicky had gone I went downstairs and sat in the study, a small room that contained nothing but a desk, a chair, a filing cabinet and bookshelves. I sat at the desk, flipped open the laptop and switched it on. Immediately in front of me was a framed photograph of Nicky, smiling.

While the computer was humming and churning, I opened the envelope I had taken from the Murthingtons' house in Chipping Weston and pulled out the contents. I put the photograph of Felicity, the eternal girl-woman, on the desk with the floral birthday card beside it. Why had Carlo put them into his backpack? Why now?

I took the phone out of my pocket and put it beside the card. I tapped a key. The phone beeped and its screen came to life. Kate's message was still there.

"Sorry to leave like that. You were great. Will call. Love K xxx."

Not many words but quite enough to be going on with, certainly enough for Nicky to misinterpret.

I logged on and ran a search linking Sean Fielding with Rackford. Nothing came up.

What did I have to go on? I brought up the word-processing program and made a list.

Lily was dying.

She said Kate was on the run from the police because it looked as if she'd killed Sean, her former boyfriend.

Kate was certainly acting like someone on the run—she was so paranoid that I wondered if she was mentally unstable.

Kate said Carlo had killed Sean. According to her, Carlo hated Lily and Kate because of what Lily and I had done all those years ago.

Carlo was capable of violence. Or, at least, he had been as a teenager.

Emily hated Kate. Emily thought Sean had done a runner. Emily said he had put up his car for sale, but that the police reported it had been stolen and wrecked in London.

Now the land at Rackford was potentially valuable, Kate said, and Carlo wanted it all. I wasn't sure of the legal position and, in any case, it would depend on the terms of Hugh Murthington's will. But if he had left his estate in trust while

Lily was alive, then on her death to be divided between Carlo and Kate, what would happen if Kate predeceased her mother? Would her share of the estate be transferred automatically to Carlo? If that was true, perhaps Kate was right to be paranoid.

And Lily had shown me a tarnished fragment of very fine chain with a scrap of metal hanging from it.

Looking at the list in front of me, I realized I was taking a lot on trust. I couldn't be sure that Emily was telling the truth. I wanted to believe Lily because she was dying and Kate because she was so desperate. But I wondered whether I wanted to believe them both for another reason, because on some level I felt I deserved to pay the price for what had happened all those years ago.

I highlighted the text and pressed delete.

If I could turn back the clock, I would return to the point just before everything went out of control, in other words to the moment when Lily had kissed me in the hall at Christmas. It was the first hint that she might be interested in me. Previously I had taken it for granted that what I felt could never be reciprocated in a million years. Indeed, I wasn't sure what I did feel. I had no words for it, or rather none that seemed to fit. I had no experience, no means of calibrating what was happening except the romanticized half-truths I'd picked up from films and books.

Lily had kissed me when she gave me the Christmas present. In my more rational moments I wondered whether I had misunderstood the implications. After all, I had no experience of how women worked. Perhaps it was the sort of thing a friend's mother might do out of the kindness of her heart. She might have thought I was lonely and needed cheering up. She might have been trying to fill the gap left by my own mother's absence.

But the rational moments were relatively few and far between. At school, in the months that followed the Christmas holiday, I thought about Lily constantly. Every night, as I lay in the darkness of the dormitory, I would replay the memories like a video: the first time I saw her, in the garden under the ash tree with Felicity when she had called me Jamie; the time she lay on the grass after the picnic and I watched her sleeping; and, most often of all, the kiss in the hall. Sometimes I went further than that and made up my own stories, my own videos, which left me breathless and unsatisfied. Ignorance was not bliss. It was a nightmare.

The present she had given me acted as a constant reminder. I couldn't wait until Christmas Day to open it. I tore off the wrapping paper when I was on the train to London. She had given me a watch with bold Roman numerals on a bracelet of expanding stainless steel. Heavy and obviously expensive, it clung to my wrist like a shackle. When no one was looking I would fondle it, even kiss it, and think that perhaps Lily had done the same.

As the weeks went by, I waited on tenterhooks for an invitation to stay during the Easter holidays, but I had to wait until nearly the end of term before Carlo asked me. We were smoking what we hoped was dope one Sunday afternoon when he mentioned it. I took my time answering, sucking at the joint and blowing out the sweet, acrid smoke before I said yes, I thought I could manage it. I added, "Are you sure your dad and Lily won't mind?"

He grinned evilly at me. "They think you're a good influence. If you come to stay I've got someone nice to hang around with, which gets them off the hook. They think we spend our time solving maths problems and reading Shakespeare. And if you weren't there I'd be chasing girls, smoking dope and getting pissed."

"'Once more into the breach, dear friends, once more,'" I recited. "Do you want the roach?"

So I went back to Chipping Weston during the Easter holidays of 1980. I was sixteen and a half. Carlo and I had been friends for so long that we took each other for granted. Not just Carlo—his family treated me almost as one of themselves, as a cousin, perhaps, rather than a nearer relative.

At Chipping Weston, I became a spy. I didn't want to but I had no choice. I did what I had to do and hoped that, whatever the reason for it, this strange and embarrassing state of mind would soon pass. In the two weeks of the Easter holiday, I watched Lily constantly and surreptitiously. I noticed what she was wearing and where she went. I speculated endlessly about what she was thinking and feeling.

Once I saw her in the hall as I was coming down the stairs. She was wearing a dressing gown and it had fallen open slightly at the neck. For an instant I saw her left breast. I glimpsed the darker pink of the nipple. She turned away and, tightening the belt, continued telling Felicity why it was sensible to keep your room tidy.

The glimpse of Lily's breast haunted my waking life and sometimes I saw it again in my dreams. What I felt for her had nothing to do with love. It was something inside me—in my belly, in my throat—something that yearned to escape but didn't know why or where it would go if it did. It was an aching obsession, an appetite that was almost impersonal in its nature, as inexorable as hunger but far less explicable.

Love implies a concern for the beloved's well-being. I didn't wish Lily any harm, but her happiness was irrelevant beside the urgency of my need for what only she could give me. I knew it must all come down to sex, but I didn't understand how or why. My enthusiastic exploration of masturbation and pornographic magazines seemed to inhabit a different universe, sunlit and straightforward. Why did I want *her*, for God's sake, when there was a world full of girls out there? It made no sense.

I tried with increasing desperation to engineer situations where Lily and I could be alone. Hugh Murthington, Felicity or Carlo always intruded. Nor did Lily help me. It was as if she had erased that kiss in the hall from her memory. Perhaps I had made a terrible mistake—and it really had been a friendly, aunt-like kiss that had somehow missed its way and found my lips. Perhaps I'd imagined the air of furtiveness, the secrecy. Perhaps my own desire had been so intense that I had seen it reflected in her eyes.

I saw everything refracted through my hunger for Lily. For example, I noticed that Mr. Murthington was very busy, and that he seemed abstracted—he was even quieter than usual at meals, and in the four months since Christmas he seemed to have aged as many years. I remember thinking that Lily looked young enough to be his daughter, which lent a faint respectability to how I felt about her. I liked Hugh Murthington, what I knew of him, and I didn't want to injure him, but if to all intents and purposes he was Lily's father rather than her husband there was less to worry about. The logic of lust makes strange flights of reason.

One of the hardest things to bear was when Lily talked to me and others were there. She asked me about school, about my family. She was interested in the music I was listening to—or rather, perhaps, she pretended to be—and my plans for the future. I dared not look at her while I replied. I was terrified that my face and my stumbling words must give away my feelings not just to her but to everyone else in the room.

I almost longed for the holiday to be over. The driving lessons at Rackford were particularly bad. Lily was so close to me when I was at the wheel. Sometimes she touched my hand or brushed against my leg. Carlo was always in the backseat, and usually Felicity, sometimes her friend Millie as well. At that time, Millie was a plump child who talked only to Felicity and laughed when Carlo said anything. It didn't occur to me until much later that she and I might have had something in common.

On the Thursday after Easter, while Hugh Murthington was at his office in town, Lily decided that she wanted a trunk down from the loft. She asked Carlo and me to help her.

"She probably keeps the bloodless bodies of her victims up there," Carlo murmured in my ear.

We carried a stepladder upstairs from the shed. Carlo grumbled about having to help but he'd never been in the loft before and the grumbling was more for show than anything else. The loft was at the back of the house, over the bathroom, Felicity's room and the passage from the main landing, and the hatch was in the bathroom ceiling.

Felicity, who was in her bedroom next door, was practicing the recorder. She was working her way through "On Top of Old Smoky." Her music teacher was going to give a record token to the girl who made the most progress in playing the recorder over the holidays. Felicity and Millie were both desperate to win the prize, and both of them practiced religiously every day, sometimes simultaneously and in the same room. Even now when I hear a recorder I think of Lily—of the agony of wanting someone so badly and not being able to have her. I think of Felicity too.

Carlo was first up the ladder. He pushed aside the hatch and hauled himself into the darkness beyond. His legs dangled through the opening. A shower of dust floated down to the floor.

"Is there a light?" he called down, his voice muffled.

"I don't think so," Lily said. "Hang on, I'll get a torch."

Her arm brushed mine as she left the bathroom—but with a stepladder in the middle of the floor there wasn't much space. She gave me a half-smile, as if in apology. I climbed up the ladder and poked my head and shoulders through the opening. Carlo was at the far end of the loft where the light from the hatch barely reached.

"Bloody hell," he said. "There's a wasps' nest. It's enormous."

My eyes adjusted. The loft was like a tent, its sloping roofs hung with cobwebs and gray with dirt and dust. A central gangway stretched into the shadows where Carlo was. On either side were the unwanted remnants of family life—suitcases, trunks and boxes; rolls of carpet; stacks of magazines tied up with yellowing string; pictures in heavy old frames that no one wanted to look at anymore.

"Jesus," Carlo said, "it's bigger than a football. There's enough room for a whole fucking army of them."

I heard footsteps beneath me and looked down. Lily had returned to the bathroom. She passed up the torch to me. I turned it on. The beam slid up the gangway, climbed Carlo's crouching shadow and came to rest on a dirty white globular shape clinging to the angle where the roof timbers met a chimney breast.

"It's huge," I said.

"What is?" Lily said below.

"There's a wasps' nest," I said.

"I don't think it's live," Carlo said. He scrambled back to the hatch. Even in the center of the loft, where the gangway was, there wasn't room to stand up and he had to crouch. In his excitement, he almost snatched the torch from me. He crawled back to the nest.

"Be careful," Lily called up.

He ignored her. I turned towards the sound of her voice. She was staring up at me. Felicity was still playing the recorder.

"Jamie, could you come down a moment?" She sounded breathless, almost on the edge of panic. "There's a daddy-long-legs in the basin."

"Are you OK?" I said, climbing down the ladder.

"I know it's stupid. It's just that I can't stand them."

I edged past Lily and scooped up the insect. She gave a little cry, half fearful, half admiring. I opened the window and dropped the daddy-long-legs onto the sloping roof outside. I turned. Lily was beside me. "Thank you," she whispered. "Is there something in my hair? Another? I felt something moving."

I took a step nearer and looked carefully at her dark hair. Lily shivered. She was wearing a cream silk shirt and I was aware of her breasts just inches away from me. I felt the warmth of her body. My breathing was rapid and growing faster. The recorder played on. Carlo was still moving at the far end of the loft.

"Nearer," she commanded. "You'll see better."

Her hands rested on my shoulders. Suddenly there was no longer a space between our bodies, and there was nothing aunt-like about her now. Her hands slipped down my arms and joined behind my back. She moistened her lips, and their flesh gleamed pink.

"I think it's gone now," she said, in a voice that was almost normal. "I can't feel it, anyway."

Carlo was muttering to himself. Felicity was now practicing "The Skye Boat Song," repeating the first four bars of the tune over and over again and making at least one mistake each time. Lily Murthington was kissing me, and I was kissing her.

10

NICKY HAD GONE. WHEN I WOKE UP ON MONDAY MORN-ing, the sun was shining, sending a bar of golden light across the ceiling. For two or three seconds it felt good to be alive. Then I remembered what had happened. I pushed my hand across the bed and felt a cool sheet where a warm body ought to have been.

It was the start of the working week. I got up and checked the phone for messages that weren't there. Over coffee I skimmed through my emails. There was nothing of even the slightest interest, apart from the one that Rachel had sent late on Friday afternoon containing the agenda for that morning's meeting.

There was nothing I could do, nothing that would bring Nicky back to me, nothing that would resolve the problem of Kate. In the end I walked to the station and caught the usual train into town. I needed a distraction of some sort, something to fill the front of my mind, and work was as good as any-thing. I reasoned that Nicky would expect me to go into the office. She knew how to contact me there. If Kate needed me she would phone the mobile.

The office was in the tangle of streets south of Smithfield market. The contents of my in-tray and the ritual exchanges of office life filled the hour and a half before the meeting began. Rachel broke with tradition and brought me a cup of coffee, usually something I did for myself unless I had a client with me. I wondered whether she knew or had guessed that Nicky had left me. It depended on the nature of the friendship between her and Nicky. What else was there I didn't know? Once you allow doubts into your life they don't trickle, they come in a flood.

I never said much at these weekly meetings. I said even less today. Afterwards Rachel, who had been taking the minutes, followed me out. "Are you OK?" she asked.

"Fine, thanks." I turned away to pour myself a glass of water I didn't want.

"You seem a bit under the weather."

"You know how it is—that Monday-morning feeling."

She looked at me curiously. I was uncomfortably aware of her intelligence probing my weaknesses. Perhaps she was even trying to help. For the first time it occurred to me that she knew me better than I knew her. I certainly hadn't realized how friendly she and Nicky had become.

As if catching the echo of my thoughts, Rachel said, "Nicky said something about you working late on Friday."

I sipped water. "That chapel in Queen's Park—I forgot to do some of the measurements. I had to go back."

"She thought I'd said something. You know, when you phoned in. Something that made you late, I mean."

"Crossed wires," I said. "Which reminds me, I dictated the draft report on the chapel while I was there. Would you type it up and marry it with the plans? We'll need it in presentable form by Thursday."

I tried to work but it was impossible to settle. In the end I went out early for lunch. In the street, I passed a delicatessen I occasionally used and the sight of its window gave me an idea. I sometimes bought things for supper there on the days that Nicky was working. Monday was one of her gallery days. It was just possible that even now she might be in Kew. She took her responsibilities seriously. It was one thing to leave me, I told myself bitterly, but quite another to leave her job.

I took the tube to Kew. I didn't want to phone in case she refused to speak to me. The gallery where she worked was on the main road north of the bridge. Once it had been a greengrocer's shop. Now the ground floor had been turned into a long thin display area with a small office at the back.

That was where I found Victor, with his feet on the desk. He was eating an overripe melon and the juice was running down his chin. Mahler's *Kindertotenlieder* was on the stereo, a choice of music I could have done without. Victor was wearing a pair of very short shorts, which showed off his thin, slightly bowed legs, a short-sleeved shirt and a pair of glasses with large, heavy rims. Nicky said he resembled a frog and she was right. He gazed at me with the beginnings of a frown.

"I'm James," I said, as I said every time I saw him. "Nicky's husband."

"Of course. I know. Sit down, lad, don't just stand there." Victor came from Yorkshire and believed he had a professional obligation to speak bluntly. "What are you doing here?"

I wished he'd turn off the Mahler. "Nicky's not in?"

He glared at me, swung his legs off the desk and wiped his chin with a paper handkerchief. "Of course she isn't. Why on earth do you think she might be?"

"Maybe there're crossed wires," I said, using what seemed to be becoming my formula of the day. "I must have misunderstood something she said."

"More likely you weren't listening." He hesitated. "She's off work this week. I'm surprised you don't know."

"Like I said, crossed wires."

He grunted. "What have you been doing to her?"

"I beg your pardon?"

Victor waved a finger at me. "She was upset. She phoned me yesterday evening and I knew she was. I can always tell. I feel it here." He laid his hand over his heart and patted himself approvingly. "I've a strong sense of intuition. Have you had a row?"

Suddenly I was tired of pretending. "Something like that."

"You bloody fool. A woman like that, it's bound to be your fault. I'd marry her myself, like a shot, if she'd have me. If I was that way inclined." He pushed back his chair and stood up to his full height of five foot three. "Well, she's not here, is she? Where are you going to look next?"

"I don't know."

"You could ask some of her friends."

"Which friends?"

Victor poked his tongue into his cheek. "She does have them, you know. Too many, if you ask me." He stared aggressively at me, as though I had tried to contradict him. "'I pay you to work,' I tell her, 'not to provide a floorshow of your social life.' That was after the other day, when that Miranda woman descended on us."

"Miranda Hammett?"

"Could be—I don't recall."

"When was this?"

"Tuesday." He registered that I hadn't been aware of it. "You know what women are like when they get chatting. Like sparrows in your back garden. Tweet-tweet-tweet. Drives you mad if you have to listen to it for long. And Nicky kept trying to get hold of that man on the phone. My phone, I might add. He was meant to be meeting them here too."

At last *Kindertotenlieder* stopped. In the sudden silence, I said, "Who was the man?"

Victor glanced into the mirror over the fireplace and put his head on one side. His eyes met mine in the glass. "How should I know? He didn't come here in the end."

"Do you know whose friend he was—Miranda's or Nicky's?"

"I don't know anything." Victor rubbed his chin with the handkerchief again. "No, I'm wrong. I do know one thing. Miranda and Nicky were saying he'd be much better looking if he shaved off his beard."

"I'm in a hurry, James," Miranda said. "Can't it wait?"

"No," I said. "It's about Nicky."

She stopped beside the driver's door of her enormous Mercedes off-roader, the keys jingling in her hand. "Haven't you found her yet?"

"I saw her on Sunday."

Miranda's eyes were blank behind her sunglasses. "But she's gone off again, is that it?"

"I'm not quite sure where she is."

"Sorry, I can't help you." She opened the door and hauled her heavy body behind the wheel. "Wish I could but there it is. Now I must rush."

"Wait." The window was open and I rested my hand on the sill. "Maybe she's with a friend."

"Maybe. Everyone needs friends." She turned her head and looked at me. "Well, most people, anyway."

"I went to Nicky's gallery at lunchtime. Victor said you'd been there on Tuesday, and that you and Nicky were meeting a friend."

Miranda started the engine and gave a high laugh that went on for too long. "Charlie? Yes, he's in the book group too."

She revved the engine, which rumbled menacingly. "Sorry, James, you'd better ask Nicky. Look, I really must go—I've got to fetch the dry cleaning, and then I've got to pick up the kids from school. There'll be hell to pay if I'm late."

The Mercedes crept down the drive. I walked with it for a few paces. I still had my hand on the door.

"Just one thing." I hated the note of pleading in my voice. "What's his other name? Where does he live?"

The Mercedes reached the end of the drive. The driver's door was so near the gatepost I had to let go to avoid being crushed. Miranda said something, perhaps in reply, but the words were drowned by the thunder of the engine. She pulled into the road and accelerated away. She didn't wave.

I walked back to our empty house. Increasingly paranoid questions flickered through my mind like a silent movie. I knew they were paranoid but once you start asking questions, it's hard to stop, and they made a vile kind of sense. Was there a friendship between Nicky and Charlie, even an affair? Could Charlie even be Carlo? Had Carlo targeted Nicky because she was my wife? If so, how much had he told her? Because if Carlo had told her everything, it would have given her another, perhaps stronger, reason to leave me.

But no one knows everything. I didn't know what any of the Murthingtons were up to, or Nicky. The only thing I knew for certain was that I was scared.

I tried Nicky's mobile again. I went straight through to voice mail. I left a message, more urgent than before, begging her to ring for her own sake. I texted her too. I couldn't even warn her.

I thought about going to the police. But what could I tell them? Women leave their husbands every day. There was no question of her being compelled to go. I didn't have a shred of evidence to encourage them to take me seriously.

But if Kate was right, and Carlo had killed Sean, then what was to stop him killing Nicky too?

I drove to the hospice, buying flowers at a service station on the way. A nurse I recognized was chatting with the receptionist.

"Lily's awake. Do you want to go straight through?" She looked at the flowers I was carrying. "Freesias—my favorite."

"They're Lily's, too," I said. "Or they used to be."

I walked along the corridor to her room. The door was open. She was propped against the pillows. Her unopened book and a glass of water stood on the table over the bed. The news was on the radio but I don't think she was listening. I hesitated in the doorway and watched her drifting through an internal space whose geography I couldn't begin to imagine.

She caught sight of me and frowned.

"Hi," I said, suddenly as awkward as I'd been at sixteen. "How are you?"

It took her a few seconds to recognize me. "Still here."

I bent down and kissed her cheek, which seemed the natural thing to do. "I brought you some flowers."

"Freesias. Nice." She smiled, drawing back thin, bloodless lips. "You remembered."

"What shall I do with them?"

"Vases in the wardrobe. Water in the shower room."

I put the freesias in water and stood the vase on the windowsill.

"No," Lily said. "Put them here." She touched the edge of the table in front of her. "I want to see them. I want to smell them."

I obeyed her. Her eyes followed my movements. The pupils were black pinholes. She smiled at me, her lips lifting to reveal long, yellowing teeth set in receding gums. "I was dreaming," she said. "Though it didn't seem like a dream. I was remembering when I met Hugh. He seemed so old."

I said, "I've got a problem. I didn't know who else to come to so I came to you."

"He was wearing a dark blue pinstripe suit and carrying a rolled-up umbrella. I wouldn't be surprised if he had a bowler, too. Even then he looked about twenty years behind the times. As if he'd wandered out of an Ealing comedy and got lost in the future."

"Lily, I really need to—"

"He was making me old. That's why I liked you, you see. You made me young. And you were very sweet. So was Hugh, but that was different."

She wasn't looking at me any longer but at the freesias. She began to hum. There wasn't any tune to it but by the way the sounds were spaced I thought it might be "You've Lost That Loving Feeling" by the Righteous Brothers. She used to like that song. I wished I hadn't come. I wished they hadn't given her so much morphine. I picked up the biography of the dead actress. The humming stopped abruptly.

"No, not oysters," Lily said. "I don't like seafood." She smiled, this time with her lips closed and her eyes swung slowly towards me. She blinked. "Jamie. It is Jamie, isn't it? You've changed. Yes, thank you—I might read for a bit." She held out her hand.

I gave her the book. "Have you heard from Kate?"

She shook her head slowly from side to side, rolling it to and fro against the pillow. "Not for a day or two, I think. But you're looking after her. She's—she's your daughter."

"She went away on Saturday," I said. "I don't know where she is now."

"You must find her." Lily's hands scratched the blankets on top of her, trying to get a grip. "She needs you to look after her."

"Kate can take care of herself."

"Don't be silly. You will look after her." Her voice was rising in volume. "Promise me you will. Promise me. You owe her that."

I leaned forward and took her hands, trying to quieten her. "I promise," I said.

"And you'll find her? You'll keep her safe from Carlo?"

"Yes. Actually, it's Carlo I want to talk about."

"He never liked me. I thought he wouldn't come back. But he wants the money."

"Where is he?"

"Carlo? Oh, he upset Hugh so much, going off like that after the divorce. Hugh never really got over it. It was so unkind."

"It's just possible that Nicky may be with him. With Carlo. That's why I want to find him."

Lily frowned at me. "Who's Nicky?"

"My wife. She's got hold of the wrong end of the stick about Kate and she's gone off. And I can't get hold of her."

It was no use. Lily's mind was following its own train of thought. "He and Felicity used to gang up against me. And I tried so hard with them—it wasn't my fault their mother died. I was only trying to make their father happy. What's wrong with that?"

"I need to find Carlo now."

"Find him? Whatever for?"

I had learned cunning. "For Kate's sake."

Lily's face began to shake as if a small earthquake were taking place inside her skull. "He's trying to hurt her," she whispered.

"I want to stop him. But I have to find him first. Where is he?"

She shrugged. "He's come home now. He wants everything. That's why he's come."

"I know he's come home. But where—"

"I expect he's at home."

I leaned forward and took her left hand in both of mine. "Lily? Where's home for Carlo?"

"Where it always was."

"In Chipping Weston? But he's not living there, is he? Where's his real home?"

She was drifting away from me. "I do like freesias." She touched one and smiled. "Is she nice?"

"Who?"

"Your wife, of course. Nicky."

11

FREESIAS. I LEARNED ABOUT FREESIAS FROM HUGH MUR-thington. I don't think I'd even heard their name before. It was near the end of the Easter holidays and he had had to go to London for something connected with business. When I knew him, he seemed always to be busy but to achieve little. I suspect that by this time he was losing considerable sums of money. Years ago, he had promised to buy Carlo a car when he passed his test—an MGB. But one night last term, when we were very drunk on a bottle of rum, Carlo had told me that his father said there might be a bit of a delay.

"It's business, you see," Carlo had said, with a wave of the hand that somehow implied he was privy to enormous financial secrets. "You get good years and bad years. Upturns and downswings. We're in a bit of a downswing now because of the fucking unions and the change in the interest rate."

That morning in Chipping Weston, Mr. Murthington beckoned Carlo and me as he left the house, briefcase in hand, umbrella hooked over his arm. When we were in the garden, he took out his wallet, removed a five-pound note and gave it to Carlo. "Yes—ah—I'd like you to look in at the florist's. Will you do that for me?"

Carlo nodded.

"Will you buy some freesias? They said they should have them in today."

"What do you want me to do with them?"

"They're for Lily. She's—she's particularly fond of them. I thought you boys could give them to her." He hesitated, his hand on the gate, and looked back at us. "Say they're from you. No need to mention me, eh?"

He strode down the road. From the back, Hugh Murthington looked quite different—purged of diffidence and uncertainty: he was upright and commanding, a leader among men, albeit one made in a rather old-fashioned mold.

Carlo watched his father, his face expressionless. "Our little way of saying thank-you," he said. "Say it with bloody flowers."

Felicity tagged along when we went into the florist's. The freesias were waxen, yellow and purple. While Carlo was paying, I held the bunch. I had never really looked at flowers before, not as things in themselves. If I had thought of them at all, it was only as a colorful nuisance, the cause of mysterious adult obsessions and irrational prohibitions. Those freesias made me feel oddly uncomfortable. They were sensual, and part of their power derived from the fact that they looked unnatural: they were artificial like lipstick, impractical like high-heeled shoes.

Carlo pocketed the change and led the way out of the shop. Outside on the pavement, Felicity tugged at his arm. "Can we have some hot chocolate? We don't have to go back yet, do we?"

"OK by me." Carlo glanced in my direction and raised his eyebrows.

"I don't mind," I said.

"We could go to the Hot Pot." Felicity's face was pink with the urgency of desire. "Millie says it's ever so nice."

"It's miles away," Carlo said, "and I bet it's expensive."

"I'll pay. Honest, I will, whatever it costs. I'll pay for all of us."

The Hot Pot was a recently refurbished coffee shop attached to the Newnham House Hotel. Last night at supper, Lily had mentioned a rumor that David Essex had spent a night there incognito just before Christmas, which might have increased the Hot Pot's allure for Felicity: both she and Millie were in love with him. The hotel was on the London road, at least a mile and a half from where we were standing.

"It's not just the money," Carlo said. "Anyway, we can use the change from Dad. It's the distance. And then there's these bloody flowers. I don't want to carry them around all over the place. I don't want to look like a bloody pansy."

"I'll carry them," she said. "What's a bloody pansy?"

"A man who carries flowers in public. And don't swear. If you carry the flowers you'll drop them or something. Anyhow, they'll get in the way."

I pushed my hands into the pockets of my leather jacket. "I'll take them back to the house, if you want."

"You'll be ages," Carlo said.

"No, I won't. Not if I walk fast. Anyway, I need to get my baccy. I forgot it." The fingers of my left hand curled round the packet of Golden Virginia tobacco in my pocket.

Felicity smiled at me as if I'd given her a present. "We'll walk slowly, James. You'll probably get there almost as soon as we do."

"Are you sure?" Carlo said.

I shrugged. "No problem."

"You'll give her the flowers?"

"If you want."

"They're from both of us, OK? And don't say my dad gave us the money."

I nodded. Carlo handed me the flowers. I walked away quickly. At the corner I looked back. Carlo and Felicity were walking slowly in the opposite direction, very close together, her face turned up to his.

It was a crisp, fine morning, with wisps of cloud moving rapidly across a pale, pure blue sky. Besides the jacket, I was wearing new jeans and zip-up black boots. I thought I looked cool, or at least as cool as nature and opportunity allowed. I walked faster and faster. My breathing was ragged. I didn't know what I wanted anymore or what I hoped for. It was as though someone or something had taken control of my will. This wasn't the sort of thing I did. Whatever it was I was doing.

The closer I came to the house, the more unreal I felt. Lily had kissed me twice. The first time might have meant nothing but the second couldn't by any stretch of the imagination have been what someone might expect to receive from a school-friend's mother. I felt dizzy when I thought of the warm, slippery writhing of her tongue in my mouth, the pressure of her breasts against my chest, my hands running over the smooth curves of her hips. I wanted it to happen again and I was terrified it might.

The door was unlocked, which meant that Lily was at home. I heard a clatter of plates from the kitchen.

"Mrs. Murthington?" I called, and my voice emerged as a breathless squeak.

The clattering continued. I opened the kitchen door. Lily was standing at the sink, her hands in pink rubber gloves streaked with foam. She was wearing a loose white cotton top over jeans. She had pushed her hair back behind her ears but some strands had escaped.

Her eyes widened. "Jamie—you gave me quite a shock."

"Sorry."

She shook her head, smiling. "Are the others with you?"

"No, they're going to the Hot Pot."

"Very posh. Looking for David Essex?" As she was speaking, she dried the gloves on a tea towel and stripped them off. They made a sucking noise as she peeled them away from her skin. "Why aren't you with them?"

"I'm going there now." I held up the freesias. "I said I'd bring you these on the way."

"From you?"

"From—from me and Carlo. As a sort of thank-you for everything."

Her face had lost the smile. "They're my favorites."

"I know."

While we were speaking, we had come closer together. I'm not sure how that happened. The edge of the kitchen table jarred against my thigh. I gave Lily the flowers and her hand touched mine as she took them. She wasn't looking at them: she was looking at me.

"That's sweet of you. You're a clever boy, aren't you?" She sniffed the flowers. "I love their smell. Don't you?"

She held the bunch. I bowed my head over it. The flowers smelt like my grandmother's garden when a long dry spell had been followed by a shower of rain. Lily touched my hair. I gasped and shied away as if she had pricked me with a pin.

"So soft. It's like a baby's." Her fingertips trailed behind my ear and followed the line of my jawbone. "That's soft, too." She dropped the flowers onto the table. She lifted my hand to her cheek. "Is it softer than mine?" she murmured.

"No."

My senses were unnaturally alert, sucking in information as indiscriminately as a vacuum cleaner. The washing machine began to spin. The fanlight of the window was open and the curtain was swaying in the draught. There was a faint smell of fresh coffee. I noticed the fine lines at the corners of Lily's eyes. I felt her breath, warm and sweet, on my skin. I was aware of her breasts underneath the thin cotton.

She raked her fingernails down my throat. I cried out. She pulled at the neck of my shirt and drew me towards her. We pawed at each other's clothes. My jacket fell onto the floor. I tried to tug her top over her head but her arms were in the way. She clawed at my belt. I had no idea what I was doing except that I was in a desperate hurry.

Lily pulled her mouth from mine. "No. Not here."

She took my hand and we ran like children into the hall and up the stairs. She led me into the room where I slept. We didn't even bother to close the door.

What followed was short and desperate, messy and unsatisfactory. I had no idea that sex was such an awkward business. Ignorance and urgency made me clumsy, and we were both in a rush. Afterwards we scrambled back into our clothes. I was almost crying with frustration and shame.

Lily patted my arm. "Don't worry."

I tried to kiss her but she wouldn't let me. I followed her downstairs.

"You'd better get going," she said rapidly. "Carlo and Felicity will wonder where you are."

I shrugged. I didn't care about them. I didn't care about anything.

She glanced at her watch. "Oh, God, look at the time. I'd better take you in the car."

I went into the kitchen to fetch my jacket. While I was there I picked up the freesias—we must have knocked them off the table. They looked bedraggled and several of the flowers were crushed. I left them beside the sink.

We drove across town in silence. Lily pulled into a side road fifty yards from the Newnham House Hotel. I fumbled for the door handle.

She stroked my leg. "Next time, Jamie," she whispered. "Thanks. Thanks for the flowers."

I lunged at her but she pushed me away. I walked quickly to the hotel. Carlo and Felicity had found a window table in the Hot Pot. For a moment, I hesitated in the doorway and, in a sudden fit of panic, surreptitiously checked my flies. Part of me wanted to swagger, part of me wanted to run away and hide.

Carlo looked up. "You took your time. What are you having?"

"Coffee. Black."

I sat down, took out my tobacco and began to roll up.

"You gave her the flowers?" Carlo asked.

"Yeah." I licked the edge of the paper.

"What did she say?"

"She said thanks."

Felicity pursed her lips. "Is that all? You'd think she'd be really pleased, wouldn't you? It shows how cold-hearted she is. She doesn't deserve those flowers."

"Yeah, well," Carlo said. "Anything to keep Dad happy."

I don't know how I got through the rest of the day. Everything had a dreamlike quality, as though I were an observer in someone else's reality. My mind found it almost impossible to grasp what had happened. Lily and I had, after a fashion, made love. Therefore I was no longer a virgin. I had done it—now, after years of speculation, I knew what it was like. I had seen and touched a woman who had had no clothes on. And I wanted to do it again.

But it had happened so fast. Was it always like that? I wondered whether women took their pleasure instantly, at the moment of penetration, or even just before. Everyone said they weren't like men but the notion of women taking pleasure at all was not an easy one for me to understand. And was it always so disappointing for the man?

When we went home at lunchtime, Lily asked if we'd had a nice morning. Carlo grunted at her. Felicity laid the table, when asked to do so. Carlo and I took out the rubbish. Lily didn't look at me and I tried not to look at her. The flowers were in a cut-glass vase on the kitchen table.

"Thanks for the freesias," Lily said to Carlo. "How did you know they were my favorite?"

Late on Monday afternoon, I drove out of London in brilliant sunshine. But as the motorway cut through the Chilterns, the showers started. The rain continued on and off until I was on the other side of Oxford. I pulled into the first empty lay-by I could find. When I got out of the Saab, the air was full of the smell of freshly watered earth—heavy, dark and pregnant with possibilities, like the scent of freesias.

I walked up and down. A few feet away from me, cars and trucks roared and made the ground tremble. I phoned both Nicky's mobile and the Murthingtons' house. I didn't expect anyone to answer either phone. Nobody did.

It was almost six o'clock by the time I reached the outskirts of Chipping Weston. I drove straight to the house and turned into the driveway. I could no longer see any point in concealing my movements. On this occasion, in fact, I positively wanted to be seen. I wanted confrontation. I would have liked to hit someone, perhaps Carlo. What I really wanted, though, was to find Nicky.

The key was not in its usual hiding-place underneath the birdbath. I hammered on the door and rang the bell. No one came. I tried again. A couple of minutes slipped by. I walked slowly along the side of the house, peering into each of the ground-floor windows. In the kitchen, the *Guardian* was no longer on the table, and Kate's blue jacket was draped over the back of a chair. The plate and the mug on the draining-board had been joined by another mug and an upturned teapot. I didn't like the look of that second mug.

I tried the door of the shed at the back of the house. It was unlocked. The interior was cool and smelt of rusty metal and decaying paper. Apart from the area immediately inside the door, the space was filled to the ceiling with cardboard boxes, scraps of wood and redundant machinery. I recognized a lawnmower I had once pushed and a doll's pram that had belonged to Felicity. Next to it was an elderly BMX bike. The metal frame was dull and scratched but the tires were pumped up and the chain had recently been oiled.

The past ambushed me. Once there had been two BMX bikes, Carlo's and Felicity's. This one had been Carlo's. I didn't know where Felicity's bike was, of course I didn't. No one did. Felicity's bike was—

There was a noise behind me. Fists clenching, I swung round. Kate was standing on the path, barely three yards from me. I stared at her face and the shock of what I saw squeezed the breath from me. I was back in the present, and it wasn't much better than the past.

"What happened?" I said.

She opened her mouth as if to reply but said nothing. She was holding a rusty garden trowel in her right hand, raised as if she was about to hit me with it. Her face was streaked with blood: most of it had dried but some was still vivid and fresh. The skin round her left eye was swollen and discolored.

"Kate." I took a step towards her.

"Jamie," she croaked. She lowered the arm. The trowel slipped through her fingers and clattered onto the path. I leaped forward and put my arm round her. Her small body slumped against mine. For a moment neither of us spoke. She was trembling, but gradually she brought the shaking under control.

"I—I thought you were Carlo," she muttered into my chest.

"He did this? He attacked you?"

She began to shiver again. "He went for me like an animal. Hitting me. Scratching."

"But why?"

"Because he hates me." She pointed down the path beside the house. "I was by the door. He must have been round the back. He just came at me. I ran into the road and he didn't dare follow."

"Is he there now? Inside, I mean?"

"I don't think so. I saw him drive off."

"If he is in, he's not answering the door." I pulled away from her and tried to get a better look at her face. "I'll take you to hospital. You need checking over."

"No." She squeezed my arm. "I'm OK. Really."

She drew away from me. I stared at her. The bruise would probably discolor further but the eye itself looked undamaged. I wasn't sure if the scratches on her face were superficial or not. The blood made it hard to tell. "Did he hurt you anywhere else?"

"Just my face."

More questions were bubbling into my mind but now was not the time to ask them. "We need to get you cleaned up."

"We could go inside."

"Here?"

"Why not? It's my home."

"Listen," I said. "If Carlo—"

"He's not here. I told you, I saw him driving off. And he won't dare come back if you're here too."

I still didn't like the idea. The house might be a trap as well as a refuge. But the alternatives were even less appealing. At present the priority was to get Kate away from prying eyes and find out how badly she was hurt. A pretty, pregnant young woman with a bruised and bloody face would attract attention.

"Please," she said. "Please, Jamie. I just don't want to see people. I want to be here, at home."

"All right."

She pushed her hand into her pocket, pulled out a Yale key and gave it to me. I unlocked the door, thinking how odd it was that she should ask my permission to go into her own house. Odder still in that Kate did not strike me as a timid woman—quite the reverse. One question wouldn't wait.

I glanced back at her. "Was Carlo alone?"

"What? Of course he was."

"Was he alone in the car as well?"

"As far as I know. Who did you think might be with him?"

I didn't answer. I opened the door and the still, stuffy air of the house enveloped me. For a moment I stood listening on the threshold.

Kate rushed past me. "It's OK. I told you, he's not here."

"Wait. I'll bolt the door. Then I'll check the house."

She allowed me to do that at least. In the kitchen, there was fresh milk in the fridge and an unopened packet of teabags on the worktop. Carlo's backpack had gone from Felicity's bedroom. The white bucket was still in the bathroom next door but now it was empty. Someone had removed the shirt, scrubbed out the bucket and left it to drain upside down in the bath.

"You see?" Kate said, when we reached the attic. "He's not here. It's quite safe."

"When was he here?" I asked. "In the house, I mean."

"I'm not sure. Earlier today, I suppose."

"I don't understand what he was doing."

"That's because he's a bloody law unto himself." She was trembling again. "I'm freezing. I'm going to have a bath."

I went downstairs. On the ground floor, I walked through the rooms again, checking the doors and windows. I heard Kate's footsteps overhead, first running up to the attic, then down to the bathroom. The questions buzzed in my mind like flies, aimless and persistent. If she was so scared of Carlo, if he'd beaten her up a few hours earlier, why did she want to stay here? Surely it was the first place he would look.

The house was as secure as I could make it. In Hugh's study, I tried to phone Nicky again. There was no answer. I wanted her and the strength of the desire was as nagging as a stitch. More than that, even, I wanted to know that she was safe. I checked the voice mail on the home phone. There were two messages for her and none for me. One message was from Victor at the gallery and the other was from Miranda, both asking her to phone.

After a quarter of a century, my ears were still attuned to the language of the plumbing. I heard the faint sound of Kate's splashing in the bath and the groan the hot-water pipes made when the water was flowing. The house was strange, shabby and uncomfortable, too full of memories and objects that no one in their right mind would want. But it was familiar. I rather wished it wasn't but there was nothing I could do about that. The house was like Kate: it gave me no choice. If there had been a choice, I had made it a long time ago and now I was living the consequences.

When Kate came downstairs I was making tea in the kitchen. She wore a faded blue dressing gown with a pink rabbit on the breast pocket. Her hair was wrapped in a towel. She might have been about thirteen, if you edited out the bulge in her belly and the marks on her face.

"You look better," I said. "Do you want some tea?"

"Sounds good. With sugar."

She sat at the kitchen table and found her cigarettes and lighter in one of the pockets of the waxed jacket. She stacked them in front of her.

I put the lid on the teapot. "Turn your face to the window," I said. "I want to see you better."

She twisted her head and raised her chin, pretending to pout like a model. I stooped over her and examined the damage. I had been standing on the same spot when Lily had dropped the freesias on the kitchen table.

I touched Kate's chin with my finger. Her eyes swiveled towards mine but she did not respond to the contact. I tilted her face to one side so it caught the light better. The bruise was on the outer corner of the left eye. It was beginning to turn purple. A scratch raked diagonally down her right cheek, its surface now scabbing over, and there was a shorter but deeper one on the left side of her face, just below the cheekbone. The wounds were clean. She smelt powerfully of disinfectant.

"I'll live," she said.

I released her chin and went to pour the tea. She lit a cigarette. When I sat down, she glanced at me and smiled. For a while neither of us spoke. We might have been sitting side by side at the kitchen table every day for years. We might have been father and daughter, together since birth.

Kate tapped my arm to attract my attention. "Jamie?"

"What?"

"I'm so tired. And I'm scared. What am I going to do?"

12

A T THE END OF THE EASTER HOLIDAYS, THE DAY BEFORE Carlo and I went back to school, Lily took the three of us to Rackford for another driving lesson. By now Carlo handled the car quite skillfully as he drove sedately up and down the runways and along the perimeter road. He was capable of avoiding the major hazards, which were potholes and rabbits. I was a slower learner. The car still stalled unexpectedly when I pulled away or veered off the runway when I changed gear. I was furiously but secretly jealous of Carlo's expertise. I also begrudged the fact that Felicity was nearly at the same level as me. It was unfair—she was a girl, and still a child.

It was one of those warm, heavy days you sometimes get in April, an unexpected foretaste of full summer. The sun hung heavily in a bright blue sky. Despite the green shoots, the earth looked baked and tired and the heat bounced off the concrete. It was hot in the car and the sweat gathered between my shoulder blades and left damp smudges on the fabric of the seats. Lily was wearing a blue shirt-dress. Her legs were bare and the straps of her sandals criss-crossed up her calves.

Carlo and I sloped off for a cigarette while Felicity had her turn.

"Jesus," he said, as we crouched in a clearing among the brambles, sucking frantically on our rollies. "This is so boring. I wish we were back at school."

"Come off it."

He scowled. "Lily's really getting on my tits. I don't know how Felicity stands it, all year round."

I said nothing.

Carlo spat. The spittle crash-landed on a handkerchief-sized square of dusty earth amid the brambles, roots and rough grass, where it squatted like a gray, shiny slug. "She's a pain," he said. "Makes me want to puke. The way she laughs, that smile of hers." He glanced at me through narrowed eyes. "You think she's a pain, too, don't you?"

"Of course she is."

In saying this, I didn't feel I was betraying Lily. Whether she was a pain or not was irrelevant to me. I was addicted to her. But I wasn't sure I liked her. What had liking got to do with it? In those days I hardly thought of her as having an independent personality.

Carlo squinted through the smoke at me. "What are you doing in the summer? Going to your mum's?"

"Some of the time. But I'm going to Gran's first."

"Maybe I could come too—to your Gran's, I mean. Do you think she'd ask me?"

"You wouldn't like it."

"I won't know till I try, will I?" He gave a gasp of laughter. "Me and your gran might be soulmates."

"You'd be bored out of your skull. But I'll ask her, if you want."

"Good." Carlo dropped the cigarette butt onto the dry earth and maneuvered it with his toe into the spittle. "That's settled, then."

I stubbed out my own cigarette and we walked towards the runway. Behind his back I silently mouthed every swearword I could think of. I had received so much hospitality from Carlo and his family over the years that I could hardly object to a return fixture. On the other hand, having him to stay at Gran's would have been bad at any time. For me, Gran and her bungalow were something to be ashamed of in every way—socially, psychologically, materially and financially. I felt inadequate enough as a human being without having to put her on display to Carlo. And it was true that there was nothing to do there except watch TV, read books, walk half a mile through boring suburban streets to the nearest shop, which didn't even sell Golden Virginia—in any case, the woman who owned it knew Gran and had a nasty habit of reporting my purchases to her.

Now there was another, even stronger reason not to go there: the thought of not seeing Lily next holidays made me feel physically ill. If I couldn't be with her, I didn't want to be with anyone, even Carlo.

The Rover was coming up the runway towards us. Felicity was driving and she was revving the car too high in too low a gear. We waited for them in the shadow of the control tower. The car slowed as it approached us. Felicity braked hard. The engine stalled. The car juddered. The driver's window was down and I heard Felicity saying, in a cold, clear, calm voice, "I hate driving."

She and Lily joined us beside the control tower.

"So, who's next?" Lily said brightly.

"James," Carlo said, although it was his turn.

Felicity touched her brother's arm. "Can we go down to the stream? Please?"

Carlo yawned. "OK."

"But why, darling?" Lily asked.

"Because there's lots of flowers there."

"Well, I suppose so. But don't get muddy, will you? You've got your best sandals on." Lily glanced at me. "So, it's your turn, Jamie. Maybe we should have a look at the Highway Code. It's about time you got to grips with the theory."

Carlo and Felicity walked away. Lily watched them for a moment, then climbed into the front passenger seat. I opened the driver's door and got behind the wheel. My body felt weak and a little unreal, as though it was fighting a fever. Lily opened her handbag and took out a copy of the *Highway Code*. She turned her head towards me again and we looked at each other. We were so close that I could make out the down on her cheek.

"The seats are so uncomfortable and the car's like an oven," she said. "Perhaps I should test you somewhere else. Somewhere in the shade." She pointed through the windscreen at the huddle of Nissen huts beyond the control tower. "In one of those, do you think? The one over there might still have some chairs in it."

I swallowed. "OK."

Lily picked up the *Highway Code* and got quickly out of the car. She walked away briskly, leaving me to follow. The material of her dress was thin and soft. A woman's walk can be the sexiest thing in creation: I couldn't tear my eyes off her hips swaying from side to side, rocking gently across the direction of travel. She went directly to the second hut on the left. So, this was not a spur-of-the-moment decision. She had known exactly where she was going.

She opened the door and went inside. When I joined her, she was standing at the far end near a window opaque with grime and cobwebs. The hut contained a long metal table and a calendar for 1954. The air was warm and dry.

"God, it's hot." She took hold of one end of the table and abruptly abandoned her role as driving instructor. "Help me with this."

We pushed the table against the door. She smiled at me and held out her hands. I went blindly towards them. This time it lasted longer. I remembered the cool metal on bare skin, the roughness of the concrete floor.

"I wish I was a cannibal," I said. "I want to eat you all up."

She bit me. Our bodies rose and fell together, like complementary parts of a perfectly designed machine. At the same moment we cried out. At the same moment we lay still. When I looked into her face, her eyes were as blank as smoked glass in a car window.

Afterwards she touched my cheek. "We must hurry."

We went back to the car, moving furtively like scouts in hostile terrain. My jeans were smeared with dirt from the table but Lily's dress seemed spotless. We were just in time. As I closed the driver's door, Carlo and Felicity came into view two hundred yards away at the other end of the runway.

"Start the engine." Lily pulled down the sun visor and examined her face in the mirror mounted behind it. "You can drive over and offer them a lift. Check your mirror first, then signal and move off."

• • •

There was hardly any food in the house except for a few rust-spotted tins in the kitchen cupboards. I wondered when Kate had last had a proper meal.

"We need to go to a supermarket," I said.

"There's a Waitrose," she said. "Go back to the bypass, then come into the town from the west. It's faster than going through the center."

"You'd better come with me."

"Like this? You must be joking."

"You can get dressed."

"I'm not going out like this in public. I look like a battered wife. Everyone will think you've been bashing me about."

"You could stay in the car."

She shook her head. "I'm tired. I don't want to have to get dressed. It's all right, I'll lock up and put the bolts across. He won't want to make a row because the neighbors would hear."

"That didn't stop him beating you up."

"That was different. He lost his temper. Can you get me some grapefruit juice?"

"I'm not leaving you here by yourself. It's as simple as that."

We glared at each other. For an instant a suspicion eddied in my mind: surely she wouldn't really want to stay here alone if Carlo had attacked her only an hour or two ago. But Kate had a habit of doing the unexpected. Or perhaps it was vanity.

Suddenly she smiled and touched my arm. "You sound like a father."

"I mean it. I'm not leaving you here."

"All right, I'll come. I'll wrap a scarf round my face and lurk in the car."

Fifteen minutes later we drove over to the other side of Chipping Weston. I left Kate smoking in the car. My mouth watered as I wandered up and down the aisles of the supermarket. Since Friday lunchtime I had survived on coffee, wine and the occasional snack. With increasing urgency I plucked items from the shelves and filled the trolley with food and drink.

The place was crowded. The queue at the checkout tested my patience to its limits. I found myself trapped between two trolleys at the end of a long line. One contained a toddler who was full of rage against the universe. The other supported a very old lady with an irresistible desire to teach me the finer points of her shopping technique.

"I wait for the special offers, that's the secret. You can save pounds and pounds. My daughters gave me a freezer for Christmas so it's no trouble. Most of the ladies know me and sometimes they . . ."

It was then that I noticed a young woman with short dark hair on the far side of the store. She had just come through the checkout nearest the exit and was carrying a bag in either hand. She hesitated at the sliding doors.

"The best time to come is around now," my instructor was saying, "or perhaps a little later, because that's when they go round the perishable stuff and put the reduced stickers on the ones that are nearly out of date."

For an instant I glimpsed the woman's face in profile. Emily Fielding? It was hard to be sure because she was wearing different clothes and there was no sign of Maisie and Albert.

"Excuse me," I said to the old lady. "I can see a friend of mine over there. I need to have a word with her."

But it was no use. The old lady continued talking. The toddler continued howling. I used the trolley to force my way out of the gridlock, but by the time I reached the sliding doors, Emily had disappeared. A line of cars was streaming steadily onto the main road, and one was probably hers.

I returned to the queue, which had grown longer since I had been away. The toddler had been placated with chocolate and the old woman had found another pupil. I couldn't be certain that I had seen Emily Fielding. I reminded myself that I hardly knew her. I was hungry, worried and scared. All in all, I wasn't a reliable observer. I wasn't a reliable anything.

When I reached the Saab, Kate's eyes gleamed at the sight of the supermarket bags. I had bought a French stick and she fed us with handfuls of it as we drove back to the house. We went into the kitchen and continued eating. We stuffed the food into our mouths—bread, cheese, ham, olives and fruit. Kate drank half a liter of grapefruit juice, straight from the carton. It was a picnic without table manners, without conversation. I didn't mention Emily to her, then or afterwards. If I was wrong about seeing her, there was no point. If I was right, I needed time to think about the implications. When I had eaten enough, I put on the kettle. I spooned coffee into the cafetière.

Kate lit a cigarette. "Can I have tea?" she said. "I can't stand the taste of coffee at present. Everything's upside down. I never used to like grapefruit juice either."

I reached for the teapot. "How are you feeling?"

"Better. Much better. The bath helped, and the food even more."

"So, what was Carlo up to? Why did he go for you like that?"

She tapped ash into a saucer. "He lost it. This isn't just about money, you know. He hates me. I don't know—it's like I'm a symbol of all that's gone wrong in his life. Everything from his mother dying onwards."

"What was he doing here? And why were you here too?"

"Why shouldn't I be here? This is my home."

"That's what your mother said. I suppose it's Carlo's home too."

She began to empty the remaining carrier-bags. "I came back because I wanted to collect some clothes. Some of Mum's jewelry too. I don't want to leave that sort of thing lying around for Carlo to grab. I thought I'd be safe if Sean hadn't been found. I was just going to pick up the stuff, then go back to London and lie low for a bit. I'd have phoned you, honestly."

I wondered whether she was telling the truth, and also why I cared.

"The trouble was," she went on, "Carlo was here too."

"For God's sake," I said, suddenly angry. "I don't believe it. Why run the risk of coming back here? You must have known that Carlo—"

"I'm not going to let him frighten me away forever. Besides, I checked—I phoned the house. I looked through the windows."

"You said he drove away. Was his car in the drive?"

"He'd parked in the road."

"You didn't notice on your way in?"

"I don't notice cars much. Anyway, he was in the back garden." She winced. "I told him he was a vicious, mean-minded prick and he said I was a greedy little bastard. But that was just warming up. Sort of like the adverts before the main feature." She grinned at me.

I smiled back. I wasn't sure that Kate was my daughter, but there were many things I liked about her and her sense of humor was one of them. Maybe this was one of the side benefits of having children—when you grew to like them as well as love them, when pleasure and biology marched together side by side, just as they should in the moment of conception.

"I need to know more," I said. "Your mother kept going on about him wanting everything. And why did it all come to a head on Friday?"

"Because I found a letter from a property developer. It came here by mistake—it should have gone to Carlo in London. My mother's not even dead yet and Carlo's already trying to sell the airfield. He had a meeting set up for Friday morning, at Rackford, and he hadn't told me about it. He was planning to sell the place over my head. So I phoned Sean, got him to come and pick me up. I thought I'd give Carlo a little surprise in front of witnesses." Her lips trembled. "And I did. And then he gave me a surprise too."

"He's full of surprises."

She nodded, avoiding my eyes. She lined up items of shopping on the table top—pasta, oil, soup, coffee—adjusting their positions so they made a crescent-shaped curve. "But what about you?" she said suddenly. "How come you just turn up out of the blue when I need you?"

"I was looking for Carlo."

What happened next unnerved me. My throat constricted, as though it was attempting to force back a tide of emotion welling up from deep inside me. Something of this must have shown in my face. Kate frowned. She put down a shrink-wrapped pack of apples and came round the table to where I was standing by the kettle. Neither of us spoke. She took my head between her hands, stood on tiptoe and stared at me as though I were a book she wanted to read.

"What is it, Jamie? Something's happened, hasn't it?"

"Nicky's gone," I said. "Maybe Carlo's got something to do with it."

Kate's brown eyes had amber flecks in them. Her hands were dry and warm. Her smell was familiar, a blend of soap and talcum powder, a reminder of childhood, of a time before everything went wrong. "What?" She released my face. "What's he up to?"

"There's someone called Charlie in her book group. She never mentioned him. Does Carlo ever get called Charlie?"

"Not that I know of."

"Apparently he's got a beard. Like Carlo."

"So have lots of men. Jamie, this doesn't make any sort of sense."

I shrugged. A shrug is a convenient response in that you let the other person provide the interpretation. If Carlo knew what I knew, and what I suspected Lily knew, he would have a very good reason to want to hurt me through Nicky. But I didn't intend to share this with Kate.

"Are you sure he's got your wife?"

"No," I said, "and in a way that makes it worse. I can't be sure of anything. The last time I saw her, yesterday, Nicky said she wanted some time by herself. She thinks we're having an affair."

"Us? You and me?" Kate gave a snort of laughter.

"She's not been in touch. She's not answering her mobile."

"So? She's pissed off with you. She doesn't want to talk. You're reading way too much into this. There's nothing to show that Nicky isn't by herself. I can't see why Carlo would want to go after her. And I don't see why this Charlie has to be Carlo."

I let out my breath. "You're right. Probably."

"Of course I am." Kate smiled at me. "Jamie, don't look so worried. Dads are meant to be cozy and reassuring, OK? I know you've not had much practice but it's never too late to learn." She saw me smiling back. "That's better."

I sat down. Nothing had changed but I felt a little less miserable than before. "Your mother thought Carlo might be here."

Kate sat down opposite me. "She said that to you yesterday?"

"Today."

"How is she?"

"No real change. She's comfortable, but rambling a bit."

"You're taking your new responsibilities seriously. Me and Mum."

"One of the nurses said that Carlo went to see her on Saturday afternoon and she had a bit of a setback after that."

"We should get him banned from visiting. We should—"

"Your mother thought you might have gone to Sean's so I went there first. That was yesterday."

"Sean's? But how did you know where he lived?"

"His address was in your mother's diary. Kate, I met Emily."

"At Sean's?" Her face was full of hard lines and sharp angles, like a fox's. "What was she doing there?"

"Looking for him. Apparently the police phoned her and said they'd found his car. It had been stolen. It turned up in Peckham. Someone had set it on fire."

Kate reached for her cigarettes. "I left it in Harlesden on Friday afternoon with the keys in the ignition before I came to your house."

"Why did you leave it?"

"Because it tied me in with Sean." She shook out a cigarette. "Jamie, I was in such a state I couldn't think. You understand? Like you with Nicky? I drove up to London in his car on Friday afternoon. He'd driven me over to Rackford in the morning, you see, and when Carlo killed him, I made a break for it." She was shaking so much she couldn't get the cigarette into her mouth. "It was either that or let Carlo kill me." Then she straightened her spine and looked at me with startled eyes. "So you met Emily? You talked to her?"

"A bit."

"I hope you didn't believe a word she said." Kate managed to find her mouth and light the cigarette. She inhaled twice, holding the smoke in her lungs. "I'll tell you about Emily. She made Sean's life hell. She was always wanting things. That was what cost him his job. And when he didn't have a six-figure income she just didn't want to know him."

"She put a rather different slant on it."

"She would, wouldn't she? Had she got the children with her?"

I nodded.

"I feel sorry for those two. She takes them everywhere. Have you noticed how mothers with little kids use them to get their own way? You can't teach Emily anything about emotional blackmail."

"Emily thought that some of Sean's things had gone. His bank stuff, ID, that sort of thing. She said it looked like he was planning to go away, maybe for good."

"Maybe he was. He didn't want to pay child support for the rest of his life. He wasn't cut out to be a dad. I always knew that if we ever had kids, I'd end up a single parent. But I didn't expect it to happen this way."

She was trembling again. I got up and put my arm round her. She nestled against me. We stayed like that for a minute, perhaps ninety seconds. I thought about the baby that was living inside her clean, pink body, feeding and moving and growing as a child should. It was a child that would lack a father, just as I had done, or as Carlo and Felicity had lacked a mother.

"You can't be sure that Sean's dead," I said. "He might have gone back to his house after you last saw him. Maybe Carlo's the reason he's gone away."

"He's dead," Kate whispered, trembling more violently than before. "I know he is. I saw him, he was covered with blood. He wasn't moving. I know what Carlo's like."

I thought about that, and I remembered Emily saying that Sean hadn't been in contact with his mother, and how that had surprised her. I said, "If the police find Sean's body, the evidence will point to you?"

"Yes. I think so."

"Thanks to Carlo?"

"Yes. I told you."

"So if they don't find the body, or if the evidence isn't there, you're off the hook?"

"In theory. But what about Carlo?"

I didn't know the answer. All I could do was hold Kate until she stopped trembling.

13

PART OF ME ASSUMED I WAS STILL IN THE NORMAL, PRE-dictable world where two and two made four, I went to work five days a week, and Nicky was beside me when I went to sleep and when I woke up. Another part wondered whether I had slipped without realizing round a mental corner and arrived in a place where nothing made sense.

That night I used my old room at the Murthingtons' house, although I didn't do much sleeping. Before we went to bed, Kate and I checked the doors and windows. Afterwards, as she climbed the attic stairs, I noticed a claw hammer in her hand.

"Just in case," she said.

My bedroom smelt of stale perfume. Every surface was gray and feathery with dust. The air was cold and had the dead, sad quality you find in rooms where nothing happens except the passing of time. The floor was a jumble of suitcases and furniture, and everywhere there were possessions large and small that were too old or battered to use but too good to throw away.

The top of the single bed was covered with clothes, men and women's, some on hangers, some in carrier-bags, some loose. I dumped them on top of a treadle sewing machine in front of the empty fireplace. I didn't undress but lay down with a blanket over me for warmth. I thought about Nicky most, but also about Carlo, Kate and Sean, about Lily dying in the hospice and about a younger Lily lying with me on this bed. If the room had a memory, the shapes of our warm, naked bodies were imprinted there. Nothing could be forgotten, nothing could be eradicated, nothing could be changed.

For the first time in twenty-five years, for the first time since I had decided to remake my life without the Murthingtons in it, I could not see a way forward. I did not have a plan for the future. I wanted my old life back and I hadn't the faintest idea how to get it. Most of all I wanted Nicky. My need for her was a form of hunger. I clung to the idea, as an article of faith, that it was better to be hungry for Nicky, even to starve for want of her, than never to have the hope of eating.

At two o'clock I turned on the light and tried to read. There was a pile of yellowing paperbacks on the shelf above the fireplace. I remembered some from previous visits. I opened one and found myself looking at C. *Murthington* on the flyleaf. I turned the pages and found the first chapter.

But the words wouldn't hold my attention. It was almost with relief that I heard Kate's footsteps coming slowly and carefully down the attic stairs. She passed my door and continued along the passage to the bathroom. A few minutes later the lavatory flushed. Her footsteps returned. They stopped and she tapped on my door. When I told her to come in, she opened the door a few inches and slipped through the gap, as though she was trying to make herself as small as possible.

She was still wearing the dressing-gown. In the harsh electric light, the bruises and scratches on her face looked like garish imitations of what they really were, like the accidental by-products of a child playing with a paintbox. She was carrying the hammer. An absurd fear flashed into my mind that she would hit me with it.

"Do you mind if I come in?"

"It's not easy to sleep, is it?"

She picked her way through the debris on the floor. "It's not just that. I need to pee all the time. The baby's pressing on my bladder."

I drew up my knees, making room for her on the end of the bed. She sat down and balanced the hammer on top of the pile of clothes over the sewing machine. It seemed impossible that such a childlike person should have another life growing inside her. She hugged her belly and rocked gently to and fro.

"I expect you'd like to see your mother soon," I said.

The rocking stopped. "I'd like to, of course, but that's where Carlo will expect me to go."

"It didn't stop you coming here."

"I know."

"Then you're not making sense."

"Don't be angry." She glanced at me and her face was now thin and worried. "It's—it's not just that. I'm scared of Carlo but this is something else. I—I don't like people who are ill. It makes me feel—Jamie, I hate to see her dying. I don't think I can bear it. Should I go and see her?"

"I can't tell you that."

"But what does she want?"

"Most of all she wants you to be safe. If you went, you might not catch her in a lucid moment. She's in and out of consciousness. At one point she thought I was your—" I broke off and smiled at her "—your father. Hugh."

Kate rubbed her eyes like a sleepy child. Then she nodded at the window. "Do you think Carlo's out there? In the garden, I mean, watching us. Waiting for the right moment."

"I don't know about that either."

"There's him and there's Emily. It's strange when you know there are people who hate you. Really hate you."

"When did you last see Emily?"

"Just before Sean and I split up." Kate wrinkled her nose. "But she phoned me once or twice after that. Just to remind me of what she thought of me."

I was on the verge of asking whether she'd been to Sean's house after she left the chapel but she forestalled me. "Jamie, I've got this huge favor."

"OK."

"Promise you'll think about it even if you don't say yes right away."

I nodded.

"I need to go back to Rackford. Will you take me?"

"What—now?"

"Tomorrow. I'm not sure I could find my way in the dark. Listen, it's my one chance. If I go back to where—where Sean is . . . My handbag's there. If I can just get it, there'll be nothing left to link me to his body."

"Except that you used to live with him and you're eventually going to own the place where he's found. And that's leaving aside the chance that someone saw you with him, or that you left something else behind."

She tossed her head. "I can't help that. But I can help my bag being there."

"I don't think it's wise, Kate. Once you start tampering with the evidence—"

"I just—"

"You'd only make matters worse. And you're tired and upset and this is the middle of the night. It's not the best time to make a decision. No one thinks straight in those circumstances."

"Don't say no," she hissed. "Please." She leaned towards me, her face sharp and gray like old carved stone. "Don't say no."

I sat up. Her vehemence alarmed me. "OK. I won't make up my mind, and you won't make up yours. We'll talk about it tomorrow. How's that?"

Suddenly she was a child again, made of flesh and blood. She rubbed her eyes. "All right." She slipped off the bed and picked her way across the room to the door. "And, Jamie?"

"What?"

"Thank-you. Goodnight."

The door closed behind her and I listened to her bare feet padding up the stairs. I dropped the paperback on the floor and turned off the light. I lay there in the darkness. I didn't know whom to trust. I had no idea who was telling the truth or when they were telling it. I didn't even know whether Kate was my daughter or not. As far as the Murthingtons were concerned, I had only two certainties: that Lily was right when she'd said I owed her something, and that Kate was scared and pregnant.

That was another reason I missed Nicky—she had a way of making things clearer. I remembered her saying when we were in the process of buying our house and I was afraid that the seller would withdraw at the last moment, "You know what your problem is, James? You never trust anyone. You never just shut your eyes and jump because you're always afraid someone will take away the safety net."

• • •

At last it was Carlo's turn. Short of feigning illness or making a scene, there was no way he could get out of driving with Lily that afternoon. I'm not sure he wanted to. He loathed Lily but he liked driving.

I hoped Felicity would go with them. I wanted to be alone with my memory of what had happened in the hut. Like a miser I wanted my privacy, so I could count every single golden coin in my hoard. I wanted to relive what I'd seen and smelt and heard and tasted. I was the holder of secret knowledge and I revelled in it. I knew now that those first fumbles in the spare bedroom at the Murthingtons' house were not really what sex was about after all. I pitied people like Carlo and Felicity, who did not know how wonderful it could be, who had not experienced it.

But Felicity had other ideas. "Come on, James—Carlo promised you'd help."

"Help with what?"

"The den, silly. We're building a den."

I glanced at Carlo. He was watching me. I couldn't tell what he was thinking. I was instantly afraid that he knew or guessed what Lily and I had been doing, that somehow it had marked my face like a smudge of lipstick.

"I can't do it by myself, you see," Felicity went on, in a sweetly reasonable voice. "We need to get branches across the stream. It's a two-person job."

"Try not to get too muddy, dear," Lily said to Felicity. "It's not just your best sandals. Those are your new jeans as well."

Carlo sighed in a gusty, melodramatic way. He opened the car door and got behind the wheel.

"See you later," Lily said, aiming the remark somewhere over our heads. "We'll honk twice when we've finished and you can come up to the road."

Carlo started the engine and drove off, working his way up through the gears with a smoothness I envied. Felicity and I took the path leading from the runway to the section of the road near the western boundary of the airfield. At first neither of us spoke. We crossed the perimeter road near the airfield's side entrance. Felicity dived into the belt of trees and bushes separating it from the fence along the lane.

The track zigzagged downwards, following the logic of four-footed animals rather than two-footed ones. Felicity went first. I sniffed my fingers. They smelt of Lily. There was another surprise—I had not realized that even smells could be charged with eroticism.

"Look," Felicity said. "There's a wood anemone. Isn't it sweet?"

I grunted.

"And see that tall green one with the purple-spotted leaves? That's called lords-and-ladies. Or cuckoo pint."

"How do you know all this stuff?"

"Mum used to tell me the names." Felicity looked back over her shoulder. "My real mum. Flowers are interesting."

I grunted again. Felicity was no longer looking at me, which was a good thing because I thought I might be blushing. The first Mrs. Murthington was rarely mentioned, or not in my hearing. The mother of Carlo and Felicity was not quite a taboo subject but she came close to it.

The ground levelled out. There were few trees down here. The bottom of the valley was clearer than I remembered—the last time I had come, with Carlo at the end of last summer, the ground had been thick with bracken that masked much of the stream. Now I could see that the water followed a wavering course and, except in the narrowest parts, it was only a few inches deep. On the other bank the slope of the land rose much more steeply than on this one. Felicity came to a stop beside the widest part of the stream. We had water on three sides—we were inside a bend shaped like a horseshoe.

She pointed. "There's my den."

On the other side of the stream a shelf of land was shaped like an orange segment. Behind it the ground rose almost perpendicularly. The shelf was about three yards wide and no more than two yards deep at the maximum. An untidy pile of branches filled one end.

"Carlo started building a sort of frame," Felicity said. "Can you see? He's pushed that curved branch into the bank at the back—that will be the doorway—and that long straight branch on top goes all the way from the opening to the back. We've just got to get more branches, pile them up and make a wall and a roof."

I took out my rolling tobacco and began to make a cigarette. "It's not very big."

"Big enough to sit or lie in."

"What are you going to use it for?"

"It's a den. I can do anything there. Anything I want to."

"OK." I licked the edge of the cigarette paper and folded it over. "What do you want me to do?"

"You haven't got time for that now, James. Can't you smoke it afterwards? Carlo says we must get it weathertight by the time we leave." Felicity nodded across the clearing at an uprooted birch, the casualty of a miniature landslide. "He broke off some of the branches. We need to get them over the stream."

"It's too wide to do it there. We'll have to get across where it's narrower."

"That's why there have to be two of us. I'll get on the other side and you can pass the branches over. Then, if you go round to where the den is, I can float them down to you on the current."

It was a sensible plan, in its way. Felicity worked hard and expected me to do the same. It wasn't long before we were both wet and muddy from the knees downwards. When she judged we had enough materials, we constructed the den itself, building up the walls and roof with branches. All the while, the sound of the car's engine ebbed and rose in volume as Carlo drove round and round the perimeter road and up and down the runways. I knew he was driving faster than usual.

"Look—there are some bluebells."

I glanced across the stream. Halfway up the bank a clump grew underneath the branches of a beech.

"They're the first I've seen." Felicity sounded unusually excited. "Do you know what they mean?"

"Spring is here?"

"No—what they *mean*. Flowers have meanings, didn't you know?"

"Sort of symbolic? Like horseshoes mean good luck?"

Felicity stared across the stream. "They mean constancy," she said, in a quiet voice, "everlasting love."

"Say it with flowers," I said, trying to make a joke of it, echoing Carlo the other day. "So, what do freesias mean?"

"I looked them up the other day. They mean innocence."

I laughed and turned away to put another branch on the roof of the den.

"So I don't know why they're Lily's favorites," Felicity went on. "Do you like her, James?"

"I don't know," I muttered. "She's nothing to do with me. Pass me that branch."

Felicity handed it to me. "It's funny that everyone gets married sooner or later."

"Some people don't."

"Most people do. I suppose—I suppose I might one day."

"I expect so. What do you want to do about the doorway?"

"Just leave the opening for now. We'll find something we can drag across it. Or bring a blanket or something from home. The trouble is, I don't know who I'll marry."

I smiled at her. "You'll find out."

The car's engine stopped. There were two blasts on the horn.

"Come on," I said. "We'll finish it later."

"Yes," Felicity said. "We've got plenty of time."

The phone woke me. I hadn't been asleep for long and I was down in the depths of a dream from which I was glad to escape. Half awake, I rolled off the bed. The phone rang on. *Not the mobile.* So it couldn't be Nicky—she didn't have the Murthingtons' number.

I blundered from the room, across the landing and into the big front bedroom. There was a telephone on the side of the bed that had been Hugh's. Perhaps Nicky had got the number from Directory Enquiries. But it was far more likely to be someone else.

I picked up the handset. All I heard was the faint background hum of an open line. I covered the mouthpiece with my hand in case my breathing was audible at the other end. I waited. Seconds crawled by.

"Kate?" It was a man's voice. "Kate, are you there?"

I said nothing.

"Kate?"

"Who's speaking?"

The man at the other end put down the phone. I broke the connection and dialled 1471. I listened to the recorded voice telling me that I had been called today at 07.45 hours and the caller had withheld their number.

I listened but there was no sound of movement in the attic. I wasn't sleepy anymore. I phoned Nicky and the call was transferred directly to her voice mail.

I wandered downstairs and prowled through the ground floor of the house. Nothing had changed. There was no sign of Carlo or anyone else. Sunlight filtered through dusty windowpanes. The fears of the night receded. In the kitchen I filled the kettle and plugged it in. The room smelt of stale tobacco. I opened the back door. The long grass was silvery with dew. I stood on the doorstep and took a deep breath of morning air.

Then it hit me. The back door had already been unbolted.

I knew I had checked all the locks and bolts before we went to bed last night. The lock was another self-closing Yale, and I had put the catch down so it couldn't be opened from the outside. But the catch was up now.

In the garden, a gray squirrel scrambled up the trunk of the ash tree and ran out along one of the branches. Birds sang. The door of the shed was ajar. It was possible we hadn't closed it yesterday afternoon. I pushed the door open. For a moment I thought the interior of the shed was unchanged. Then I realized my mistake. Carlo's BMX bike was gone.

I closed the shed door, went back to the house and walked upstairs, first one flight, then the next. I stopped outside the attic door and knocked. There was no answer. I hadn't expected there would be. I opened the door and went in. The bedroom was empty, and so was the little boxroom next door. The duvet had been pulled up. Kate's suitcases were still there. Some of the clothes she had worn yesterday were on the chair in the corner. The dressing-gown with the pink rabbit was hanging on the back of the door. There was nothing to show where she had gone or when she would be back. Or whether she planned to come back.

Suddenly I discovered I was angry. I was tired of being manipulated and taken by surprise. I was tired of not knowing whether Kate was telling me the truth. Self-pity washed over me. I was being treated abominably by everyone. Kate was the worst offender but she wasn't the only one. I'd had enough. Most likely she had gone to Rackford to look for her handbag. Well, she could do what she wanted without any help from me. The sooner I left this house the better. If I was going to be unhappy I might as well be in the comfort and privacy of my own home.

I gathered up my belongings, locked up the house and left. Things weren't any better now, but at least they were simpler. When I reached Oxford I drove into the center, bought a paper and had breakfast in a café near Magdalen Bridge. The place was full of chattering students who weren't much younger than Kate. Food made me feel more cheerful.

I was on my second cup of coffee when the phone rang. I lunged at the mobile, missed, knocked it onto the floor and spilled my coffee. A girl at the next table picked up the phone for me. It was still ringing. But it wasn't Nicky's number on the display, or even Kate's.

"James? Is that you?"

It took me a moment to place the voice. "Yes, Victor, it is."

"At last. A real person. I thought I was the only one left in this poor bloody universe." He sounded older, and more querulous, on the phone and his Yorkshire accent was more pronounced: he had become a caricature of himself. "If I hear another recorded message I'll go mad."

"Nicky's not with you, I suppose?"

"Of course she's bloody not. That's why I'm ringing. I want to know where she's put the VAT return."

"I'm afraid I can't help you. She's—"

"It's most inconvenient, lad."

"The thing is, I'm not sure where she is, and her mobile seems to be out of range."

Victor snorted. "It's a funny sort of marriage you've got. Is there anyone I can ring who might know? What about these other numbers?"

"What numbers?"

"On this list of hers. I found it in the drawer of her desk. That's how I got yours. They're not work numbers, I can tell you that. I just hope she doesn't spend all the time ringing up for a chat when I'm not here. I don't pay her—"

"Who else is there?" I interrupted, and I must have raised my voice because the girl at the next table looked at me curiously. "What are the other names?"

"That Miranda woman."

I took a deep breath. "Is someone called Charlie there?"

"No. But there's a Charles. Charles Browning. Will he know where she is? Shall I give him a ring?"

"No," I said. "I will. I want a word with Charlie."

14

IF GOD EXISTS, HE MUST BE LONELY, FOR EVEN A LITTLE knowledge cuts you off from those who do not possess it. So omniscience must leave you with no one to confide in.

When I went back to school for the summer term of 1980, I was lonely. Over the years I had gradually acclimatized myself to the institution. But now it had become alien. I still conformed to its rituals. I did what was expected of me. But I was detached from the place and its inhabitants. They had become part of my past. I was like the grown-up joining in the games at a children's party, the only one who knew that they really didn't matter.

Real life lay somewhere else, somewhere as yet ill-defined. All I knew for certain about my real life was that it would have to contain Lily and lots of sex. I was desperate to finish school. At the time I thought I had well over a year of it left, and it stretched ahead of me like an endless wasteland. What I didn't know was that I had already begun my last term.

I think Carlo sensed something had changed. One day he started to talk about our plans for the summer. We had just had lunch and were walking away from the school dining hall.

"Why don't we go abroad?" he suggested. "As well as to your gran's, I mean."

"I thought you wanted to have driving lessons."

I was confident that this tactic would work. Carlo had turned seventeen in May, and had immediately applied for a provisional driving license. His father and Lily had given him a course of ten lessons for his birthday, which he was going to take over the summer. I knew, because Carlo had told me on many occasions, that he was particularly keen to pass his test because then he could be much more independent at Chipping Weston, and he wouldn't have to rely on Lily to drive him when he wanted to go anywhere. I also knew, because I knew Carlo, that he wanted to be the first in our year to pass his test, and that being first mattered to him in a way it rarely did to me.

"I want to get away," he said. "That's more important."

"Don't you want to spend some time at home?"

"I'm sick of Lily. She's always bloody watching us."

"Where would we go?"

"Who cares? Somewhere with lots of girls. Ibiza, maybe, or a Greek island."

"It'd cost money."

"My dad wouldn't mind." He raised his eyebrows. "And wouldn't your mum be only too glad to fork out a hundred quid or so?"

I shrugged. "Maybe."

"What's got into you?"

"Nothing."

Carlo stopped and stared at me. "I could always go with someone else, you know."

Usually at this point we'd wander off and have a cigarette. But not today. He scowled and walked rapidly away without another word.

This left me with a practical problem. Carlo was no longer the most important person in my life. Now that I was older, now that Lily had changed my entire universe, he had become no more than a means to an end. But in that way he was still important. If I wanted to go back to Chipping Weston, if I wanted to see Lily again, I would have to woo Carlo. I didn't care. They say that love—if that's the right word—is blind. What I realized then, at the tender age of sixteen, is that love is amoral as well. Or at least the sort of love I felt.

I was entirely cynical. I even took a sinister pleasure at the almost immediate success of my program of manipulation. I offered Carlo a cigarette when it was his turn to offer me one. When we played the guitar together, I encouraged him to do the lead vocals. I let him copy my physics homework.

When I wrote the obligatory weekly letter to my mother, I mentioned the idea of going to Greece with Carlo. In her reply, my mother was unexpectedly enthusiastic. It would be ideal, she wrote, if we were to go in the second half of the holiday, perhaps during the last two weeks in August. That was when she, my step-father and their children were flying to Seattle to spend some time with my step-father's parents, and to help them celebrate their golden wedding. My mother thought I really wouldn't enjoy that very much so it would be nice if I could do something I really wanted to do with Carlo instead. After all, I would be nearly seventeen by then, and she knew she could trust me to behave responsibly.

One problem solved—but there was another, more difficult one to deal with. This was the danger that we would spend most of the rest of the holiday at my grandmother's. When Carlo decided to be obstinate, it was hard to shift him. My mother and my grandmother, who were both aware of how much hospitality I'd had from the Murthingtons over the years, had agreed to this without hesitation. I tried pointing out the drawbacks to Carlo.

"No," he said, "it'll be fine. We'll lay in some booze and fags on our way down. She can't expect us to stay in the house all the time, so we can walk down to the seafront. There must be some sort of nightlife down there in summer." He rolled his eyes and intoned in a deep, solemn voice: "And girls."

Nothing I could say dented Carlo's enthusiasm for my grandmother's bungalow. As far as he was concerned, it might have been in outer Siberia. Its main attraction was that it wasn't his home in Chipping Weston.

As the term drew towards its end, it was a measure of my increasing desperation that I even prayed to the God I had never really believed in. As if to show how wrong I had been all these years, the prayer was answered. Just before the end of term, my grandmother tripped on her back doorstep and broke her left leg in two places. She would still be in hospital at the beginning of the holidays and would probably go from there to convalesce in a nursing-home. There was even a question of whether she would be well enough to return to the bungalow and live an independent life, let alone invite teenage boys to stay. I felt guilty enough to sell three of my least favorite records and use the proceeds to send her a bunch of roses by Interflora.

When Carlo heard the news he said, "Oh, shit—can't we go by ourselves? Sort of look after the house while she's in hospital?"

"I can ask," I said, safe in the knowledge that the answer would be no.

I was right. And God continued to be obliging: Hugh and Lily said I'd be welcome to come to Chipping Weston for the first part of the holiday. Carlo reluctantly accepted the need to make the best of a bad job. He fixed all of his hopes on the second half of the holiday, when we were going to Greece. Lily had arranged this on our behalf. We were to spend a fortnight in Lindos on the island of Rhodes. We would share a villa room. A schoolfriend in the year above had been to Rhodes the year before. He told Carlo the Dutch chicks were really hot and a lot of them went around topless. Also, cocktails were as cheap as cups of tea.

"Fuck me," Carlo said, not once but many times. "I can't wait."

I did my best to appear excited. It seemed to me that Carlo was behaving like a kid—he was excited in the way a child is excited on Christmas Eve, expecting something magical and unreal. The anticipation I felt, for Lily and Chipping Weston, was something altogether darker and more urgent. It wasn't a matter of enjoyment and I believed I had no more choice in the matter than the moth does when it flies towards the candle flame or the lemming when it heads for the cliff edge.

But I did have a choice. I know now that there is always a choice.

Nicky's Mini Cooper wasn't outside the house when I got home midway through Tuesday morning. But, then, I hadn't expected it to be. I hadn't expected there to be a message from her either, and there wasn't. I felt grubby, as though the dirt and dust of the Murthingtons' house had got under my skin. I shaved, had a shower and found clean clothes. I put on the kettle and made yet another pot of coffee. Then, when I could put it off no longer, I went into the study and sat down at the desk. I pulled the telephone directory from its shelf and flipped it open. I took out the piece of paper on which I had written the name and number that Victor had given me.

Charles Browning. The number was a landline. And the area code was the one for Greyfont.

I could have phoned on my way from the café in Oxford. But it's easy enough for someone to say on the phone that another person is not there, even if that person is in the same room as them. And if I'd talked to Nicky, it's always easier to put the phone down on an unwanted caller than to show him the door.

There was a Browning, C. J., listed in the residential section of the phone book, and he had the same number as Nicky's Charlie Browning. He lived at 3 St. Ann's Lane, which was in the old part of town near the church. Early nineteenth-century terraced cottages, I remembered, two up and two down, most with extensions at the back and some with converted roof spaces; the front doors opened directly onto the street. They weren't cheap—nowadays nowhere in Greyfont was. They were the sort of houses that attracted single professional people or young couples with two jobs and no children.

I was scared about what I might find there so I found a reason to delay going. I remembered I had a job. I phoned Rachel's direct line at the office.

"Hi—it's me."

"James! How are you?"

"Fine. Well, no, not really, not a hundred percent. So I'm afraid I won't be in for a day or two. Maybe longer."

"Are you OK?"

"Nothing a little rest won't cure. Gareth will cover for me if there's anything you can't handle."

"Have you seen a doctor?"

"No. It's not like that."

"I think you should. What does Nicky say?"

"She's away, actually."

Rachel did not reply.

"I wondered whether she'd phoned you." I risked a lie. "She said she might."

"No, she hasn't. James, are you sure you're OK?"

"Yes, of course."

There was a short, uncomfortable silence. I didn't know how much Nicky had told Rachel.

"I'd better go," I said. "There's someone at the door."

Once the lies start, they come easily, and the more you lie the more easily they come. The only person at the door was me and I was leaving, not arriving. I grabbed my jacket and keys from the hall and set off for the center of Greyfont. I walked quickly. My mind was blank. I didn't have a plan. I met no one I knew, which was just as well because I couldn't have found anything to say to them.

St. Ann's Lane sparkled in the morning sun. Number three was near the far end. There were pansies in the window boxes and the front door was painted eggshell blue. Just beyond the single window on the ground floor a covered passageway ran through the terrace to the gardens or yards behind. Screwed to the wall beside it was a painted sign: CHARLES BROWNING. After the name were the letters MSTAT, a qualification I didn't recognize.

I rang the doorbell. I waited for what seemed like three years and rang it again. Still no one came. I tried to peer through the ground-floor window, but it was covered with an off-white linen blind. I walked down the passageway, which was paved with old bricks. Behind number three there was a tiny yard full of shrubs and flowers in pots, and at the far end, a modern single-story building with long clean lines that should have clashed with the setting but complemented it.

A man was standing on the other side of a half-glazed door at its left-hand corner and his face was a blur through the glass. The door opened. He was tall and fair, with a neat little beard and narrow, sloping shoulders. Neither his face nor his figure had any resemblance to Carlo's, apart perhaps from the beard. An ambiguous feeling, somewhere between relief and despair, swelled inside me.

"Yes? Can I help?" The voice was light and pleasant. It sounded as if it had started life in Manchester but hadn't been home for some time.

"I'm looking for Nicky."

His face changed. His mouth lost its smile and a couple of frown lines appeared on his forehead.

"You are Charles Browning?"

He nodded.

"Nicky's my wife," I said, and took a step nearer to him.

"Yes, I guessed that. You must be James." He was standing very still and looked relaxed. Perhaps dealing with aggrieved husbands was part of his everyday life. "She's mentioned you."

"You're in the same book group, I understand?"

"That's right. That's where we met."

"Do you know where she is now?"

He said nothing.

"Is she here?"

"No, she's not." He smiled. "Come and see for yourself."

He locked the door of the single-story building and walked slowly down the path. When he passed me he came so close that I saw the silver threads in the fair hair at the temples and smelt a hint of aftershave.

He led me into a large, airy kitchen and through an archway to the sitting room at the front of the house. It was an uncluttered room. Bookshelves filled the alcoves on either side of the fireplace. The only pictures on the walls were monochrome photographs of flowers. A couple of sofas faced each other across a coffee table. He waved at the nearer. "Do sit down."

I stayed on my feet, looking around. Nothing was particularly expensive—most of the kitchen's contents had come from IKEA—but it was a home that someone had planned with care and affection.

"You're Charlie, aren't you?"

He scratched his neat little beard. "Yes. That's what my friends call me."

"Nicky does."

"Not just Nicky. Lots of people." He smiled at me again. "I was half expecting you."

He sat down on the other sofa and nodded at the one opposite. This time I took him up on the offer.

I gestured around the room. "What do you do?"

"I teach the Alexander Technique."

"You teach people how to stand? Give them exercises?"

"That sort of thing."

"You teach Nicky?"

He shook his head.

I stared at him. Charlie Browning was being far too nice. He should be asking me to leave rather than giving me quiet reasonable answers. I wanted to smash the coffee table over his head. Or possibly over my own. So here was the man that Nicky liked—sensitive, kind and caring; nice enough looking, as far as I could judge these things, and at least five or ten years younger than me. Equally disturbing was the fact that I had constructed a paranoid fantasy over the last few days on the strength of a similar first name, a beard and my own insecurities. It was hard to believe that I had allowed myself to entertain the possibility that Charlie Browning might be Carlo Murthington.

Charlie cleared his throat. "I don't want to hurry you but I have an appointment in a moment."

"I've been trying to get in touch with Nicky." I waited but he said nothing. "She's not been returning my calls," I went on. "I think she's switched off her mobile."

"Maybe she wanted a breathing space."

"Has she come here?" The question came out almost as a snarl.

"Yes."

"When? How long?"

"On Sunday. That's when she arranged to use our cottage."

There was a pause long enough for a couple of heartbeats. I repeated, like a parrot, "Our cottage?"

"It belongs to my partner and me."

Neither of us spoke for a moment. Then Charlie got up in one slow, fluid movement and went into the kitchen. While he was out of the room, I glanced at the spines of the books nearest to me. Paperback fiction mainly, with a couple of shelves of larger-format books below. I recognized two that Nicky had read in the last few months, including *The Turn of the Screw*.

Charlie came back with an unframed color photograph in his hand. It showed a dark, compact man lying on the sofa where I was sitting. He was smiling at the camera and showing rather a lot of chest hair. Charlie was standing behind the sofa, leaning over it and holding the man's hand.

"Your partner," I said slowly. "I see." Apparently I had been even more of a fool than I'd thought. "I—I want to find Nicky. Can you tell me where the cottage is?"

"I'm sorry. No."

"She's my wife."

"It wouldn't be fair to her." He hesitated. "But I'll pass on a message if you'd like. Would that help?"

I should have liked to strangle Charlie until he told me where the cottage was. On the other hand, if I tried, I should probably discover he was a martial-arts expert as well. In the end I said, "Would you tell her I'm worried about her and I miss her? Ask her to ring my mobile if she can't get me at home." I wanted to add, "Tell her I love her," but I felt awkward saying this in front of a stranger.

Charlie put the photograph of his partner on the mantelpiece. "I'm sorry to hurry you but we'll have to say goodbye now."

I stood up. He opened the front door that led directly from the room to the street. Neither of us offered to shake hands.

"Thanks," I said. "I'll be in touch."

"Look after yourself," he said. "This must be a very difficult time."

I didn't reply. It's humiliating to be on the receiving end of someone else's compassion.

Charlie Browning closed the front door behind me. I turned right and walked down the lane towards the church. A door slammed. I glanced towards the sound and saw Miranda climbing out of her enormous Mercedes. She lowered herself heavily to the ground and waddled across the lane. She was wearing tight white trousers and a pink top that told me altogether more about her figure than I wanted to know.

"Hallo, sailor. Fancy seeing you here."

"You knew about Charlie all the time," I said. "Didn't you?"

She opened her little eyes as widely as they would go. "Didn't Nicky mention? That's funny. I've been doing the Alexander Technique for ages. It was me that brought Charlie to the book group."

15

AT THE HOSPICE, LILY WAS SLEEPING. I SAT BESIDE THE bed and watched her. The freesias were still in the vase, which was now on the windowsill. They were beginning to look the worse for wear. Nobody had brought Lily any other flowers. I wished I had remembered to buy more. I should have liked to search the room for the chain but she was sleeping too lightly for that, and people were coming and going along the corridor. But perhaps the chain didn't matter anymore. It only mattered if you knew what it had been, what it meant.

I had come here partly because I didn't want to stay at home. Our house felt like a prison. Nicky and I had moved into it three months earlier and promised ourselves it would be a place for a new beginning. It had turned into a place for an ending.

At least Lily couldn't ask me too many awkward questions. She was lying on her back. Her mouth was open and her right arm rested on her chest. The sleeve of her nightdress had ridden up. The arm was very thin now and surprisingly hairy. Even in the last few days she had altered. The window was open and everything was very clean but still there was a hint of decay in the atmosphere. She was dying quietly, and alone.

I got up to go. The chair creaked and Lily opened her eyes.

"Jamie." She licked her lips, which were dry and flaky. "I was dreaming about Hugh. Isn't that funny?"

I held a glass of water for her and supported her with my arm while she drank. A tall thin clergyman passed across the open doorway. Lily glanced at him. "Is that Hugh?"

"No, it's not," I said. "Hugh isn't here."

"Hugh's dead." Lily pushed the glass away. "I wish he wasn't."

I put the glass down. "I must go. I only dropped in to see how you were."

"Much the same but worse." She bared the yellow teeth in what I think was a grin. "Hugh never really got over it."

I knew at once what she was talking about. "I'm sorry."

"But Kate helped, of course. She was the only one who could make him forget. Not for long, but it was something. I want Kate, Jamie. Where is she?"

"I don't know."

"Tell her she must come and see me. She's my daughter." Lily sniffed and frowned. "Have you found your wife yet? What's her name?"

"Her name's Nicky. No, I haven't."

"Hugh said marriage is for life. You shouldn't just give up on it if it goes through a sticky patch. He's such a nice man, you know. He's somewhere here. I know he is."

Lily stared at the doorway, as though willing Hugh Murthington to stroll into the room.

"Why did you choose me?" I said. "For Christ's sake, why did it happen?"

"You and me? Because you changed. It was very sudden. One day you were just a boy, and then suddenly you were something quite different. And you were *young*. I couldn't stop it happening. Because I wanted someone young. That was the one thing Hugh couldn't be. I think he was born aged thirty."

I said, because I suddenly needed to know: "Tell me, was I the only one? Or were there others? Was I just one of a series?"

But I was too late. Though her eyes were still half open she was no longer aware of me. For a moment I wondered if she had died. Then I saw the muscles at the corners of her mouth were twitching. I had asked her a similar question a long time ago and I had never understood what her answer meant.

I left her sleeping and drove back to Greyfont, to the house that wasn't a home. I wished I had someone to talk to. I had colleagues and business partners, and people who shared the same interests as I had. Before I'd met Nicky there had been lovers as well. But I had never had anyone to talk to except Nicky.

At home, I planned my afternoon. I was going to mow the lawn. Then I was going to dig the long flowerbed at the far end of the garden, which was trying to revert to primeval jungle. It would be boring, back-breaking work but at least at the end of it I should be tired, perhaps tired enough to sleep properly. I went upstairs to change. I had pulled on a T-shirt and was zipping up a pair of jeans with holes in the knees when the doorbell rang. I ran barefoot down the stairs. I don't know why I ran. I knew perfectly well that if it was Nicky she would let herself in with a key. I opened the door.

A strange man was standing in the middle of the drive-way, staring up at the house. He brought his eyes down to me—slowly, like a panning camera. He was tall, with very short hair and a very short beard. He wore a gray suit, a white shirt and a bright blue tie. He was carrying a briefcase made of shiny black leather, like his shoes. For an instant I thought he'd come to sell me something I didn't want, like double-glazed uPVC windows or the keys to the Kingdom of Heaven.

"Hello, James," Carlo said.

He looked tanned and fit. He was Carlo but he was also someone else. Our shared past had evaporated, leaving only a sour sediment behind.

"Aren't you going to ask me in?"

I wouldn't have known his voice. It was the sort you hear every time you turn on the radio or the television—a voice without tribal or geographical roots apart from a hint of outer London.

I said, "Who told you where I live?"

"It's not much of a secret. Your company lists you as a director on its Web page. You're in the phone book. You answered the phone at Chipping Weston this morning but you weren't there when I called round at the house. This was the obvious place to come next."

I held open the door. Carlo stepped into the hall. He glanced round it, his face indifferent yet attentive, like an estate agent's. I led the way into the sitting room. I offered him a chair but he prowled up and down, looking at the pictures and the ornaments. I stood on the hearth rug and waited. I was acutely conscious of the disparity in our sizes. I wished I was wearing shoes. My bare feet felt vulnerable.

Carlo came to rest at the window overlooking the drive. He touched Nicky's raku bowl with the tip of his forefinger and turned back to me. "Nice place. I expect you're pretty comfortable."

"I get by."

"More than that, I should think. No kids?" He waited and, when I didn't reply, went on: "Except our Kate, of course. Or rather your Kate. Yours and Lily's."

"What do you want?"

He ignored the question. "I never liked her, you know. She never felt like my sister. Not one little bit. Not surprising, really."

When in doubt, I thought, say nothing. Nothing does less damage.

"I only found out on Thursday," Carlo went on. "And you want to know how?"

Again I made no reply.

"Felicity told me."

A shiver ran through me as though I'd been touched unexpectedly by something cold. "I don't understand."

"That's your problem."

"It was all a long time ago, Carlo. We—we were different people then."

"You don't get out of it that easily." He picked up the raku bowl and held it to the light. He turned it this way and that as though studying the glaze. "Where is she?"

"Kate? I don't know."

"She's a sly little bitch. You want to be careful with her." He added, with an odd emphasis on the words, "You can't believe a thing she says."

"Is this true about Rackford?"

"Is what true?"

"That it's potentially much more valuable than it was."

Carlo nodded. The bowl gleamed in the light. He ran his finger round the rim.

We no longer had anything in common but a shared past. Over the years he had become a creature of my memory, someone who was never more than seventeen; someone who was, in a sense, my creation. Now I had a large, angry, middle-aged man in my sitting room. To all intents and purposes he was a total stranger. But he was also Carlo.

"Look," he said suddenly. "It's just not fair. Rackford was my father's. He bought it before he even met Lily. He left it to his children. But Kate wasn't his child so she's got no earthly right to it."

"I don't know if a lawyer would agree with you."

"Sod lawyers. I'm talking about what's right."

"You can't be sure. Your father thought Kate was his. Perhaps she was."

He shook his head. "I'm having a test done. Not that there's any doubt about it."

"And your father accepted her as his. Surely that's the point?"

Carlo did not reply. He stroked the inside of the bowl with a fingertip, working his way down in a spiral. Then he sighed and relaxed his grip on the rim. The bowl slipped from his fingers, fell to the floor and shattered.

He looked up at me. "Oh dear. Sorry."

I glanced sideways. We had an open fire sometimes and there was a poker in the hearth. I remembered how Carlo had behaved at the ten-pin bowling center on his birthday. I remembered the boy he had beaten up in the park. Carlo would suddenly snap and become quite another person when his anger reached a certain level. I had always assumed that he couldn't know the whole story of that last afternoon at Rackford. But I was no longer sure.

"What exactly do you want?" I said.

"To warn you. Kate's planning something. She'll probably try to use you."

"Planning what?"

"Work it out. When she was a kid she was greedy. She hasn't changed. She wants it all."

"Rackford? She says the same about you."

He picked up a vase from the bookcase. I tensed.

"Are you married?" I asked. "Have you got children?"

He sighed. "No children. I'm not married now either. I tried it once but it didn't work out. And you?"

Carlo put down the vase on the bookcase. He walked slowly across the room to the door. Shards from the raku bowl crunched and crumbled beneath his feet. In the doorway he stopped and looked back.

"Yes," I said. "Her name's Nicky."

So Carlo and I went down to Chipping Weston in the summer of 1980. Occasionally, even now, I find myself imagining that somewhere in another universe there exists a version of me who didn't go down to Chipping Weston that summer. It wouldn't have taken much, after all—if my grandmother hadn't fallen on her doorstep, for example.

I know now that to expect too much is dangerous. On our first evening at Chipping Weston, Lily was wearing jeans and a sweatshirt, and her hair was scraped back from her face. She was slim and sexy and apparently uninterested in me.

"Felicity's just got a brace on her teeth," she said to Carlo and me when she collected us at the station. "Try not to mention it. She gets terribly self-conscious about how she looks.

And I've got you a present for her. You can pay me back later. She doesn't know I bought it, by the way."

Lily gave Carlo a little package wrapped in silver paper and tied with a purple ribbon. Carlo grunted. Felicity's birthday had been at the end of June and he had failed to buy her a present. Lily had volunteered to deal with it for him.

Carlo gave Felicity the present as soon as we got to the house. Her face turned pink with pleasure. She ripped off the wrapping paper and found a small box made of rosewood. Inside it was a silver pendant in the form of a leaping fish. In a way, the fish was like Hugh Murthington's freesias—another gift with a deceptive provenance and unintended consequences.

"It's gorgeous," she said, and hugged him. "It's beautiful." She made him fasten the chain round her neck and admired herself in the hall mirror. "I'm going to wear it always," she said. "For the rest of my life."

"What a lovely present," Lily said, edging away from me. "Well done, Carlo."

That evening I hardly exchanged a word with her. I spent more time talking to Hugh Murthington than anyone else.

"Ah, James," he said, shaking hands, frowning as though quarrying my name from the depths of his memory. "How is your—your grandmother coming along?"

I said she was as well as could be expected. He plied me with further questions about her, about my parents and my plans for university. If I had been a better person, his kindness would have made me feel guilty. Instead it made me impatient. He was nothing more than yet another obstacle between me and his wife.

I hoped at least for a kiss from Lily and tried to maneuver myself into situations where this might be possible. But she seemed to take an almost calculated pleasure in treating me as a sort of appendage to Carlo. I tried to steal a moment after supper but Lily avoided being alone with me and in any case I had reckoned without Black Maria.

Felicity, now thirteen, had recently learned to play Hearts, the card game whose object is to avoid winning tricks containing cards of the hearts suit. She especially liked a version called Black Maria, in which the queen of spades is an extra penalty card. Each heart is worth one negative point but the queen of spades scores thirteen, which makes it as undesirable as all the hearts together.

We played Black Maria on the first evening—and every day after that, while I stayed at Chipping Weston during that last summer. Felicity was a persistent child. Unfortunately the game requires a minimum of three players, which meant there was rarely an occasion when either Lily or I was not playing. And Black Maria wasn't just a game. It became an elaborate joke designed to ridicule Lily.

"I know why you like this game," Carlo said to Felicity on the second evening, when he and I were playing with her after supper.

"Oh, no, you don't." She stuck her tongue out at him. "Why?"

"Because it's Black Maria. She's nasty by nature and thirteen times as unlucky as anyone else."

He stared at her, his face blank and innocent, and she stared back. They started laughing at the same moment.

I looked from one to the other. "Is this a private joke or can anyone join in?"

"Black Maria," Felicity said, in a stage whisper. "She eats babies for breakfast."

"And raw snails," Carlo added.

"And cat's poo."

At that moment the door opened and Lily came in. "What are you laughing about?"

"Nothing," Carlo said. "James was telling us a joke."

"Dad and I are going out now. I'll leave the Millers' number on the hall table in case you need us."

Carlo grunted. Felicity gave no sign that she had heard. I glanced at Lily. She was wearing a dress and high heels. I smelt her perfume. As the door was closing Carlo began to hum a tune from *The Sound of Music*. It was called "How Do You Solve a Problem Like Maria?"

Still humming, he selected a card and put it down on the table. It was the nine of clubs. I had to follow suit so I put down a ten. Felicity gave a whoop and slammed down the queen of spades.

"Your trick. Poor old James." It was the third time in three rounds that I had been left with the queen of spades. "You just can't get away from Maria."

She began to laugh, and Carlo joined in. I laughed with them, although I didn't like losing any more than they did, and I didn't like the way they were looking at me.

So Maria became our code name for Lily, which gave both of the others much pleasure. Felicity constructed a fantasy Maria to extend the joke's potential. At breakfast the following morning, for example, she confided to Carlo that Maria smelt.

"Really?" he said. "Yes, now you come to mention it I suppose she does."

"It's very bad," Felicity went on. "And getting worse."

"Pooh." He held his nose. "What a stink!"

She began to giggle and both she and Carlo glanced at me.

"Who's Maria?" Lily asked. "Anyway, perhaps she can't help her body odor."

"Just a girl I know," Felicity said. "Not a very nice one. I don't think she washes very much. Madame Stinker has only herself to blame."

"That's not very nice, dear. How would—"

"Can we go to Rackford today?" Carlo interrupted. "I need all the practice I can get."

Carlo had become deadly serious about his driving. If we had to spend the first half of the summer at Chipping Weston, he was going to use the time to pass his test and he had arranged to take the lessons he had been given for his birthday. He had booked a driving test, too, four days before we were due to fly to Rhodes.

The first lesson was scheduled for the afternoon of our third full day at Chipping Weston. I hoped this would give me an opportunity to be alone with Lily but Felicity ruined that plan. First she wanted a game of Black Maria, which involved all three of us, and then Lily sent us out to buy vegetables. I was furious.

Felicity and I walked into the town center together. On the way we met her friend Millie. Since I had last seen her at Easter Millie had acquired small but unmistakable breasts, twin mounds that poked at her shirt, creating an oddly enticing gap between two of the buttons.

"This is James," Felicity said, laying her hand for an instant on my arm. "You remember him, don't you?"

"Of course I do." Millie giggled. She was no longer plump, either—she was much taller than Felicity, and her long red hair framed a face with green eyes and a big mouth. She grinned at Felicity. "How could I forget?"

"We're just doing a bit of shopping."

She giggled again. "I like your pendant. Is it new?"

"Carlo gave it to me for my birthday." Felicity touched the silver fish. "It came in its own wooden box. Where are you off to?"

Millie said that she was going home but she was thinking of going to the cinema later in the afternoon. "Do you want to come?" Her eyes flicked from Felicity to me and I realized with a shock that I was included in the invitation. "Maybe Carlo'd like to come too?"

"What's on?"

"*Kramer vs. Kramer.*"

"I've seen it. Anyway, we've got things to do, haven't we, James?"

Felicity glanced at me and I nodded automatically. For the first time I noticed that she was wearing eye shadow and very pale lipstick. I hadn't known that she used cosmetics. I was sure she hadn't been wearing makeup when we were playing cards. She must have put it on just before we came out. It looked rather odd with the brace on her teeth.

"See you, then," Millie said. "Maybe I'll come round later." And she smiled at me and swung her hair across her face like a veil. "Nice seeing you again, James."

"OK." Felicity touched my arm again. "Let's go."

It seems so obvious now. But at the time I was almost willfully blind. That summer I found myself spending almost as much time with Felicity as with Carlo. I didn't have the first idea what was going on in her head. I knew she sometimes made me uncomfortable. I knew I didn't particularly want to be with her. But what I didn't know, not then, was that in some sense she had fallen in love with me.

16

MY MOBILE RANG WHILE I WAS SWEEPING UP THE FRAGments of Nicky's raku bowl. I ran to answer it. It wasn't Nicky but a nurse from the hospice.

"I'm afraid Lily's taken a turn for the worse," she said.

"I'm sorry," I said, then wondered what I was sorry for.

"We'd like to get in touch with her children but we're not having much luck with the numbers we've got."

"What are they?"

She recited the Chipping Weston number, followed by those of two mobiles I didn't recognize. I scribbled them on the cover of the phone directory. "I've got another for her daughter," I said. "If you hold a minute I'll try it." I used the landline to call the mobile I had given Kate. There was no answer. I left a message and went back to the nurse.

"Lily's really not at all well," she said. "I know you've already seen her today but is there any possibility you could look in again?"

"Is she—is she conscious?"

"Drifting in and out. She keeps asking for Hugh."

"Her husband. He died last year."

"I know."

The nurse said nothing else. I listened to the silence that filled the house like a cloud of feathers, to the expectant silence at the other end of the line. Lily had been the sort of woman who accumulates friends and admirers. Now all she had left was a daughter who was afraid to see her, a stepson who hated her, and me. I glanced at my reflection in the hall mirror and saw a thin, pale man who looked faintly familiar.

"All right," I said. "I'll come over."

The traffic was heavy and it was after six by the time I reached Wembley. At the hospice, Lily was asleep. Small and shrunken, she lay on her side with her knees drawn up and a drip trailing away from her like a thin, plastic tail. She didn't look quite human anymore. It was as though she was in the process of migrating into another species. The biography of the dead actress was no longer on the bedside table.

I had bought her another bunch of freesias on the way, which was just as well because the old bunch had gone. Once I had found a vase for them, there was nothing else to do so I sat down and gazed at the figure on the bed. But I didn't think about her. Instead I drifted into my mind and thought about Nicky.

I had left a note on the kitchen table at home in case she came back. It said where I had gone and also gave her the name of the patient I was visiting. I tried to visualize Nicky's face, as though by doing so I might will her into existence and bring her through the doorway. It was surprisingly hard to remember her features. It was as though I knew her so well I no longer saw her face but something beyond it, something closer to the essence of her.

"Jamie."

I got up and stood by the bed. Lily stared up at me but I wasn't sure whether she saw me. I touched her shoulder. "Can I get you anything?"

"Jamie, where's Kate? You were going to fetch her."

"I can't reach her. I don't know where she is."

Lily began to cry. They were the weary tears of old age that slid almost unnoticed from the corners of her eyes. Sobbing takes effort, and effort was now a luxury she couldn't afford.

"I want Kate," she said. "She's my daughter."

"I'll try to find her. I promise."

"But it's too late. I can't bear it anymore. Will you do something for me?"

"If I can."

"Hurts too much now," she said. "I've had enough."

"I'm sorry," I said. "I wish—"

"I want to go. I can't wait for Kate anymore. I want you to put a pillow over my face."

"What?"

"A pillow over my face."

"Don't be foolish."

Her lips curled into something that was almost a smile. "Not foolish. Not for me. I asked them to give me something, but they won't."

"You can't do that," I said. "And I won't help you."

"Why not?"

"It's obvious."

"I wouldn't have thought it would bother *you*."

I noticed the slight stress on the last word. "Well, it would."

Her lips curled again. "I need Carlo."

"Carlo? Why?"

"He'd do it like a shot. Been wanting to for years."

I said nothing.

"He'll kill somebody one day, if he hasn't already. And he damn nearly did before, didn't he?" Her voice was becoming slurred now. "So, why not me?"

"What do you mean? Who was it?"

She didn't reply. Pain twisted her features. Her eyes closed. Gradually her face relaxed.

"Who did he nearly kill? What happened?"

Her chest rose and fell. Each intake of air made a soft, wheezing sound, but when she breathed out the flow of air seemed to hop and skip like a shallow stream flowing over stones.

I shook her shoulder gently. "Lily. Wake up. What happened? What did Carlo do? It's important—for Kate's sake."

The eyelids fluttered but remained closed. She said something else I couldn't distinguish. Then she added, quite clearly: "Kate knows. And Millie, of course."

Two hours passed. In that time Lily said nothing more, or nothing that I could understand. People came and went—I was rarely alone with her for more than a few moments.

The nurses were kind but professionally reticent. Lily was balanced between living and dying and the scales were swaying, first one side up and then the other. People die as they live, in ways unique to themselves. A Church of England priest came and sat with us for a while. When she left the room I followed her into the corridor.

"Do you think Lily knows what's happening?" I asked her. "Is she really asleep?"

"I don't know," she said, "but people are often like this. Neither one thing nor the other. I like to think there's a rhythm to it, that they go when they're ready."

I said nothing.

"You look tired."

"It's a difficult time."

"She's in good hands."

"I think I'll go home," I said. "I've got things to do."

I drove back to Greyfont, thinking about Carlo rather than Lily. At home, the driveway was empty and the grass still needed cutting. Inside the house, I turned on the heating and checked the voice mail for nonexistent messages. Five minutes later a frozen pizza was thawing in the oven and I was sitting at the kitchen table, drinking wine and watching my laptop flicker into life. I logged on. The only emails I had were from work, and I didn't bother to open them.

I fired up the search engine. I found nothing relating to "Charles Murthington." Could I trust what Lily had said? It was certainly plausible. If Felicity's friend Millie knew about it, it must have been something that happened at Chipping Weston. I couldn't remember Millie's surname, if I'd ever known it.

I thought of what Carlo had done to the boy by the swings in the playground all those years ago, the one who had bullied Felicity, and to the other boy at school, the one who had jostled me in the changing room. But Lily hadn't known about those episodes, or about the girl at the Eagle on the night the fox died. So whom had Carlo nearly killed? And when? The threat of violence, usually concealed, had always been part of Carlo's charm. You knew it was there, part of his fabric, something hard and awkward like a knot in the grain of a plank. People don't change: they just find new ways to be themselves.

Why hadn't Kate or Lily told me before? As soon as I'd framed the question, I glimpsed a possible answer. I was their reluctant helper at the best of times. Perhaps they had feared that telling me more about his history of violence would make me even less enthusiastic.

Too late to think about that now. I felt queasy with fear. During the evening I drank most of the bottle of wine and forced myself to eat a third of the pizza. I went to bed early. At the back of my sock drawer was a packet of mild sleeping tablets that the doctor had given me a couple of years ago and I had never used. I swallowed a couple before I turned out the light.

I'm not sure I needed them. I slipped into a dreamless sleep and stayed there for seven and a half hours. When I woke up, I drew back the curtains. It was a gray, windy morning and the sky was spitting with rain. Somehow my sleeping mind had made a decision.

It was still early, before nine o'clock. I didn't bother to shave or eat breakfast. I drove into the center of Greyfont, the old village, and parked in the lee of the churchyard wall. I turned into St. Ann's Lane. Most of its residents would have left already for work. At Charlie's house, blinds covered the windows at the front, upstairs as well as downstairs. Tucked up against the guttering was the metal oblong of a burglar alarm.

I rang the doorbell and waited. Nothing happened. I rang the bell again. Just to be sure, I tried phoning him. I stood on the doorstep with my mobile and listened to one phone ringing in my ear and another somewhere in the house. After a while Charlie's phone stopped and his voice mail cut in. I broke the connection.

The street was still empty. I walked swiftly down the passageway leading to the little gardens at the back of the terrace. The curtains were drawn across the windows of the studio. There was an outside tap beside the back door and a crowd of plants in pots clustered round it, like chickens waiting to be fed. I tried the door. It was locked. I peered through the kitchen window but a Venetian blind covered most of it. All I could see was a stretch of worktop and the edge of the sink.

It was a dead end. Even if there hadn't been a burglar alarm, I doubted I had the courage to break into somebody else's house in broad daylight. As I turned to go, my eyes ran over the dustbins beyond the tap. I hesitated, rubbing the stubble on my chin. Then I raised the lid of the nearer one. It was empty. I replaced the lid and opened the second. It contained a black plastic sack, neatly secured with a double knot.

I didn't give myself time to think. I bent down and pushed my fingers under the knot. I hooked the bag like a fish. I put the lid back but in my haste I let it slip from my hand. It fell with a clatter onto the concrete path. I left it there and plunged into the gloom of the passage.

A door opened behind me. There were footsteps. A woman said, "Hey—you! What d'you want?"

I didn't look back. At the street, I turned right and fixed my eyes on the church tower at the far end. As I walked, the plastic sack swung to and fro as though it was trying to escape me. It banged against my leg. I thought I heard footsteps pursuing me. Panic rose like nausea. I broke into a run. At the end of the lane, I didn't look back. I flung the rubbish bag onto the floor of the car. I started the engine but it stalled when I tried to move off. I heard myself swearing with a childish violence that even in my panic-stricken state amazed me. At my second attempt I managed to drive jerkily down the high street. An old man shouted at me and I realized I had jumped a red light at a pedestrian crossing.

The neighbor had seen me mainly from behind. She might have glimpsed my face in profile, but only for an instant. That was what mattered. As for the rest, I was wearing jeans and a dark coat with the collar turned up against the rain. There wasn't a great deal to describe. Anyway, I told myself, it was unlikely that the police would be interested in the theft of a bag of rubbish. These were reassuring arguments and made perfect sense. Nevertheless, when I reached home, my pulse was still racing and my hands were clammy.

I took the black sack into the garage and set it down in the middle of the concrete floor. I put on a pair of rubber gloves and teased apart the knot. I spread out sheets of newspaper and emptied the contents onto them.

There are people who make their living by going through other people's rubbish. I suppose you must get used to it, this intimate acquaintance with the waste products of someone else's life. I picked my way through crumpled tissues and egg-shells, torn packaging and emptied tins. There were papers, too—mainly flyers and junk mail. I studied them all. There was a rash of special offers at the local supermarket; some-one was pleased to inform Charlie that he had been pre-selected for a ten-thousand-pound loan; and someone else was full of excitement about a plan to pedestrianize part of the center of Greyfont. It was no good. All I'd achieved by going through Charlie's rubbish was to make myself feel physically and emotionally grubby. I began to shovel the debris back into the sack.

But the loan letter caught my eye as I picked it up again. Not the letter itself but Charlie's name above his address. In particular, what caught my eye was the middle initial, which was X. It was sufficiently unusual to distract me for an instant. Xavier? Xerxes? But the X was probably a mistake. He had been Browning, C. J., in the phone book.

X. A single letter was all it took. The second glance gave me time enough to see the rest of the address. I sat back on my heels and made myself read the words very slowly, just to make sure I hadn't invented them: *Mr. C. X. Browning, Wyesham Cottage, Larks Hill, Farleigh Pemberton, Bath, Somerset.*

Charlie's cottage, the one he shared with his partner, the cottage he had lent to Nicky. I abandoned the pile of rubbish on the garage floor and went back to the car with the letter in my hand. I found Farleigh Pemberton in a road atlas. I could be there in ninety minutes.

My instinct was to start the engine and go. But I forced myself to return to the house and make toast and coffee. After breakfast, I looked up Farleigh Pemberton on the Internet and discovered that its population was fewer than two hundred, that the church was late medieval, that the post office had closed two years ago, and that there was a farmers' market on the first Friday of every month. While I was online, I checked to see whether there was any news of Rackford. There wasn't.

It was still raining when I left Greyfont. I took an overnight bag containing a change of clothes and my laptop. The traffic was heavier than I expected. I cut down to the M4 and drove westwards. The weather seemed to mirror my state of mind.

More than once I considered turning round and going home. Even if Nicky was there, she might not want to see me. And, for all I knew, she was long gone. She was not a person who vacillated.

The rain became heavier. The wipers slapped to and fro. The wind was blowing out of the south-west and throwing the rain against the windscreen. I switched on the heater. It felt more like February than May. But part of me wanted the journey to go on forever.

I turned off the motorway and drove south first towards Bath, and then east into a network of smaller and smaller roads. At last I came to Farleigh Pemberton. The village was strung out on the side of an escarpment that faced west. Most of the houses were tucked below the road. A few, however, were on the higher ground, linked to the road by lanes carved into the hillside like old men's wrinkles, and running with rivulets of grimy rainwater.

Larks Hill was one of these deep-cut lanes. At the end of it, near the top of the hill, a five-bar gate was set in a tall yew hedge. I stopped the car in front of it and got out. On the other side of the gate was a stretch of gravel with a trim little garden to the left and a low stone cottage on the right. Nicky's Mini was parked on the gravel. Next to it was a Renault Mégane.

For a moment, I leaned on the gate and studied the place. Rainwater trickled down my neck. There were cast-iron grilles over the cottage windows and enough hanging baskets to stock a small garden center. An ornamental wheelbarrow with a cargo of pansies stood by the front door, and on the lawn was the sort of well that had nothing to do with water. A puddle the shape of Italy had formed on the gravel, and the rain was making the water dance.

I heard the sound of a car in the lane. I turned slowly. A black VW Golf came round the corner. The driver braked sharply when he saw the Saab. He switched off the engine and got out. It was the man I had seen in the photograph at Charlie's house in St. Ann's Lane: the man who was lying on the sofa, smiling and showing his chest hair. Today he was wearing a shiny black leather jacket and he wasn't in a good mood.

The Golf's passenger door opened. Nicky climbed out. She was wearing jeans and a black moleskin coat that fitted snugly over her hips. She frowned at me. "What are you doing here?"

I didn't answer, partly because the answer was obvious and partly because the words had dried in my throat. I had forgotten how beautiful she was, how elegant, how delicate.

"Well?" she prompted. "What do you want?"

Charlie unfolded his long, thin body from the back of the car. He smiled at me. "Hi."

I ignored him. "I want you to come home."

Nicky shook her head. "I'm going on holiday."

I took a step backwards. I stared at her and tried to find the right words. There were raindrops in her hair.

"We're going to drive down to Montpellier." She glanced at the man in the leather jacket. "We're just about to leave."

"You're going to France with these two?" I said.

"Why not?"

Charlie reached into the car and found a black umbrella. He opened it and held it over Nicky. He said, "Jason's got a friend who's lending us a house. There's plenty of room. This is Jason, by the way."

I nodded at Jason, and he continued to scowl. "Your car's in the way," he said. "Would you move it?"

"I'd like to talk to Nicky."

"That depends on her."

"I'm not sure we've got time," she said. "And I'm not sure I want to talk to you."

"Please."

"Whatever you're going to do," Jason cut in, "can you move that car out of the way? I'm getting soaked."

"Anyway, there's nothing to say," Nicky said.

"There's everything to say. Can't we talk in private?"

"I didn't say we could talk at all."

"We do need to get out of the rain," Charlie said gently.

Nicky combed the wet hair from her forehead with her fingers. "I'm not talking to you."

"For God's sake—" I began.

"I don't trust you anymore."

"Just a few words. That's all I want."

"And I want to get the car inside so I can load it up without getting even wetter than I am," Jason said.

"He's right, you know," said Charlie, the voice of reason. "No point in getting wetter than we need to." He unlatched the gate and pushed it open. "James, if you drive over there, near the steps up to the lawn, that will give Jason plenty of room to turn and reverse up to the front door."

Nicky glanced at him. "You think I should talk to him?"

He didn't answer.

She turned back to me. "Two minutes."

While I was parking, Nicky and Charlie went into the cottage. Jason maneuvered his car back to the front door. He caught up with me in the porch.

"You know something?" he said. "I hate Charlie's lame ducks."

The cottage wasn't large: one room deep and perhaps two or three rooms wide. A vase of lilies stood on the hall table and filled the air with a heavy funereal perfume. The wallpaper had Regency stripes. The cottage wasn't like Charlie's house and it didn't fit with what little I knew and guessed about Jason. But people are full of surprises.

"You can go in there." Jason nodded to the room on the left, a sitting room with pink peonies on the three-piece suite.

At that moment, Nicky came out of the room on the other side of the hall. She had shed her coat and somehow found time to tidy her hair. She followed me in and sat on a hard chair in front of a bureau. I stood by the window and looked at the rain.

"I've not decided what to do," Nicky said. "That's why I'm going to France with Charlie and Jason. I need time to think."

She had left the door open. Charlie and Jason were moving in and out of the hall with bags and boxes. Jason was explaining something about timetables with mind-numbing thoroughness.

"Nicky." I stopped and glanced at the open door. "Nicky, it's very difficult to say anything like this."

"Why? Because of them? You don't think they're interested enough to listen, do you?"

"Yes."

"Then don't say anything at all." She started to get up. "Anyway, there's nothing more to say."

"Nicky. I love you."

Her head jerked towards me as though tugged by an invisible rein. But she sat down again.

I said, "You must let me try and explain. I know I haven't handled this well but if I could make you understand—"

"That's the trouble," she interrupted. "I do understand, and how do you think it feels? You felt like a change. Your old model's not quite what it was, it's showing its age. And it's got a big drawback you didn't know about when you got it. A fault in the design. So you've moved on to something a little more up-to-date."

"It's nothing like that."

"That's what it amounts to." She sounded harder and sharper than I had ever heard her before. "A sordid little midlife crisis."

"That's nonsense."

"Maybe you've given it a pretty name, like falling in love. But really it's just one of those things that middle-aged men are always doing. Like—like getting high blood pressure or turning into pompous old bullies. And the real losers are the poor bloody women they're married to."

"You needn't lose anything. Especially not me."

"I know. In a way it's my fault. I can't give you what you most want and maybe that's the real reason. But do you know what's worst? I feel such a fool. I'd actually persuaded myself you were different, that you weren't like the rest."

Jason was on the phone now. He was postponing an appointment with his dental hygienist.

"Can't we talk alone?" I said to Nicky. "Please."

Nicky sighed and knotted her fingers together and studied them. I realized with a lurch of dismay that she wasn't wearing her wedding ring.

"Nicky. Darling. You're what I most want."

She looked at the bureau, not me.

"The Monday morning's out," Jason said. "Afternoon?"

"I'm not sleeping with her," I went on. "She's not my lover."

"I don't even have a name for her." Nicky turned to face me again. "'Love K.' That's what it said on the text message. 'Sorry to leave like that. You were great. Will call. Love K.' Kiss, kiss, kiss."

"It's not what you think."

"Miranda was right about you. All men are bastards and it's just a matter of how much and when they reveal it." She shook her head. "It would be funny if it weren't so sick."

"No," Jason said. "I can't do the Tuesday, either."

"Her name's Kate," I said. "According to—"

"You always did like the name Kate," Nicky said. "I remember you saying that if we had a daughter maybe we should call her—"

"That's it. That's just it."

"That's what?"

"All right, then," Jason said. "If there's nothing else it'll have to be four thirty."

I moved away from the window and stood beside the bureau. I looked down at Nicky and said quietly, "According to her mother, Kate is my daughter."

17

I T WAS LILY WHO HAD ORIGINALLY PUT THE NAME INTO MY mind, and it was such a tiny, insignificant thing that I had failed to erase it along with everything else. The four of us were in the car, on our way to Rackford. Carlo and Lily were in the front and Carlo was driving because now he was seventeen he had his provisional driving license. Felicity and I sat in the back with as much space as possible between us. Felicity was telling Carlo about a friend of hers, who had just acquired a baby sister called Kate.

"I rather like the name Kate," Lily said, over her shoulder. "It's one of those names that never go out of fashion."

"Like Maria, you mean?" Felicity said.

Carlo snorted. The car veered towards the nearside of the road.

"Careful," Lily said. "We nearly went up on the curb."

"All right," Carlo muttered.

"And put the windscreen wipers on. It's starting to rain."

"I don't like the name Kate much," Felicity said. "It's almost as bad as Maria. Sounds nasty and angry, like the one in the film."

"The film?" Lily said.

"*The Taming of the Shrew.*" Felicity looked and sounded smugly superior. "Shakespeare, you know."

Carlo drove on. We left Chipping Weston behind and threaded our way through the network of lanes north of the town. Hugh Murthington had taken Felicity to see the Zeffirelli film of *The Taming of the Shrew* because she was due to study the play the following term.

"Ow," Carlo said.

"What is it?" Lily asked.

"Nothing."

From where I was sitting I could see the side of Carlo's face. He had poked his tongue into his cheek and the skin was puckered at the corners of his mouth and eye.

"Toothache again?"

"Just a twinge. That's all."

"You must see the dentist," Lily said.

"It's all right," Carlo replied. "I'll have some aspirin when we get back."

"No, you must have it seen to," Lily persisted. "Think what it would be like if it got worse when you were in Greece. You wouldn't know what to do."

"Don't fuss," Carlo said. "It feels fine now."

The car began to slow. He indicated right. We turned into the airfield entrance and drove past the ruined guardpost.

"Look!" Felicity said. "There's a fox—near the control tower."

We all looked. No one else saw it.

"It was there," Felicity said. "It was. I'm sure it was."

"We saw a fox here once," I said. "Ages ago."

She smiled at me. "Yes, we did. I was there too." Her mouth was full of jagged teeth like white rocks roped together by the silver wire of her brace. "It was my first lesson."

I nodded. "I remember."

"Yes," she said, still smiling. "Just the four of us. You, me, Carlo and Dad."

"Your father wasn't there," Lily said. "It was me."

All of us drove that afternoon but Carlo most of all. After all, he needed the practice. It wasn't much fun for the rest of us because he paid obsessive attention to each maneuver. I had not realized that so much could go wrong with parallel parking, reversing round corners, three-point turns and emergency stops. And it was not enough for Carlo to get them right. They had to be perfect.

Even Felicity started snapping at him. As far as I was concerned, the real torture was that I was so close to Lily and yet, for all the good it did me, she might as well have been in another country. I was sitting immediately behind her. I could have leaned forward and nuzzled the nape of her neck. I could have stretched my hands over her shoulders and touched her breasts. Even the thought of these things, impossible though they were, aroused me and I had to keep my jacket draped across my lap so the signs of this were not obvious to Felicity. The rain continued, though it was never much more than a half-hearted drizzle. As the afternoon wore on, I became increasingly hot and uncomfortable—increasingly angry, too: it was as though the Murthingtons had somehow banded together to make me feel ridiculous.

Felicity said, "This is so boring. Can I go down to the stream for a while?"

"But it's raining, dear," Lily pointed out.

"So what? A little water won't hurt me. Anyway, it's not raining very hard." She turned to me. "Do you want to come?"

"OK."

Felicity's face broke into another smile, all teeth, brace and pink gums. By then I think I would have agreed to anything that enabled me to get away from Lily. I didn't particularly want to go with Felicity but if we went down to the stream at least I could have a smoke. Carlo drove us round the perimeter road to the entrance on the western side of the airfield.

"We'll honk when we need you back," Lily said.

Felicity and I climbed out of the car and followed the path through the belt of trees to the stream. The bracken had grown since the spring and the bottom of the little valley was green and crowded with vegetation. On the other side of the water was the ledge with Felicity's den.

"It's come on a bit since last holidays," I said. "Your den, I mean."

Felicity glanced at it. "I suppose so. I don't use it much nowadays." She made it sound as though the den belonged to another era in her life, one that was unimaginably far removed from now. "Are you going to have a fag?"

I nodded.

"Can I have one?"

I stared at her. "I didn't know you smoked."

Her thin shoulders rose and fell. "You do now. Can you roll it for me?"

The rain had stopped. I took out my tobacco and squatted down. I was conscious of her watching me while I rolled the two cigarettes. Vanity made me work a little harder than usual to make the white cylinders neat and even. As I was licking the gum on the second cigarette I looked up at her. She was still staring at me. In that instant it struck me what an intimate thing this was, rolling someone else's cigarette. When

Felicity put this in her mouth, I thought, my spit would mingle with hers. That was a repulsive idea. But if it had been Lily's mouth rather than Felicity's, the prospect would have excited me.

"Are you sure you want this?" I said. "They're not good for you."

"You smoke them. So does Carlo."

"We're older."

She said nothing. Her mouth was a tight, straight line. She held out her hand for the cigarette. I gave it to her and lit our cigarettes from the same match. When she bent over the flame the silver fish round her neck swung forward and brushed my cheek. She screwed up her face when she drew in the smoke and held the cigarette gingerly, between the very tips of her fingers. She did not inhale.

The packet of Golden Virginia was nearly empty so the tobacco I had used for our cigarettes was dry and powdery. A shower of burning shreds fell from the end of her cigarette. Two or three burning flakes landed on the front of her pale blue shirt.

"Look out," I said.

Felicity brushed them away. But she was too late to prevent one burning a small, dark-rimmed hole in the material.

"Oh, bugger," she said. "Oh, shit."

It was the first time I had heard her swear like that, too. I wasn't sure I liked the new Felicity. I preferred the old one, the predictable child.

I relit her cigarette. We stood there smoking, watching the water dripping from the leaves and the clouds moving sluggishly across the sky. I didn't want to look at Felicity, or talk to her. She smoked silently, as children do, and with obvious concentration, as though engaged in some religious rite designed to appease an obscure god. She smoked fast, too, so she had finished before I had half smoked mine. She flicked the butt into the stream. The current caught it. It slid across the surface of the water, turning slowly, and came to rest on the opposite bank.

"Do you want to see something?" she said. "Something I found the other weekend."

"What is it?"

Her eyelids fluttered. "You'll have to come and find out."

She set off along the bank downstream. There wasn't a path—it was a matter of scrambling through the gaps between the bracken, the brambles and the saplings. Still smoking, I followed her. Her bottom swayed from side to side. She was beginning to walk like a woman. I stopped to tie my laces. When I looked up again, Felicity had vanished.

I called her name. There was no answer. I made my way further along the bank. The hems of my jeans were getting wet. The stream curved into a sharp, right-hand bend. The land on my right rose more sharply. I walked on.

I heard Felicity laugh. She was above me somewhere. I scanned the trees and bushes that masked the slope. A second after my eyes had noted it, my mind registered a variation in tone and texture. There was something up there that looked like stonework, a fragment of wall. Roughly squared blocks of limestone were bound together with ivy. Not much of it was visible.

"James. Up here."

I couldn't see her. I worked my way up the slope towards the stones. I found traces of her—footprints in the mud and downtrodden nettles. As I drew nearer, I discovered that the stones formed a low archway that seemed to lead into a tunnel to the depths of the earth. Mortar crumbled and oozed from the joints between the stones. There were brambles on either side of the archway and ivy trailed down from above so the opening was much smaller than the archway itself and there was little light within. I took a step towards it. "Felicity?"

She didn't answer. I was suddenly afraid. Suppose there was some sort of mine or pit in there. Suppose she had fallen. Suppose she was lying hundreds of feet below me in the darkness with her bones broken. Suppose she was dead. In the same instant that these thoughts flashed through my mind I saw myself blamed for the terrible accident, my life blighted because I had allowed Felicity to fall to her death.

"James."

She was standing in the green frame of the archway. Only her top half was visible, which meant the ground inside was lower than outside. She was smiling, the whiteness of her teeth bright in the green gloom, and holding out her hands.

"What do you think? It's much better than the den we made, isn't it?"

"What is it?"

"I don't know. A sort of cave, I suppose."

"Can't be. It's man-made. I think it's a kiln." I wasn't entirely sure. "A sort of oven."

"There was another higher up the slope but it fell down. It's covered up with bushes now."

I pushed aside one of the bramble suckers and peered into the dark interior. It was smaller than I had expected, walled and roofed with the same stone as the archway itself. There was a strong and unpleasant smell I couldn't identify. The roof was curved and, like the walls, tapered towards the back where the space ended in a crude apse. Roots poked through from the trees and bushes above. As my eyes adjusted I saw roughly squared pieces of masonry on the earth floor. The roof was slowly collapsing.

"For Christ's sake!" I seized Felicity's wrist and yanked her back into the open air. "That ceiling could come down at any time."

"What would you care?" she said, sounding angry.

"What?"

"What would you care?" she repeated.

"Of course I'd bloody care." My mind had instantly replaced the falling-into-a-pit nightmare with an alternative version in which Felicity lay buried alive, her body mangled beyond recognition by the pile of masonry on top of her.

"Would you care?" she said, in a softer voice. "Would you really?"

I was still holding her wrist and the bones felt tiny and delicate. She was looking at me with a peculiar intensity that made me uncomfortable. The brace glinted in her mouth. Her cheekbones were beginning to poke out and her face was no longer soft and rounded like a child's. At that moment, half to my relief, half to my annoyance, we heard the sound of the horn.

"Oh, shit," Felicity said softly.

I let go of her wrist. Without a word we made our way down to the stream and walked along the bank in single file. I turned left up the path leading to the perimeter road.

"James," Felicity said, behind me, "you won't tell anyone, will you?"

I glanced back. "About what?"

"About the cave. Or whatever it is. And about what happened. Even Carlo."

"Why not?"

"Oh, because I want it to be a secret, and—" The horn sounded again. "Can't she bloody shut up?" she added, with a sudden spurt of anger. "She must know we heard her. Bloody Maria."

We plodded upwards in silence. The car was parked at the side of the perimeter road with its engine running. We climbed into the back. Lily was in the driving seat. I knew, though I'm not sure how, that she was furious. It was something to do with the way she was sitting, the set of her head on her shoulders.

She rammed the gear lever into first. "You took your time."

"We came as soon as we heard," Felicity said.

Lily turned to her for the first time. "Look at the state of you. What have you been doing? Rolling in the mud? Isn't it about time you started to grow up?"

Felicity said nothing but the color drained from her face. She seemed to shrink into the seat, as though making herself as small a target as possible. Carlo said nothing: usually he would have found some way to defend Felicity. I said nothing because I was hideously embarrassed, I didn't know what to say and I didn't want to draw Lily's anger towards me.

Lily looked more closely at Felicity. "And what's that on your shirt? It's not a burn hole, is it?"

Felicity hugged herself.

"Have you been smoking?" She glanced at me with cold, remote eyes, then back at the girl. "Have you? I want the truth, Felicity."

No one spoke. I longed to be somewhere else. Lily glared at her step-daughter. My throat was dry. Felicity licked her lips and I glimpsed the jagged teeth and brace.

"It was me," I said, and the words came out in a whisper.

"What?" Lily turned the glare on me.

I cleared my throat. "It was me who was smoking. Felicity wasn't."

Carlo let out his breath. Felicity stared at her knees.

"A bit of tobacco fell on her shirt," I went on. "That's how the hole got there. So it was my fault. I'm sorry. I'll pay for a new one."

Lily's foot must have slipped off the clutch. The car jerked forward. The engine stalled. She muttered something under her breath and turned to face the front.

"Easily done," Carlo said, to no one in particular. "I've done it myself sometimes. Stalled, I mean."

I didn't turn my head but I could see Felicity at the edge of my range of vision. I saw her hands relax and draw apart, her arms fall to her sides.

Oh, fuck, I thought. What have I done? Oh, fuck.

Nothing more was said about the cigarette burn, then or later. During the drive back to Chipping Weston, in fact, nobody said anything at all. For the rest of the day, I waited for something to happen. I was convinced that Lily or, more probably, Hugh Murthington would tell me that they were sorry but the trip to Rhodes was cancelled and I would have to go home immediately, wherever home might be—the school, perhaps, or over to the States to my mother and stepfather.

But everything went on as before. Lily behaved to me as she had throughout the holidays, as though I were a semi-detached extension of Carlo, not quite family, not quite friend, not quite adult, not quite child, not quite anything. Felicity didn't say anything either, although sometimes I found her looking intently at me in a way that made me uncomfortable. Hugh Murthington was just as he always was—vaguely benevolent but with at least half of his attention elsewhere.

After supper, Carlo and I walked into the town and went to the Black Lion, where the landlord was relaxed about the ages of his younger drinkers. When we went out to pubs, Carlo and I bought rounds alternately, a routine we adhered to strictly and carried over to the next session. This evening it was my turn to buy the first round but he insisted on buying me a large vodka and a packet of Golden Virginia.

"There's no need," I said, as he put the drinks and the tobacco on the table.

"This is like a birthday," he said. "So it doesn't count."

I pushed the tobacco across to him. "Thanks."

Carlo sat down and took a sip of his drink. He opened the packet and began to roll a cigarette. "Was she?"

"Was she smoking? Yes."

"Bloody hell. They start younger and younger."

"She asked me to roll it for her."

"She's just a kid. Is she smoking dope too?"

"I don't know. No sign of it."

"Oh, fuck." His hand flew to his cheek.

"What is it?"

"Bloody tooth. It's OK."

"Listen," I said, "I could have said no, but what was the point?"

He shrugged. "If she's going to smoke, she's going to smoke. But why did you say it was you?"

"I don't know." I thought about what had happened in the kiln that afternoon, about the way Felicity had stared at me with that strange expression when I held her wrist. "I felt sorry for her, I guess. Do you think Lily will tell your dad?"

He frowned as he lit the cigarette. "I doubt it. She doesn't like going to him about us. It's like a—what do you call it?"

"A confession of failure?"

"Something like that. Anyway, you're OK. They like you. They wouldn't want to change their minds about you being a good influence on me."

He laughed and soon it was my turn to buy us a drink. The alcohol helped, as it often does for a time, and it was good to sit with Carlo on a small, masculine island, surrounded by a sea of chatter, tobacco smoke and loud music. They were playing an old song by 10cc on the jukebox—"I'm Not in Love." It seemed to say everything I felt. I wasn't in love with Lily. I just happened to be obsessed by her—or, rather, by my desire to make love to her. That's all, I told myself, I'm not in love, I'm not in love.

When the pub closed, we walked home slowly. The air was still warm. The clouds had cleared. It was a fine, dry night and despite the yellow haze of the streetlights you could glimpse the stars.

"Maybe we'll sleep on the beach when we're in Lindos," Carlo said. "With a couple of girls to keep us warm, eh?"

We wandered, a little unsteadily, through the streets. The Murthingtons' road was less well lit than the town center.

There was a crescent moon like a bright fingernail. We stopped in a patch of shadow a few doors away from the house so we could finish our cigarettes.

"Fucking Maria," Carlo said. "She's really got it in for Felicity."

I flicked away the cigarette end, an arc of sparks swallowed by the blackness of the hedge.

"We've got to do something." Carlo swayed towards me. "Teach the bitch a lesson."

I shivered. "How?"

He prodded my chest with a finger, forcing me to step backwards. "Got to be careful, though. Because of Dad. But can't let the bitch get away with it."

His voice was thick and slurred, the words tumbling over each other, like rocks in a landslide. He sucked hard on his cigarette and flung it onto the pavement. He ground the butt under his heel.

"I don't see what you can do," I said.

"Nor do I. Not yet. But I know what I'd like to do." He touched my arm, gently this time, and his voice fell to a whisper. "I wish she was dead."

He staggered on and I followed him. When we reached the Murthingtons', the usual miracle happened: suddenly we found ourselves capable of appearing sober, at least for short periods. Felicity was already in bed. Hugh and Lily were watching television. We went upstairs, played our guitars for half an hour and went to bed early.

Time passed. I heard Hugh and Lily coming up to bed. I wondered whether they would have sex. Slowly the house settled. The more I tried to sleep, the more awake I became. It was hot, which didn't help, and neither did the possibility that Lily was making love with her husband. I threw off first the blankets on my bed and then the top sheet.

As time went by I thought more and more about Carlo's threats against Lily. I wasn't sure how seriously to take them. Carlo had a tendency to go one step further than everyone else. I sometimes thought he wasn't quite sane. Nor was I, of course—not where Lily was concerned.

At a little after one o'clock I got out of bed. I stood by the window, to one side so I could see more of the garden. The moon had moved and, though it was so small, it cast a gray light over the trees, grass and flowerbeds and gave them a faintly luminescent quality, like pearls or wet shells. I pulled on a T-shirt and jeans, then checked that I still had tobacco and matches in my pocket. I picked up my sandals, tiptoed round the end of the bed and opened the door.

Houses at night are different from their daytime selves: their spaces fill with silences into which noises drop like stones in a pool. The air is cool and still. Houses at night become the homes of unfamiliar dreams. Maybe, I thought, I would meet someone else on Rhodes, someone who would take the place of Lily, someone who wouldn't hurt so much.

The landing window was uncurtained. There was enough light for me to pick out the head of the stairs. I moved slowly across the carpeted floor. I could have found my way in complete darkness. I knew the Murthingtons' house as well as I knew anywhere, certainly better than I knew any of my mother's homes. If I was careful I should make very little noise on the stairs, so long as I avoided the third step down and the second step from the bottom.

I took the precautions automatically. My mind was else-where, bouncing unsteadily on the turbulence of the last few days, perhaps helped by tiredness and the alcohol in my system. I padded down the hall and into the kitchen. I unbolted the back door and slipped outside. I did not put on my sandals until I was on the grass, which was already wet with dew. I walked across the lawn to the little summerhouse where I had first met Lily and Felicity. By the time I got there, my feet were cold and wet.

The summerhouse was a grand name for what was no more than a rectangular wooden platform, perhaps three yards wide and two yards deep, which formed the base for a three-sided shelter with a pitched roof. The fourth side was open and faced the lawn. I perched on the narrow bench that ran round the inside of the walls and began to roll a cigarette.

The cold and the dark made my fingers clumsy. I couldn't see what I was doing. More by luck than good judgement, I managed to create a misshapen cylinder. I was just about to light it when I heard the click of the back door.

I pushed myself back into the shadows, into the corner furthest from the moonlight. In front of the summerhouse, the lawn shimmered: it seemed to shift and move like mist. For the first time I noticed there were two lines of darker smudges on its surface—my footprints in the wet grass.

One moment the lawn was empty. The next moment she was there, moving slowly towards me, treading in my footprints. The light was so poor that at first the figure was little more than a blur. But I knew at once it was Lily. She came closer and closer. I held my breath. Suddenly a blinding light filled my eyes. My fist curled around the unsmoked cigarette. I wanted to run away.

"Jamie." Lily lowered the torch. "What are you doing out here?"

"I couldn't sleep."

"I thought you might be sleepwalking."

I shook my head, forgetting she couldn't see me in the darkness. "Sorry if I woke you."

"You didn't. It's too hot. I couldn't get to sleep."

"Nor me."

She stepped into the summerhouse. "It's cooler here. Were you coming out for a smoke?"

"I—well—"

"Oh, come on, Jamie." She giggled softly, a low, throaty sound that ran down my spine like a small nocturnal animal. "You and Carlo stink of tobacco. You're always nipping off for a smoke. You can hardly miss it."

For a moment neither of us moved or spoke. I wondered whether Lily would mention Felicity and the burn on her shirt. Instead she sighed.

"What is it?" I asked.

"I don't know. It's a bit chilly, isn't it?"

"There's the rug over there." In the darkness I waved towards a wicker basket that stood in the far corner. "You know, the picnic rug."

I wondered whether she really did know—whether she remembered. The picnic rug was made of heavy cotton with a red-and-white checked pattern. We had used it when we had the picnic at the falconry center the previous summer. The first time I had seen Lily properly, as opposed to Carlo's stepmother Mrs. Murthington, was when she was lying on that rug at the falconry center. I had thought she was asleep until she opened her eyes and caught me staring at her.

I opened the basket and pulled it out. It was heavier than I expected and slightly damp. I shook it out and draped it over Lily's shoulders. She stood there with her head bowed and her hands dangling at her sides, like a child allowing a parent to dress her. Our roles had mysteriously reversed. In the near-darkness of the night, she had become another person, someone smaller and more vulnerable than her daytime self.

"Why?" I asked.

"Why what?"

"Why haven't you been—why haven't you been talking to me this holiday?"

I was standing in front of her now, still holding the rug because otherwise it would have slid from her shoulders. I did not see her shrug but I felt it.

"Talking?" she said. "Is that what you call it?"

"It's not fair. I'm going mad."

"No, you're not, Jamie."

I brought my face close to hers. "Is there someone else? Is that what it is?"

She drew in her breath. "I'm cold, Jamie. Wrap me up."

Her arms glided round my waist. She drew me towards her. Her fingers dug into the small of my back and pulled apart, as though she were trying to tear the flesh from my spine, to fillet me like a kipper. Our mouths collided. I tasted blood. The rug fell to the ground. She was wearing a cotton nightdress. Her thin body rubbed and twisted against mine.

She pushed me into the back of the summerhouse, as far away as possible from the pale shadows on the lawn. Between us, somehow, we spread the rug, lay down and wrapped it over us. I pulled at the neck of the nightdress and heard the sound of tearing cloth. She fumbled at the waistband of my jeans.

I don't know how long we took. I remember crying out because Lily was holding me so tightly, and her hushing me by covering my mouth with the palm of her hand. I remember how the smell of her was unlike it usually was, because we were making love at night, whereas before we had always made love in the day when her face was made up and she wore perfume. I remember the hardness of the wooden floor, the way the rug rubbed like sandpaper against my skin and the desperate urgency of it all.

I was no longer cold. We pushed the rug aside. My clearest memory of all is of Lily on top of me, rearing up like a pale gray ghost in a pale gray world that was only one remove from darkness. For an instant I felt as though a winged beast had trapped me with her wings and I would never escape. Then she made a wordless sound, a groan wrenched from deep inside her, and her body crumpled.

Afterwards we dressed in silence. I didn't know what she was feeling or even whether I had satisfied her. She stepped down onto the lawn.

"Is that it?" I hissed.

She stopped. "I need to get back."

"But aren't we going to talk? Aren't we—"

"There isn't time." She was barely visible now, reduced to a shadow. "Wait five minutes and then go to bed."

"Do you do this often, then?" The words burst out of me before I knew they were in my mind. I hadn't realized I felt so abandoned, so angry.

"What do you mean?"

"All this." I waved my arm in a gesture I hoped embraced the summerhouse, the rug, the hardness of the floorboards and the ritual that had just absorbed us. "You know—having boyfriends. Making people fuck you."

"No," she said quietly. "No, you stupid boy. How can you be so stupid?"

18

WHEN THE MOBILE RANG I WAS ONLY FIVE MINUTES away from the M4 and driving too fast through the rain. I braked sharply and pulled into a lay-by. An articulated lorry swept past me, flashing its lights and sounding its horn in a long, sonorous reproof.

The other lorry, the road monster, sounded its horn on our way back from Rackford on the night of the fox, the night of the baby punk, and that was also the evening when Felicity cried, the only time I saw her cry.

I braked again, harder, and the Saab came to a stop, rocking on its suspension. The phone, still ringing, shot forward from the seat beside me onto the floor. I scrabbled among old newspapers and empty mineral-water bottles. It was still ringing when I found it.

"James?" Nicky said.

"What is it?"

"I've changed my mind."

"So we can meet?" I said. "You'll let me explain?"

"What?" Her voice was very far away. "What?"

"The line's breaking up." I opened the door and got out of the car. "Is that better?"

"A bit. I'm not making any promises, James. All I'm saying is that I'll come and talk to Kate. Then I'll probably fly down to Montpellier tomorrow. What's the address?"

"It's in Chipping Weston. I'll take you there."

"No. I want to drive myself."

I said, "I'm not exactly sure where Kate is."

"Really? That's very convenient. So maybe I should go with Jason and Charlie after all."

"No, don't—the odds are she'll be staying at her parents' house."

"Her parents?" Nicky said, with a hint of sarcasm.

"She wasn't there this morning," I rushed on. "Or if she was, she wasn't answering the phone. But it's the obvious place to start. She—she's probably left a note." I hardly knew what I was saying. I would have said anything to keep Nicky on the phone, to keep some sort of future for us, even if it only lasted a couple of hours.

"Anyway," Nicky said, "we're going in two cars."

"All right. We could meet at a service station and go on from there."

"What? Service station?"

"The line's breaking up again. Can I phone you back?"

"No—I'm at the cottage still. I'm using Charlie's line. The battery on my mobile's flat."

"Meet me at Membury services on the M4," I shouted, as though by raising my voice the quality of the connection between us would magically improve.

Nicky said something I couldn't hear and broke the connection. I stood in the rain staring at the phone, while the traffic streamed past me almost within touching distance, heading for the motorway. At least we were talking again. At the cottage, when I'd told her who Kate was, she had told me to leave. I tried to explain but she wouldn't listen. She'd walked out of the room, and a moment later Jason had ushered me off the premises.

When I reached the M4, I made myself take the slow lane and settled down behind a pair of caravans. There was no point in hurrying. If Nicky had phoned from the cottage, I would be at Membury long before her.

At the service station, I parked the car, left a note for Nicky on the windscreen and went inside the building. I bought an in-car charger for Nicky's phone, a sandwich and some coffee. It had stopped raining so I took my lunch outside. I stood by the main entrance and watched the cars drifting in and out of the parking area, and the people drifting in and out of the cars. Too much time went by—enough for another cup of coffee and a lot more worrying. When at last the Mini Cooper nosed into the car park, it was after three o'clock. I glimpsed Nicky, pale and ghostly, hunched over the wheel. She parked several ranks away from the Saab. I waited for her to get out but she stayed inside the car.

I walked towards her. When I reached the Mini, she was still sitting in the driver's seat. Her eyes were fixed on the car parked in front of hers. She had been expecting me to come to her, I thought, and she had no desire to meet me halfway. I stopped beside her window, which was open.

"I nearly didn't come," she said, without looking at me.

"I was beginning to think you wouldn't. I'm glad you did."

"You know what really scares me? That you're lying again. That this woman isn't your daughter after all."

I rested my hand on the sill of the window. "What I said at the cottage was the truth. But not the whole truth."

Nicky transferred her gaze from the windscreen and stared up at my face. She looked older than I'd ever seen her look before. Something turned inside me. I had made her look like that.

"You mean there's more?" she said. "Or just more lies?"

"Kate's half-brother is someone I was at school with. That's how I knew the family in the first place. Kate says he's trying to kill her."

"James, you can't seriously—"

"He's got a history of violence," I said. "Kate thinks he killed her ex-boyfriend. There's quite a lot of money at stake. And when I saw her on Monday her face was covered with scratches and bruises. He attacked her—that's what she said."

"For God's sake! Don't be such an innocent. If there was any truth in all that she'd go to the police."

"There's a reason she can't go to the police."

"I'm sure there is. The reason being she's telling a pack of lies."

"Kate says it looks as if she killed the boyfriend, not Carlo."

"Carlo," Nicky said, dangerously calm. "He's the brother?"

I nodded.

"Either you're lying or she's taking you for a ride."

"I'm not lying. Nicky, there's one more thing."

"Just the one?"

I ignored the sarcasm in her voice. "It's the only other thing that's important now. Kate's pregnant."

There was a silence. Nicky lowered her head. She said something but I couldn't make it out. I asked her to repeat it.

She fiddled with the neck of her shirt. "I said, that's all I needed. Are you sure that wasn't a lie too?"

I hesitated. "She's about five months gone. So it's showing."

"Well—either you take me to see this woman right now or I'm going to Montpellier on the next flight I can find. What's it to be?"

"Shall we drive in convoy?" I said.

"OK."

"This is for you." I passed the phone charger through the window. "I don't want to lose touch."

She tore at the packaging. "That may not be up to you." She hesitated and, at last, raised her head. "You know, James, even if all this is true, all this nonsense, I don't understand why you've got involved. It really doesn't make sense. This woman you used to know phones you up out of the blue. OK, she's dying, and maybe you've got some sort of sentimental attachment to her. But that doesn't explain it, does it? Why you're acting like this—it's just not like you."

"I—I suppose the fact that Kate's pregnant—"

"That's unkind, and you know it. And it's not the truth, either." Then she raised her voice and mimicked me: "'Or if it is the truth, it's not the whole truth.'"

She was right. I said nothing. Then, right on cue, it started to rain again, more heavily than before. Within thirty seconds my hair was running with water and the shoulders of my jacket were dark and wet.

"We'll finish this later," Nicky said. "You're getting soaked."

"But you'll come?"

"Yes. But for God's sake, go and find your car."

Pursued by the rain, we drove north through the afternoon. On the road I phoned Kate's mobile twice but there was no answer. I wasn't sure whether to be glad or sorry. At least, I thought, even if Kate isn't there I can show Nicky the house. Words are treacherous, slippery things. But you can't argue with a house. You can't misinterpret something made of bricks and mortar and slates. The house might not prove the truth of what I had claimed but at least it would be a form of independent testimony.

We reached the A40 and joined a line of lorries moving sedately westwards. I kept glancing in the rearview mirror to make sure that Nicky was still there. I was gambling my future with her. I had no way of knowing whether I would be successful. More than that, I had no way of knowing what constituted success. Not now—because the rules had changed. The one thing I did know was the nature of failure: if I lost the gamble, then I would lose Nicky.

By the time we got there, Chipping Weston was crowded with cars and people going home. We turned into the Murthingtons' road. At the house, I pulled into the driveway and Nicky parked on the road. The landing window was open. I got out of the car and checked the birdbath where the spare key was kept. It wasn't there. I went into the porch and rang the bell.

Nicky came to stand beside me in the porch. "No one in?" She said it in such a way that suggested she hadn't expected there would be. "So what do we do now?"

I rang the bell again and didn't reply. We listened to the silence. After a moment, she touched my arm but there was no need because I had heard it too—footsteps on the other side of the door. Nicky drew a slow, deep breath.

Then came another sound, quieter than the first. Somewhere in the house a child was crying.

· · ·

I hate it when children cry. I saw Felicity crying only once. It was in the evening, a few days before Carlo was due to take his test. By that time, of course, she was hardly a child but she still cried like one, letting the emotions run unchecked through her and making no attempt to wipe her eyes. She even stamped her foot.

It was a Friday and the three of us were alone in the house. Millie's parents had taken Hugh and Lily to Cheltenham to see a play at the Everyman Theatre, and afterwards they were going out to supper. We had already eaten our meal and were sitting in front of the television.

As usual I was thinking of Lily. We had made love twice more since the time in the summerhouse. On one occasion we had done it during the day, writhing and panting on the sitting room carpet while Hugh was at work and Felicity and Carlo were visiting a friend of their mother's—their real mother. On another, when Hugh was spending the night in London, she had come to my room in the early hours and woken me.

"Wake up," Carlo said. "Let's go for a drive."

I blinked. "Now?"

"Why not? We'll drive out to Rackford."

"You want to go to the airfield?"

"Don't be stupid—it's Friday night. Party time. We'll go to the Eagle and have a drink."

"We could go for a drink in town instead. Then we could walk."

"I want to go to Rackford."

"But you haven't passed your test. You wouldn't be insured."

"You sound like my dad," Carlo said, with a grin that wasn't entirely friendly. "No—you sound more like Lily."

"Black Maria, you mean," Felicity said. "Yes, let's go to the Eagle."

Carlo turned to her. "I wasn't talking to you."

"But I want to come."

"You can't. Anyway, they wouldn't let you in. You're too young."

"I could sit in the car. And you could bring me a drink and some crisps. Please, Carlo."

He shook his head.

"I'm not sure this is a good idea," I said. "What happens if the cops stop you?"

"They won't. They're not going to stop me unless I'm driving dangerously."

"Or if you have an accident."

"Are you saying I'm not a safe driver?"

"No. I'm just saying—"

"You're chicken," Carlo interrupted.

"I'm not. I'm—"

"Prove it."

We stared at each other. I sensed that something more was at stake than whether we drove to the Eagle and had a drink. I couldn't put it into words then but I can now. Carlo was testing my loyalty as well as my courage. Also, he wanted to shock me and perhaps Felicity as well. The ability to shock people is, after all, a way of exercising power over them.

"Please," Felicity pleaded. "I'll do the washing-up when it's your turn."

Carlo didn't look at her. "No." He hit my arm with his open hand, and the blow was a little too hard to have been merely playful. "Well? Are you on?"

"If you don't take me, I'll tell," Felicity said.

Carlo towered over his sister. "If you tell anyone we've taken the car—*anyone*—I'll never talk to you again. Got it?"

The brother and sister stared at each other. Felicity's mouth opened. Her face crumpled, as though the bones had turned to jelly. That was when she started to cry. Carlo watched her for a moment. He made no move to comfort her and neither did I.

He turned back to me. "Are you coming?"

Felicity stamped her foot. "It's not fair!"

Carlo ignored her. He raised his chin and stared down his nose at me. "Well?"

"What the hell? All right."

Felicity shrieked, "I hate you. I hate you both." She ran out of the room. We listened to her feet pounding up the stairs. Her bedroom door slammed.

"Women." Carlo grinned at me as though we were the best of friends again. "Christ. They're all the same."

"Shouldn't you go up? See if she's all right?"

"No point. She'd just start yelling again. We'll let her cool down in her own time." He tapped my arm again but this time his touch was gentle. "Come on. I'll buy you a drink."

It was a fine evening, and to the west the sky was streaked with red. Carlo drove to Rackford with great care. We didn't speak. When we reached the village, he didn't turn into the pub car park but left the Rover on the street.

"Don't want to get boxed in," he said, elaborately casual.

I knew that really he was doubtful of his ability to maneuver the car in tight spaces. I followed him into the Eagle. The place was heaving with people, most of them young. It took us some time to reach the bar. We ordered Carlsberg Special Brews and drank them in a corner by the fruit machine.

There was too much noise for us to be able to talk easily and perhaps we hadn't much to say to each other. Instead we smoked furiously, sipped our beer and eyed the girls. In one corner of the bar it was somebody's birthday party.

"Christ," Carlo shouted in my ear. "I wouldn't mind a bit of that one."

"Which one?" I shouted back.

He nodded towards the birthday corner. "The baby punk with big tits."

Baby punks were what we called people who played at being punks, the ones who kept the spikes and chains and safety-pins for weekends, and who scrubbed themselves up and smoothed themselves down for schools or offices on Monday morning. The girl in question was probably fifteen or sixteen. She wore a frayed denim skirt, a torn T-shirt and a leather jacket festooned with chains. She had a pink, plump face and someone had sprayed golden glitter over her hair. I didn't fancy her, but she had indisputably large breasts. The leather jacket was so skimpy that it enhanced rather than concealed them.

Carlo's lips moved. I couldn't hear him but I knew what he was saying: *She isn't wearing a bra.*

He was right about that too. I bought another round. The noise, the smoke and the alcohol were making me dizzy. Carlo kept glancing at his watch in the intervals between staring hungrily at the baby punk. I was only halfway through my second bottle when he suggested it was time for us to go.

I finished the lager and followed Carlo towards the door. As we threaded our way through the crowd we came close to the birthday corner. Carlo leered at the baby punk. She ignored him. But she looked up at me over the rim of her glass and smiled. Despite the breasts, she wasn't much taller than Felicity. The glitter on her hair and shoulders looked like golden dandruff.

Carlo and I came out into the yard at the back of the pub. By now it was twilight and the air was cool. The noise and light of the pub receded. The yard was full of parked cars and shadows.

"I need a pee," I said, and sheered away to the gents', which had a separate entrance from the bars. No one else was in there, which was a relief, because I had drunk the lager too quickly and thought I might be sick. I waited, swaying, for several minutes, willing the nausea to pass.

I heard a faint scream, swiftly muffled.

I staggered outside. For an instant I thought the sound must have come from someone in the bar. But I heard movement beyond the toilets, on the far side of the yard where the shadows clustered most thickly. "Hey?" I called. "Where are you?"

There was no answer, but the movements continued and I thought they sounded urgent and violent. *Someone's beating up Carlo.* I ran across the yard. There wasn't much light but there was enough for me to see Carlo pushing someone against the wall. He was grunting and snarling—but quietly, which somehow made it worse. I heard the chink of metal on stone, and suddenly I knew exactly what was happening, and to whom.

"Stop it! For Christ's sake!" I grabbed Carlo's shoulders and pulled him away. He resisted for an instant, then went slack. The baby punk was pressed against the wall. Her skirt was round her thighs and her breasts, no longer covered by the T-shirt, poked out like a pair of pale bombs.

"Quick, come on." I broke into a run, pulling Carlo after me. I expected the baby punk to scream. But she didn't. She started crying instead.

I had to remind him to put on the lights. He wasn't used to driving in darkness; and twilight, with its treacherous, shifting shapes, was even worse. We left the village and drove fast along the narrow, winding road that ran round the western boundary of the airfield. The other road was faster, but that would have meant turning the car round. There hadn't been time for that.

"Fucking cock-teaser," he said. He was panting like a thirsty dog.

"What happened?"

"She came out after me. She was asking for it. Then she pretended she didn't want it." Carlo glanced at me. "Sometimes they do that. They like you to be rough."

"Slow down," I said, fumbling to fasten my seat belt.

Carlo accelerated. The Rover plunged onwards. "It'll be dark by the time we get back," he said.

"I hope Felicity's OK."

"Of course she bloody is. You didn't mention my name, did you?"

"In the pub? I don't think so."

"Then we're OK. That stupid girl can't do anything."

"Do me a favor," I said. "Just think about driving."

Carlo was hunched over the wheel. I hoped he was right about the baby punk. We came round a shallow left-hand bend on the wrong side of the road. A fox was standing in the middle of the lane directly in our path.

"Fuck," muttered Carlo, and swerved.

For an instant I saw the fox clearly in the headlights, which were on full beam. For no good reason, I automatically assumed it was the one we had seen at Rackford earlier in the summer. Its eyes blazed, reflecting the headlights. Still looking at us, it started to run, moving towards the airfield's perimeter fence.

The car lurched onto the narrow verge. The driver's side scraped along the hedge. But Carlo was going too fast and the fox was running too slowly. There was a jolt as the nearside front wheel went over it.

"Oh, Christ," Carlo said. "Oh, shit."

I turned in my seat. The headlights had dazzled me. I wasn't sure whether I saw or imagined a small patch of darkness on the roadway behind us. It was only a glimpse. Almost at once we were careening round a right-hand bend, and Carlo was fighting for control of the car. Afterwards the lane straightened. He cut the speed to less than thirty m.p.h. We passed the side entrance to the airfield.

"Bloody thing," he said. "Nothing I could do. Shit. Stupid animal."

"Maybe it's OK. Just a bump."

He didn't reply. Neither of us suggested that we should go back to see if the fox was alive. I thought that if it wasn't dead it was dying. I thought about how quickly it had happened, how quickly the ginger fur, the flesh, blood and muscle, the blazing eyes and the fluid movements had been converted to a ragged smudge of shadow on the Tarmac. I wanted to be back inside the Murthingtons' house with the car parked blamelessly outside.

Carlo was having trouble managing the headlights. Several cars flashed us and one lorry honked its horn, a long, deep, booming sound like an outraged sea monster. By the time we turned into the Murthingtons' driveway, my back was sticky with sweat. But at least I was no longer feeling sick.

Carlo turned off the lights and switched off the engine. "There," he said, and his voice trembled slightly. "Safe and sound. Told you it wouldn't be a problem."

We got out of the car. I wondered whether there was blood on the bumper or the wheel arch but I didn't want to look. Carlo glanced at the side of the house. All the upstairs windows were in darkness. "Felicity's asleep."

"Maybe you should go up and check," I suggested.

He unlocked the door. "Or maybe you should," he said over his shoulder. "She likes you."

I followed him into the house. "You go. You're her brother."

He stopped in the hall and stared into my face. He smiled, as though what he saw there was a source of amusement. There were flecks of golden glitter on the shoulder of his shirt.

"OK," he said. "But it's been quite an evening. Let's celebrate. Why don't you get some glasses and some ice? I fancy a vodka."

When he came down, we took the drinks out into the garden so we could smoke.

"Was she asleep?" I asked.

"Yeah."

"She got really worked up." I wasn't sure which girl I meant, Felicity or the baby punk, or perhaps both.

"Women. She'll be fine in the morning. You'll see." He took a swallow of his drink, and suddenly his mood changed. "She's been acting really weird lately. Have you noticed?"

I turned my head so he couldn't see my face, which was ridiculous because it was too dark to see it properly in any case. "What do you mean?"

"Always uptight about something. Did you hear her yelling at Lily the other day? I mean, that's understandable, everyone should shout at Black Maria, but Felicity went way over the top."

"She's growing up," I said.

"She's just a kid."

I let a silence grow between us. Felicity was using makeup more often, especially when she was with Millie. She had started wearing a bra since the Easter holidays.

"Shit," Carlo said. "Everything's changing. Dad's looking about sixty-four. Felicity's acting like a keg of dynamite. Lily's even more of a bitch than usual." He hesitated, then said, in a lower voice that seemed not to have quite as much breath behind it as it needed, "Even you're different."

I turned so I could see the glow of his cigarette, his dark profile and the gleam of his glass. "Everything's the same as it always was."

"I don't know." He sounded almost ashamed of himself, which was not an emotion I associated with Carlo. "You just seem—not like you were before. It's not Lily, is it?"

"Lily? Of course not. Why should it be?"

"No reason." The cigarette tip burned brightly and I saw his face, intent and red as the devil's. "I just thought maybe you liked her."

I crossed my fingers behind my back. "She's a cow. Black Maria. The queen of the bitches."

Carlo was standing so close I felt his breath on my cheek. "Just wait till we get to Rhodes, eh? All those chicks. It's going to be great."

"Yeah, it's going to be great," I echoed, and thought of Lily splayed out before me, but then the picture was spoiled because she turned into the baby punk against the wall.

"So, things are OK?"

He was making me uncomfortable. "Sure they are—of course." I saw lights moving along the hedge that bordered the road. "Look out, I think that's your parents."

We flicked the cigarettes into the darkness and carried our glasses into the kitchen. We finished what was left in them and rinsed them in the sink. I heard footsteps in the hall.

"Nothing's changed," Carlo said under his breath, as though trying to convince himself. "Nothing's changed at all."

But Carlo was wrong. More than one thing changed that night.

At about two o'clock in the morning, Lily scratched like a cat on my door. I hadn't expected her because Hugh wasn't away. We went into the moonlit garden and across the lawn to the summerhouse. For the first time I couldn't do anything. My body, the one thing I thought I could rely on, betrayed me.

"It doesn't matter," Lily whispered. "It really doesn't matter."

I heard her speaking but I listened only to the silence around the words. She held me in her arms and stroked me but still nothing happened. I was helpless again, reduced to childhood.

"You're just tired, Jamie," she said. "It doesn't matter."

But of course my failure mattered. So did the baby punk up against the wall and the fox in the lane. So did Felicity crying. Everything mattered.

"Don't worry," Lily said, easing herself away from me and standing up. "It happens. Next time it'll be fine. I'm going back to bed. Give me five minutes, OK?"

I didn't reply. She loomed over me, dark against the gray of the sky, and the world was silent and full of misery. She sighed and walked quickly across the grass to the house. I waited for as long as I could. At last, when I could bear the cold no longer, I went back into the house and climbed the stairs.

On the landing, I thought of Lily and Hugh, side by side, perhaps touching each other, within a few feet of me. A sour rage washed over me. I wished they were dead, like the fox. I was about to slip into my room when I heard a sound, the sort of click the lock of a door makes when it closes. It came from the back of the house—the bathroom, perhaps, or Felicity's room.

Yes, Carlo was wrong. Something changed that night and nothing was ever the same again.

19

T HE MURTHINGTONS' HOUSE HADN'T CHANGED MUCH in twenty-five years, apart from growing older and dirtier and more crowded. But there was one innovation I hadn't noticed on my last visit: the fish-eye lens of a spy-hole set in the door. Someone was looking at us. I heard bolts rattle. The door opened a couple of inches, then stopped. It was on the chain. The child's crying increased in volume. A face appeared.

"Hi," Emily said. "I can't remember your name."

"James."

"I'm still looking for Sean. You haven't seen him, have you?"

"No. May we come in?"

"Who's this?"

"My wife. Nicky, this is Emily."

The crying stopped as the distant child began to shriek instead. "Mummy! Carry me!"

The door closed. I waited for the bolts to shoot home. Instead there came the rattle of a chain.

"Who's Emily?" Nicky hissed. "Another of your young women?"

The door opened again. Emily was lopsided because she was carrying Albert on her left hip. He was holding her hair, and in his other hand was a wooden spoon, which he was waving to and fro very slowly and regularly like a metronome.

"Do you at least know where Kate is?" she said, in a voice that wobbled.

"No, I don't. May we come in?"

Emily nodded listlessly and stood back. She was wearing blue dungarees and a torn T-shirt. She hadn't brushed her hair recently and her complexion had the pale, slightly grubby quality that faces acquire when their owners spend too much time indoors eating the wrong sort of food and thinking the wrong sort of thoughts.

"I'm looking for Kate too," I said. "How did you get in?"

"I broke a window at the back." She glared at me, challenging me to object. "We found some food. And chocolate biscuits. You liked those, Albert, didn't you?"

"Tick," said the little boy. "Tock."

"I *need* to find Sean," Emily said loudly, as though explaining something so obvious it shouldn't need to be spelled out. "The car broke down and I haven't any money. I had to go somewhere."

As she was speaking, she turned away and began to walk down the hall to the kitchen. We followed. By the time we got there the crying had stopped. Maisie had emptied out what looked like an entire packet of cornflakes onto the kitchen table. Some had fallen onto the floor. She was cramming them into her mouth with both hands.

"Oh, Maisie," her mother said.

The child continued eating.

"Will you please tell me what's going on?" Nicky murmured to me.

But Emily had heard. "You don't know either? Nor do I."

"Then why are you here?" Nicky said, in a voice so gentle it made the question inoffensive.

"Because this is where Kate Murthington lives." Emily looked at me. "Have you told her?"

"Not about you."

"She broke up my marriage," Emily said to Nicky. "I'm trying to find my husband and remind him he's still got some responsibility to our children. And to me, if it comes to that."

"She's still living here?" I asked. "You've seen her recently?"

"She was here on Monday. She tried to scratch my eyes out. Her things are upstairs so I presume she's still living here."

"Kate attacked *you*?" I said.

"Yes—on Monday. She's *vicious*," Emily added, as though stating an inalienable truth to one of her children.

I remembered the scratches and the bruise on Kate's face. Kate had told me that Carlo had attacked her—but had it been Emily? And who had attacked whom?

"I thought I saw you on Monday," I said. "At the supermarket on the other side of town."

She nodded. "We stopped on the way home."

"What happened to your car?"

"I don't know. It's completely buggered, I can tell you that. It's in a car park off the high street. We drove over from Bedford this morning, and I stopped there to get us a drink. But when I tried to start the car again, it made this horrible noise and smoke started coming out of the engine. So we walked here. No one answered the door and—Maisie, stop doing that." Emily swooped on her daughter and lifted her away from the table. She began to heap the remaining cereal into a pile. Meanwhile the cornflakes on the floor crunched beneath her feet. "Oh, God," she said. "Kids make such a mess. You can't leave them alone for a minute."

"Let me help," Nicky said. From somewhere she found a dustpan and brush and began to sweep up the cereal.

One of the panes of the kitchen window was broken and there were shards of glass still in the sink. I cleared them away and cut a piece of cardboard to make a temporary cover for the broken pane. I pulled out the overflowing pedal bin that festered under the sink and took it outside to empty into the dustbin, which was also overflowing.

Five minutes later, a degree of order had been restored. Nicky put the kettle on and we sat round the table. If any of us thought it strange to be doing this in somebody else's house, none of us said so. Albert sat on his mother's knee and continued to murmur, "Tick, tock," but more quietly than before. Maisie practiced writing on the back of an envelope she had found on the worktop. She wouldn't look at us. She was pretending we didn't exist.

"What are you going to do?" I asked Emily.

"Wait for Sean. I know he's been here. And he must be coming back."

"What makes you say that?"

"Because his jacket's over there." She looked towards the corner by the door, where there was a chair against the wall. A blue waxed jacket was draped over the back. Her face crumpled. "We both got one—we bought them in Cambridge. I was pregnant with Maisie. And I know it's his because of the tear in the left sleeve. He did that when he was pruning one of the apple trees at the farm."

I picked up the jacket. It was definitely the flyweight Barbour Kate had been wearing when I first met her; I recognized the tear in the sleeve and the smudge of paint on the left shoulder.

"So I knew he must be here," Emily said. "That's why I broke in. And I was right."

I glanced back to her. "How do you mean?"

She delved into the bib of her dungarees and pulled out three scraps of paper, which she put on the table, slapping them down one by one, as though showing her cards in a game of poker. "These were in the pockets."

They were slips from automated teller machines. On Sunday, someone had drawn two hundred pounds out of Lloyds TSB's Chipping Weston branch. The second withdrawal, also for two hundred, had taken place yesterday at a cash machine in Paddington. The third, for a hundred and again at Chipping Weston, had taken place this morning. There was now £39.53 left in the account.

"See?" Emily tapped the table with her fingertip. "That proves it. And he told me he was broke. I mean, Christ, we could live for weeks on five hundred quid."

"So it's definitely his account?" Nicky said.

Emily nodded. "I'm staying here till he comes back."

"And if he doesn't?"

"I'll wait till he does. We'll camp outside on the pavement if we have to."

"Poo," Albert said. "Tick, tock. Poo."

Emily peered down the back of her son's waistband and glanced at Nicky. "I'll take him up to the bathroom. It's a bit messy."

Maisie abandoned her drawing and clung to the leg of her mother's dungarees.

"Is there anything we can do?" Nicky asked.

Emily shook her head. "Albert's very unsettled, aren't you, darling? It's all the stress. He's forgotten everything he ever knew about toilet training."

She left the room with Albert in her arms and Maisie, still attached to the dungarees, trailing after her. Nicky and I listened to their dragging footsteps on the stairs.

"There's a lot you haven't told me," Nicky said. "Too much."

"There hasn't been time."

She looked at me, her face unsmiling. "So, is the husband alive?"

I shrugged. "Sean's jacket doesn't prove anything. Kate was wearing it when I first met her."

"And Sean's the ex-boyfriend? The one the brother's meant to have killed? But if Emily's right, it looks as if he's been here. And it also looks as if your precious Kate has been telling you a lot of lies."

"Not necessarily. It's—"

"You're not trying to tell me Kate was attacked by both Emily and Carlo, are you? Though from what I'm hearing it's more than likely that Kate was the one who did the attacking."

"I don't know what to believe."

Nicky got up. To my surprise she stretched out her hand and touched my shoulder. "You look bloody awful, too. I don't know what Kate's up to, or what you're doing with her, but I do know that it's not agreeing with you."

"I've told you the truth," I said. "I can't do anything else."

"You can show me the house."

"What?"

"Show me the house," she repeated. "It doesn't matter if Kate walks in—you're her father, aren't you?"

The question had a mocking edge. It didn't need an answer. I opened the door to the hall.

Nicky paused in the doorway. "Are you really telling me the truth?"

"As far as I know it myself."

She grimaced. "You should have been a lawyer."

We walked slowly through the crowded, dust-laden rooms. Nicky stared without comment at all the possessions that were no longer worth possessing. She looked out of place, a stranger in a country with inexplicable rituals and a lower standard of living than her own. The last room on the ground floor was Hugh's study. Nicky glanced at the photograph of Felicity but she didn't ask who the girl was. She picked up the card with the hospice's address and flicked it between her fingers.

"All in all, your Kate doesn't seem much of a victim to me," she said. "More of a hellcat."

"It's complicated."

"I'm worried about Emily and those poor children."

"Emily's not much more than a child herself."

Nicky nodded.

I smiled at her. "So we can agree about that, in any case."

She didn't return the smile. "I don't think you should leave her here."

"I don't think we've got much choice."

"But Kate's already attacked her once. And you say that brother of hers is violent. Do you think it's true what Emily said, about having no money?"

"I only met her on Sunday, at Sean's house in St. Albans. She says they used to be quite well off. Then Sean started having the affair with Kate and a little later he was sacked. I don't think either of them has much money now. Emily thought he'd come back for his passport. She couldn't find his bank stuff either. So the implication is that either he decided to disappear or someone wanted to make it look as if he had." I shrugged. "But it's their lives. It's you I—"

"But it's not just them, is it?" Nicky interrupted. "It's the kids."

"What do you think we should do?"

She said nothing for a moment. Then: "It's your problem."

"It's a mess." I waited.

"You can't just leave them here. Not the children. We could contact social services."

"Once they get involved, God knows what would happen. They'd probably notify the police, for a start."

"So it's back to you."

"What are you suggesting? That we take them home with us?"

She shied away from that idea. "No, I was thinking—perhaps a hotel. Just for a night, so the kids can calm down and everyone can take stock. Have you got a better idea?"

I stared at her, wondering whether I should take her words at face value or treat them as ironic. But Nicky was always serious about children.

"There's a place called the Newnham House Hotel on the London road," I said slowly. "We used to go there for coffee."

"You and Lily?"

"No. I went with Carlo." I didn't mention Felicity. "The thing is, will Emily agree?"

Nicky nodded. "Leave her to me."

"Thank you," I said.

She was already in the doorway. "I'm not doing this for you. It's for the children's sake."

"I know," I said, and I heard the bitterness in my voice. "I know."

By the time I had left the others at the Newnham House Hotel, the rain had petered out and the sky was a fresh, clean blue with wispy streaks of red cloud in the west. It was one of those clear, bright May evenings that seem to go on forever.

Nicky and Emily were putting the children to bed. We had taken a family room for Emily and the children and a double for Nicky and me. I drove up to the main road, then north, following the familiar route to Rackford. At the entrance to the airfield I slowed, but at the last moment I couldn't face it. I went on to the village and parked outside the Eagle.

Before I left the car, I called the hospice and asked how Lily was. No change, they told me. She had spent most of the day asleep. No one had come to see her.

Suddenly I was ravenously hungry. I went into the bar. The place was much less crowded than it had been on my previous visit. I ordered a chicken salad and a glass of red wine from a well-maintained blonde with faded, puzzled eyes. While I waited for the food to come I nursed the wine at a table in the corner of the room—the corner where the baby punk had sat with the birthday party.

Three indeterminately middle-aged men were celebrating the end of the working day near the window. A young couple talked in an undertone, their heads almost touching, at a table next to mine. At the bar, two elderly men were sipping whisky. They wore well-cut tweed jackets and neatly pressed corduroy trousers; they had unlined pink faces and scanty but neatly trimmed hair—they might have been brothers. Everything was ordinary. No one was talking about a murder.

The food came. The chicken was leathery and tasteless. I ordered another glass of wine to go with it.

"House prices," said one of the old men at the bar. "That's the big unknown."

"It's the traffic that's the problem," the other replied. "The village is crowded enough as it is. More houses mean more cars."

"It's not just a matter of houses. If the golf course goes through, every Tom, Dick and Harry for miles around will be coming here. More traffic. They'll all be in a hurry. You mark my words, there'll be accidents."

"The golf course, though." The other man drained his glass and slid cautiously off the stool, holding on to the bar for balance. "That can't be bad, not for house prices. It'll add a few thousand on."

The two walked out unsteadily. A little later, I said to the woman behind the bar, "So, you're getting a golf course?"

She wrinkled her forehead. "There's talk of it. New houses, too."

"Where are they going to go? I wouldn't have thought there was much room in the village."

She jerked her thumb in the direction the old men had taken. "Over the hill. There's an old airfield up there."

"Have they got planning permission?"

"Not yet. Haven't even applied. But they'll probably get it if they do." She laughed, automatically cynical. "Sooner or later. If they grease the right palms."

"Good for trade if it goes through."

She smiled at me and leaned forward across the bar top, resting her elbows on the counter. "So long as they're nice houses. We don't want any riffraff here. This is a nice village."

I smiled warily back. "I'm sure it is."

"I've seen you before, haven't I? Weren't you in a few days ago?"

I nodded.

"On holiday, are you?"

"Not exactly."

"On business, then."

"Family business." I finished my drink and stood up, abandoning the salad. "What do I owe you?"

For an instant, the woman looked surprised, as if I'd failed to live up to expectations. I paid the bill and left. I had been a fool to go back to the Eagle, I decided, and a fool to strike up a conversation with a woman who remembered me from my last visit. When I drove away, I turned left out of the village rather than right, so I wouldn't pass in front of the window of the bar and risk the woman seeing the car.

But turning left brought me back to the airfield, and this time I was approaching it on its western side. For the first time in twenty-five years I drove along the lane where Carlo had killed the fox. It still zigzagged, a left-hand bend and a right-hand bend. The fox had died between the bends. I accelerated hard into the second bend and the nearside of the car scraped the hedge. I felt the prickle of sweat along my hairline and in the small of the back.

I've done it. I've done it.

The hedges were higher on the right, and on the left, where the airfield was, the tangle of vegetation that sloped down to the stream had grown into a small forest. The lane had been resurfaced, and the fresh Tarmac overlaid the memory of blood. The side entrance, the one we used if we were going directly from the airfield to the village, was blocked with coils of rusting barbed wire. A buzzard hung in mid-air, wings outstretched, floating in defiance of gravity.

I skirted the boundary of the airfield and worked my way round to the main entrance on the eastern side. A clump of brambles masked the location of the guardpost. I pulled over onto the concrete apron. Further in there was a gate, new since my last visit, which was standing open. Without giving myself time to think about it, I let out the clutch. The car crawled through the gateway, jolting in and out of potholes.

The surface of the perimeter road had deteriorated and most of the runways had vanished beneath the spreading tide of green and brown. The buildings were still there, but at some point the control tower had caught fire and only blackened wall remained. The surrounding land had been sown with what looked like cereal crops.

I parked beside the tower and got out of the car. It was very quiet—apart from the ticking of the Saab's cooling engine, the only sound was the distant murmur of traffic on the main road. I walked from one building to the next. All the doors had gone and I didn't see an unbroken window. In the Nissen hut where Lily and I had once made love, the metal table was still there, coated with rust. The calendar for

1954 had disappeared. I remembered how Lily had walked in front of me into the hut that afternoon, and how her hips swayed under her dress; and I remembered what we had done inside. But it no longer seemed very important. Revisiting the past diminished it.

Revisiting the past . . .

I went back to the Saab and drove round the perimeter road to the western side of the airfield, to the patch of woodland that sloped down to the stream and then up to the boundary fence along the lane. I left the car on the disused access road leading to the blocked side entrance. The path to the stream was still there, though narrower and less clearly defined than before. I followed it downhill.

In the little valley at the bottom, the stream was shaded oppressively by the bushes and trees on either side. I struggled along the bank to where Felicity had shown me the stone arch. I knew exactly what it was now—a primitive kiln, probably late-eighteenth or early-nineteenth century, where they would have made quicklime.

Revisiting the past . . .

But the past was no longer there. A pile of masonry marked the site of the kiln. Saplings and bramble shoots sprouted among the stones. In front of the ruin, the ground was relatively clear beneath the overhanging branches on either side. There was a cider can and a crisp packet, so old that the weather had bleached away the colors and made them ghostly. Someone else had been here more recently, perhaps several people—the ground underneath the archway and just in front of it was muddy, churned up by the movement of feet. There was nothing as straightforward as a footprint. I saw no sign of Sean.

Slowly my eyes adjusted to the green gloom under the trees. I scrambled higher up the slope and found another heap of stones, probably the remains of the second kiln, which Felicity had mentioned but I had never seen. On my way back, a speck of white caught my eye. It was the remains of a cigarette caught in the angle between two of the fallen stones. I stooped and picked it up. Just above the filter was the word Marlboro.

Kate smoked Marlboro Light. So did a lot of people. But, unlike the can, the butt had not been here long. I dropped it on the ground and wiped my fingers on my trousers.

I walked back to the stream. I felt an unexpected and perhaps undeserved sense of achievement. I hadn't found Sean and I hadn't found Kate. On the other hand, it was a relief not to have stumbled over Sean's corpse. I had confirmed Kate's story that a developer was interested in the airfield and discovered a possible trace of her at the kiln. Also, perhaps most importantly, I had driven down the lane where Carlo had killed the fox and I had come back to the airfield, back to the stream and the kiln. I couldn't wipe out the past—I couldn't rewrite the memories and reroute the chain of cause and effect. But something had changed. Kate had done me a favor without intending it. There was nothing to be frightened of anymore. The past was over. Maybe, I thought, maybe one day I can tell Nicky what happened. Maybe.

I followed the bank of the stream to the point where the path climbed up towards the perimeter road. The sun was low in the sky and some of its rays had found their way through gaps in the foliage. Bars of gold slanted across the stream where it curved into a bend. I glanced across, following the light to the opposite bank. I saw the spot where Carlo and I had helped Felicity build her den in that strange time when she was neither child nor teenager. Nothing remained of the den now and the ledge on which it stood had either been eroded or buried since I had last seen it. But there, outlined in the shaft of sunshine, was a square of cherry red, as vivid as blood against the browns and greens surrounding it.

On the other side of the stream, no more than five meters away from me, was what looked for all the world like a small red handbag—a simple rectangular shape with two loop handles. One loop had caught the end of a branch. The bag dangled above the water, close to the opposite bank.

In that instant, the bar of sunlight shifted. Where the handbag had been there was only a patch of shadow.

20

AT THE NEWNHAM HOUSE HOTEL, THE FIRST PERSON I recognized was Carlo. The second was Nicky. They were sitting opposite each other in the bar that opened out of the reception area and drinking white wine. Nicky was laughing at something Carlo had said.

She was laughing because she was really amused, not because she was trying to be polite or because she couldn't think of any other response. Carlo looked relaxed too, and he was smiling. There seemed nothing left of the hard, dour man who had broken the raku bowl in the sitting room of our house in Greyfont. Instead I glimpsed someone who had once been my friend.

Slipping the red handbag under my jacket, I made a U-turn and headed for the door. I went back to the car park, where I locked the bag into the boot of the Saab. When I returned to the bar Nicky and Carlo were still where I had left them, and she was still laughing. I walked towards them. At almost the same moment, they looked up. I watched their faces change. Carlo pushed back his chair and stood up, holding out a hand. I shook it. He had an uncomfortably firm grip.

"Nice to see you," he said, with an affability wholly at odds with his behavior at our last meeting.

"I was about to phone you," Nicky said.

I looked at Carlo. "How did you find out we were here?"

"The neighbor saw you and your car. He mentioned a Saab. It wasn't hard to put two and two together."

I knew, without quite knowing how, that he was lying. "But how did you find us here—at the hotel?"

He glanced at Nicky and smiled, inviting her to share his amusement at my skepticism.

"Emily," Nicky explained. "The neighbor heard her saying something to the children as we were leaving. He was in his garden on the other side of the hedge. Something about a hotel, and that it wasn't far."

"So I thought I'd ring round on the off-chance," Carlo said, signalling to the barman for another glass. "Might have known you'd try the Newnham House."

"Where's Emily?" I said.

"Upstairs with the children. She and Albert are a bit under the weather."

The barman brought me a glass. An uneasy silence settled over the table. The three of us hadn't any small talk. The strangest of strangers are those you once knew well.

Carlo cleared his throat. "I was saying to Nicky—I've come to apologize."

"What I really find amazing is that you haven't mentioned him until today," she said to me.

"You came to apologize," I said to him, my voice sounding harsh in my ears. "What for?"

"For barging in on you the other day. I was under a lot of strain." He turned up the palms of his hands and studied them. "I'm afraid I wasn't very diplomatic."

I thought of the raku bowl and nodded.

"I also wanted to say sorry that you had been dragged into our little family dispute."

"I know about Lily," Nicky said. "James told me this afternoon."

He smiled at her. "Whatever happened between James and my stepmother is ancient history. I only found out myself on Thursday. I came across something that gave me the hint when I was going through my father's things."

He paused, and I waited for him to drop Felicity's name into the conversation. He glanced at me and I thought I saw malice in his eyes.

"A hint was all it needed, really," Carlo went on. "I think on some level I already knew. Kate and I have always been like chalk and cheese—and, looking back at that last summer James had with us, it's no surprise. All the signs were there, but I didn't know how to read them."

"It must have been terrible," Nicky said.

Carlo shrugged. "It's a long time ago."

"Do you think your father knew?" she asked.

"I'm not sure. It's quite possible he didn't. He was very fond of us all but he wasn't an observant man. Anyway, it all came to a head last Thursday," Carlo continued, directing his words to Nicky. "I haven't seen much of Kate lately—I'm living in London these days—but we happened to coincide here. We don't see eye to eye about my father's estate and then this business with Lily came up, and that was the last straw. We had a row."

"By her account, you terrified her," I said.

"She terrified me," Carlo said. "She's a little vixen when she's angry. And I must admit, if she's not my father's daughter,

I find it hard to see what moral right she has to a share of his estate."

"The fact that he treated her as his daughter? That's ignoring the very real chance that she is his child."

"As to that, we'll soon know." He turned back to Nicky. "I'm having a DNA test done. Not so much for the legal side of it—I don't think it would be of much use in a court of law—but for my own satisfaction. I like to know where I stand. Especially where my family's concerned."

After a pause I asked, "And how does Kate feel about the test? You can't alter the fact that she's grown up thinking you both have the same father."

"She doesn't know I'm doing it," Carlo said. "Unless you've told her."

"Why are you two like this?" Nicky asked.

"Like what?" I said.

"Like a couple of dogs trying to pick a fight."

"You're right. This isn't helping anyone." Carlo raised his glass. "So, let's have a toast. To sweet reason."

Nicky picked up her wine and looked at me.

I left my glass on the table. "What's going to happen?"

"With what? With Kate?" Carlo was still looking at Nicky. "I wish I knew—I don't even know where she is."

"She thinks this is about Rackford."

"The old airfield? And why should she think that?"

"She said she saw a letter from a property developer. A letter to you."

"It's true I've had a preliminary discussion about what we could do with the land, but it's no more than that."

"Who've you been talking with?"

"I don't think we need to go into that now."

"And what about Sean?"

"The boyfriend? I assume that's his wife and children up-stairs. Was she the one who broke the kitchen window?"

"Yes," I said. "But what about Sean?"

"What about him?"

"You didn't see him on Friday? At the airfield?"

"I didn't even realize he and Kate were still an item. Are they?"

I gave up that line of questioning and tried another angle. "As I understand it, your father left his estate to you and Kate, but Lily has a life interest."

Carlo nodded.

"What happens if one of you predeceases her?"

As I asked the question, he was taking another sip from his wine. He coughed and put the glass down.

Nicky said, "James, are you sure you—"

"If Lily dies first, we divide the estate into equal shares," Carlo said. "But if one of us predeceases her, then the other gets the lot when Lily eventually does die."

"And what happens if one of you dies before Lily, and that person has a surviving child?"

His lips moved. He was trying to smile but his muscles weren't cooperating. "Then that child would inherit the parent's share."

"And neither of you has any children yet—is that correct?"

"Perfectly." Carlo leaned forward and rested his elbows on the table. He was smiling now, back in control. "Kate's been letting her imagination run away with her. She was always inclined that way. She was asked to leave one of her schools because she had a habit of making up stories. Anyway, I don't see what you're getting at. Lily's dying. There's no debate about that. After she's gone, and I'm afraid it probably won't be long, Kate and I will see what we can do with Rackford. It's all quite straightforward and above board."

Carlo made it sound so reasonable. And perhaps he was right. Perhaps Kate had let her imagination run away with her. It wasn't as if I had discovered Sean's body at Rackford. All I had found was a cigarette butt and a cherry-red handbag. If Emily was to be believed, Kate had lied to me about Carlo attacking her. And, also if Emily was to be believed, Kate had had a far more predatory relationship with Sean than I had understood from Kate's version of it. The only thing I didn't doubt was Kate's pregnancy. I had seen the curve of her belly and the glow on her skin.

"Anyway," Carlo said, "I'm so glad we've all had a chat. And I hope we've cleared up some of the problems." He smiled at Nicky. "We must all have dinner sometime. I'll give you my card."

He took out his slim black wallet and produced a business card, which he slid across the table. The card described him as a marketing consultant and gave an address in Hendon.

"You know what puzzles me," I said. "It's that you got in touch with me, out of the blue, at the same time. All of you— you and Kate and Lily."

"No mystery there." Once again, Carlo seemed to be talking to Nicky rather than me. "In a manner of speaking it was my fault. As I told you, I had come across your company on the Web and seen your name, and just gone from there. You know how it is—you get curious about people you used to know. And then on Thursday, when all this blew up, I blurted it out to Kate. So it's my fault you got involved. Sorry."

He shook hands with us again, smiled at Nicky and patted me, briefly and awkwardly, on the shoulder. "I'll be in touch," he said. "And if you need me for anything, my phone number's on the card."

Nicky watched him leave the bar, walking through Reception and out of the revolving doors at the front of the hotel.

"Well?" I said. "What do you think of him?"

"I rather liked him. He seemed straightforward. It was nice to hear a bit of plain speaking." She paused. "Nice-looking, too."

I sat down and picked up the glass of wine. "He's up to something."

I was grateful that at least Carlo hadn't mentioned Felicity. On the other hand it also made me wary. Sooner or later, Nicky would have to know. I didn't want Carlo to be the one to tell her so the sooner I told her the better. I turned over in my mind the words I would use. I was about to open my mouth when one of the reception staff came into the bar area and made her way towards our table.

"There's a message from Mrs. Fielding," she said to Nicky. "She phoned down and asked if you could go up to her."

I stood up but Nicky shook her head. "You might as well stay here and finish your drink. I'll phone down if we need you."

I watched her walking through the lobby to the lifts. When she was gone, I went through the french windows at the end of the bar and walked round to the hotel's car park. The important point, I thought, was that I hadn't found Sean's body at Rackford. I had found the handbag and the cigarette butt, both of which supported the rest of Kate's story, but the significant thing was the absence of Sean. He might still be alive. His fight with Carlo might never have happened.

In that case, was I looking at this whole business from the wrong angle? Was it some sort of conspiracy between Kate, Carlo and perhaps Lily with me as its intended victim? The ownership of Rackford might have nothing to do with it. Maybe some or all of the Murthingtons simply wanted to destroy my life.

I opened the Saab's boot and took out the handbag I had found at the airfield. It was a jaunty affair—rather like a small, squashed leather bucket. The top was held together by a zip which had been open when I found it. I emptied the contents onto the floor of the boot and felt the bag's lining. There was nothing there. I worked my way through Kate's possessions. There were crumpled paper handkerchiefs, a phone without any charge on it, and a bunch of keys, which looked as if they belonged to the house. A foil-wrapped stick of sugar-free chewing gum had wedged itself into the bristles of a small hairbrush. A blue leather purse contained a collection of receipts, five debit and credit cards and a driving license. The driving license was one of the newer sort with a photograph of the holder. In the miniature picture, Kate looked improbably pretty, like a Barbie doll or a face on a television screen. There was no cash whatsoever.

I put everything except the phone back into the handbag and tucked it into the box of tools I kept in the boot. I went back to the hotel. On my way upstairs, I asked the receptionist to have the phone charged for me.

Nicky was not in our room. Her suitcase was on the bed but she hadn't unpacked it. I called the extension for Emily's room. Nicky answered.

"Everything OK?" I asked. I heard a child wailing in the background.

"Albert's got an upset tummy," she said, in a resolutely cheerful voice. "I'm giving Emily a hand."

I heard Emily shouting something. "Anything I can do?"

"Not really—oh, wait a moment, maybe there is. I don't suppose you'd like to read Maisie a story?"

"Of course I will," I said, without enthusiasm.

"I'll bring her along to our room. She's got a book with her. And afterwards she may want to have a little sleep on our bed."

"Of course." I liked the way Nicky had said *our bed*. I cast around for the sort of hospitality that might appeal to a small child. "Would she like a drink of something? Shall I look at the room-service menu?"

Nicky gave a snort of laughter. "A fruit juice from the fridge will be fine. Not a Coke, though. If she wants milk, you could phone down for it."

A little later there came a knock on the door. I was unexpectedly nervous. I wasn't used to being responsible for a small child and I wasn't sure how you did it. Nicky led Maisie into the room. Maisie was carrying a green plastic satchel, a grubby white blanket and the purple monkey I had seen at Sean's house. She stared up at me as if she didn't like what she saw.

Nicky presented me with a book whose cover showed a youthful wizard standing on tiptoe to stir an enormous cauldron. "James will read to you now," she said to Maisie. "He'll get you a drink if you want, but you must remember to do your teeth afterwards and then you'll have a rest. Mummy or I will come and fetch you in a bit."

The child wandered into the room and stopped in the middle of the carpet. Nicky jerked her head at me, summoning me into the corridor.

"I'm afraid Emily's in a bit of a state. On top of everything else, Albert's got rampant diarrhea and I think she's going down with it too."

"What about you?"

"I'm fine." In fact, Nicky looked more cheerful than I had seen her for weeks. "The toothbrush is in the satchel, if you need it. Do try and encourage Maisie to get some sleep. The poor kid's exhausted."

When I went back into the room, Maisie was standing at the end of the bed with the blanket and the purple monkey pressed to her mouth. She was wearing pajamas whose colors had faded from too much washing. The top was too short to cover her plump little belly. I had a moment of complete panic. "Well," I said brightly. "I suppose we'd better do some reading."

Maisie said nothing.

I piled the pillows at the head of the bed. "We'll sit here. We'll be more comfortable."

There was no response so I put my arm round her shoulders. She allowed me to steer her. I thought I would have to lift her up but at the last moment she decided to climb on herself. I covered her with the duvet. She wedged the satchel against her body and pinned it in place with her arm.

Sitting next to Maisie seemed a little too intimate for the length of our acquaintance so I sat on the side of the bed. All the time she held the purple monkey and the blanket up to her mouth. I wasn't sure but I thought she was probably chewing her fingers.

The youthful wizard turned out to be very good at finding things because he had one spell that made invisible objects visible and another that operated as a sort of occult sonar. He was a nauseatingly smug child who, according to the illustrations, wore an oversized green dressing-gown and carried a wand like a policeman's truncheon. The story lasted ten minutes, and by the end of it I was exhausted.

Unfortunately Maisie was not asleep. She was still staring fixedly at the book, with the monkey and the blanket against her mouth.

"Would you like to shut your eyes for a bit now?" I suggested.

She muttered something I couldn't catch.

"What was that?"

"Again."

"You want me to read the story again?"

"Yes. With the pictures."

This involved a certain amount of rearrangement. I sat beside her on the bed and held the book so she could see the pictures. The weight of my body drew her towards me, and it would have been natural for her to nestle against me. But she pulled away.

I began to read. As the story progressed, I was aware that Maisie was drawing slowly closer. She examined each picture carefully and on two occasions grunted furiously when I tried to turn over before she had finished her inspection. First the blanket slipped away from her mouth, then the purple monkey.

When I had finished the second reading, I suggested again that she might like to settle down. She said she wasn't tired so I offered her a drink. Her eyes gleamed when I opened the minibar. Before I had time to object, she seized a can of Coke, opened it and retired to bed with the purple monkey, the blanket and the book.

While she drank, she turned the pages. She turned again and again to a picture of the wizard's house, a small pink building with a tower. It nestled on the slope of a mountain, its windows overlooking a lake in which the wizard had found several items his neighbors had lost.

"Do you like the lake?" I said, to break the silence.

She nodded.

"What do you like about it?"

"Granny lives near a lake."

"Really? What's it called?"

She shook her head. "It's a nice lake. It's much bigger than this one. It's as big—as big as America."

"I'm sure it is."

"It's the biggest in the world. Daddy took me there."

"That must have been nice."

"We went to see Granny. We went in a boat on the lake."

"So Granny's your daddy's mother not your mummy's?"

Maisie nodded. "Mummy hasn't got a mummy. Or a daddy." For the first time she looked directly at me. "I know a secret."

"What's that?"

"I can't tell. It's a secret. It wouldn't be a secret if I told you."

"But if you told me and I didn't tell anyone it would still be a secret."

She thought about this specious suggestion, which seemed to satisfy her. She leaned towards me and her hair brushed my hand. "Mummy doesn't like Granny. She told me."

"Do you like Granny?"

"She smells funny. But it was nice being with Daddy. It was just us, him and me. And it was nice on the lake." She twisted on the bed and hugged the purple monkey to herself. "I've got a picture."

"Have you? Can I see?"

She dug out the green satchel, which had become entangled with the duvet. She opened the strap and emptied a jumble of toys, crayons and crumpled drawings onto the bed. The envelope was there too—the one she had been using to practice writing in the Murthingtons' kitchen. She had written her name, Maisie, all over it in letters that staggered up and down in a variety of sizes.

"Nice writing," I said.

I turned the envelope over. There were more Maisies on this side, and I admired those as well. I also noticed that the envelope was addressed to Mr. Charles Murthington at the Hendon address on the card he had given us earlier this evening. The postage mark on the envelope was dated at the beginning of last week and had the company logo of Tarborough's beside it.

Tarborough's. I knew the company—we had even done some work for them over the years. They were London-based with a head office near Moorgate.

Maisie squealed with triumph and dug out a dog-eared color photograph from among the drawings. She passed it to me. It showed her with a man I had never seen before in the stern of a small boat on a stretch of gray water. Maisie was on the man's lap and she was wearing a yellow lifejacket. He had his arms wrapped round her and his chin resting on the top of her head. He had a round face, gold-rimmed glasses and a receding hairline. It was hard to get an impression of his size from the photograph but I thought he was probably small.

"So, that's your daddy?"

"Yes." Maisie lifted the purple monkey to her mouth and began to chew her fingers again. She added something I didn't catch so I asked her to repeat it.

"We're going to go back one day," Maisie said. "We're going to sail from side to side in a big boat. There's a monster that lives in the lake. And Daddy says we're going to find it."

21

FOR YEARS I THOUGHT OF MYSELF AS A MONSTER. YOU can't change the past: you can only try to forget or forgive what you were, what you did. I tried both tactics, first one then the other, but neither worked.

There are few things more obtuse than a teenage boy with sex on his mind. Looking back, I remember that Felicity didn't smile much in those last few days and that she spent a lot of time by herself. When I was with Lily, however, she often contrived to be with us. Jealousy feeds on what causes you pain. It also makes you preternaturally observant. A scorned woman is no less terrifying, no less vulnerable and no less perceptive if she is only thirteen years old.

I overheard Lily and Hugh talking about Felicity while they were having tea in the garden on Sunday afternoon. They were sitting on the lawn in front of the summerhouse, the scene of my humiliation on Friday night. Lily was doing most of the talking, as was usual when she and Hugh were together. Carlo was having an extra driving lesson at the time, at vast expense because it was Sunday, and Felicity was spending the day at Millie's house.

I didn't mean to eavesdrop. I had been into town by myself to buy tobacco from the garage shop. I came through the gate at the back of the garden so I could have a quiet smoke in the old vegetable garden where nobody grew vegetables anymore. I was on the other side of the hedge from the Murthingtons, no more than five yards from them. I had no idea they were there until Lily began to talk as I was rolling a cigarette.

"Felicity will need some clothes before school starts," Lily said. "I thought I'd take her to Cheltenham or perhaps Oxford." There was a pause. "Of course, London would be better."

Hugh muttered something I couldn't catch.

"I can't help that," Lily replied. "Growing up's an expensive time. At least she'll be worth it in the long run."

"What do you mean?"

"In a few years' time she'll be quite an elegant young woman. Clothes will look good on her."

"Oh, Lord. Boyfriends."

Lily laughed. "Not for a while. Anyway, my bet is she'll be more elegant than sexy. So perhaps the boys won't go for her."

I thought the last remark had a touch of complacency about it. A silence followed, broken by the chink of china.

"You mustn't be so possessive," Lily went on, sounding amused, though Hugh hadn't said anything. "She's not going to be your little girl forever. Just be glad you're not Millie's father."

"Why? Nothing wrong with Millie, is there? Rather—ah—rather clumsy, poor kid, but—"

"Early developer," Lily said. "You just wait. She'll soon have boys round her like wasps round a spoonful of jam. It won't last—she'll be running to fat by the time she's in her twenties. That sort always does. But not Felicity."

I licked the gum on the edge of the paper, rolled the cigarette and slipped it into the pocket of my shirt. Hugh said something else I couldn't hear.

Lily laughed. "Jamie? Well—who knows?"

Overhearing that conversation made me feel uncomfortable, as though I was at fault. In a sense I felt guiltier about listening to Hugh and Lily chatting than I did about making love to Lily. I suppose eavesdropping on a conversation between a friend's parents was something I'd been brought up to think of as socially inappropriate, while what I was doing with Lily had nothing to do with society. It was hidden away, a thing apart that existed in a different place from the rest of my life, a place without rules.

I turned, intending to retreat as quietly as possible to the gate. That was when I saw Felicity. She was standing in the gap between the hedge and the greenhouse. Her hand was pressed against her mouth and her eyes were fixed on me. She was wearing Carlo's present, the silver chain with the fish pendant. The chain round her neck looked like a piece of Christmas tinsel decorating a plucked bird hanging in the butcher's window. I had no more wish to touch her than I would an uncooked chicken.

Felicity stared at me in silence.

What strikes me now is how callously I behaved towards Hugh Murthington. At the time he seemed barely important. In retrospect, to make matters worse, he was clearly such a nice man. I never heard him raise his voice, I never saw him act unkindly. There's a dark irony in that if he hadn't been so considerate I would not have gone to Rackford on the day before Carlo's test.

We were due to fly to Rhodes at the end of the week, on Saturday. Carlo's driving test had been booked for Tuesday.

It was arranged that Lily would take us both out for a drive on Monday afternoon: I would drive at the airfield for a little and Carlo would practice on the roads.

In the morning, however, Carlo's toothache grew suddenly worse. It had been troubling him all summer but he had tried to ignore it. He never admitted it but I think he was afraid of the dentist. By Monday he could no longer endure the pain and Lily made him an emergency appointment for the afternoon.

Hugh came home for lunch. It was a hurried meal, partly because of Carlo's appointment and partly because Felicity was due at Millie's house by two p.m. She left while we were clearing up, and I saw her wheeling her BMX bike past the kitchen window. She was wearing a white T-shirt, which showed off Carlo's fish. Hugh waved to her and she waved back.

"Ah—what about James?" Hugh asked, when Felicity was out of sight. "Will you still take him out for a drive?"

"I hadn't really thought," Lily said.

"No reason not to," he said. "I'll be around if Carlo needs someone."

"I suppose so." She sounded unenthusiastic. "It's very hot."

I didn't dare look at her.

"And Felicity won't be back till this evening," Hugh went on. "If Carlo wants a drive later on, I'll take him out. If he feels up to it."

Lily glanced at me. "What do you think, Jamie? Maybe you'd rather stay here?"

I stared at my plate. I knew she didn't want to go. "No, thanks," I said. "I'd rather have a driving lesson, please. If you don't mind."

. . .

On the way over to Rackford, neither of us spoke. It was very hot. Lily turned on the radio, and classical music poured out of the speaker, preventing conversation. I stared sideways at her with fascination, longing and loathing. *Why hadn't she wanted to come this afternoon?*

We drove on to the airfield. The runways quivered in the heat. The Rover drifted round the perimeter road and glided to a halt beside one of the dispersal bays near the western boundary, not far from the stream and the side gate to the lane. Lily turned off the radio. Without a word we got out of the car. I heard the distant throb of a tractor engine. Somewhere in the trees, wood pigeons were cooing.

"I've got a bit of a headache," Lily said. "Do you want to drive?"

"You know what I want," I said, and my voice was thick, heavy and sticky like black treacle.

"Jamie." Lily waited in silence until I had turned to her. "This can't go on."

I looked at her across the roof of the car. "Why can't it go on?"

"Because I'm married to Hugh and you're Carlo's friend. Because you're sixteen and I'm old enough to be your mother. That's why."

"Doesn't matter. None of that stuff matters."

"It does. I shouldn't have let things get this far."

I knew Lily was right, and not just for those reasons. But it didn't matter. I walked round the car to where she was standing by the driver's door. I gripped her arm between elbow and wrist. She flinched, just a little. I enjoyed that. But

I didn't want to be like Carlo with the baby punk so I let go of her. "We can't just stop," I said.

"We can." Her color was high and she was breathing hard. "We should never have started in the first place."

"Lily—please. Just once more."

"No. We should—"

"We could go down by the stream. I know somewhere really private. No one would ever see. You must." I was gabbling and the sweat was running down my face. I knew that it was over, that we would have to stop. I didn't care. I just wanted her now, and I wanted her all the more because this had to be the last time. I wanted to take her down to the kiln and make it last forever. "Please, Lily. It'll be so good, I swear. Once more. Just once."

"Stop it," she said. "Sooner or later you're going to meet a girl of your own age and you'll want to be with her. You'll probably find someone waiting for you on Rhodes." Her mouth twisted. "You don't want someone like me. You're young, Jamie. You've got it all in front of you."

"I don't want anyone else. I want you."

"Don't be silly. Let me go."

I realized I'd taken hold of her again. I let go of her arm. I hated her. She made me feel stupid. She was treating me like a child. She rubbed the bare skin where I had gripped her. She was still breathing hard.

"Well," she said brightly, "shall we go home or do you still want to do some driving?"

I felt a surge of rage at the unfairness of it all. Lily had wanted me to make love to her, had wanted me to be an adult. Now she'd had enough and she expected me to return to being a child. Shaking with anger I opened the driver's door and slid behind the wheel. I twisted the key in the ignition and watched her moving through the heat to the passenger door. I touched the central-locking switch and the locks slammed home.

"Jamie." She rapped on the window, which was an inch or two open. "That's enough. Don't be stupid."

"I'm not a child," I said.

"What are you doing?"

"Going for a drive," I snarled. "That's what you want me to do, isn't it?"

"Jamie, just calm down. That's enough. All right? You've made your point."

I'm not a child.

I let out the clutch. For once I had perfect control, and the Rover moved slowly and smoothly forward. Lily was still holding on to the door. First she walked, then she broke into a run.

"Jamie," she shouted. "Stop. We'll talk."

I didn't reply. In my head I was saying over and over again: *I'm not a child, I'm not a child.* I changed up to second gear and suddenly she was gone. I accelerated, changing up to third. Exhilaration flowed into me. I changed up to fourth. I was going faster than I'd ever driven before. I followed the perimeter road to the main gates. I slowed, changed down and drove past the ruined guardpost.

I'm not a child. If Carlo can do it, so can I.

The exhilaration changed into something dark and bitter, an emotion I had never tasted before. I was going to make Lily squirm, I thought, I was going to show her who was boss, show her I wasn't a kid to be pushed around. I decided to drive round the airfield, up to the village and back. She'd think

I'd left altogether. She wouldn't know what to do. But then I'd turn up at the airfield, driving perfectly. I'd slow down beside her and ask, oh-so-casually, if she'd like a lift. Then I'd say that if she wanted a ride, there was a price to pay. And there would be nothing she could do about it.

I'm not a child, I'm not a child, I'm not a child.

I drove into the lane without stopping to see if anyone was coming. I pressed the accelerator. Driving was easy. I followed the twists and turns of the road. The Rover roared past the airfield's side entrance. *I'm not a child.* On the left was a high, unkempt hedge and on the right the rusting boundary fence. Everything was noise and movement. The car slid over to the right and careered round a sharp left-hand bend.

This is where Carlo hit the fox. Oh, Christ—

In front of me was an old green tractor parked against the hedge. In front of the tractor was Felicity. She was running, trying to get away from the oncoming car. But she hadn't expected the car to be on the wrong side of the road. I swung the wheel to the left. Her mouth was open but the noise of the engine drowned all other sounds.

I'm not a child.

A moment later I saw the silver fish quite distinctly. It was an instant of extraordinary clarity. Sound and movement stopped as though someone had thrown a switch and the surrounding details dropped away. All that was left was the fish, like a silver stain on Felicity's pale skin, a stain that could never be removed.

Nothing else. Just the silver stain on Felicity's skin, in the middle of an immense silence.

22

MY HEART LIFTED WHEN NICKY CAME BACK INTO THE room. It was nearly midnight and I was lying on the bed with the laptop open in front of me.

"I'm not staying," Nicky said. "I promised Emily I'd go back."

"You're going to sleep in her room?"

"There are twin beds. It's a family room so there are a couple of smaller beds for the kids." She picked up her bag, which she still hadn't unpacked. "I know we should talk but she really does need me."

"What's wrong?"

"She's in a dreadful state. On top of everything else she's gone down with whatever Albert's got."

I closed the laptop. "And Maisie?"

"Fast asleep." Nicky hesitated at the door. "You did a good job."

I felt ridiculously pleased and tried not to show it. "She's a nice child. What do you intend doing?"

"I don't know. Where's Kate? That's why you brought me here, remember?"

"I wish I knew. Lily needs her too. The best thing I can do is look for Sean."

"You think he's alive?"

"I went to the airfield but I didn't find his body. If he's alive it changes everything."

"He hasn't got any money," Nicky pointed out. "Not if Kate's been using his cards."

"But I found Kate's handbag there. At the airfield."

"Why didn't you say?"

"There hasn't been time, remember? Her mobile was in it, and her wallet. But no cash. So he could have taken that."

"But I thought you'd already tried his house."

"I didn't search it." I pushed the laptop away from me and sat up. "I told you—Emily said Sean's passport had gone. And what she called his bank stuff."

"You think he's abroad?"

"Maybe. Or he could have gone home to Mum. If he's alive, Nicky, then Kate's off the hook. And so am I, and so's Carlo, and we can all go back to normal." I decided not to mention the conspiracy theory, not yet. "I'd also like to know what really happened on Friday, and he's probably the only person who might be able to tell us."

"If he's alive." Nicky put down the bag and perched on the end of the bed, poised for flight. "Emily said she'd already tried Sean's mother."

"That doesn't mean Sean's mother was telling the truth. Her name is Fielding, by the way, initials L. M. She's a widow and she lives near Inverness."

Nicky raised her eyebrows. "You've been busy."

"Maisie went up there with her dad. Just the two of them. According to Maisie, Emily doesn't like Granny. Maybe it's reciprocated."

"How did you trace her?"

"Maisie said she lived near Loch Ness." I touched the laptop. "It's easy to find a residential address if you've got a surname and an area, and if the person isn't trying to be discreet. Mrs. Fielding's been on the electoral roll up there for the last three years. And her landline number is in the memory of Kate's mobile."

"You seem very sure he's there."

"Not really. But if he's alive, he has to be somewhere. Maybe he's the sort of man who needs a woman to look after him. And the best person to do that is always your mum."

I paused. Into the silence came an unwanted snapshot of my own mother: her image was grubby now and blurred, like someone seen through a dirty windscreen on a misty day. Nicky was looking at me and there was something in her face I didn't want to see.

"And then there's the passport," I went on quickly. "Sometimes you need photo ID for internal flights in the United Kingdom. Something official like a passport or a driving license. If Kate's got his bank cards, maybe she's got his driving license too. So perhaps he went and fetched his passport from St. Albans. Luton airport's only a few miles away. There are direct flights to Inverness. The airline insists on photo ID."

"It's a long way to go on what's probably a wild-goose chase."

"Have you a better idea?"

"You could go and have another talk with Carlo."

"I don't think he'll tell me anything. Or nothing I want to know."

Nicky sighed. "He's the first person I've met who knew you when you were a boy. I asked him what you were like. He said it was all too long ago. It was hard to remember. But he said he trusted you. And then he said he felt he'd never really known you."

I picked at a loose thread on the duvet cover.

"Believe me, I know how he feels," she went on, letting out her breath in a great rush of exasperation. "I just wish you'd talk to me sometimes. And I wish I knew what you were really up to." She opened the door. "We'll talk in the morning."

"I'll probably leave about seven."

"Then phone me from the airport. If you want to."

"I will," I said.

In the event I was up at five thirty and left the hotel a little after six. There wasn't much point in staying in bed when I couldn't sleep. I drove through steadily thickening traffic to Greyfont, where I picked up clean clothes, checked the mail and listened to the messages on the phone. One was from Rachel. She wanted to know when to expect me in the office. Colleagues and clients had been asking. She sounded worried and her voice was uncharacteristically tentative, as if she was unsure of the response she would get and whether she would like it.

I drove to the airport. After I had checked in, I called Nicky from the departure lounge. She had been up for most of the night with either Emily or Albert. I didn't ask what her plans were. There was a fragile truce between us, based on other people's needs. I thought if I pressed her too hard it would fly apart.

Next I phoned the hospice. Lily was still sleeping. There was no change since yesterday evening. Finally I rang Rachel.

"How are you? Are you better?"

"Yes," I said, belatedly remembering that I was supposed to be ill. "But not out of the woods yet. I'm afraid I can't come into the office for a few days. You'd better cancel my appointments for the rest of the week."

"But they're—"

"It can't be helped. And there's something I'd like you to do for me."

"Where are you?" Rachel asked.

I ignored the question. "You know Brian Valden?"

She was there at once: "The guy at Tarborough's? He's on the board now, isn't he?"

"That's the one. See if you can find me a number for him—a mobile for preference, or his home."

"OK."

"And text it to me. And, Rachel, I'd rather the people at Tarborough's weren't aware of this. So don't go through the switchboard or call his PA."

I knew this would strike her as unusual but not necessarily strange. There was often a need for confidentiality in our work, usually because our clients demanded it. I thanked her and rang off.

Time in departure lounges moves more slowly than elsewhere. I bought a paper but was unable to concentrate on other people's news. Kate's phone was in my overnight bag. I dug it out and switched it on. She hadn't bothered to protect it with a password.

Once again I scrolled through her contacts. There were thirty or forty names on the list. Carlo's home number was there and so was his mobile, as were St. Margaret's Hospice, Sean's house in St. Albans and Mrs. Fielding's in Scotland.

I checked the call register. No calls had been logged since the previous Friday. Before that, in the fortnight before she had lost the phone, Kate had used it mainly to stay in touch with Sean, the hospice, Carlo and a mobile number she had labeled "Regine." She hadn't saved any text messages but one from Regine had arrived on Saturday while she had been at the chapel. "Got to stay till Thursday. Bloody builders. Can we make it Friday instead? XXXXXXX."

The Inverness flight number came up on the screen. I turned off the phone and joined the queue waiting to board. During the flight, which lasted a little over an hour and a half, I had the newspaper open in front of me but I didn't read much. I tried not to think either. I was going to Inverness on the strength of a hunch that Maisie had planted in my mind the previous evening. There didn't seem much point in thinking about it because the more I thought the less plausible it seemed. On another level, I knew I had to keep moving because I was afraid of what would happen if I stood still. My life at present was like riding a bicycle. If I stopped pedaling for long, the bike would drift to a halt and fall over, taking me with it.

But if Sean was alive, everything changed.

The plane arrived a moment or two after one o'clock. The weather was fine. As we were coming in to land, the country below looked cleaner, greener and somehow more clearly defined than the fields around Luton.

I had phoned ahead to hire a car. Now I was there, I was suddenly in no hurry to find out whether I was making a fool of myself. I drove into Inverness, where I bought a map and had lunch in a pub where they were playing country music and where the main activities were drinking lager and staring at strangers.

I switched on Kate's mobile, opened the address book and found Regine's name. I pressed the call button. The phone didn't ring. It went straight through to voice mail—an anonymous woman recited a recorded announcement. I couldn't understand a word of it—I think she was speaking Spanish. I didn't leave a message.

After lunch I drove southwest out of town on the A82. A mile or two outside the city, the Caledonian canal and the river Ness flowed into the northeastern tip of the loch. The road hugged the western bank. I drove with the windows down. The water was a long slash of blue between the road and high ground on the far side. Suddenly life seemed not just cleaner but simpler too. Nicky and I had once had a holiday up here. I remembered smoking endless cigarettes to keep off the midges, the brightness of the stars, and early-morning air that tasted as though it should be bottled and sold in Harrods and Bloomingdale's.

After I turned off the A82, the road narrowed and began at once to climb. It was fenced on either side. Beyond the fences were fields, rough grazing studded with outcrops of rock and, behind them, the dark green shadows of conifer plantations. I passed a scattering of houses, most of them isolated, set back from the road, and a small, reed-fringed loch whose water was the sheer, blinding blue of the sky.

The road came to a junction. I took the left fork. The road wound on, mile after mile. Just before another plantation of pines, I came to the mouth of a track on the left-hand side. Tightly confined by fences, it ran down for a hundred yards to a white-painted cottage, its little garden backed by the dark curve of the forest.

I drove cautiously towards it. A long time ago someone had surfaced the track with coarse gray stones. I pulled up in front of the house. No one was visible. An elderly Nissan Micra was parked in an open shed that leaned against one gable wall of the cottage. I switched off the engine and climbed out. It was very quiet, as though the place were holding its breath. I felt I was being watched.

The front door was painted pink but most of the color had leached out of it. I knocked and waited. No one came. I knocked again. This time I heard footsteps inside. A woman opened the door. She was small and broad, with long gray hair scraped off a wide face and held at the back with a comb. She wore a paint-stained fisherman's smock with black trousers and sandals below. Her feet were grubby and her toenails looked like jagged, yellowing teeth. She could have been any age between sixty and eighty.

"I'm working," she said.

"I'm looking for Mrs. Fielding."

"You've found her." Her accent was English, Home Counties with a hint of the West Country in the background.

"I need to have a word with your son."

"He's not here."

She began to close the door. She hadn't asked me my name or what I wanted with him or why I had turned up unannounced on her doorstep.

"Do you know where he is?"

"No."

My eyes went past her, over her right shoulder to the whitewashed wall behind. A painting of a little girl with a watering can hung there. "That's Maisie," I said.

The door stopped moving. "What?"

"Isn't that a picture of Maisie?"

The woman stared at me. I saw something in her face that had not been there before, a sort of hunger. "Who are you?" she said.

"I'm a friend of Kate's mother."

"Kate. I see." Mrs Fielding looked as though she would have liked to spit on the ground.

"I'm not here for Kate." I glanced to the east, the way I had come. I couldn't see the water from there. "Maisie showed me a photograph of herself and your son. They were in a boat on the loch, looking for Nessie."

She flushed. "I took that photograph."

"She misses her dad. That's why I came."

There was a pause. Then Mrs. Fielding stood back, opening the door wide. "I suppose you'd better come in."

I followed her across the tiny hall into a long, low room, also painted white, with a small fire burning in the granite hearth at the far end. The place was simply furnished with a table and a couple of sofas. The air smelt of woodsmoke and cigarettes. The walls were hung with paintings in a variety of frames.

"Where are they?" Mrs. Fielding asked.

I turned back to her. "At present your grandchildren and Emily are staying with my wife and me." That wasn't quite the truth but it wasn't far off. "I need to talk to Sean about what happens next."

"But why are they with you? Emily's got a home of her own."

"She's having a difficult time," I said. "There are problems with money—"

"That girl couldn't manage a doll's house," Mrs. Fielding said. "The only thing she can do with money is spend other people's. Why Sean ever—"

"The thing is, we need to decide what's best for the children."

"What's all this got to do with you?"

"I told you, I'm a friend of Kate's mother. She's very ill." I bent the truth once again, this time a little further: "And she's very concerned about the children. Your grandchildren, I mean."

"She probably feels guilty about the effect her daughter's had on them."

"Emily's been trying to get in touch with Sean," I went on, "but he's not at his house. And he's not answering his phone either. His car was stolen and ended up a wreck in London so, naturally, she's concerned. And then there's the question of the children's welfare. As you say, Emily's not a good manager, but at least she's their mother. Believe me, if social services have to be called in, it won't do the children any favors."

Alarm flared in Mrs. Fielding's eyes. I glanced round the room. The afternoon sun was slanting through one of the windows: it reached the fire and reduced the flames and the smoke to pale, wispy wraiths. The sunlight touched the mantelpiece, too, and picked out a packet of Marlboro Light. I turned. There were two placemats on the table, each with a scattering of crumbs beside it, as if two people had sat down to lunch and nobody had yet cleared away.

"I just want to speak to him for a moment," I said softly. "For the children's sake. That's all."

"He should have brought them here," she hissed. "If he had had any sense at all, he would have brought them to me."

Muscles worked in the leathery cheeks. Her mouth twisted as though she was chewing something vinegary. "Maisie, especially—that child loves it up here."

"Maybe they will come," I said. "They have to go somewhere."

She sighed. "All right. I'll see if he'll talk to you. No promises, though. You'd better wait here."

Mrs. Fielding left me alone. Unable to settle, I walked up and down the room. Excitement surged through me. I'd found Sean and he was alive. At last there was a glimmer of light, a chance I might find out what was really happening.

I looked out of the window but there was no sign of anyone. While I waited, I examined the pictures, searching for clues about the Fieldings' lives. Other people's dreams are always mysterious. Most of the paintings were portraits of people with stiff, unconvincing faces and lifeless bodies. The colors were dull. The frames had been hung without thought to their combined effect. I wondered whether Mrs. Fielding had dragged herself up to the Highlands in the hope that the place would make a proper painter of her.

I recognized some of her subjects. There were two portraits of Albert and four of Maisie. There was one of Emily and Sean together and, to judge by their clothes, it might have been based on a wedding photograph. I counted no less than six portraits of Sean, one of which showed him as a boy and another as a slim, sulky teenager.

A door opened in the back of the house. Mrs. Fielding came back alone. I waited.

"He asked if you'd come outside," she said abruptly. She turned, and I followed her into a kitchen beyond the living room. "He doesn't want me listening in," she flung back, over her shoulder. "He's afraid of what I'll say." She pointed accusingly at the back door, which was standing ajar. "He's over there."

I went outside. The sun was on this side of the house and for an instant the light dazzled me. The area immediately in front of the door was paved with slabs of what looked like granite. On the left, a lawn sloped down gently from the cottage. On the right, the ground rose at a sharper gradient towards the plantation.

Sean Fielding was standing against the fence that separated this upper area of the garden from the trees. His dark green shirt and olive army-surplus trousers blended into the browns and greens behind him. For a moment I could hardly believe he was real, and not a trick of the light.

I walked slowly towards him. There was little trace of the sulky teenager. He was a compact man, already running to fat, with one of those round faces in which the flesh begins to drown the features as middle age approaches. He had fair, ragged hair and he hadn't shaved for a day or two. What I noticed most of all, though, was his posture: although he was still, there was nothing relaxed about him. As I drew closer I stared at his face, half hoping and half fearing to see something that supported Kate's story of Carlo attacking him.

"Sean," I said. Surnames seemed redundant in this context. "I'm James."

"My mother said you're looking after Maisie and Albert."

"My wife's giving Emily a hand with them."

"Why?"

There were several possible answers to that. I said, "Emily's broke and Albert's ill."

He didn't pursue it. "So you're a friend of Lily's?" He gave a yelp of laughter. "In a manner of speaking. Kate told me you're her father. Does my mother know?"

"I haven't told her. But that's why I'm here."

"Where is she?"

"Kate? I don't know. Do you?"

He shook his head. "I hope I never see her again. But I thought Emily and the kids were out of this. I thought they were safe."

"When you disappeared, they came to Chipping Weston to look for you."

"Oh, Christ. The stupid cow."

"Emily thought you'd be with Kate."

"We've not been together for months."

"What about Christmas?"

"What about it?" He grimaced and, for a moment, bore a startling resemblance to his mother. "Kate fancied a quick one for old times' sake but that's all it was."

"Your choice or hers?"

"Hers. I didn't hear anything from her after that until Thursday last week when she rang me up. Friday, really—it was in the early hours. She was at her parents' house in Chipping Weston, and she was scared shitless. Which made a change." He glanced at me. "You know Carlo?"

"Yes."

"And you know he'd found out that Kate's not really his sister—that you're her dad? And now he wants all of his father's estate, not fifty percent." Sean swallowed. "He's angry. Know what I mean?"

"Yes," I said impatiently. "I know all that."

"I tell you, she was fucking terrified. Which I guess wasn't surprising if what she said was true."

He hesitated. He was on the verge of adding something but evidently thought better of it. It struck me that Kate wasn't the only one who was terrified.

"Why did she phone you?" I asked.

"She wanted me to come down and fetch her because she hadn't got a car. But when I got to Chipping Weston she said we had to go to the airfield. Have you been there?"

Again I nodded.

"It could be worth a lot of money if they build on it. That's what Carlo really wants. He'd fixed up a meeting with a developer there on Friday morning—Kate had only just found out about it. She wanted to go too. She wanted a witness, in case things got nasty. So we drove over there and met Carlo."

"Was he expecting you?"

"No." Sean stared at me but I think he was seeing someone else. "Anyway, the whole thing was a waste of time—Carlo said the guy had phoned to say he couldn't make it." Sean licked his lips. "And he and Kate started arguing again. He hit her. I tried to stop him and he beat me up."

I looked at Sean—small, out of condition, reluctant to be involved. Carlo was a big, powerful, angry man.

"I lost a tooth somewhere along the line and there's a bruise on my jaw. There was a hell of a lot of blood—but some of it was his: I made his nose bleed. I think a couple of ribs are fractured—anyway, they're bloody painful. And there's another bruise on the back of my head. Look."

Sean came closer and displayed his injuries to me. One of his front teeth was missing. Now I was closer I could see that his lower lip was swollen, and there was a bruise under the stubble on his jaw. He parted his hair with his fingers, revealing a larger bruise and a patch of broken skin among the hair roots at the back of his head. "That's the one that must have knocked me out," he said, with pride in his voice. "I probably hit a stone or something when I went down. But I don't remember any of that. I do remember telling Kate to run. Next thing I knew, I woke up and I was alone. I had a bloody awful headache and I was lying on top of Kate's handbag."

"You were brave." I watched him preening himself. "Where did this happen exactly?"

"I told you—at the airfield. Near where we parked."

"Yes—but where exactly?"

"Near a stream, which was in a little wood on the edge of the airfield. It wasn't far from one of the entrances. That was where we parked, just off the lane. You couldn't drive into the airfield that way anymore but you could get through a gap in the fence. Kate must have run back to the car and driven off. The trouble was, my jacket was in the boot, and my wallet and phone were in the pockets."

"But you had Kate's bag."

"Just as well. The phone was dead—she'd forgotten to charge it—but I took the cash. I needed money to get away. It was her fault I was there in the first place." His eyes wouldn't look at me. "But I didn't go at once. I was in too much pain, and I didn't know whether Carlo was still around. So I cleaned myself up as best I could in the stream. Then I hid in the wood and waited a couple of hours."

"Where exactly?"

He frowned. "Under the trees near some ruins."

The lime kiln. I remembered where I had found the cigarette end and the handbag. Everything fitted. Everything came back to the lime kiln, sooner or later.

"I walked into the village and phoned for a taxi to take me to the station," Sean went on. "I told the guy I'd fallen off my bike. I went straight home, got a few things and came up here."

"Kate's been using your bank account."

He laughed, and for a moment I almost liked him. He laughed so hard his whole body shook.

"What's so funny?" I asked.

"Because it's typical of her and it's typical of me. I never changed the PIN number, you see. It was the date we first met. Our special anniversary. She knew that. That's what comes of being sentimental—you get ripped off. She'd never make that mistake."

"What are your plans?"

He shrugged. "I've stopped having plans. They don't seem to be much help. I've given them up." He was talking faster and faster, the words bumping into one another. "I used to have a spreadsheet for everything. Everything in my life was planned. But it didn't work, not after I met Kate. In the last twelve months I've lost my job, my home, my wife, my kids. And for a while last Friday I thought I was going to lose my life. I tell you one thing, though—I'm not going anywhere near Carlo or Kate ever again. They're off their fucking heads."

Neither of us spoke for a moment. Someone was using a chain saw half a mile away. I looked back at the cottage. I thought I saw movement at one of the windows.

Sean said softly: "At least I've stopped wanting her now, since Rackford. Sometimes I felt I was addicted. Do you know what I mean?"

I thought of Lily all those years ago. "Yes. I do."

"I didn't want her but I had to have her. The bitch." He glanced at me. "Sorry—she's your daughter."

"And Maisie's yours. She misses you."

His face brightened. "How is she?"

"She seems OK. A bit confused, maybe. She showed me a picture of you last night—the two of you in a boat on the loch."

He smiled. "I remember it."

"Maybe you should talk to Emily," I suggested. "About the kids."

His eyes became slits. "Maybe."

I took out my wallet and gave him a card. "There's my number. I'll tell her where you are."

"I can't stop you doing that."

"What I'd really like to do now is find Kate. You know she's pregnant?"

"She made damned sure I knew. She says it's mine."

"And is it?"

"Who knows?" He didn't sound very interested.

"I need to find her before Carlo does."

"She's not worth it."

"The baby is."

"Not to me." He stared at me, mouth slightly open, and a muscle jumped below his left eye. "Anyway, I told you—I've no idea where Kate is and, frankly, I couldn't care less. I just don't want to get involved."

I looked past him, up into the trees. A red squirrel was perched on one of the pines, perhaps thirty yards away from us. I had never seen one before because they were extinct in most of the country. I took it as a good omen. "Tell me," I said. "Who's Regine?"

He blinked. "Who?"

"Someone Kate knows. Regine." I spelled the name.

Sean's face was blank with willed incomprehension. "Never heard of her."

"Maybe it's a shop or something."

"I haven't the faintest idea," he said.

"A Spanish friend?"

"God knows."

I knew he was lying. The squirrel skipped along a branch and leaped onto a neighboring tree. It climbed up the trunk, higher and higher, until it vanished. I said goodbye and began to walk down the slope to the cottage. After a few steps I glanced back. Sean was standing where I had left him. "You said Kate was terrified on Thursday night, and that it wasn't surprising if what she said was true."

I waited but Sean said nothing.

"What *did* she say?" I said, and took a step towards him. "Why was she so scared?"

He flung up his hands, palms out, as if he was trying to push me back. "I thought you knew. She said Carlo raped her."

23

PERHAPS, I THOUGHT ON THE PLANE BACK TO LONDON, Sean had been lying. Or perhaps Kate had lied to him—after all, lying seemed to come naturally to her. The trouble was, I thought they were both telling the truth.

It was Friday morning. As the plane cruised noisily through the blue world above the clouds, I argued the matter out with myself yet again. Neither Kate nor Sean could know what I knew—about the boy in the school changing-room; about the other boy who had bullied Felicity; and, most tellingly of all, about the baby punk at the Eagle. They didn't know about Nicky's raku bowl either. The notion that Carlo had raped a pregnant woman was unexpected but it fitted a pattern that was familiar to me. It also explained why Kate was so terrified of him. I remembered our conversation in the chapel, and how I had wondered even then whether she was holding something back.

Kate screwed up her face and rocked to and fro, her whole body nodding. "You don't know what Carlo's done," she said, in time with her nodding body. "You just don't know what he's capable of. I do."

If actions speak louder than words, then what the rape said was this: *You are no longer my sister. You are in my power. I hate you.*

If I was right, the next question was: how far would Carlo go? What distinguished the sort of violence that came with such frightening ease to him from the sort that ended in murder? Or was there no distinction at all? Was it simply a matter of degree? After all, most murders are not only domestic affairs but also by-products of something else, as unplanned as a pregnancy after a one-night stand with a former lover.

First things first. Rachel had texted me Brian Valden's number. I had called him before leaving Inverness and set up a meeting later in the day. When I got back to London, I phoned the hospice. Lily wasn't well, they told me, which was their way of saying she was worse. She was asking for her daughter. I said that I'd do my best to bring her and I would come myself as soon as I could.

A few hours later, I walked through blazing afternoon sunshine along the north side of Fleet Street. I turned into the Gaunt Tavern and was swallowed into its gloom. The place was a superior drinking-hole, once the haunt of journalists and now much patronized by lawyers. At present it was in the brief lull between lunch and early evening. I searched the labyrinth of rooms arranged on either side of the low, stone-flagged hallway. There was no sign of Brian so I ordered a glass of water and sat at a table with a view of the entrance.

While I waited, I rang Nicky. She hadn't phoned me since yesterday and I hadn't phoned her. She answered on the second ring. She was still at the Newnham House Hotel with Emily and the children. She hadn't seen Carlo. "I'm taking them home," she said.

"To Bedford?"

"No—to Greyfont. Just for a day or two."

"You make them sound like stray kittens."

"Would you mind?"

"No." I glanced at the clock behind the bar. "But it's no answer, is it? Not in the long term."

"Of course it isn't," Nicky said. "But I'm not talking about the long term. I'm talking about the short term. That's what matters."

"OK. If that's what you want. To go back to Carlo—"

"What about him?"

"There's something I heard. He may be dangerous." I heard Nicky sigh with what sounded like impatience. "I'll explain later. But try to avoid him, if you can. And don't be alone with him." I saw Brian in the doorway. "I've got to go." I waved at Brian and he shambled towards my table, then veered away in the direction of the bar. "One last thing, does the name Regine mean anything to you?"

"No."

"Will you ask Emily? It's someone or something to do with Kate."

We said goodbye. Brian was leaning on the bar counter, examining the list of wines chalked on a blackboard. He was a big man who carried a lot of weight although he wasn't fat. He had a red face, rumpled hair and the perpetually sur-prised expression of someone who has just awoken from a deep sleep. He shook hands without taking his eyes from the blackboard.

"What are you having?" I said.

"The Chilean Cabernet Sauvignon? If I remember rightly, it slips down quite nicely."

I ordered a bottle and we took it to the table. Brian drank most of his first glass in one mouthful. He sat back on the settle, thrust his feet under the table and loosened his tie. "Thank God for the weekend," he said. He glanced at me over the rim of his glass. "You look as if you could do with the break, too."

"You know how it is," I said, hoping he didn't.

He cocked an eyebrow. "My spies tell me you've been off work."

"One of these bugs. It's on the way out now." I guessed that he had tried to phone me at the office. "How's the family?"

"How should I know? The children just want me to sign checks nowadays and, anyway, they live with their mother when they're not drinking themselves senseless in the cause of higher education." He spoke without rancor, even with a trace of amusement. "You don't have kids, do you? Wise man."

We drank a couple of glasses apiece and talked about nothing in particular. I didn't know Brian well but I realized he didn't want to be hurried. And both of us were aware that he owed me a favor—last year I had worked over a weekend so that he could complete a time-critical contract that Tarborough's had on the Isle of Dogs. Gradually the conversation meandered to a discussion of the chancellor's last budget and its possible implications for Tarborough's and my own company.

"Too early to tell, really," Brian said, "but we're slowing down on new projects for the time being. Unless the funding's in place."

"I heard a whisper that you were looking at a site near Chipping Weston."

"Oh, yes?"

"A bit outside your normal range, isn't it?"

"And yours, perhaps." He smiled at me and his face disintegrated into folds and wrinkles. "Are you fishing? Between ourselves, we're a long way from putting it up for tender."

"This isn't work, not for me. A friend has an interest."

"Ah." He topped up our glasses. "I take it we're talking about the same place?"

"A former airfield near Chipping Weston. Golf course, housing development."

"That's it. Good road access, mainline railway station in Chipping Weston, and they tell me the demographics look good."

"Planning?"

"The council's playing cautious but they'll probably come round in time. It's broadly in line with the county structure plan. But it's very early days. I believe we've only had a few preliminary discussions. So, you know the owner?"

"Not exactly. I know someone who has an interest in it."

Brian rubbed his finger down the stem of his glass, considering the distinction. "Not my project. As far as I recall, the landowner contacted us off his own bat."

"Charles Murthington?"

He nodded. "But you're saying that someone else has an interest?"

"The land's part of an estate held in trust. Murthington's the executor."

"I think we knew that."

"But were you aware that there are two residuary legatees, with equal shares in the estate? Murthington's one of them."

He reached for the bottle. "How very interesting. Who's the other?"

"His half sister."

"Your friend?"

I sidestepped the question. "There's not much love lost between them."

"You don't mind if I pass this on?"

I shook my head.

"I wonder if that explains it," Brian went on. "I seem to remember there was a site meeting set up at the end of last week. Apparently the chap canceled at the last moment."

"Murthington canceled? Not someone at Tarborough's?"

"It was definitely Murthington. Very last minute, too. One of my colleagues wasted his morning on the M40 and he wasn't happy."

We drank in silence for a moment. So, Carlo hadn't expected Kate to come to the airfield; he hadn't known that she knew about the proposed meeting, and almost certainly he was unaware that she had been in touch with Sean. Suppose he had got to Rackford first. Suppose he had seen them arriving. His instinct would have been to cancel the meeting because the last thing he would have wanted was Kate queering his pitch with Tarborough's. No wonder he had been angry.

"As I say, it's all at a very early stage," Brian said. "If there's a possible problem with ownership it may not be worth the effort of pursuing. Not in view of the last budget."

"Yes," I said. "It's not really the climate for risk-taking, is it?"

Brian grinned and raised his glass in a silent toast. "Better safe than sorry. Plenty of other fish in the sea."

The phone in my jacket pocket gave two bleeps. Someone had sent me a text message.

. . .

Regine Wilder's skin resembled cracked, tan-colored leather in need of polish. She had shoulder-length platinum blonde hair with gray roots, and her lipstick was the color of blood. I thought her mouth pouted naturally rather than from petulance.

"Yes?" She glared up at me. She wore a long, tight-fitting dress made of some shiny green material. She was carrying a packet of Marlboro Light in one hand, and in the other a half-smoked cigarette.

"May I see Kate, Mrs. Wilder? Kate Murthington."

"She's not here." Regine began to close the door in my face, just as Mrs. Fielding had done the previous afternoon. "Sorry."

"She's either here or you know where she is."

The door slammed in my face. "Bugger off," Regine said, on the other side. "I know your sort."

"All I want to do is—"

"If you don't go now, I'll call the police," she said, in a voice that ran out of breath before the end of the sentence.

"I'm going to give you my phone number." I found a card, crossed out the office numbers and wrote my mobile number on the back of it. "Ask her to ring me, all right? This is for her sake, not mine."

There was no reply. I fed the card through the letterbox. I walked down the steps from the front door and glanced up at the façade of the neat terraced house. No one was visible at the windows. I began to walk in the general direction of Clapham Common. I felt oddly relieved.

Then I heard Kate call my name. I turned. She was on the pavement outside Mrs. Wilder's house. I walked back slowly. She was wearing a loose dress that made her seem more pregnant than before. I stopped at the gate. She kissed my cheek.

"You've been drinking," she said.

"Just a glass or two."

"How did you find me?"

"Your phone was at Rackford. At the airfield."

She held onto the gate and swayed.

"It's all right," I said. "It was in your handbag. The handbag was there but Sean wasn't."

"Then what's happened to him? Have they found the body?"

"He's alive and well and living with Mum. I saw him yesterday."

Her face changed. "He's in Scotland? With the Loch Ness monster? The rat. He could have let me know."

"He's trying hard to pretend you don't exist. I don't know who terrifies him more, you or Carlo."

Carlo. The name hung in the air between us.

Kate touched my arm. "It's good to see you. I—I just thought it would be safer for everyone if I wasn't around. I'm trouble, you know? I don't want to be but I am. But I still don't understand how you found me. Did you phone Regine? She didn't say."

"I didn't talk to her. I just listened to a Spanish voice mail message. No—you've got Emily to thank. She remembered Regine's surname, and the road she lived in. She said she came here once."

"It was just after she found out about me and Sean. Regine rents out the basement flat and I lived there for a bit before I moved in with Sean. I wasn't here when Emily came. She had a go at Regine but she didn't get very far."

"Why come back here now?"

"I had to go somewhere safe, somewhere where no one knew where to find me. No one ever came here except Sean and Emily, not even Mum. And Regine's always been kind to me. I'd have come before if she hadn't been in Spain." She opened the gate. "You'd better meet her properly."

I followed her into the house. There were two large suit-cases in the hall. Regine was smoking a cigarette in the little sitting room on the left of the front door. The three-piece suite and the television had been designed for more spacious sur-roundings. Kate settled with a sigh into an armchair and waved me towards the sofa.

Regine looked hungrily at her and sucked the cigarette. "Well, who's this, then?" she demanded.

"He's my dad," Kate said.

"I thought your dad was dead."

"He is. Jamie's my biological father. I didn't know about him until last week. No one did, except my mum. And he didn't know about me."

Regine glanced at me through a haze of smoke. "Why have you come?"

"Kate's mother asked me to. She's very ill."

"You never told me," she said. "Kate, why didn't you say?"

Kate reached for the cigarettes on the glass-topped table beside Regine's chair. "I didn't want to worry you."

"What's wrong with her?"

"She's dying," I said. "Cancer. She's in a hospice."

"I can't believe you never told me."

Kate lit the cigarette and tossed the match into the ash-tray. "You've got enough on your plate."

"Yes, but your *mother*." Regine seemed shocked, even hurt. "Where is she?"

"Wembley," I answered. "I've come to take Kate to see her."

For a moment I thought Kate would refuse. But Regine was nodding, as though what I had said was the most natural and sensible thing in the world, which in a way it was. Kate opened her mouth. I expected her to protest but instead she blew one of her smoke rings.

"You need something to eat before you go," Regine said. "Or a drink at least. What about a nice cup of tea and a sandwich?"

Kate shook her head. "I'm all right," she snapped. "Don't fuss."

Regine winced. I wondered how often this had happened before, not just with Regine but with other people, Sean included, and perhaps Lily and Hugh. Kate made people love her, and then she hurt them. But it would never happen with me, I thought—I knew what was happening: I had a choice.

"I've got the car," I said. "I've parked a few streets away."

"I'm taking Kate to Spain with me," Regine said, seemingly out of the blue. "I've got a villa in Marbella. Now the builders are out it's really nice. She can get a bit of peace and quiet, and there's a pool. Be good for her and the baby."

Kate said nothing. I had the feeling this had been said before and it was being said again for my benefit.

"Of course, you'll want to do what you can for your mum first," Regine went on. "But the place is waiting when you're ready."

Kate stubbed out her cigarette. "I'll get my bag, then," she said.

Regine and I sat in silence and listened to Kate's feet on the stairs. Regine fiddled with the gold bangles she wore on her right wrist. Her face was like a painted wooden mask but the faded eyes were alive and swimming with moisture. "She's in trouble, isn't she?"

"There are family problems."

"That brother of hers? She told me about him. Nasty piece of work."

"It's a difficult time for all of them."

"She's a sweet girl. People can be so unkind." Regine patted her hair and the bangles slid down her thin brown forearm. "Money, eh? It brings out the worst in people. I'd like to help her. I'd like to take her away from all this."

"I know." I hesitated. "But first she needs to sort a few things out."

"I haven't got any children of my own, you see," she said, as though I had asked her a question and this was the answer. "Me and Keith—he was my husband—we weren't able to have them. We'd have liked to."

There were footsteps on the stairs. We both stood up and went into the hall.

"You look as if you've come to arrest me," Kate said. She smiled but it wasn't quite a joke. She kissed Regine on both cheeks. The older woman clung to her. "I'll be back soon, sweetie," Kate said. "You look after yourself."

"You're coming home this evening, aren't you?" Regine said, looking from Kate to me.

"I don't know." Kate gave her a hug and released her. "There may be a few things to sort out for my mum. I'll phone and let you know."

I said goodbye. Regine's hand was small and dry, and trembled slightly in mine. I knew that as we walked silently away she was standing on the doorstep, watching us. Kate didn't turn round, didn't wave.

24

I OPENED THE PASSENGER DOOR OF THE SAAB AND KATE eased herself carefully inside. Scented air wafted out. She looked up at me, smiling her thanks. "You've been buying flowers," she said.

I could smell them even on the pavement. "Freesias."

"Mum's favorites."

"I know." I closed her door, walked round the car and opened the driver's door. Inside, the smell was overpowering. I let down the windows.

"I can't say I like them myself," Kate said suddenly. "They're so waxy they look unreal. And the smell makes me think of rotting fruit."

I remembered what Felicity had told me all those years ago. "In the language of flowers they stand for innocence."

Kate drew in her breath sharply. "You're full of surprises. Carlo knew about the meanings of flowers too."

I wondered whether the language of flowers had a word for rape. "I saw him the night before last. He's in Chipping Weston."

"What's he doing there?"

"Passing through." I started the engine and edged into the traffic. "Looking for you, probably. A lot's been happening since you left. Talking of which, why did you leave?"

"You mean on Tuesday morning?" Her voice was wary. "I'm sorry, Jamie."

We drove in silence for a few minutes. The smell of the freesias slowly diminished.

"You could have let me know you were OK," I said.

"I wanted to, honestly. The thing is, I thought it would be safer if I had nothing to do with you. Safer for you, I mean. I thought Regine was coming back on Tuesday morning—she had a flight booked. If you wouldn't take me, I couldn't go to Rackford to look for the handbag. So I took the bike down to the station, caught a train to London and came here. The trouble was, the house was all shut up and I didn't have Regine's mobile number—it was in my phone."

The story fitted with the ATM slips that Emily had found in Sean's jacket at Chipping Weston. According to the second slip in the sequence, someone had withdrawn money in London on Tuesday. And according to the third, the next withdrawal had been in Chipping Weston.

I said, "And then you came back to the house."

"How do you know?"

"The jacket."

"I had to go somewhere," she said, in a voice that was almost a wail. "I knew I had Regine's number in Spain in an address book in my room. I wanted to pick up more of my things. And—and there was also my mother's jewelry. I didn't take it last time, and I didn't want Carlo to get his hands on it."

I kept my eyes on the line of cars moving sluggishly in front of us along the Upper Richmond Road.

"Why don't you say something?" she demanded. "For Christ's sake, I'm trying to tell you the truth."

"But you haven't told me the truth," I said. "Some of the time you've told me lies. You told me Carlo attacked you on Monday afternoon. But he didn't. It was Emily. And for all I know you attacked her and she was just defending herself."

I remembered how Kate's face had become sharp and startled when I'd mentioned meeting Emily at St. Albans. She hadn't expected me to talk to Emily, and she must have been calculating the implications at desperate speed.

"All right," she said. "That was a lie, and I'm sorry. The thing is, I needed your help and that seemed the best way to get it. I thought Emily would just be a complication—I didn't even know you'd met her. And when I did find out it was too late. Anyway, in a sense it wasn't a lie."

I blinked. "What do you mean?"

"Because Carlo really is out to get me. You know that."

"Oh, come on. That doesn't begin to justify it. And it doesn't explain why you ran away from me, either."

She made a muffled sound, half sob, half groan. Then she said, "I know it makes me sound as if I'm just out for what I can get, but it's not like that, I promise. I'm trying to be honest with you now. I'm just trying to do the best I can for me and the baby. That's all I care about. That's all I've ever cared about."

I risked a glance at Kate. She wasn't beautiful anymore. Her face was red and her features were distorted. I felt an enormous tenderness for her. She was one of those people who roll like grenades through the empty rooms of other people's lives. She was capable of doing untold damage and probably would. "I'm not trying to judge you," I said.

She sniffed.

Neither of us spoke for some time. We turned right and drove up to Kew Bridge. On the other side of the river, we passed the gallery where Nicky worked. I caught a glimpse of Victor, still in his shorts, arranging a sculpture in the window. He looked inherently improbable, like a creature from another galaxy in your garden shed.

The traffic was even worse on the North Circular. The tired air smelt of diesel and Tarmac. The city was sweating. We crawled in fits and starts through a series of roadworks. Kate lit another cigarette.

"Have you found your wife yet?" she said.

"Yes."

"And?"

"Nicky's more or less convinced that you and I are not having an affair."

"So it wasn't Carlo who took her?"

"He had nothing to do with it. She's met him now, though."

"I don't understand."

"It's a long story and I don't think I understand it either. We met on Wednesday evening in Chipping Weston. She rather liked him. If she had to make a snap choice about whether to believe you or him, she'd probably go for him."

"What's he up to?"

"I don't know."

There was too much to talk about and not enough time to say it. And I didn't know how far I could trust Kate. We had to take this one step at a time. Most of the decisions could wait until after Lily had seen her.

"So he didn't kill Sean?" she probed, unwilling to let it go. "That's good, I suppose. But he still wants me out of the way. And the baby. Because if Mum dies after me, and the baby's already been born, then my share will go to the baby."

Was that another reason for raping her? In the hope of inducing a spontaneous abortion? But this was already the second trimester of the pregnancy so the baby should be well established, its hold on life as secure as—

"I've made a will, it's all sorted," Kate said suddenly. "It's with my bank. Barclays, in Chipping Weston."

"I don't know," I said. "For what it's worth, I think he may be potentially violent. But I don't think he's the sort of man who would sit down and plan how to kill somebody."

"He could easily do it on impulse, though. He might just lose his temper. He knows the advantages of having me out of the way, and he's always hated me. It wouldn't take much, would it? He just has to lose his temper and let it happen."

"Is that what happened last week? When he realized you weren't his sister?"

Kate said nothing. Her fingers played with her cigarette packet.

"Did he lose his temper then?" I asked.

"Yes. Of course he did." She turned her head towards me. "Oh—I see. You've been talking to Sean. He told you."

"But is it true?"

"That Carlo raped me?" She let out her breath in a rush. "Yes."

"Why didn't you say? Why didn't you go to the police?"

"Because he was clever. There were no marks. He came into my room. He wrapped me in the duvet. He—he made sure there was nothing left behind."

I said, as gently as I could, "So, it would have been your word against his." Allegations of rape were notoriously difficult to prove, and perhaps this one, with its extraordinary ramifications, would have been harder than most.

"I kept thinking what it would do to Mum," Kate said, in a high, wavering voice, "if she heard."

"You could have told me."

"I didn't want to tell anyone," she shouted. "Why are you so stupid? It's gross. It leaves you feeling like shit. Can't you understand that? The last thing I wanted to do was talk about it. I wish I hadn't told Sean. I wish—"

"Kate, stop this. It's better that I know. But we'll talk about it later. See your mother first."

She lit a cigarette. The traffic crawled along a few more hundred yards while we breathed foul air and thought foul thoughts.

"She's worse, isn't she?" Kate said. "I can tell by the way you're speaking about it. I hate hospitals and places like that. I hate seeing her ill."

"It'll be all right. Everything will be all right."

"Are you sure?"

"Yes."

I glanced at her face. She was looking happier, I thought, which was absurd. She had taken my assurances at face value. Then I realized that it wasn't absurd at all: in a sense, it made me responsible for ensuring that what I had said was no more than the truth. When you help someone they put themselves in your power but at the same time, and by the same transaction, you put yourself in theirs. It's the classic weapon that the weak use against the strong, that the child uses against the parent.

After Hanger Lane, we drove in silence up to St. Margaret's. I found a space in the hospice car park and turned off the engine. Kate angled the vanity mirror and tried to repair her makeup with a paper handkerchief.

"You should go in alone," I said.

Her eyes widened. "I thought you were coming to see her too."

"I am. But later. If she's awake she'll want to see you. She won't want me there."

"And if she's not awake?"

I shrugged. "Even so. She's your mother."

"You won't be long?" She bit her lower lip. "You won't be long—promise?"

"Five minutes or so."

She picked up her bag. "I don't like these places. I really don't."

Kate struggled out of the car, the extra weight making her ungainly. I watched her walking across the car park and through the doors. My mind was clogged with images I didn't want to see. Carlo could well be twice as heavy as Kate. The duvet must have trapped her like a net.

I twisted round and scooped my jacket from the backseat. I patted the pockets, looking for my phone. Just as I found it, I glanced through the windscreen.

A woman came out of the hospice. She tottered with surprising speed across the car park and gestured imperiously at a silver M-class Mercedes, which obediently flashed its lights at her. She wore a tent-like dress covered with little flowers and high-heeled sandals that seemed too fragile to bear her weight. Her face was partly concealed by dark glasses.

She hauled herself into the driving seat of the Mercedes. Despite the glasses, there was no mistaking her shape, the way she walked or the car she drove. The engine growled.

She maneuvered the heavy vehicle out of the car park and turned onto the main road. She passed within a couple of meters of the Saab but she didn't turn her head.

Miranda Hammett had just paid a visit to St. Margaret's Hospice.

The smell of the freesias was growing stronger and stronger. The heavy scent was suffocating me. I wrenched the door handle and scrambled out of the Saab. I felt dizzy, almost drugged. I leaned against the car and phoned Nicky. The call was answered on the third ring but the voice belonged to a strange woman. "Who's that?" I said, suddenly on the edge of panic. "Where's Nicky?"

"It's Emily. Nicky's driving. Who is it?"

"James. I need to speak to her."

A few minutes later, Nicky phoned me back. "What is it? Emily said you sounded as if you'd been running."

"I'm fine," I said. "Are you OK?"

"Of course I am. We're on the way to Greyfont now."

"I'm at the hospice."

There was a pause. "Seeing Lily?"

"No, not yet. I'm in the car park. I let Kate go in first."

"Kate's with you?" Nicky's voice was cold.

"I found her at Regine's. Listen, the hospice is called St. Margaret's and it's in Wembley. Kate went in a moment ago, and I was sitting in the car, just about to phone you. And Miranda came out."

"Miranda? Miranda Hammett?"

"Yes. She just climbed into her car and drove off. She didn't see me."

"But what was she doing there?"

"I wondered if you knew. Does she know someone who's a patient?"

"I talked to her yesterday, and the day before," Nicky said slowly. "She didn't mention it. Would you like me to ask her?"

"No need. *You* didn't say anything to her, I suppose?"

There was a silence at the end of the line. Then: "Are you asking if I sent her to spy on you?"

"No," I said, and my voice sounded feeble to me. "At present I don't know what to believe. But please don't mention this if you talk to her."

"OK. But I really don't like it."

"Nor do I." Suddenly Felicity was in my mind, sauntering about because she belonged there, an unwanted ghost who had earned her place the hard way. "Nicky—when I see you, there's something I need to tell you."

"If you and Kate—"

"It's nothing like that. I promise. It's about a mistake I made a long time ago."

"Can't you tell me now?"

"No. Sorry, I've got to go."

I told her I loved her but I'm not sure she heard because she broke the connection. I picked up my jacket and the freesias, locked the car and went into the hospice. I asked after Lily.

"Her daughter's with her now," the receptionist said. "She's having quite a busy day."

"She's had other visitors?"

"Her daughter-in-law was in a little earlier. You've only just missed her."

For the second time that evening, the earth shifted uncomfortably on its axis.

"That's nice," I said, clinging to my character as an old family friend and wondering who had been telling lies to whom. "I'll try not to tire her. Is she in the same room?"

The receptionist nodded. "I see you've got her some more freesias. She loves freesias, doesn't she? She'll be so pleased."

You could tell the receptionist was pleased as well. Lily might be dying, she might be one among many patients, but still the staff knew her likes and dislikes and wanted to please her. There was a shelf of books near the desk, donations from patients, and among them I noticed the biography of the dead actress, the one Lily had been reading.

"Isn't that Lily's?" I said.

"It was—her daughter-in-law said she'd finished with it."

I walked along the corridor, feeling curiously calm. I paused in the doorway of Lily's room. She was lying back with her eyes open, her head and shoulders propped against a stiff mound of pillows. She seemed to have grown less substantial, as if time and illness were gradually diminishing her, reducing the flesh, bringing the bones nearer to the surface, nearer to their final dissolution. Kate was sitting beside her, holding her mother's hand in both of hers.

Lily looked up and saw me. She frowned. But she raised her other hand, beckoning me in.

"I can come back later," I said.

"No—stay," Kate said. She had been crying. "I'm not being much use at present."

"Freesias," Lily said, in a voice that rustled like the wind in dry grass. "How lovely."

"I'll find a vase," Kate said, and stood up.

I pulled up a chair to the other side of the bed and sat down. "How are you?"

Lily ignored the question and ignored me. She watched Kate moving around the little room, finding a vase, filling it with water.

Suddenly she sighed and looked at me. "At least we did something right."

I glanced at Kate, then back to Lily and smiled. The urgency I felt, the fear, the confusion, dropped away. The company of the dying makes you view life through the other end of the telescope. Kate put the vase of freesias on the table at the end of the bed where Lily could see them. She returned to her chair. Once again she took Lily's hand.

"I gather you had another visitor today," I said.

Lily glanced at me. "Who?"

"Miranda."

"Oh, yes," Lily said. "Miranda."

"Really?" Kate sounded surprised. "I didn't know she was still around."

"I haven't seen her for years." Lily frowned. "She just turned up. She was asking after you, darling."

"What did you tell her?"

"I think I said I hadn't seen you. I can't remember. I can't remember what I said. Or if I just thought it."

"How do you know Miranda?" I put in.

"She used to be married to Carlo," Kate said. "It was ages ago. They divorced when I was a kid."

"That's the trouble with marrying young," said Lily, her voice suddenly vigorous and authoritative. "She was only just eighteen, and Carlo wasn't much older."

"I remember the police coming round and talking to you and Dad," Kate said. "I remember thinking I ought to feel sorry for her."

Lily's mind was elsewhere. "She's put on a lot of weight. I always said she would."

"I didn't realize they were still seeing each other," Kate said. "You'd think she'd never want to clap eyes on him again."

"She was besotted with him." Lily fought to retain her concentration. "She's married again now, and they've got children, but she's never quite given up on Carlo." She made a dry, malicious sound that was almost a laugh. "He nearly killed her once, you know."

"Broke her nose and her arm," Kate said, glancing at me. "And pushed her out of a first-floor window. Didn't he injure her spine as well? He was drunk and he thought she'd been carrying on with someone."

"But she wouldn't press charges." Lily stared at her right hand, as though she hadn't seen it before. "Worshipped him like a dog," she muttered. "Still does."

I leaned forward, elbows on knees. "Miranda is Carlo's ex-wife? I had no idea he even knew her."

Lily's brown, incurious eyes met mine. "But you know her too, Jamie. Don't you remember Miranda Miller? You know—Millie. Felicity's best friend."

25

I TRIED TO SUMMON UP THE MEMORY OF MILLIE'S FACE AND impose it on Miranda Hammett's. I couldn't do it. There's a huge gap between a thirteen-year-old child and a middle-aged woman. Anyway, I hadn't noticed Millie much in the old days—apart, of course, from the last time I'd seen her, which was at the hospital.

She had been Felicity's friend, after all, much younger than Carlo and me, a nonentity, at worst a minor irritant. I remembered wondering whether some of the guilt had rubbed off on her. After all, Felicity had been going to spend the whole afternoon with her and something must have happened to change her plans. Perhaps they had quarrelled.

According to Millie, when I saw her at the hospital the following Wednesday, Felicity had decided to go home because she had a headache. The story was that she cycled away into that hot August afternoon, and that was the last Millie saw of her—the last anyone saw of her.

But I saw her—just for an instant—when I drove round the bend of the lane, too fast and on the wrong side of the road. There she was, open-mouthed, with the green tractor behind her. The sunshine sparkled on the silver fish that dangled from the chain around her neck.

I'm not a child.

After that, the rest is darkness. I wasn't wearing a seat belt. When the Rover hit the tractor, the impact flung me forward. It drove my forehead into the windscreen, and my rib cage into the steering wheel. The edge of the rearview mirror caught the corner of my eye. I deduced this after the event from the nature of my injuries. I don't remember the crash or its immediate aftermath. That is quite normal. In some cases the memory returns, but often it doesn't—and not in my case.

"Open the door," someone was screaming. "Open the door."

Lily was next to the car. She was hammering on the window. I opened the door and she pulled me out. I wasn't in pain, not then. She was crying, and my blood was on her dress. There were cuts on my face and hands from the broken glass.

"You stupid boy, you stupid, stupid boy."

The engine had stalled. I watched Lily reach into the car and turn off the ignition. I propped myself against the warm metal and felt the blood trickling down my face.

I heard a faint rumble, a ripple of sound in the hot, heavy air. Then everything was silent. Not even the birds were singing.

"That's all we bloody need," Lily muttered. "A bloody storm. What happened?"

"Felicity—" My mouth was full of blood and I choked as I said her name. I stopped and swallowed. The blood tasted of salty metal. "Fox," I said firmly. "There was a fox."

There was blood on the side of the Rover Vitesse, and blood on the ground by my feet. There was even blood on the other side of the lane, by the side entrance to the airfield. Puzzled, I staggered towards it like a sleepwalker, leaving a trail of blood behind me with every step. How had my blood got all the way over there? I leaned against the fence and stared down at it. More of my blood dripped down to join what was already there.

Something nibbled at my memory, then slipped away when Lily spoke. "I was driving," she said sharply. "Got that?"

"What?"

The sounds failed to make sense. Nothing made sense. She took my arm in both hands and shook me. There was an explosion of pain in my shoulder. I yelped. "Listen to me," she said, bringing her face very close to mine. "I was driving." Her mouth was a jagged pink hole. "Listen to me, Jamie. I was driving. Do you understand?"

I rubbed my cheek. "All right." I looked at my hand. There was blood on my fingers. The watch that Lily had given me for Christmas was still on my wrist. There was blood on that too.

"We were going to buy something to drink in the village. We came round the corner and found some idiot had left the tractor in the way."

"You were driving? You were?"

"Yes. You bloody fool. Otherwise the insurers won't pay up and you'll be prosecuted. So who was driving?"

"You were," I said.

"And what happened?"

"Some idiot left the tractor there. You went up the back of it."

"Good boy. It was nobody's fault, except maybe the tractor driver's. There was nothing we could do. *And I was driving.*"

"The tractor," I said, looking at the blood. "The tractor."

"Yes, the tractor," she repeated. "It was in the way."

Lily made me say the words after her until she was sure I had understood them. She had analyzed the situation quickly, and she tried automatically to minimize the damage by molding the truth into a shape she believed would suit us better. On one level, I am sure, she would have preferred to say that I was driving but that would have meant admitting that she had lost control, that she was no longer the responsible adult. And once she admitted that I had been driving, there would be the risk of further questions, of the details about our relationship emerging, of my blurting out the sort of truth that couldn't be molded.

But at other times I wonder whether she did it for me— whether she was trying to spare me the consequences of my actions. The possibilities aren't mutually exclusive. People aren't simple: they do things for more than one reason. In my more cynical moments I think that for her, truth was an entirely plastic commodity, infinitely adaptable to her changing requirements.

The sequence of events immediately afterwards is blurred. There was a white-faced man, the tractor driver—I think he was the son of the farmer who rented the land at the airfield. He drove away on the tractor, the engine whining like a mad thing, to the nearest telephone.

Later the police came, followed by an ambulance, which took us to a hospital near Swindon. By that time the anaesthetic of shock was wearing off. I had broken my collarbone and several ribs. My face was bruised and cut, and I was concussed. I had a blinding headache. They put me in a ward full of men who coughed and groaned and spat; and somewhere in the background a television chattered to itself.

At one point, Hugh Murthington was stooping over me. His face was thin and very pale, corrugated with wrinkles. I shut my eyes because I couldn't bear to see him. When I opened them, he had gone and the headache was worse.

That night, it was as though I had been thrown into a black well where there was neither light nor movement nor thought. I woke with a thick head and a dry mouth. I thought I heard thunder. It might have been a dream, but it was still enough to wake me up.

The sky was full of light but no one was awake in the neighboring beds and I wasn't sure how to call a nurse. For some reason it seemed desperately important to discover what time it was. I opened the cupboard by the bed and found my watch. The blood had dried to a rust-colored stain. The glass was broken and the hands were no longer moving. Time had stopped at 3:19 in the afternoon.

At times like this you rely on the kindness of strangers. Later in the morning, one of the nurses told me that my friends hoped to come and see me soon but a problem at home was holding them up.

Just after lunch, Hugh Murthington peered through the porthole of the door at the end of the ward. I watched him striding towards my bed, where he perched like a sad gray bird and stared out of the window at a sky so blue it belonged over a Mediterranean island. I tried to speak to him but he wouldn't listen.

"Ah—James. Um. How are you feeling?"

He said kind things in a flat, dull voice. Everyone sent good wishes. He was so sorry I had been involved in the accident. But there was something else he needed to talk to me about.

"It's Felicity," he explained. "She—well, she's disappeared."

"I don't understand."

"Nor do we. She didn't come home from Millie's yesterday. I don't suppose you've any idea . . . ?"

"No," I said. "I thought—I thought she was at Millie's."

"Yes—we all did. Anyway, we've had to call the police. Do you think they could have a quick chat with you? Just in case."

There were two officers, a man and a woman, both in plain clothes. The sweat was pouring off me. After they had asked how I was, the officers wanted me to confirm what they had already been told about Felicity—what she was wearing, where she was going, what had been on her mind recently.

The policewoman said, "Does she have a boyfriend?"

"She's just a kid," I said.

"Someone said she rather likes you."

"She's just a kid," I repeated. "It's not like that."

The policewoman smiled. "When they're that age, it's all in the mind most of the time, isn't it?"

"Yes," I said, flattered.

"So you didn't have an argument? Something that could have upset her? It might have meant more to her than to you."

"No. Everything was fine. I've known her for years. She's—she's like a kid sister."

"I see."

She smiled, and so did her colleague. They thanked me for being so helpful and went away.

The next time I saw Hugh Murthington was later that day, Tuesday, in the evening. He came over with Carlo.

"Any news?" I said.

"No, I'm afraid not. Not as far as Felicity's concerned. No sign of her or her bike. But I—I'm afraid I've got some rather sad news for you."

I gaped up at him.

"I'm so sorry. We had a phone call from your mother. Your grandmother's died."

"Oh," I said. "Oh."

"Your mother's flying home now, and if you're up to it, she'll come and fetch you tomorrow. There'll be the funeral and so forth." He swallowed, and for a dreadful instant I thought he was about to start crying. "At times like this, families have to stick together." He held out his hand. "But I'm sure we'll see you soon."

While I was still trying to find words, he marched away, radiating soldierly purpose, until he reached the door, where he blundered blindly against the frame and stumbled into the arms of a passing porter. I never saw him again.

"Christ, what a mess," Carlo said, when we were alone. "It's a fucking nightmare."

"Felicity?"

"She's just buggered off."

"I hope she's OK."

We couldn't find words to say to each other. In a moment he mumbled goodbye and wandered off in search of his father. I was relieved when he went. Too late, I remembered that his driving test had been booked for that day.

My only other visitor was Millie, who came on Wednesday morning. I was sitting in a chair by the window. I had my eyes closed because it hurt to have them open. I heard footsteps beside me. I opened my eyes, expecting to see a nurse. Millie was standing very close to me and the rust-colored hair swung on either side of her face.

"What are you doing here?" I asked, too surprised even to try to be polite.

"Mum's come to see my auntie."

"Any news?"

"About Felicity? No." She took a deep breath. "I just want to say I hate you."

"That's not—"

"I told those cops, you know. I said that was why she was in such a mood on Monday. It was because of you."

"Listen, I was—"

"Don't you know how she feels about you? Why can't you be nice to her? If she's dead, it's your fault."

She turned on her heel and stormed out of the ward. I realized she had spoken loudly enough for people in adjoining beds to hear what she had said. Everyone pretended not to have heard, and I pretended that I didn't know they had heard.

In the afternoon, my mother arrived. She looked tanned and glossy, a creature from another planet. She drove me to my grandmother's bungalow. I sat in the back, pretending to doze. We didn't speak a single word during the journey.

Carlo and I didn't go to Rhodes. He rang me once at my grandmother's bungalow, and we exchanged a few letters. The Murthingtons were in a terrible state. No one had seen Felicity leaving Chipping Weston. Nothing connected her with Rackford on the Monday afternoon she disappeared. There were several unconfirmed sightings of her—one in Glasgow, two in Manchester and one in Brittany—but they came to nothing. The BMX bike didn't turn up. The local police force sent an officer to interview me again: he covered the same ground as the others.

I didn't think too much about it. There was no point. I convinced myself I couldn't be sure I had seen Felicity in the lane beside the airfield. Even if she had been there, she'd obviously gone somewhere else. Telling the police wouldn't help them find her. It would just let everyone know that I'd been driving the car by myself, and that Lily and I had lied.

Lily didn't try to get in touch—either in the hospital or afterwards. She had cut me out of her life. So I had to cut the Murthingtons out of mine. I did not go back to school. I couldn't, because of Carlo, and I made such a fuss that my mother agreed to let me leave. I went to London to finish my A levels at a sixth-form college in South Kensington. My mother arranged for me to live in Hammersmith, at the house of a friend of a friend. It was a business arrangement. The friend of a friend rented me a room, made me breakfast every day and left me alone for the rest of the time. That suited everyone.

I never told Carlo where I was living in London. He had the address of my grandmother's bungalow, and he wrote to me there. In December, my mother at last succeeded in selling the bungalow and I didn't give my address in London to the new owners. I didn't send Carlo a Christmas card. If he sent me one, I didn't receive it.

I worked harder than I had ever worked in my life. I had nothing else to do. In that year I reinvented myself as someone who had never been to Chipping Weston, who had never known anyone called Murthington. In that year I learned to live with my own company. I learned to keep silent.

One summer while I was at university I went to Crete with a girl whose name I can't now remember. She was studying classics and she liked visiting ancient sites. I remember a ruin on a headland. I don't know what it had once been. Stone walls baked under an unbearably hot sun. The girl wandered round with a camera. I sat in a patch of shade beneath an olive tree. I smoked a cigarette and watched a lizard sunning itself on a rock.

I heard a distant rumble. The ground shook slightly. I looked up at the sky, which was a serene and cloudless blue. I heard the girl calling my name, and as I stood up she came running towards me.

"Did you hear it?" she gasped. "A whole chunk of wall fell down. Just like that. No warning. It was only a couple of yards away. Jesus, I could have been killed."

"It sounded just like thunder," I said.

Lily's mind was drifting away from us.

"Mum? Do you want to feel my bump?" Kate picked up her mother's hand and placed it against her belly.

"What?" Lily said.

"It's the baby."

"What baby?" Lily closed her eyes and began to snore quietly.

"Mum—"

I touched Kate's arm. "It's the morphine. She needs to rest."

Kate put her mother's hand gently on the bed. She stooped and kissed her cheek. At the touch of her daughter's lips, Lily stopped snoring for a moment and nodded, as though agreeing with an inaudible proposition. Kate glanced at me and, after a moment's hesitation, I kissed Lily's forehead. She did not react. She smelt of urine and decay. The skin was waxy.

At the doorway, Kate glanced back at the little figure on the bed. "Mum?"

Lily did not respond. Her eyes were open. The top of her nightdress was unbuttoned. Her neck looked as though a child could snap it by flicking a couple of fingers.

Kate left the number of her mobile at Reception and asked them to call her if there was any change. She seemed composed until we reached the car park. Then she began to cry quietly as we walked side by side across the Tarmac. She got into the car, folded her hands across her belly, bowed her head and continued to weep. After a moment I leaned across and found her a paper handkerchief in the glove compartment. She wiped her eyes and blew her nose.

"Why does it have to be like this?" she said at last. "Why can't they just switch us off like a light?"

I thought of Felicity, alone in her darkness.

"What's up?" Kate said suddenly. "Jamie?"

"It's OK."

"I wish I'd gone to see her more," she said. "I should have done, shouldn't I?"

"You've seen her today."

"I can't stand it when people are ill, when they're dying. When I was young, Carlo used to tell me stories where everyone died. They terrified me. I had nightmares for years."

"He knew you were scared?"

She nodded. "That was the whole point of it. He's always had it in for me. I could never be good enough for him—I couldn't be Felicity, could I, the one who disappeared? Besides, he hated Lily, and I was Lily's daughter. Once he shut me in the cupboard under the stairs, in the dark, and left me there for a whole afternoon. I was three years old. It was Felicity's fault."

"How come?"

"I'd found an old recorder that used to be hers and I was trying to play it. That was what set him off."

I groped for a change of subject, anything to escape the ghostly echoes of "The Skye Boat Song" and "On Top of Old Smoky."

"Where do you want to go? Regine's?"

"It's too far. They might need me." She glanced at the hospice and gave a little shiver. "How about a hotel or something?"

"Do you want to come to Greyfont for an hour or two? It's nearer than Regine's and if there's a call I can drive you or you can borrow the car."

"What about Nicky? Won't she mind?"

"The sooner you meet her the better. One thing, though— Emily's there with the children."

Kate laughed, a harsh, jarring sound. "Then maybe it's not such a good idea."

But I wanted Nicky to discover for herself that Kate was who I said she was. There was also the point that Kate needed company. I said: "Let me ring her—Nicky, I mean. See what she thinks."

I got out of the car to make the call. Kate let down the window and lit a cigarette. I walked to and fro while the phone rang on and on. When Nicky answered, she sounded harassed. I explained the situation.

"You can bring her if you want," she said.

"What about Emily?"

"There's no need for them to meet, not if it's just for an hour or so. Emily's upstairs in the bathroom being sick. Whatever she had has come back with a vengeance. She wouldn't notice if the roof fell in."

I heard the television in the background and a child shrieking. "Are you OK?"

"I'm fine," Nicky said. "We may need a new carpet in the sitting room but that's a minor matter. I can't stay and chat, I'm afraid, because I'm trying to borrow a cot for Albert. He's decided he's afraid of beds."

I said goodbye and returned to the car.

"That's all right."

Kate brushed a fleck of ash from her leg. "So, what's Emily doing there?"

"She's staying for a day or two with the children. She's run out of money and her car's broken down. She's not well so you probably won't see her."

"Doesn't Nicky mind having her to stay?"

"It was her idea."

Kate looked at me but said nothing. Nor did I. I wasn't going to explain, not to her.

She gave me a hint of a smile. "You're very loyal." She dropped the cigarette out of the window. "Which is just as well for me."

26

Nicky's mini cooper was parked, as neatly as ever, in front of the garage doors. I let the Saab roll to a halt beside it.

"I'm nervous," Kate said. "It seems stupid at a time like this, but I am."

So was I. I unlocked the front door and we went into the hall. From the sitting room came the sound of music, full of synthetic excitement and gaiety, of hurdy-gurdies and fairgrounds. A discarded beaker and a small pile of crisps had been deposited on the antique Caucasian saddlebag I had given Nicky for her last birthday. A trail of Lego led from the kitchen to the sitting room door.

Albert ran into the hall from my study. He was wearing nothing but a pair of pants and a single sock. He hugged the newel post and stared at us with huge, worried eyes.

"A man's come!" he howled. "Nicky!"

Nicky appeared behind him. She swung him up and rested his little body across her hip. He laughed and touched her cheek with a small hand smeared with a brown substance that I hoped was peanut butter.

I kissed her other cheek. "Nicky, this is Kate."

The two women shook hands. I watched with an unexpected sense of anticlimax. Albert's legs curled round Nicky's hip and he dug his heels into her waist. Still laughing, utterly confident that she would keep him safe, he arched away from her body like a bareback rider at a rodeo. *Ride her, cowboy.*

Nicky glanced down from Kate's face to the curve of her belly. "How's your mother?"

Kate grimaced. "Not very good. I'm sorry to turn up like this."

"The more the merrier. Although I hope James has warned you—we've got Emily and her children here, and Emily's not very well."

Kate nodded.

Nicky drew Albert back to her side, tucking him under her arm. She swayed, her body automatically rocking him, and turned back to me. "By the way, Miranda's here too. She's—"

"Miranda?"

"I told you—Albert needs a cot. She brought one round."

Nicky's face changed. She was looking over my shoulder. I turned. Miranda Hammett was coming down the stairs.

"James. Hi. I see you've found Nicky at last. That's nice for you." She reached the hall and said to Nicky, "I've put it up. It's a bit stained in places but there's nothing wrong with it. A cot's a cot, eh?"

She stopped abruptly. She had just seen Kate standing beside me.

"Hi, Miranda," Kate said. "I haven't seen you for ages."

"Millie," I said quietly. "Millie Miller."

Miranda opened her mouth, then closed it.

I smiled at her. "Why didn't you say?"

She wriggled her heavy body and laughed; for an instant I glimpsed the red-haired girl with the two little mounds beginning to grow on her chest. "I didn't want to stir up old memories," she said. "You know how it is. Some things are best left, aren't they?"

"But now you've changed your mind."

"Yes. Especially since this afternoon."

Albert buried his head in Nicky's shoulder. Kate had her hands on her hips and a scowl on her face. Somewhere upstairs a lavatory flushed.

Nicky looked at me. "I don't understand. What's going on?"

"Miranda lived in Chipping Weston when she was a girl," I said. "I've only just found out. She was a friend of the Murthingtons, and I knew her slightly. Everyone called her Millie because her surname was Miller. I didn't know her real name was Miranda."

"She married Carlo," Kate said. "My brother. But it didn't last."

I continued, speaking to Nicky, "But she and Carlo still see each other. That's how Carlo found me."

"Is this true?" Nicky said.

Miranda shrugged.

"It explains a lot," I went on. "I think she told Carlo that Kate had come here on Friday evening. And she must have told Carlo that we'd gone to the Newnham House Hotel on Wednesday. But long before that she did her best to stir up trouble between you and me."

"That's balls," Miranda said. "I don't know what you're talking about."

I remembered when she came to see me in hospital, twenty-five years ago. *I just want to say I hate you.* I said to Nicky, "For her this is a sort of revenge."

Nicky murmured in Albert's ear: "Why don't we go and find Maisie and see if she'd like to watch cartoons with you?"

The child nodded. He had two fingers stuffed into his mouth. Nicky carried him into the sitting room. I heard her talking to Maisie. Miranda picked up her bag from the hall table.

"Well," she said, to no one in particular, "anyway—I must be going. The children will—"

I leaned against the front door. "We need to talk."

"We shall. But not just now."

I guessed she wanted to see Carlo first, to show him the chain, which was almost certainly in her bag. "Wait till Nicky comes back."

"That may not be a good idea," Miranda said.

"And why's that?"

"Because she may hear something you'd rather she didn't."

"About what?" said Nicky, coming back into the hall.

Miranda smiled in triumph. "About Felicity."

"Who?" Nicky looked confused, then suspicious.

Miranda pointed at me. "He knows all about her, don't you, James?"

"Carlo's sister," Kate said to Nicky. "She would have been my half sister but she disappeared before I was born. It's terribly sad, of course, but that's all. What does it matter now?"

"Of course it matters," Nicky said. "What happened?"

"It was in the summer holidays—she was spending the afternoon at Miranda's house. They were best friends. She cycled off and no one ever saw her again."

"But there's more than that," Miranda said. "Much more."

"Wait," Nicky said. "Let me get this straight. Are you saying you recognized James when we moved here?"

"Yes. But he obviously didn't recognize me and I didn't see why I should tell him. I thought I'd see what sort of man he'd turned into."

"What about Carlo?" I asked. "Did you tell him?"

"I mentioned it, yes. He agreed with me—best not to say anything. To be honest, he didn't have very good memories of you, the way you left him high and dry, the—"

"You're still in love with him," I said. "Had that got anything to do with how you acted?"

"Oh, for God's sake!" Miranda tossed her hair away from her face. "You're letting your imagination run away with you."

"So Dave knows about this, does he?"

She flinched but said nothing.

I turned back to Nicky. "Miranda made a pass at me a couple of months ago. You remember? When we went round to the Hammetts' and the Furstons were there? She tried to grab me in the hall. I thought she was just drunk and that the best thing for all concerned was to forget about it."

"I don't see why I should stand here and be insulted," Miranda said.

Nicky looked at Miranda. "So getting friendly with me was all—"

"No. It wasn't like that." She had the grace to look embarrassed. "All right, at first it was, but not later. I've nothing against you. Quite the reverse. And you ought to know the truth about James and Felicity. I can't believe he's never mentioned her."

"It's best to leave it," I said.

Nicky shook her head. "I'll be the judge of that."

"No one knows what happened to Felicity," I said. "After she disappeared, there were sightings in Manchester, Glasgow and—"

Miranda's breath hissed between her teeth. "She never went more than a few miles away from home. And if it wasn't for you, I reckon she'd still be alive. I went to see Lily this afternoon and she told me something very interesting."

"About what?" I said.

"My mother is dying," Kate shouted. "She's off her head on morphine and God knows what else. She doesn't know what she's saying."

You can argue with the words of a dying woman, I thought. But you can't argue with a tarnished chain and its pendant.

"You were driving the Murthingtons' car in the lane near the airfield," Miranda said. "You were on the public road and you were all by yourself. You were only sixteen and you didn't even have a provisional license."

Nicky touched my arm, then snatched away her hand. "I want you to tell me what happened, James. I want *you* to tell me."

"Felicity was in love with you," Miranda put in, as if that made it worse. "You were so nasty to her. Sometimes she—"

I looked at Nicky. "Felicity was only twelve and—"

"Thirteen, actually."

"—I hardly had anything to do with her."

"Because you were only interested in Lily," Miranda put in.

"She was giving me a driving lesson at Rackford," I said. "It's an old RAF airfield, and Hugh Murthington owned it. Carlo was at the dentist that afternoon. Felicity was meant to be at Millie's. Lily said it was over between us, that we had to stop. I lost my temper. I drove out of the airfield and into the lane. I was trying to scare her, I suppose. I came round a corner and there was Felicity straight in front of me. I couldn't avoid her."

"Oh, God," Nicky said.

I dared not look at her face. "A tractor was parked at the side of the road. The car smashed right into it. I blacked out. When I woke up, Lily was there, and she said we had to say she'd been driving. Because of the insurance, because she was afraid everything would come out. And there was no sign of Felicity."

Blood near the gate to the airfield, the sound of thunder on a fine day?

"I didn't even know she'd disappeared until the next day. I was in hospital then. I was concussed, and my memory was patchy. I thought I'd imagined seeing her or she'd just walked away."

"Isn't it amazing?" Miranda said. "Just listen to him. I can't believe he never told you. I think you hit her. I think you and Lily did something with the body. And I know that because—"

"Stop it," Kate said. "I can't stand this anymore. You're a bloody hypocrite. I'm glad my father can't hear all this shit that's coming out of you."

"Your father?" Miranda laughed. "*Your* father? That's a joke."

Kate advanced on Miranda. She was much smaller but Miranda took a step back. "My father had his own way of dealing with things. So do I."

Miranda scowled. "Felicity tried to tell him about Lily and James. Did you know that? She painted a card for his birthday. Carlo found it a week or two ago in his father's things. He didn't understand what it meant but I did. That was when we knew how far they'd gone. That's when we knew about *you*."

"The card? The one on your desk in the study?" Nicky put her hand on my arm. "With flowers in watercolor?"

"That's the one," I said.

"So it was you who stole it?" Miranda said. "Carlo thought it was Kate. He was furious."

Nicky ignored her. "Maisie found it. She said it was pretty."

"It is."

"I had a book about the language of flowers when I was a kid," Miranda said. "I've still got it, in fact. It's Victorian—it belonged to my great-grandmother. Felicity borrowed it just before she died, and Lily gave it back to me afterwards. But I didn't see the card until Carlo found it."

Nicky slipped into the study. Through the open door of the sitting room came the chatter of the television. Maisie laughed. Albert was singing to himself, a song without words and a very simple tune, three notes repeated over and over again. When Nicky came back she had Felicity's card in her hand.

Miranda came to stand beside her, and Kate moved to her other side. The three women read the message inside the card, then studied the picture like a panel of judges assessing an entry for an amateur painting competition.

"That's a lily," Nicky said. "The one on the left."

"Yes, it reads from the left, I think," Miranda said, confidence flowing back into her voice. "The lily's obvious enough.

But it's yellow, and that's important, too. A yellow lily stands for falsehood or gaiety. We can guess which it meant here."

"What's next to it? An azalea?"

"Yes—a sort of rhododendron, sometimes called rosebay. It means beware or danger. And next to it there's a variety of mimosa, acacia. That's secret love in this context."

My mouth was dry and my knees were weak. Felicity was in the hall with us. The ghost of a thirteen-year-old child had come to accuse me. A child who had once loved me.

"She was quite good, wasn't she?" Nicky said. "I know the scale's all wrong and there's no real perspective but the colors are lovely, and it's so delicately done. What about this one? It's a bit like Solomon's seal."

"Jacob's ladder," said Miranda. "It means come down." She looked at me. "Perhaps you used to meet downstairs at night, and she saw you. But it's more than that. It's the clincher."

"Jacob," Nicky said, in a high, strained voice. "In other words, Jacobus, which is, of course, the Latin for James."

"And the last one," Miranda went on, "is colt's foot, which means justice shall be done. I think she was planning to tell Carlo or her father. Maybe she was going to tell her dad when she gave him the card. But by the time Hugh's birthday came round she was gone."

"It's all crap," Kate said, drawing away from the other two women. She folded her arms across her chest and glared at Miranda. "Total crap. For all we know you painted it yourself. I mean, what was the point of Felicity doing it? Dad wouldn't have known what it meant. And I don't think Felicity even knew about my mother and Jamie."

I saw Felicity's face with hallucinatory clarity—the watchful eyes, the long hair framing adult features emerging from puppy fat. I blinked and she vanished.

"James." Nicky was beside me. "What is it?"

"Felicity did know about Lily and me," I said, "but she couldn't tell Carlo because they'd quarrelled. He made her cry, and that was just before she found out. So she did the card for Hugh instead."

I closed my eyes and I was with Felicity again on the last Sunday afternoon of her life, back in the ruined vegetable garden behind the summerhouse; and Lily Murthington was talking to her husband about children growing up, about Carlo and Felicity, about Millie and me. But by now I was no longer eavesdropping on their conversation, and neither was Felicity.

I hurry away. I know Felicity is following. She catches up with me at the garden gate and follows me onto the path beyond. The gate closes behind her with a click, and I remember another sound, the one I heard on Friday night when I came in from the summerhouse after failing to make love to Lily.

I turn to face Felicity. The silver fish is resting on her flat chest. She is carrying a book, an old hardback with a red cover and a torn spine.

"Hi," I say, and for the first time I am anxious about her. I am aware of the need to win her over. "I thought you were at Millie's."

"I came back." She hesitates and then adds, with an emphasis I do not understand, "I borrowed a book from her."

"*I've just bought some more tobacco. Do you want to go and have a smoke somewhere?*"

Felicity wrinkles her nose as though she smells something that disgusts her. "*I saw you from the bathroom window,*" *she says.* "*You and fucking Maria in the moonlight. You fucking lying bugger.*"

27

I OPENED MY EYES AND FOUND NICKY LOOKING AT ME. I HAD no idea what she was thinking, whether this would be an ending or a beginning.

"You never told me," she said softly. "You never told me about Felicity. You never told me *anything*."

"I didn't want to lose you."

"I need to sit down," Kate said suddenly. "Sorry—would you mind?"

"Yes, of course—we'll go into the kitchen." Nicky avoided my eyes. "I'll just check on the children and Emily. Why don't you see if the others would like something to drink?"

In the kitchen, Kate asked for herbal tea, and Miranda for white wine. Kate sat down at first but after a moment she went out into the garden so that she could smoke a cigarette. Miranda stayed at the table, her face stiff with disapproval, and watched Kate through the window. "I just don't understand how people can smoke when they're pregnant," she said. "The poor baby. There's no excuse."

I set down the glass of wine in front of her. "I don't understand how people can do a lot of things."

"And I wonder what Nicky will think about Kate's baby." Miranda picked up the glass. "What with her not being able to have children. So sad."

"It always struck me as strange," I said, "the way you got friendly with Nicky so quickly. And all your other friends have kids. Now I know."

"Poor Nicky. So brave of her, trying to make a new start in Greyfont. But such a waste." Miranda took a swallow of her wine. "I never liked you when we were young," she said, in the same conversational tone. "You were so stuck up, so conceited. Nothing changes, really, does it?"

I didn't reply.

"If I was Nicky I'd leave you. It's the best thing she can do."

I turned aside to fill the kettle. It is easier to face anger than malice. Malice has a way of finding your weaknesses.

"You can't expect her to stay," Miranda said. "Not now."

Kate's mobile started playing a tune, penetratingly audible through the half-open window. She fumbled in her bag and moved further down the garden to take the call.

While her phone was making its insistent noise, the doorbell rang. I turned off the tap and put down the kettle. I was halfway across the kitchen when I heard Nicky's footsteps in the hall and the sound of the front door opening.

"Oh—hi," she said.

A man's voice replied.

"You'd better come in," she went on. "We're in the kitchen."

"Nicky!" Emily called down the stairs, and her voice was wavering on the edge of hysteria. "Can you give me a hand? Sorry, I've made a bit of a mess."

"You phoned him," I said to Miranda. "You told him to come here."

She smiled at me. I wanted to strangle her.

Carlo's big body filled the kitchen doorway. He glanced from me to Miranda. "You've seen Lily?"

"Yes," Miranda said. "James knows. I've told him about the card."

Carlo's eyes slid back to me. Nicky was climbing the stairs.

"And I've found Kate for you, too," Miranda went on, and now her voice was soft, almost pleading.

I glanced through the window over the sink. Kate was standing by the herb bed that Nicky had planted and she was talking into her phone. I moved a little closer to Carlo so he wouldn't be able to see her through the window.

"Best of all, though, we've got something else." Miranda sounded breathless. "From Lily. We've got proof." Her face blazing with triumph, she stabbed her finger in my direction. "It was him. It was James. He killed Felicity."

"You?" Carlo said. "*You?*"

"No. It wasn't like that at all." I spread out my hands. "You remember the car crash? Felicity was there. She was in the middle of the lane. It was like you and that fox."

He stared at me. "But Lily was driving."

"No. I was. She wasn't there. I'm sorry."

"Why?"

"Why what? Why am I sorry? Isn't that obvious?" I felt a sustaining spurt of anger. "Or do you mean why was I driving? I was driving because I was angry with Lily. I wanted to upset her."

"But Felicity—"

"Lily didn't know Felicity had even been there. She can't have been badly hurt. I think she ran off, and I don't know what happened to her after that."

Blood near the gate to the airfield, the sound of thunder on a fine day?

"He's lying," Miranda said. "You can see it in his face. He killed her, and then Lily helped him hide the body. And now we've got proof. Look at this. It's Felicity's fish, the one you bought her."

The one that Lily bought for Carlo to give to her.

Miranda opened her bag and took out the white envelope. She emptied the tarnished chain and pendant onto the palm of her hand and held it out to Carlo. His face intent, he rubbed the fish between thumb and forefinger as though trying to bring it back to life.

"Lily said Kate found it years afterwards—at the airfield," Miranda went on. "Lily wasn't making much sense by then, but I'm sure she said that."

Carlo put the fish on the table and took a step forward. For a moment I thought he was going to lunge forward, grab me by the neck and shake me. I remembered him in the playground at Chipping Weston, towering over a smaller boy while he kicked and punched him for Felicity's sake. I remembered him naked and dripping in the changing-room at school, ramming a boy's head against a brick wall, doing the wrong thing for the wrong reason. I was terrified, and he knew it, and he knew that I knew it.

"Why did Lily take the blame?" he asked.

"Because if it came out that I was driving on a public road, she'd have been blamed anyway and the insurers wouldn't pay up. Because she was afraid that the truth would come out about us." I paused. "And because she didn't want to hurt your father and you."

"That's a joke."

"I promise you she had no idea Felicity was there that day. Not till Kate found the chain, and that was years afterwards."

"So that was why you went away. That was why you left school. You felt guilty."

I bowed my head. Of course I felt guilty, then and now. But now I also felt angry—specifically with Carlo. I hated him. There's nothing like injuring someone to make you hate him, and when you're afraid of him too, you hate him even more.

"You can't hide from the truth," Miranda said smugly.

"Shut up," Carlo said.

She shied away as though he'd threatened to hit her. She looked down at her hands. They were cupped round the wineglass, which was now almost empty. Carlo gave a shout of laughter.

"What is it?" I snapped. "For God's sake, what's so funny?"

"You've no idea how ironic this is. That's what's so funny. So what really happened to Felicity?"

"I think she had an accident. I think she came to Rackford to spy on Lily and me. She had a special place she showed me once, an old lime kiln near the stream. Kate found the fish in the ruins. So I think Felicity left her bike in there. And I think she went back there after the crash, and the roof collapsed on top of her."

"Just like that?"

"It was dangerous. It could have come down at any time. I told her."

That was why Felicity went there. Because I'd told her it was dangerous. Maybe she wanted the roof to fall in. Maybe she made it fall in.

I shook my head. "Anyway, no one looked for her there because no one had any idea she was at Rackford."

"No one except you."

"I didn't even know she was missing until twenty-four hours later."

Carlo walked slowly towards me. I was aware of many things all at once—the distant sound of the television, Nicky's feet moving across the guest room immediately over the kitchen, Miranda raising the glass towards her lips, and above all Carlo himself, his height and breadth, and the way the bones of his face stood out as though the skin that covered them was thinner than it ought to be.

"Yes, it's ironic," he repeated, drawing nearer. He ran his left hand along the worktop, his fingertips palpating the surface, searching blindly for cracks and stains. It reminded me of how he'd touched Nicky's raku bowl with a fingertip, caressing the glaze, just before he let it fall to the floor and shatter.

"Are you planning to share the irony with us?" I asked.

"I was coming to tell you you were off the hook. I had the report today."

"What report?"

"The DNA test." He came to a halt in front of me, and now his fingertips drummed a miniature tattoo on the marble worktop. "You'd forgotten, hadn't you? It wasn't even important enough to remember."

"Of course I remember, but I've had other—"

"I paid extra to have it done by express," he interrupted. "Five working days. They phoned this afternoon and confirmed it by email."

I turned aside, plugged in the kettle and switched it on. I moved with infinite caution like a drunk pretending to be sober. "And?" I said.

"You don't have a daughter after all. There's something like a ninety percent probability that Kate and I have a parent in common."

Miranda slammed down the glass on the table. Wine slopped over the brim. "So he's not Kate's father? Hugh was?"

"I'm afraid so," Carlo said.

I stared at him. "You're afraid? Why?"

"Because it complicates things in one way and makes them too simple in another."

"It's certainly more complicated. It means that when you raped Kate last week, it was incest as well."

"What?" Miranda said. "*What* did you say?"

"You killed Felicity," Carlo said. "Is that simple enough for you? It is for me."

I took a step backwards. The movement gave me a clear view through the window and down the garden. Kate was still talking on the phone. I couldn't see her face. I wished I could think of a way to warn her.

"I didn't kill her," I said. "It was an accident."

"The point is," Carlo went on, fingertips still tapping on the worktop, "I had it the wrong way round, didn't I? I thought you'd given me a sister. A fake one, of course. A fraud—a sister I didn't want. But now it turns out you're not Kate's father after all. You didn't give me a sister. You took one away from me instead. My real sister—the one I did want. *You killed Felicity.*"

"It was an accident." My voice sounded shrill. "I wish I could go back and change it, just as I wish I could turn back the clock and stop you raping Kate. But I can't. What do you want me to say?"

He didn't answer. He rocked to and fro between the balls of his feet and his heels. He smiled. Then he hit me.

It was a backhanded blow with the left hand. He wore a ring on his wedding finger and I felt it smack against my cheekbone. My body slammed against the worktop. I knocked over the kettle. Lukewarm water splashed over my arm, flooded across the marble and poured onto the tiles below. I tried to scramble backwards, away from Carlo, but my feet slipped away from me. I lost my balance and sprawled on the floor. Carlo kicked my ribs. I curled into a ball, trying to minimize the target. He stamped on me twice more and then he crouched and punched my face.

"You keep out of it, Kate," I heard Miranda screaming. "Fuck off. You're not wanted."

Carlo knelt on me with his full weight and placed his hands round my neck. He looked at me, his face serious but also calm, as though I were an algebraic equation that it was important to solve. His hands began gently to squeeze.

"It's the hospice," Kate said—not loudly but I heard her clearly, despite the blood pounding in my ears.

The fingers tightened round my neck. I tried to struggle but Carlo had pinned me into the angle between the floor and the line of cupboards below the worktop. He trapped me like a lover.

"My mother's dead," Kate said. "They phoned to tell me she's dead."

"Good," Carlo said. "Good, good, good." He banged my head against the floor in time with the words.

"No," Miranda shouted. "No."

Through the pain, I thought, Thank God, Miranda's trying to stop him.

Carlo's weight collapsed on top of me. The air rushed from my lungs. Everything was black.

Miranda screamed. Feet ran down the stairs. Nicky, I thought, keep Carlo away from her. And I tried to say the words aloud but Carlo's chest was pressing down on my head. He coughed and spluttered. I squirmed and saw a patch of daylight and part of the door of the cupboard. A fine red spray had appeared on it.

"James," Nicky said. "James—where are you?"

I summoned up all my strength and wriggled away from Carlo. Water was soaking into my clothes. It wasn't only water. There were streaks of dark red, of pink, of a variety of shades between them. I raised my head and tried to take in what had happened. Kate was standing over me, her hands wrapped around her full belly. Miranda was still screaming. I wished she would stop. I couldn't think with all the noise.

Carlo lay beside me in an untidy sprawl. He was coughing and choking. More blood spattered out of his mouth. His legs jerked and his feet tapped on the floor in a petulant, ineffectual dance.

A knife with a black handle jutted out of his back, a little to the left of the spinal column. It had come from the block beside the kettle. I recognized the welt of scarred plastic on the handle where I had left it by accident on a cooker hob and turned up the heat, in another life long before we moved to this house. It was the one with the biggest blade, long and tapering, which we used for carving.

"It won't come out, Jamie," Kate said, shouting to be heard over the noise Miranda was making. "I tried to pull it out but it just won't come."

The blade had penetrated the rib cage. It had hit the lung and probably the aorta or the heart itself. Now the ribs and muscle spasm gripped it like a pair of pliers, holding it in the wound.

Carlo gasped. His body twitched. Then at last he stopped moving. For an instant the room filled with blessed silence.

Miranda shrieked, her voice rising higher and higher. Nicky closed the door. She slapped Miranda first on one cheek, then the other. The screaming modulated into a wailing sigh.

"You must stop," Nicky said. "You mustn't frighten the children."

"How can you say that?" Miranda sobbed. "Kate's mad, she's out of her fucking head."

I climbed slowly to my feet, holding on to a chair for support. There was blood everywhere now, and it was spreading across the floor, a red tide.

Nicky took my arm. "Are you all right?"

I was looking down at Carlo. "I think so. Nothing hurts." I knew the pain would come later, when the anesthetic of shock receded, just as it had after Felicity died.

"I didn't mean to do it," Kate said, in a small voice. "Honestly. I was just trying to stop him hurting you. He was going to kill you."

Honestly?

"She picked it up and stabbed him," Miranda said. "With both hands—I saw her. You all did. She came rushing in from the garden and killed him. Why don't you call the police? She's—"

"Shut up," Nicky said. "Just shut up."

"It was an accident," Kate said. "I had to stop him somehow. He was going to kill Jamie."

"You've got what you wanted now, haven't you?" Miranda said, in a voice that had shrunk to a ragged whisper. "Your mother's dead, and so's Carlo. It's all yours now, the house, Rackford, everything. It's so fucking obvious. Can't you see it?"

No one answered her. The red stain spread further and further across the tiles. Miranda groaned and fell to her knees beside Carlo. She shook his shoulder. I think she was trying to shake him awake. I tried to calculate how many inches of the blade were buried in his body. Five? Six? Who would have thought that Kate had all that strength?

"Jamie," she said urgently. "It *was* an accident. You do believe me, don't you?"

Nicky was moving towards the door. "The children. They mustn't come in. I'll take them up to Emily."

"Children first," I said. "You take them up and I'll phone for an ambulance."

"Jamie." Kate hugged my arm tightly against her, and I felt the gentle curve of her belly. "You won't leave me, will you? Whatever happens, you won't leave us?"

"No, of course I won't," I said.

My wife was at the door.

"Nicky?" I said. "Nicky?"

But it was too late. She had gone.

"An accident," Kate murmured. She sounded drowsy. "Honestly."

But, honestly, who did you really kill him for? For me or for you?

Still on her knees, Miranda looked up at her. "You're a murderer."

"I'm not," Kate said. "I was just trying to make him stop hurting Jamie, wasn't I?" She turned her face to mine. The amber flecks glowed in the brown eyes. "An accident, Jamie, an accident."

Writing *A Stain on the Silence*

It used to be said of Harold Macmillan that as prime minister he marched steadily towards the left, with his eyes to the right. During the last ten years I have sometimes felt that as a crime novelist I have been lurching steadily forwards with my eyes looking backwards over my shoulder. From the middle of the 1990s, after *The Four Last Things*, all my novels have been set in the past, mainly in the 1950s. *The American Boy* [published in the U.S. as *An Unpardonable Crime*] was set in the early nineteenth century.

Steadily the urge grew on me to write a book about a place that barely existed when I wrote *The Four Last Things*—this brave new world of ours where mobiles chatter and trill like birds, CCTV cameras perch on every corner, and people go Googling on svelte laptops that no longer need to be attached to the rest of the world with wires.

Some authors methodically prepare for the novels they write by researching, planning, visiting locations and assembling material. Others, including me, go about it in a less rational way. The first drafts of my novels evolve rather as a plant grows. Like a gardener, I can do a certain amount to facilitate the process—to extend the analogy, I can prepare the soil, water the seedling and pray for the right sort of weather. But, also like a gardener, I have to accept that there are elements I cannot control. (The rearing of children and the writing of novels have much in common.)

The title came first: my wife heard it on the radio, an un-attributed phrase floating on the ether. Thanks to the helpful staff of the Scottish Poetry Library, I eventually tracked it down to a remark made by Samuel Beckett on several occasions near the end of his life. For him, he said, his work was the only thing that made life worthwhile, his way of leaving a stain on the silence. My immediate reaction was to think that, for many people, the stain on their silence is the children they leave behind them. This led to the next thought: what happens if for some reason those children go missing?

Suddenly I had a theme. Though the novel's setting is contemporary, its dilemmas are as universal as love and death. I knew it would be a book about children and parents, and especially about missing children. Children go missing in many ways. Their parents may lose them. They may lose themselves. They may fall victim to one of the anonymous predators that stalk through every parent's nightmares. They may even be missing without having been born, when their potential selves haunt the minds of those who might have been their parents.

Two more ingredients came to the surface of my mind. Both of them were triggered by true stories. The first was a report in the press about a murder trial in which a woman was accused of killing her lover. The case turned not so much on the forensic evidence as whether you believed what the woman said. The real-life outcome was irrelevant to my purpose. What mattered was the issue of credibility: are you inclined to believe what an attractive woman says, for all the wrong reasons?

The second story concerned a middle-aged man looking back to an affair he had during his schooldays. He had barely hit puberty. The woman had been in her twenties. He had not seen her since their affair had been discovered, and she had been sent away. For the moment I ignored the legal and moral dimensions of the relationship. The question that came into my mind was this: what if the woman had been pregnant?

Out of all this came *A Stain on the Silence*. The novel starts with three very simple questions: what if a childless man in his forties discovers that he has a daughter, the result of an affair twenty-five years earlier? What if the daughter herself is pregnant? And what if she's on the run for murder?

That's all I had at the beginning—the story gathered itself in the writing, like a snowball rolling down a hill (and in this case a snowball pursuing a rather erratic course). Now another novel is rolling down another slope. I know the title—*Bleeding Heart Square*—and I know at least one of the themes, two of the settings and many of the characters. Almost certainly, there will be no mobile phones in this book, and no laptops either. But I can't be absolutely sure. Not until the snowball reaches the end of its run.

ANDREW TAYLOR

© Caroline Silverwood Taylor

ANDREW TAYLOR is the award-winning author of numerous novels. His first novel won the John Creasey Award, and he has also been shortlisted for the Gold Dagger and the Edgar. The only author to receive the CWA Ellis Peters Historical Dagger Award twice, Taylor lives in England.